"You have given me your word, Archer, and I will believe it." It was a true answer. But not the whole truth. "I will not run from you."

The wool of his frock coat whispered against marble as he turned to fully face her. She stared back, unguarded for a pained moment. Warmth filled his eyes. He understood. He took a quick breath and his voice dropped thick and unsteady. "You've no notion of the effect you have on me."

The words gave a hard tug to her belly. She closed her eyes and swallowed. "If by effect, you mean finding yourself in uncharted waters, wondering whether you are coming or going…" She stared at his shirt, watching his breath hitch. "Then I fear you have the same effect on me, my lord."

Cool quiet surrounded them, highlighting the soft rush of their mingled breathing. Slow as Sunday, his hand lifted, and a wash of heat flowed over her as she thought he might touch her. But his hand moved to the hard mask at his face. The mask came off with a small creak and a burst of Archer's freed breath. Light hit his features, and Miranda froze.

Praise for **FIRELIGHT**

FIRELIGHT

Kristen Callihan

FOREVER

NEW YORK   BOSTON

Copyright © 2012 by Kristen Callihan
Excerpt from *Moonglow* © 2012 by Kristen Callihan
All rights reserved. Except as permitted under the U.S. Copyright Act of 1976, no part of this publication may be reproduced, distributed, or transmitted in any form or by any means, or stored in a database or retrieval system, without the prior written permission of the publisher.

Forever
Hachette Book Group
237 Park Avenue
New York, NY 10017

www.HachetteBookGroup.com

Printed in the United States of America

First Edition: February 2012
10 9 8 7 6 5 4 3 2

Forever is an imprint of Grand Central Publishing.
The Forever name and logo are trademarks of Hachette Book Group, Inc.

The publisher is not responsible for websites (or their content) that are not owned by the publisher.

ATTENTION CORPORATIONS AND ORGANIZATIONS:
Most HACHETTE BOOK GROUP books are available at quantity discounts with bulk purchase for educational, business, or sales promotional use. For information, please call or write:

Special Markets Department, Hachette Book Group
237 Park Avenue, New York, NY 10017
Telephone: 1-800-222-6747 Fax: 1-800-477-5925

For my husband, Juan. Your unwavering faith gave me wings. Without you, none of this would be.

For Rachel. You know what you did. A better friend I could not have.

And for Maya and Alex. Always.

Acknowledgments

If you are lucky, you'll find yourself supported by the best, the sort whose talent only makes you look better. I consider myself very lucky.

First and foremost, to the two people who helped make my dream a reality: my agent, Kristin Nelson, for being part cheerleader, part wolverine, and all heart; and my editor, Alex Logan, whose elegant editing skills and generosity made my first foray into publishing a pleasure. Every day, I thank my lucky stars that I have you both in my corner.

Thanks to editorial assistant Lauren Plude for your support and infectious enthusiasm. To cover designer Christine Foltzer for a kick-ass cover. To copy editor Lynne Cannon Menges. And to Amy Pierpont and all the talented people who make up the Forever/Grand Central Publishing team.

My eternal gratitude to the best friends and writing partners a girl could hope for: Claire Greer, Jennifer Hendren, Susan J. Montgomery, and Rachel Walsh, who held my hand, encouraged and cajoled me day after day, from concept to completed work. You've all helped me more than I can say. My love always.

Many thanks to beta readers Deniz Bevan, Rhianonn Morgan, Kait Nolan, Precie Schroyer, and Carol Spradling.

Huge thanks to Diana Gabaldon, who inspired me to write and is more of a mentor than she'll ever know. To Jo Bourne for answering many newbie questions, and for being one of the best conveyers of craft I've ever met. To the wonderful writers who hang at the CompuServe Books and Writers Forum; you will not find a more welcoming and supportive writing community.

To the home team: my sisters Karina and Liz for listening to endless writer-related babble and all-around sister support. My friends Christine Child, Eileen Cruz Coleman, Kerry Sheridan, and Amy Smith for much of the same. To Jim and Christine Mollenauer for watching my babies countless times so I could write. And to the three who make up my heart: Juan, Maya, and Alex, for understanding when I was holed up in the office, for being my inspiration, for making it all worth it.

Lastly, thank you, Hilde and Herb, my mother and father, who taught me to love books, gave me the gift of storytelling, gave me life.

FIRELIGHT

Prologue

It was the mask engaged your mind,
And after set your heart to beat.
— W.B. Yeats

London, November 1878

The knowledge that Archer would soon end the life of another cut at his soul with every step he took. The miscreant in question was a liar and a thief at best. That the whole of the man's meager fortune now rested at the bottom of the Atlantic did little to rouse Archer's sympathy. On the contrary, it only ignited his fury. A red haze clouded Archer's vision when he thought about what had been lost. Salvation had almost been his. Now it was gone because Hector Ellis's pirates had raided Archer's ship, stealing that which might cure him and hiding it away in their bloody doomed clipper ship.

Mud-thick fog hung low on the ground, refusing to drift off despite the crisp night breeze. It never truly went away, ever present in London, like death, taxes, and monarchy. The ends of Archer's cloak snapped about his legs, whipping up eddies of the foul yellow vapor as his mouth filled with the acrid taste of coal, filth, and decay that was the flavor of London.

Archer rounded a corner, moving away from the street lamps and into shadow. The sharp staccato of his footfall echoed over the deserted cobbled streets. Far off on the Thames, a mournful foghorn wailed its warning. But here all was quiet. The constant clatter of coaches and the occasional shout of the night watch calling the hours had faded away. Darkness swallowed his form, as it always did, both a comfort and a reminder of what he'd become.

The neighborhood around him was old but fine. Like all places that housed those whom fortune touched, the streets were empty and desolate, everyone having long ago tucked into their well-tufted beds.

Ellis's house was near. Archer had walked the streets of London long enough to move without hesitation through its perverse network of twisted alleys and endless avenues. Anticipation, cold and metallic, slid over his tongue. To end a life, see the incandescent light of a soul slip from its house—he wanted that moment, *craved* it. The horror of such craving shook his core and his step faltered. *Never do harm.* It was every doctor's creed, his creed. That was before he'd forfeited his own life. Archer took a cleansing breath and focused on the rage.

A garden lay ahead, large and walled in, its pleasures solely for the benefit of those who had the key. The seven-foot wall loomed up before him. It might as well be only four feet. He vaulted himself lightly up and over, landing on the soft grass below with nary a sound.

He rose, intent on his mission, when the sound of steel slicing against steel stopped him. Odd. Sword fighting had long fallen out of fashion. London fops now settled matters with law and courts. He rather missed the days of his youth when grievances had started with the slap of a glove and ended in first blood. He gazed over the dark garden and found the swordsmen as they moved under the weak haloed light of the gas lamps cornering the central court.

"Come on!" taunted the fair-haired one. "Is that your best effort?"

They were boys. Archer slipped into the deep shadows by the wall and watched, his unnatural eyes seeing as well as if he'd been ringside. The blond could not be more than eighteen. Not quite a man, his limbs held the lankiness of youth, but he was tall enough and the timbre of his voice had dropped. He was clearly the leader as he paced the other boy round the slate-lined court in the garden's center.

"Keep your arm up," he coached, coming at the younger boy again.

The younger boy was nearly as tall as his compatriot, but altogether delicate in form. His legs, peeking out from an ill-fitted frock coat, were mere sticks. A ridiculous bowery hat was crammed down upon his head, so low that Archer saw only a flash of white jaw as the pair sparred about *ala mazza*.

Archer leaned against the wall. He hadn't seen such eloquent sparring in a lifetime. The elder boy was good. Very good. He had been trained by a master. But the little one, he would be better. He was at the disadvantage being lighter and shorter, but when the blond attempted a *Botta-in-tempo* while the youth was tied up in a bind, the little one sprang back with such quickness that Archer craned forward in anticipation, enjoying himself more than he had in decades. They broke measure and came back again.

"You'll have to do better than that, Martin." The youth

laughed, his steel flashing like moonbeams in the purple night.

Martin's eyes shown with both pride and determination. "Don't get cocksure on me, Pan."

Martin thrust once then cut. The youth, Pan, crossed to the right. To Archer's delight, the boy leapt upon the thin wrought-iron railing that surrounded the court and, in a little display of daring, slid along the rail a distance before landing just behind Martin. He gave a swift poke to the elder boy's backside before dancing away.

"I *am* the god Pan," he sang out, his youthful voice high as a girl's. "And if you don't watch yourself, I'll stick my flute right up your blooming arse, ah—"

The silly boy toppled backward over the boxwood hedge he'd overlooked in his gloating. Archer grinned wide.

Martin's laugh bounded over the garden. The boy doubled up with it, dropping his small-sword to hold his middle. Young Pan struggled to rise, holding his absurd hat in place while grousing about English hedges under his breath.

Martin took pity and helped the boy to his feet. "Call it quits, then?" He offered his hand once more in peace.

The youth grumbled a bit then took the proffered hand. "I suppose I must. Take the sword, will you? Father almost found it the other day."

"And we mustn't have that, hum?" Martin tweaked the boy's nose.

The two parted ways, each going toward opposite garden doors.

" 'Night, Martin."

" 'Night, Pan!"

Smiling, the blond boy watched his little friend leave the garden and then left.

Archer moved through the shadows, heading toward the door where Pan had gone through. Prickles of unease danced over his skin. Fighter or no, the boy was too fragile to walk alone and unarmed in the dead of night. A rare bit of entertainment certainly earned the boy a safe passage home.

He stalked him easily, staying to the shadows, keeping well behind. The boy moved through the night without fear, a jaunty near swagger in his step as he turned from the sidewalk into an alleyway.

Thus his squeak of alarm was all the louder when two grimy older boys slipped out of the shadows and blocked his path.

"An' who's this?" The fellow was a big brute, short and wide. The type, Archer thought grimly, for he was in no mood to throttle children, who always wanted a fight.

"Hello," said Pan, stepping back one pace. "Don't mind me. Just out for a stroll."

The taller one of the two laughed, showing a large gap between his teeth. " 'Out for a stroll,' " he parroted. "Who you think you are? Prince Bertie?"

Pan was quick to rally. "Eh? Can' a man use the Queen's English now an' then?" he chided, slipping into street tongue as smooth as plum pudding. "Especially when it helps wit me fannin'?"

Young Pan eased around them, slyly moving toward the back of a large town house. There lied safety, Archer realized. It was the boy's home. It was Ellis's home, he realized with a little shock. Who was this boy?

"Them marks always appreciate a kind word," the boy went on.

Archer had to appreciate the boy's flair with the common tongue; he hardly understood a word. But the lad was putting it on too thickly. The young roughs knew it, too.

"You think we're flat?" one of them snapped.

The youth backed up as the older boys closed round. "Here now, no need to kick up a shine..."

"Need a slate, do ya?" The taller of the two roughs cuffed the boy lightly on the head. The boy's hat flew off, and Archer's heart stopped short. A silken mass of fire tumbled free, falling like molten gold down to the boy's waist. Archer fought for breath. Not a boy, a girl. And not thirteen, but closer to eighteen. A young woman.

He stared at the mass of red-gold hair. He'd never seen hair so fine and glorious before. Titian hair, some would call it. That ineffable color between gold and red that captivated artists and poets alike.

"Keep back!"

The high pip of a voice pulled Archer out of his reverie. His urchin moved into a defensive stance as her attackers loomed in with interest. Surprise had overcome the two roughs as well but they recovered quickly and now sought a new opportunity.

"Aw, come on, luv. No need for tantrums. We didn't know you was a dollymop, now did we?"

They moved in, and the hairs lifted on the back of Archer's neck. A growl grew in his throat. Archer took a step, then another. They wouldn't hear him yet; he was too quiet, his form steeped in darkness.

"Show us your bubs, eh?" said the shorter one, and clearly the first who would feel the business end of Archer's fist.

Surprisingly, the girl didn't appear as afraid as she ought to be. She stood defiantly, keeping her fists raised and her eyes trained on the boys. The idea was laughable.

"Leave off," she said with iron in her small voice.

The street roughs laughed, an ugly sneering sound. "Oh right, leave off, she says."

The taller one snorted. "Listen 'ere, toffer, behave an' we'll leave you intact."

Green eyes blazed beneath her auburn brows that arched like angel's wings.

They were green, weren't they? Archer squinted, his abnormal eyes using what little light there was to see. Yes, crystalline green ringed with emerald, like the cross section of a Chardonnay grape. Yet he swore he saw a glint of orange fire flash in them.

"Leave now," she demanded, unmoved, "or I'll turn you both to cheese on toast."

Archer could not help it, mirth bubbled up within, and he found himself laughing. The sound echoed off the cold stone houses and brick-lined alley. The young men whirled round. The fear in their faces was clear. They weren't up for an exchange with a grown man, most especially any man who'd be out on the streets at this hour. Archer knew their cut, cowards who preyed on the weak and fled at the first sign of true danger. He came close enough for them to see his shape and the toes of his Hessians, preferring to stay in shadow until necessary.

"Hook it! This 'ere's our business," said the tall one with forced confidence.

"Stay a moment longer in this alleyway," Archer said, "and your time in this world will come to a swift end." His voice was not his own. A pale rasp after his last battle, it had been torn by injuries that should have robbed him of his ability to speak. But he would heal. Soon.

They sensed the unnaturalness in him—the street wretches always did—and stood gaping at him like dead fish.

He cracked his knuckles. "Or perhaps not so swiftly. I do enjoy playing with my prey."

The pair gathered their wits and ran, the rapid patter of their footfall clamoring on the cobblestones of the street beyond.

They'd gone but the girl had not. She stood, frozen it seemed, in her ridiculous stance of defense.

The bones beneath her alabaster skin were exquisite, with high curved cheeks, graceful jaw, and straight, delicate nose. Michelangelo might have sculpted her. And a blow from one man's fist would smash that beauty in an instant.

"Go home," he said to her.

She flinched slightly but stayed set, swaying a bit as though dazed.

He sighed. "Go, before I decide to teach you a lesson."

That snapped her out of it. She eyed the wall behind her, where the safety of her home lay, and then the alleyway to her side. She didn't want him to know she was home, but had no desire to run off down that alley. Was she a servant? No, she hadn't the hands of one. Nor could Ellis afford a servant. But he had daughters. Three that Archer knew of, and only one that remained in the home. *Miranda.* His mind rolled over the name, savoring it like wine.

"Leave," she squeaked. "And I'll go home."

He bit back a smile. Had defiance ever been so intriguing? Youth so beguiling? She was old enough to marry. He blinked, clearing his mind of that insane thought. She was an innocent. He would not think of her as seductive. But she would be—someday. Would that mouth grow lusher still? The slight baby softness at her cheeks melt into greater delicacy?

He watched her, momentarily entranced by the golden strands of hair that swirled about her angular face like flames.

"Who are you?" she snapped.

The sharp query brought him to attention. He made a courtly bow.

"A concerned subject of the Crown."

She harrumphed but did not drop her fists. Shockingly, she came closer. He backed away into the dark and collided with the alley wall. The deep-hooded cloak hid the mask he wore. Even so, he didn't want to scare her. A ridiculous notion, considering she tracked him like a falcon, drawing near, sensing his reticence and acting on that weakness. Admiration filled him.

"Lower your hood. Let me see your face."

He should walk away. Leave her be. "No."

Heated energy flared around her, almost palpable in the cold air. Anger made her lovely, powerful.

"I could make you."

In the shadows, he grinned. He could not account for the utter confidence in her, yet it made him...exhilarated. "An intriguing idea. Perhaps you ought to try."

Had he been a normal man, her movement would have been a blur. Even so, it shocked him how quickly she was upon him, a knife in her hand shoved firmly against his ribs. He ought to teach her a lesson in taking on strange, large men in the night, but the sweet, grassy scent of her distracted him, and he was curious as to what she would do.

"Turn around." Her voice was forged iron. "Your hands to the wall."

When he simply stood there amused, she flushed. "I don't care who you are as long as you go. But I will check you for weapons before I send you on your way."

Foolish girl. He really ought to set her straight. "Of course," he said.

The damp on the bricks seeped through his gloves as she reached around to skim her hand over his chest. The moment she touched him his senses snapped to attention. A light shiver passed over him. He tapped it down, thought of the Queen, pickled eels, or...the fact that no woman had been this close to him in years. For a moment, he was dizzy.

"Quality clothing. Carrying the scent of the sea. The sea and..." She trailed off with a noise that made him wonder what she detected. Did the unnaturalness in him carry a scent?

"You're here to harass my father."

His head snapped up, and she made a sound of annoyance.

"You are not the first to ooze from this alleyway in the dark of night, nor will you be the last." Her hand slid over his belly. His gut grew twitchy, aching. "I assume he owes you money. Well, it is gone. There is nothing left. You cannot get blood from a stone, and I won't let you take his blood in payment."

He winced at the hurt in her voice, at what she had to face for the deeds of her father. It changed nothing; save he wanted to keep her away from her father's inevitable demise. Tenderness warred with the deep, tight-chested anger that was his constant companion.

"How am I to respond?" he asked. "Deny it, and you accuse me of lying. Admit it, and you cut my throat."

The tip of the knife dug in a little farther as her soft voice rumbled at his ear. "I may do both yet."

He could only chuckle. "I am honored. You had this pig sticker in your boot, and you saved it for me."

"I hadn't the opportunity to use it on those fools. Not with you blundering in my way. But make no mistake, I would have done so."

Brusque pats flanked his side. The touch was impersonal, and driving him mad all the same. His flesh tensed before each hit, waiting for the contact with taut anticipation.

"They might have taken your point to heart had you pulled out the knife from the first."

He could feel her head shake. "Not those two." A smile hid beneath the professional tone of her voice. "They would have leapt at the opening. They wanted the fight."

Archer had to agree.

"Besides," she said crisply as she ran a hand down his outstretched arm, before kneeling to check his boot. "I do not particularly like violence."

Ha! "I'd say you excel at it."

Her breath puffed warm against his thigh, making his quadriceps twitch. "Sweet talk won't save you."

He affected a sigh. "My own folly for protecting a child."

"Child," she scoffed. "I am nineteen years old. Older than most Mayfair debutantes offered up for sale. Hardly a child."

Ah, yes, and didn't he know it.

Cautiously, she felt along his right leg, before moving on to his left. Oddly, she didn't pick his pockets. She left his money purse alone.

"Pardon, *madam*." He glanced down to watch the top of her head bobbing about like a copper globe by his upper thigh. Illicit thoughts flared hot at the sight. He struggled to keep his tone light. "Save when one has lived as long as I, nineteen years is little more than a flicker in time."

Amusement danced in her voice. "You're an old lecher, are you?"

He was thinking of becoming so. Should she, say,

move her hand a few inches to the left...He cleared his throat. "Old enough."

She made a noise under her breath. "Liar." She was at his left hip now. "Your form doesn't feel elderly in the least." *If she only knew.* "You're musculature is quite—"

He felt the precise moment when everything changed— the subtle increase in tension in her hand, a stutter in the efficient way she moved, the shift in her breathing from strong and determined to light and agitated. The answer in him was instant, painful arousal. For a moment, he couldn't think. He hadn't been noticed as a man in so long that his mind barely held the echo of such memories. But his flesh...his flesh remembered the pleasure of touch all too well.

Slowly, her slim hand smoothed over the swell of his buttock, lingering there. A shocked laugh choked his throat, the sound muddled by a stifled groan that her intrigued touch elicited. The saucy little *sneak thief* was copping a feel. He felt inclined to turn around and let her get a handful. Christ, this was madness.

Her breath came in hard rasps, audible and so like those of a woman being tupped that Archer's head grew light, all available blood surging down to the throbbing pain in his cock. His forehead fell against the brick wall with a thud. Bits of mortar drifted like dust over his wrists as he clung to the wall like a buoy.

Inquisitive fingers combed his inner thigh, testing its hardness, and surely feeling the trembling there. His cock swelled, drawing so tight and hot it quivered. *Sweet Christ.* This time he could not bite back the low groan that filled him. It broke whatever spell she was under. Her breath caught sharply, and she snatched her hand away as if scorched.

He forced himself to turn, grateful for the protective cover of his cloak. She stood gaping at him as if she couldn't quite understand what had happened. A lovely rose tinted her cheeks, her fiery hair swirling in the cold wind. Already she was fading away, stepping back into the moonlight. The heat in him cooled, leaving him with a familiar hollowness just under his breastbone. His throat closed in on him.

"No weapons," she whispered.

"No." He clenched his fist to keep from reaching out.

"Well, thank you, then." She backed up another step. "For speaking out. Unnecessary, but kind."

"Wait."

She halted.

He stared blankly for a moment, not knowing what to do. When she looked as though she might move, he fumbled with his pockets. *Give her something. Make her stay.*

"Here." The coin in his hand flashed in the weak light as he held it out. "Take it."

She did not hesitate. One second it was between his fingers, the other it was gone. He watched as she inspected it, the red wings of her brows knitting together. "West Moon Club?"

"It isn't proper currency," he said as the frown grew. "Just a silly trinket made by men who have nothing better to do with their time. I've no use for it any longer." No, because they had cast him out. The emptiness in him became pain. He hated the coin and everything associated with it. Of all the things he could have reached for in his haste, why had it been that?

One red brow rose as she glanced up at him, considering.

"It is pure gold." He was babbling like a maiden.

Irritation flushed within him. He bit it back. "Melt it down and sell it when you have need." The idea gave him a certain joy.

Her fingers closed around the coin. "You think I'm too proud to take it?"

His lips twitched. "On the contrary. I think you pragmatic enough to make good use of it." He didn't offer her the wad of bank notes he had in his pocket. A gift was one thing. Charity was another.

Green eyes slanted up at him. "Silver-tongued devil. But you're wrong. I don't take gifts from strangers."

He opened his mouth to protest when she flicked her wrist. The knife in her hand hissed through the air, embedding itself with a thud into the wall next to him.

"A trade, however."

Oh, he liked this girl. Keeping his eyes on her, he pulled out the knife with ease. The slim, black-enameled hilt was warm from her touch. That she trusted him with the knife left him oddly expectant, as if for once the next sunrise might be a welcome sight. "A trade it is," he rasped.

"Go on, then," she said. "I'll not leave until you're well out of here."

Deliciously peremptory. His gut tightened and went hot.

Come with me. He'd take her to a tavern, buy her ale and bread, tease her simply to hear her talk, to watch her all night and revel in the way she commanded those in orbit around her. Only then she'd see him. And run. The heaviness in his chest was a crushing thing.

"As my lady wishes."

She gave a start. She hadn't truly thought he'd obey, and it made him chuckle. God, he hadn't smiled this much in years. The muscles along his chest ached from his recent laughter. When had he last laughed? He could not remember.

Desperate yearning returned, for in her unflinching stare, the way she did not hesitate to speak to him, he saw the reflection of his own salvation. A man no longer cast out to the shadows, but seen. If there was a greater gift in this world he knew not of it. Archer was not fool enough to turn away from a gift.

Hector Ellis's daughter. So the man would have to live. Archer turned a new plan over in his mind. One Archer knew Ellis would agree to, for a man such as him would agree to anything to save his own skin. A little time was all that Archer required.

Taking a deep breath, he made himself say the words he must. "Good night to you, fair Pan."

Chapter One

No, no, farther down...yes, that's the one...there!" Satisfaction pulled at her lips. "Ah, how lovely."

The man at the counter flushed in pleasure. His gaze strayed to her smiling lips and held for a moment past propriety. "The loveliest I've seen, Miss."

His small boldness sent another wash of red over his fair skin. Miranda leaned farther into him. The glass countertop beneath her elbows gave a small groan, and the clerk swallowed hard, his gaze flittering between her mouth and the swells of her breasts that plumped over her bodice. His grip tightened on the ruby bracelet he held in his hands.

So easy, really, to seduce a man with the simple act of arching one's back. A woman ought to feel satisfaction in the sight. Miranda only felt as she always felt: dirty, wrong, empty.

"Set it down," she murmured before clearing her throat delicately. "Let me see it in the proper light."

Gently, he set the bracelet among the others, dozens of necklaces and bracelets strewn out over the small counter. Too many wares pulled out for display than was prudent or proper. So very accommodating. And a mistake only a befuddled clerk would make.

Miranda set her chin upon her hand, the act bringing her arm against the side of her breast, lifting it further into view. The clerk smothered a noise, his eyes riveted to the sudden increase in displayed flesh. Her skin crawled. She did not flinch, only looked up at him with a small secret smile. *You and I understand this forbidden desire between us*, it said to him. Her free hand settled with the lightness of a feather upon the pearl necklace lying near her ribs.

"Any one of these jewels would do you credit, miss."

Her finger hooked over the row of pearls. *Slowly. Slowly.* Countless times she had done this, yet every time felt like the first. Every time filled her with terror. *Never let it show.*

She mocked a wounded pout. "The *jewels* credit me, sir?"

His thin mouth worked as he flushed. "You misunderstand. They pale against your beauty. Were I a ruby, I would despair at being noticed while in your presence."

A genuine smile tugged at her lips. Plain and bashful, he might be, but the young man had a romantic heart and the beginnings of a poetic tongue. It was his whey-face and quick blushes that had made her select this shop that rested at the edge of respectability. The little shop specialized in fine jewels pawned by aristocrats whose wealth was dying. A place new wealth bought baubles for their town-kept mistresses. A place where a young, unescorted woman might go, pretend to shop for jewels far past her means so that she might flirt with the young clerk she had her eye on.

It was the role she played. Letting him see her walk by his window once a week. Making eye contact before turning away with a blush. And then working up her courage to finally enter. She dipped her head and blushed.

"You are too kind, sir," she murmured.

He fairly glowed with pleasure, and her heart ached. Too good a boy to ruin. For he would be ruined when his master found out what he had let happen here. But she could not return empty-handed. It had been too long. On the inside she screamed. *This is my life, and I hate it. I hate it.* She returned his smile.

The shop bell trilled, and the young man started as if caught with his hand in the biscuit bin. Two plump matrons entered, giving him a curt nod. Like Miranda's, their gowns were slightly out of date and well-mended, but unlike with Miranda, the clerk took notice and did not jump to assist them.

Miranda trailed a gloved finger down her neck.

"W-would you like to try one of them on?" he asked.

She licked her lower lip, a tiny flicker of pink tongue that kept him riveted. "I don't think I should." It took no effort to make her lips tremble. In truth, she felt like crying.

"Merciful heavens!"

The matron's exclamation made them both turn. The older woman pressed her hand upon her ample chest and grabbed hold of her companion.

"Oh, Jane, look who it is!"

Her friend paled and made an attempt to support her friend. "Who, Margaret?"

"The Dread Lord Archer! His coach is coming up the street!"

"No!"

Both women craned their wrinkled necks to peek between the gold lettering upon the shop window. Miranda stopped short of rolling her eyes. *What a pair, these two.* Her fingers tensed to take her prize but she held firm. *Slowly. Slowly.* Marks always felt it if one rushed. It was instinctive.

"I've seen him," hissed Margaret. "Late one night on the way home from the theater. He walked along Piccadilly as if he had every right to do so. I swear I nearly swooned from fright!"

"You poor dear. What has the world come to when men such as he are permitted to roam the streets?"

Miranda had never heard such censorious drivel.

"My dear, he is aristocracy," said Margaret, "and as rich as Croesus. Who would dare question him? I heard he has sent at least four men to hospital for simply looking at him in the wrong light."

The conveyance came flush with the shop window. Miranda caught a glimpse of the black top hat and cloak of a coachman, a black coach with a white shield upon its door.

"Heavens, he looked at me..." Jane shuddered, and with a moan, her eyes rolled up in her head.

"Jane!" Her friend tried to grab her as the woman began to topple.

"Here! Here!" The clerk jumped up, running to catch the hare-brained woman.

There was something to say for flighty females. Miranda acted, slipping the necklace into her skirt pocket as she rushed to aid, *accidentally* brushing several necklaces off the counter in her haste. "Oh my," she exclaimed, frantically trying to gather the jewels and succeeding in making a muck of it. Ropes of gold and gems fell to the floor, a hopeless muddle.

The clerk wavered between assisting her and struggling to help the matron on the floor. *Perfect.*

"What a mess I have made!" Miranda pressed a shaking hand to her brow. "I am sorry. And you have your hands full!"

She reached the door, her heart pounding. It pounded every time. Every time.

"Wait, Miss!" The clerk buckled, his hand outstretched as if he would pull her back.

Hand twitching on the doorknob, she shot the clerk a regretful smile. "Good-bye. I *am* sorry."

His words were drowned out by the bell.

Outside, the coach in question was gone, swallowed up by street traffic and drifting fog. Only now did the gaping pedestrians begin moving on. Unsettled murmurs rippled along the streets before being drowned out by the usual clatter and clang of hacks, omnibuses, and coaches rattling along the cobbled road. Miranda decided she did not want to know what the unfortunate Lord Archer looked like. She had experienced enough horrors in her meager lifetime.

The slight weight in her pocket felt like a ton as she made her way home. Miranda's steps stuttered to a stop as she saw the sleek, black double-brougham stretched out like a coffin in the front portico of the house. Thick whorls of yellow-green evening fog rose from the cobbled drive, ghosting over the coach's large spoke wheels and coiling like snakes round the spindly legs of the matched black Friesians that stood placidly waiting.

Dread plucked at her insides. Long gone were the days when their drive filled with endless lines of landaus, barouches, and phaetons as nobility and gentry alike called upon father to purchase his wares.

With a jostle of rigging and the smart clip of hooves, the coach turned, and the crest upon the door flashed in the waning light. A white shield bisected by a heavy black cross bore the words *Sola bona quae honesta* upon it. Four sharp arrowheads slashed across the white planes of the shield. The hairs along her arm stood at attention, and she knew the source of her disquiet. *The Dread Lord Archer.*

The coach drew near, and the form of a figure, no more than a broad black outline of shoulders and the glimpse of an arm, appeared behind the window glass. As the coach pulled away, a finger of ice slid along Miranda's spine, for someone was staring back.

"I shall not!"

Her shout bounded off the bare stone walls of the dark, cramped kitchen. High and rather thready, nothing like Miranda's normal voice. She struggled to tone it down.

Her father moved around the battered wooden table that stood between them. His small brown eyes flashed. "You most certainly shall!" He slammed his fist to the table. "My word is law here!"

"Bosh." She slammed her wooden spoon down as well, sending a splatter of mutton stew across the pudding. "Your control over me ended the day you sold Daisy off to the highest bidder."

The wrinkled mask of his face went pale as Irish linen. "You dare!" His hand rose to strike but held, hovering in the air and shaking, when she did not flinch.

"Please try it," she said quietly. Her eyes held his as the air about her began to coalesce, heating and stirring with an almost expectant agitation. "I beg of you."

Father's hand quivered then slowly lowered. "I'm sure you do, daughter." Spittle slicked the corners of his shaking lips. "See me writhe and burn."

Miranda shifted, heat and pain mingling within her belly, a surge that wanted out.

"Always calling upon the fire to protect you." He took a step closer, his eyes burning into her. "Never mind the price."

Like a flame in a draft, the heat snuffed, and with it, her father's confidence seemed to swell.

"The worst of it is that I do this for you," he coaxed, leaning in. "You're not a lass anymore. Not for years. Did you think to live here forever with me?"

"No, I—" Her mouth snapped shut. She had not given the future much thought but simply lived from day to day. Surviving. No point exchanging the hell one knew for the hell one did not.

"I think you must believe so. You've scared off every lad that's come this way ever since that fool Martin..." He swallowed down his words aware, for once, that even he might have gone too far. But he rallied quickly, and his bushy brows formed a white V. "It cannot have escaped your notice that this is the finest meal we've had in months." His weathered hand swept over the meager meal of mutton stew and simple brown bread pudding that Miranda was preparing. "Who do you think provided the money for this meal?"

"I thought perhaps you'd sold the wool—"

His dry cackle cut the air. "With the price of wool being as low as it is, and the debts I owe, we'd be lucky to dine on fish-head stew. My creditors will take the house before the year is out," he said quietly. "And you will have no home to come to."

A home? She almost laughed. She hadn't a true home in years. Not since her sisters had left.

"Doesn't take much to imagine what trade a beauty like you will find," he went on. "But once that beauty fades? 'Tis hardly fittin' to say what's to come of you."

"Oh, stop!" Miranda snapped. "You paint a very grim picture, indeed. And one that's hung over my head for years."

"Bloody hell!" The pudding crashed to the floor in a mess of brown scum and broken crockery. "You owe me, Miranda!" Rage colored him red as he pointed at her. "If it weren't for that fire, I'd have half my fortune! By God, you destroyed my bloody warehouse!"

"Years I have paid penance for my mistake!" she shouted. "Still, it is not enough. Well, I am done with it." Her hand slashed the air as if the motion could somehow sever their conversation. "You cannot make me do this!"

Father's thin lip curled into a sneer. "Aye, I cannot," he agreed with sudden calmness. "The agreement states you must go willingly, or it is void." He took a step closer, pressing up against the wooden table, and pointed with a trembling finger. "But I'll tell you this: Should you refuse, you'll no longer live here."

Her throat closed, red-hot pain forming a large lump there. The lack of a home was one thing. The lack of proper shelter was another beast entirely. "You cannot seriously . . ." She swallowed.

The yellowed whites of his eyes flashed in the lamp-light. "I'm done with you. I would not have kept you as long as I have if I weren't waiting for this moment. So you've had a disappointment with Martin. I'm glad for it! I was a fool to even consider it. Some promises are too dangerous..." He swallowed audibly. "Your bags are packed, either way," he snapped.

So it had come to this. Miranda's lower lip quivered before she bit down hard. There was little love lost between them. But he was her father, and he was prepared to toss her to the wolves. Pain radiated across her chest, seeping into her bones.

Father's eyes were flat. Dead. She knew that look. His decision was made. Even so, she could not but try.

"I cannot believe you would—"

"You will marry Lord Archer!" he shouted out, his temper breaking like glass. "Devil take it, the man is one of the richest nobles in the kingdom. I cannot believe your stupidity for even refusing. Of all the bleeding stubborn—"

"But why?" A wretched sob escaped before she could swallow it down. Hateful that she should be weak before him.

He stopped short and blinked at her. "Why what?"

"Why does he want me?" She wiped a hand over her mouth. "I am nobody. I've never heard of the man before today. How can he know me?"

Father's expression froze for a long moment before he broke into an incredulous laugh. "I may be a failed man, Miranda Rose. But I have one jewel left in my coffers." He came round the table, his expression almost fond. She backed away from him, bumping up against the worktable. Father stopped but the satisfaction in his smile remained.

"Lord Archer has wealth, power, and land. A man such as that need not look to nobility for a bride. Overbreeding has left their rank chinless and small-eyed. You, my dear, are a diamond in a sea of cut glass." A familiar gleam lit Father's eyes, the glint of a transaction well played. "The finest feather for his cap."

For a moment, she saw red. "I will go to Poppy or Daisy."

A terrible silence fell between them, and her father's confident expression withered. He went pale as cream. "They won't want you. Never have."

"They've offered before." Her sisters had pleaded with her, in truth. And she had refused out of a misplaced sense of obligation toward Father. Penance, really, because she had been the one to start him on the road to ruin. How gratifying to know that she had finally reached her limit on guilt. But she didn't want her sisters' pity, nor to be their burden. The very idea made her insides pitch.

Father raised his hands in disgust. "He has paid handsomely for the right to you, Miranda. If you plan to forfeit the agreement, then I am leaving." He straightened his tattered waistcoat and smoothed his disheveled hair. "I suggest you do the same. Believe me when I say that Lord Archer does not take kindly to being cheated."

"Oh, I believe you." Something told her his being cheated by Father had put her into this mess in the first place.

They stared at each other for a long minute, her finger tapping an idle rhythm against the counter while her father waited in stony silence. She ought to hate this Lord Archer for buying her like a commodity. Save he'd only done the same as nearly every gentleman in England did. Marriage was a business. Any sensible girl knew this. It was only when they had come down in the world that she'd started to hope she might marry for love.

The stew bubbled brown and thick in the pot next to her, making her stomach growl. She missed having steady meals, a life free of theft and guilt. A wash of shame hit her so suddenly that she sucked in a pained breath. Lord Archer had entered into an agreement in good faith. Only to become another man her father would cheat, and she'd be a part of it.

No more. She would not become like Father. She could live a life of honor and walk with her head held up from now on.

Faced with the choice of living on the streets or doing the honorable thing, her decision was rather easy. Unfortunately, that did not stop her stomach from turning over as she forced the words from her mouth.

"All right." The vision of the silly shop matron in a swoon flashed in her mind, and a moment of pure terror wracked her body. She swallowed hard. "All right. I will do it."

He gaped at her, unbelieving. When she simply stared back, a smile pulled at his mouth. "Very good." Satisfied, Father grabbed a thick slice of bread off the counter. "On the morrow, then."

Her head snapped back. "What!"

He half-turned, his mouth already full. "He insists upon marrying you tomorrow," he said around the bread. "Everything has been arranged. Lord Archer has already acquired a special license so there is no impediment or need to wait."

The fire beneath the burners flared high for an instant. Her life had been bought, sold, and arranged quite neatly. *Bloody men.*

Her father tore off another hunk with his teeth and turned to go.

"Stop!" Miranda reached deep into her pocket and pulled out her spoils. "Take it!" The pearl choker slammed to the table. "And treasure it well, for it is the last thing I shall ever steal for you. We are more than even now, Father. After this, we are finished."

Chapter Two

Getting married was a happy dream that had filled Miranda's girlhood thoughts and promptly left as she grew older. She well knew the face that looked back from the mirror each morning. She was not foolish enough to pretend that she was without beauty. Vanity may be a sin but so was lying. She was fair of face and form, though she knew many a girl who looked better.

However, as a woman without fortune or title, she received few offers of marriage. The most consistent offers came in the form of teasing shouts from market vendors when she walked to Covent Garden each Saturday morning. How then, she thought as Daisy pinned white roses in her hair the following morning, had it come to this?

Perhaps it was a dream. The woman in the mirror didn't look at all like her. She was too pale. Her pink gown, one of many provided by Lord Archer's money, ruffled and frothed around her like a confectionary. Miranda turned away with disdain. It was the image of an innocent and a maiden. She was neither. And yet *he* had come for her. Why?

She did not believe Father's nonsense about him wanting her for her beauty. There were plenty of pretty daughters of utterly bankrupt, thus desperate, nobles for a wealthy man to chose from. What, then, did he want? *What has the world come to when men such as he are permitted to roam the streets…* Perspiration bloomed along her upper lip. And yet Lord Archer did not know precisely what he was acquiring when he took Miranda as his bride, did he?

To create fire by mere thought. It was the stuff of myth. She had discovered the talent quite by accident. And had burned through her share of disasters. Father and Mother had forbidden anyone to ever speak of it and, more to the point, for Miranda to ever use her talent again. Poppy had simply disappeared in the library to search for an explanation; she never found one. Only Daisy had been impressed, though quite put out that she did not possess a similar unearthly talent. As for herself, the question always remained: Was she a monster? Both beauty and beast rolled into one unstable force? Despite her desire to know, there was the greater fear of putting the question to anyone and seeing them turn away as Martin had. So she kept it inside. She would not tell her husband to be, no. But she took comfort in the notion that she was not without defenses.

Poppy and Daisy's mutual disregard for Father kept them at a distance as Father hovered by her elbow, guarding all possible attempts to escape. Their chatter was no more than a din, Father's hand upon her arm a ghost, as they made their way to the small family chapel by the river.

Reverend Spradling met them at the door. The brackets around his fleshy mouth cut deep as his eyes slid from Miranda to Father. "Lord Archer is..." He tilted his head and pulled at the cassock hugging his bulging neck. "He is waiting in the vestry."

"Grand," said Father with an inane smile.

"He wants to talk to Miss Ellis in private," the reverend interrupted as Father tried to walk through the doorway. "I told him it was inappropriate but he was most insistent."

The two men turned to Miranda. So now her opinion mattered, did it? She might have laughed, only she feared it would come out as a sob.

"Very well." She gathered her skirts. Her fingers had turned to ice long before, and the ruffles slid from her grasp. She took a firmer hold. "I won't be but a moment."

Slowly, she walked toward the vestry door looming before her. She would finally face the man who would be her husband, the man who sent brutes to hospital and caused women to swoon with terror.

He stood erect as a soldier at the far end of the little stone room. Women, she thought, letting her gaze sweep over him, could be utterly ridiculous.

She closed the door and waited for him to speak.

"You came." He could not fully stamp out the surprise in his deep voice.

"Yes."

He was tall and very large, though there wasn't a spare ounce of fat discernible over his entire form. The largeness of appearance came from the breadth of his shoulders, the muscles that his charcoal gray morning suit—no matter how finely tailored—could not completely hide and the long length of his strong legs encased in gray woolen trousers. It was not the elegant, thin frame of a refined man, but the brute and efficient form of a dock-worker. In short, Lord Archer possessed the sort of virile body that would catch many a lady's eye and hold it—were it not for one unavoidable fact.

She lifted her eyes to his face, or where it ought to be. Carved with a Mona Lisa smile upon its lips, a black hard mask like one might wear at Carnival stared back. Beneath the mask, his entire head was covered in tight black silk, offering not a bit of skin to view. The perversity of his costume unnerved, but she was hardly willing to swoon.

"I thought it best," he said after letting her study him, "that you enter into this union with full understanding." Black-gloved fingers ran over the silver handle of the walking stick he held. "As you are to be my wife, it would be foolish of me to try to keep my appearance from you."

He spoke with such equanimity that she could only gaze in amazement. A memory flickered before her eyes like a flame caught in a draft, a vision of a different man, in a different place. A man who also hid in shadows, whose gloriously strong body had haunted her dreams for months afterward, made her want things she hadn't the name for back then, things that made her skin heat on many a cold night. It had shamed her, the way she had coveted the dark stranger. But it could not have been Lord Archer. The stranger had a voice like shadows, rasping and weak, not like Lord Archer's strong, deep rumble.

"Look sharp, Miss Ellis!" The walking stick slammed on the stone floor with a crack, and she jumped. "Do you still intend to proceed?" he asked with more calm.

She stepped forward, and the man went rigid. "Who are you? An actor of some sort?" Her temper swelled like fire to air. "Is this some joke Father has concocted to bedevil me, because let me tell you—"

"I am Lord Benjamin Archer," he said with such acidity that she halted. His eyes flashed from behind the mask. "And it is no joke I play." The hand on the walking stick tightened. "Though there are days I wish it to be just that."

"Why do you wear that mask?"

"Asks the woman whose beauty might as well be a mask."

"*Pardon me?*"

The immobile black mask simply stared back, floating like a terrible effigy over broad shoulders.

"What is beauty or ugliness but a false front that prompts man to make assumptions rather than delving deeper. Look at you." His hand gestured toward her face. "Not a flaw or distortion of line to mar that perfect beauty. I have seen your face before, miss. Michelangelo sculpted it from cold marble three hundred years ago, his divine hand creating what men would adore." He took a step closer. "Tell me, Miss Ellis, do you not use that beauty as a shield, keeping the world at bay so that no one will know your true nature?"

"Bastard," she spat when she could find her voice. She had been beaten once or twice, forced to steal and lie, but no one had left her so utterly raw.

"I am that as well. Better you know it now."

She gathered up her train, but the heavy masses of slippery fabric evaded her grip. "I came of my own free will but will not abide by cruel remarks made at my expense," she said, finally collecting herself. "Good-bye, Lord Archer."

He moved, but stopped himself as though he feared coming too close. A small gurgle died in his throat. "What will it take?"

The tightly controlled urgency in his voice made her turn back.

"If you find my character and appearance so very distasteful," she said through her teeth, "then why ask for my hand?"

His dark head jerked a fraction. "I am the last of my family line," he said with less confidence. "Though I have love for Queen and Country, I do not desire to see my ancestral lands swallowed up by the crown. I need a wife."

The idea that she would procreate with the man hadn't entered her mind. It seemed unimaginable.

"Why not court one of your nobles?" she asked through dry lips.

He lifted his chin a fraction. "There are not many fathers who would give their marketable daughters up to a man such as me."

It irked her that his words made her chest tighten in regret.

Lord Archer tilted his head and assessed her with all the warmth of a man eyeing horseflesh for purchase. "Your appearance may matter little to me but when the time comes for my heir to enter into society, your stunning looks will help a great deal to facilitate him."

She could not fault the sensibility of his plan. Even so...

"Why do you wear that mask?" she asked again.

The mask stared back.

"Are you ill? Have you some sort of sensitivity to light upon your skin?" she prompted.

"Sensitivity to light," he uttered and then gave a short laugh of derision. He lifted his head. "I am deformed." That the confession hurt his pride did not escape her. "It was an accident. Long ago."

She nodded stupidly.

"I realize my appearance is far from ideal to an attractive young lady in search of a husband. On the other hand, I can provide a lifestyle of wealth and comfort..." He trailed off as though pained by his own speech and then shifted his weight. "Well, Miss Ellis? What say you? This is between us now. Whatever your decision, your father may keep what little funds he hasn't managed to squander without fear of retribution from me."

"And if I say no? What will you do? Is there another girl you might ask?" She shouldn't care really, but her basic curiosity could not be quelled.

He flinched, a tiny movement, but on him it seemed as obvious as if he'd been struck by a blow.

"No. It has to be you." He sucked in a sharp breath and straightened like a soldier. "To speak plainly, there is no other option left to me. As to what will I do should you say no, I will continue to live alone. In short, I need you. Your help, that is. Should you grant it, Miss Ellis, you shall want for nothing."

The man in the black mask seemed to stand alone, apart from everything. Miranda knew loneliness when she saw it. Her mind drifted over another memory, one hard repressed. One of herself standing in the very same corner of the vestry, watching as Martin cut their engagement and walked away. And it had hurt. God, it had hurt. So much so that the idea of doing it to another made her queasy.

Lord Archer had shown his weakness, given her a chance to cut their agreement. He'd given her power over him. The man was clearly intelligent enough to have done so with purpose. A chance at equality was unexpected.

Still, none of that might have mattered. Foolish was the

woman who gave away her freedom out of sympathy. No, it was not sympathy or the hope of power that prompted a decision; she felt something when in the presence of this strange man, a tingling thrill that played over her belly, the sense of rapid forward motion though her body stood still. It was a feeling long dormant, one gleaned from taking a sword in hand, swaggering through dark alleys when all proper girls were in their beds. It was adventure. Lord Archer, with his black countenance and rich voice, offered a sense of adventure, a dare. She could do nothing short of picking up that gauntlet, or regret it for the rest of her days. Perhaps, then, she could help them both. The idea of helping rather than destroying filled her with a certain lightness of heart.

Miranda collected the blasted train that threatened to trip her and straightened. "We have kept my father and sisters waiting long enough, Lord Archer." She paused at the door to wait for him. "Shall we go?"

Chapter Three

❧∼❧

It had been a brief ceremony, without sentiment. A few words spoken, and Miranda Rose Ellis had disappeared. She glanced down at her wedding ring, a glowing round moonstone held aloft by a thin gold band. Now, as Lady Miranda Archer, she rode in an elegant town coach opposite her new husband. A cantankerous grumble of thunder sounded overhead and, with it, a flash of blue light. Lord Archer's black mask gleamed for an instant, the high curves of its cheekbones and the rounded eye sockets highlighted in the dim. Miranda's heart missed a beat.

Silver streaks of rain slid down the window, obscuring the view as they crossed a small gully. She leaned closer only to have the window fog over from the warmth of her breath. She wiped it away, heedless of marring her kid gloves, and was rewarded with the sight of her new home as they turned up the long drive.

Rising up four stories, it broke from the gentle crest of land like the crags of a mountaintop. Lightning flashed above the rain-slicked slate roof, bringing the sharp gables and multiple chimneys into fine relief against the rolling sky.

Her palm flattened against the icy window. The Gothic-styled house was almost as wide as it was high. It dominated the land, lording like a great hulking beast. Large bow windows gleamed like pale jewels in a crown, but showed nothing of light or life within. Only a small lonely little light over the front portico guided the way home.

The coach shuddered to a halt, and the steady drum of the rain upon the roof abated. Lord Archer stepped swiftly from the cab and promptly took hold of her elbow. She bit the inside of her cheek and stood straight as she climbed the cold marble steps. *I shall not cry.*

Wind howled across the portico, and the brass lantern hanging high above swayed. Behind them, the four blacks stood placidly, rain dripping from their shaggy manes, steam escaping in bursts from their nostrils as they waited for the outrider to take down Miranda's traveling valise.

A not-so-gentle squeeze upon Miranda's arm made her turn around. No, she could not run to the safety of the coach. Enormous black double doors loomed high before opening to reveal the figure of an elderly man outlined in pale lamplight. More gloom.

They walked through the doors and into...light. And warmth. A large hall opened up before them, the sight making her falter. Easily the width and breadth of her old home, the hallway was filled, not with cobwebs and dank wood as she had imagined, but light and beauty. White-and-black marble floors laid out in a checkerboard design shined beneath her heels. The woodwork was painted crisp white, and the walls covered in black lacquer. Such a color ought to have made it very dark but the walls gleamed like jet under the light of crystal sconces and an elegant chandelier of cut crystal and golden filigree. Russian, she thought, looking up at it; nothing that beautifully crafted could be anything but.

Lord Archer watched her appraisal. "You were expecting something different?"

"I...yes," she admitted. "The house appeared so foreboding when we came up the drive."

"We arrived during a storm." A sudden moan of wind from the other side of the doors punctuated his statement. "Very few houses appear hospitable in such conditions, especially if they are unfamiliar."

"That is true."

"But you still expected something different," he said, studying her as though she were a specimen under a microscope.

How he knew the truth, she could not comprehend. Long before the storm, her wild imaginings had pictured dark corridors, gloomy rooms, and dusty halls laced with cobwebs.

His penetrating stare did not abate. "My home is my haven. Should I not make it comfortable?"

"Of course." Desperately, she looked to the elderly gentleman who stood as straight as a mainmast not two feet away. He'd taken Lord Archer's coat and hat when they entered, and had done so with such quiet efficiency Miranda doubted Lord Archer had truly noticed him.

Lord Archer caught the direction of her gaze and stiffened. "Hullo, Gilroy. Didn't see you there. You have everything prepared?"

"Good evening, my lord. Yes, my lord."

Around a network of wrinkles, Gilroy's kind eyes gleamed deep brown. Miranda nodded in greeting as

Lord Archer took the mantle from her shoulders. "This is Lady Archer." He handed Gilroy the mantle.

"Gilroy is our butler, majordomo, what have you," he said to her as though the idea of titles irritated him a little.

"I am honored, my lady." The man gave a short bow. "On behalf of the staff, we shall endeavor to serve you well."

"I am confident you will," she said, reaching for the same quiet dignity. The idea that she had a staff was almost enough to send her running to the carriage. Only Lord Archer would assuredly haul her back.

Lord Archer took her elbow once more and they walked down the length of the hall, past artworks of pastoral scenes and portraits of bewigged ladies and gentlemen.

"Do you have a valet?" Miranda asked, turning back toward Lord Archer as they moved past a small front parlor done up in lemon yellow and white with delicate Grecian style furnishings.

"No. I am a grown man, well capable of dressing and shaving myself. Gilroy takes care of incidentals." He waved his hand in distraction.

Poor Gilroy.

Lord Archer's eyes cut to her as though hearing the silent criticism. "It isn't as though I have lacings and coiffures to worry over," he said.

Childhood lectures from Mother ran in her head. *One never speaks of personal grooming. A gentleman should never mention a lady's toilette.* Then again, Miranda had found Mother's lectures rather stifling. "I admit surprise," she said, catching a glimpse of a library filled with blue velvet sofas and deep leather wing chairs. "I've always thought nobles considered a valet a mark of distinction.

Father said if you could, your lot would have someone wipe your..." She trailed off in a furious flush of heat.

Lord Archer looked at her sidelong. "Do go on, Lady Archer."

She stepped away to peer into a large room of powder blue, rather hoping that the floor would open up and swallow her whole. What had prompted her to speak so basely? She had deliberately tried to bait Lord Archer.

"The ladies' salon," he murmured as she gazed up at the ceiling painted like a summer sky with rolling clouds and sunbeams. The décor of the home was old-fashioned. There simply wasn't enough to appease the modern eye, no wall coverings of ornate patterning, no doilies, needlework, or bric-a-brac to fill the space. White lintels, Grecian pediments over the doors, their dentil moldings foiled with gold. Marble busts and convex mirrors adorned the simple mantels. Gothic architecture, Georgian interior, Regency décor... it was like sinking slowly back in a time long past.

"I shall give you a proper tour tomorrow." He headed toward a massive staircase of white marble. "For now, you need rest."

Miranda could wander through a house such as this all day. But she let herself be led, her feet sinking soundlessly into the carpet when they reached the second floor.

The walls were crimson. Golden candle-fed sconces and potted palms made the long hallway cheery, but the absence of servants was odd. "Where are the other servants?" she whispered. It would surely take an army of them to keep such a house.

"I keep a small staff. My privacy is more important. You shall meet most of them tomorrow."

Feeling lost, she reached out and touched his arm. He

pulled away with a low hiss, and her face flamed. "I'm sorry." She chided herself for touching him, for feeling the need to.

Lord Archer took a long breath. "No. I am." He cursed sharply. "The accident . . . my right side. I don't like to be touched on my right side." He stilled and then lifted his left arm, offering it to her. "I have offended you, the very thought of which shames me. Take my left arm. It is unaffected. Please," he added when she hesitated.

His eyes were gray, a true dove gray surrounded by thick black lashes that rivaled any lady's. It seemed an odd thing to fixate upon but she could not look away. Her heart tapped like a metronome, the palpable thing that was the force of his will and the strength of his body nearly overwhelmed her. Carefully, she placed a hand upon his arm, noting the hardness of it and the way his muscles jumped at her touch.

Her husband nodded in satisfaction, then pulled her along. He stopped before a set of doors where an elderly woman waited.

"This is Eula, our housekeeper," he said by way of introduction. "You shall want to discuss the household running with her, I should think."

By the way the elder woman was glaring at her, Miranda had grave doubts as to their working together.

Lord Archer stood stiffly between the women. "Well then, I shall see you at dinner." He gave an awkward bow to Miranda and left her alone with the scowling woman.

Coming only to Miranda's shoulder, the thin woman held herself stiffly erect and set her eagle eyes upon her. Miranda stared back squarely as the hairs on the nape of her neck bristled. The woman's bedraggled bun was the color of old ivory. The lines of her face were cragged and deep but the bones beneath the skin were strong. Something she saw in Miranda must have met her approval. One corner of her colorless lips lifted slightly.

"Well, you're no mouse. Thank God for that. A mouse has no business coming into a lion's den." Her gray brow lifted when Miranda merely held her stare. "Come along then. His Worship has bid me leave you a luncheon. I suppose a skinny bird such as yourself will be wanting some food."

Over Eula's shoulder, Miranda spied a tureen of soup and a mound of golden rolls spilling from a ceramic basket. Her stomach almost growled in anticipation.

Eula turned to shuffle into Miranda's room, leaving in her wake the smell of camphor and old sheets. "He'll collect you himself come dinner," she said over her shoulder. "And don't think of leaving these rooms by yourself."

"And why not?" Really, Miranda had no intention of wandering this night but Eula's high-handedness riled her.

"The dark hides all manner of sins here. No telling what horrors you'll encounter in some shadowed corner."

Eula's discordant cackle taunted Miranda as the woman disappeared down the hall. Heart thumping in her chest, Miranda sat heavily on a plush settee. *This was not a mistake. The evil woman only sought to scare her.* Miranda bit her lip as she stared at the empty doorway, for one thought bothered her above all others: She wished Lord Archer would come back.

Chapter Four

❦ ❀ ❦

Archer nearly ran down the hall like a frightened schoolboy. Had he some blasted malady that prompted him to act the ass at the very worst instant? Surely he must, for he'd nearly lost her before even having her. He cursed and shoved open the servant's door. A maid coming up the stairs squeaked in alarm, nearly dropping her pile of linens. Sally, was it? New maid. She'd learn.

He took the narrow stairs upward. The footman on the next landing stepped aside, well prepared for the sudden sight of the master on the backstairs. Archer took the stairs two at a time, tugging at his cravat as he got toward the top.

He burst through the door at the top of the stair and slammed it behind him, setting the panes of glass above his head shuddering. Solitude. Already he felt his disquiet ebb.

His green house. A little glass jewel hidden away on the roof of the house. The rain rattled hard upon the glass, streaking and pebbling, hiding the world from view. It was kinder here, warm and humid. Filled with potted fruit trees and velvet roses, their fresh scent as thick as the air.

The mask first. He tore it from his head, then the inner one, and allowed himself the first fresh breath he'd had in hours. The humid air collided with his sweat-soaked skin, and his nerves twitched. He raked his fingers hard through his flattened hair, scraping his scalp just to feel the blood flow beneath the surface. The rest of his clothes followed in rapid succession. Then he moved to the water tap set high in the wall and opened it.

God it was cold. Good. He needed as much. Being trapped in the dammed coach with her had been torture enough. Archer closed his eyes and let the water pour over his head, down his heated torso. And he was rewarded with the image of that blasted reverend looking at him in the church, waiting for him to kiss Miranda—of all things. Had the man any idea of just how badly Archer had wanted to?

And her voice. It no longer held that high, girlish pip, but was warm and soft—like honey in the sun. Archer shivered. That voice, haunting him for three years. He took a shuddering breath, closed the tap, and reached for a towel.

The rain petered out to a light mist as he walked to the long cot by one of the glass walls. He reclined on it with a sigh and blinked up at a cluster of peach roses in full, audacious bloom. This wasn't how he'd imagined facing her, still trapped in a mask, snapping at her like an arrogant bastard solely because, for the first time in years, he'd felt true embarrassment over his appearance. What must she think of him?

His forearm fell over his eyes. Ah God, and that utter rot about wanting her for an heir. Right-ho, when he couldn't even show her who he was. *What* he was. His mind had gone blank when she'd asked him for an explanation. The truth was ridiculous, and the height of selfishness. Because he wanted her, despite all logic, all caution. Though he could never fully be with her, he needed her near. And now? Being near her wasn't nearly enough.

How could he hide what he was from her indefinitely? His desolate laugh sounded like a stranger's. Impossible. What he wanted was impossible.

Not impossible. Only hopeful.

Archer smiled tightly as he heard the voice in his head. "Ah, Elizabeth. If only it were you."

It was a game he played with himself, talking to her as though she were here. Sometimes he wondered if talking with a memory was the final push into madness. Or the only thing that kept him sane.

You deserve happiness, Benjamin.

It was what he wanted to hear. But was it true?

A teardrop of dew rolled along the velvet edge of a rose. It hung for a suspended moment, glimmering diamond bright, before falling on his temple to skim over his brow like the stroke of a fingertip. He couldn't remember the last time human hands had willingly touched him.

Not true. Miranda had. She had touched him as if he were just a man. He had lived on those moments ever since, pulled them to the fore when loneliness threatened to suck him down and drown him. He hadn't meant to be away from her for so long. What ought to have been a year had drifted into three.

He took a deep breath. The air around was still, wet, and thick. Past the sweetness of roses came the heady scents of exotic orchids, strange plants acquired on his trips down the Amazon. All in search of a cure. His gaze drifted to the cluster of fire-pink flowers resembling a feather duster. That one had turned his piss red for a week. The purple seeds from some dark pit in Brazil that would have killed a normal man had him hunched over begging for mercy for twenty-four hellish hours. So many experiments. Trips to forgotten places. Strange concoctions made by tribal medicine men. Failures all. But he had been close.

Daoud, his valet, his trusted ally, had found it. The man's clear script burned bright in Archer's memory.

My lord, our suspicions prove correct. Alexandria held the key. I have found the answer. To be conveyed in the agreed-upon venue.

And so Archer's hope and salvation was tucked into a lacquered box and sent out on his fastest vessel, *The Karina*, only to be set upon by Hector Ellis's pirates and lost to the sea. Two days later, Daoud's body was found, his throat slit, silenced forever. Archer's return trip to Egypt to discover what Daoud might have found yielded nothing.

Frustration made him want to crawl out of his skin. "Damn it all," he hissed.

Elizabeth's voice filled his mind. *You have her now. All will be well.*

"Now who sounds hopeful?" he said, blinking up at the glass roof. But there was hope. His sources told him his box might not have sunk to the bottom of the sea, but made it to England. Thus he had returned, and had been unable to keep from claiming his bride.

Sunlight broke through the gray clouds. Shafts of light hit the glass house and filled it up. And when the first rays touched him, a familiar tingling shivered over his skin. He inhaled sharply, at once feeling the surge, the heat—and the bitter failure—for he had not been able to stay away from the light. His body hummed, the light pouring through him. God help him, he was weak. He thought of Miranda, and his fist curled tight. He needed to be stronger. For her.

Then get back down there and be with her, coward.

For a moment he thought he heard gentle laughter. Then it was silent.

Chapter Five

※～◆～※

Sir Percival Andrew, Second Baronet of Doddington, old as he was, had certain rituals preceding his afternoon nap. First, a kiss from his wife, Beatrice, who then drew the heavy brocade drapes closed and helped him don a dressing gown before retiring for a nap of her own. Marks, his valet, might have attended him but, as Bea often teased, *his* kiss was not half as sweet.

The second, a glass of port to be imbibed while sitting in his favorite chair before the fire. Today was no different. He settled down with a satisfied sigh, his old bones aching yet comforted by the warm hearth, and picked up the morning edition of the *Times*. The fire popped, and the paper rattled in the quiet. A peaceful moment shattered as a shout of pure incredulity broke from his lips upon reading the wedding announcement of Lord Benjamin Aldo Fitzwilliam Wallace Archer, Fifth Baron Archer of Umberslade, to Miss Miranda Rose Ellis.

"Son of a bitch!" He slammed the paper down in a rare display of temper. That bastard. Returning to England

when he had promised to stay away. After all the work
Percival had done to hush things up, the countless times
he had covered Archer's tracks, for the sake of all their
reputations. Now in jeopardy because Archer had a twitch
in his cock. Impertinent lot, the Archers. One and all. By
God, it was not to be borne. The impudent whelp would
have to be spoken to, firmly.

A cold wind touched his back, an icy caress from an
open window. The oddity of it barely touched his mind
before an arm slammed around his chest, pinning him
to the chair. Heart in his mouth, he caught the sight of a
black mask at the corner of his eye.

"Archer?" he rasped. Blood thundered through his
ears. His bladder had let loose, the thick briny smell cutting through the cold air as the warmth seeped over his
skin.

"Forgive me," said a familiar voice that caused Percival to convulse against the chair. "But I need you to
send a message."

Steel flashed white in the soft light. A sharp burn shot
across Percival's throat. He gagged, hot blood splashing
his shaking hands, splattering across the white marble
mantle and the faded daguerreotype of Bea on her fortieth
birthday. He took a rattling breath, tasted salt and blood
upon his tongue. *Bea*.

"Are you well settled?" Lord Archer led Miranda to
a table long enough to seat twenty, with silver candela-
brums running down its long center. The mirror-paneled
table was laden with food enough for a party. The sight of
numerous silver-domed serving dishes perplexed her as
the table was set for one. A single, lonely place setting
next to the head of the table.

He held out the chair in front of the setting and bid her to sit.

"Yes, thank you." She eyed the food with amazement as he proceeded to lift the lids himself. Wafts of steam rose from the dishes and, with it, the scent of rich warm food, too much to distinguish any one component but rather a miasma of such delectability that her mouth watered. "You are not eating?"

"Alas, I cannot dine with you," he said with a touch of asperity, for the reason was obvious. "I dined earlier."

She glanced away from the mask, wondering with chagrin if they were ever to dine together. "Then all of this bounty is for my benefit?"

"As I understand, you have forgone the pleasure of eating such foods for some time." He reached for her soup bowl. "Oyster stew or chicken soup?"

"Oyster, please." A happy smile pulled her lips. She hadn't had oyster stew in years.

Lord Archer ladled the fragrant white broth into the bowl and set it down. "Whereas I have been blessed with endless bounty, yet no one with whom to share it," he finished, handing her a small silver bowl filled with oyster crackers.

"But I could not eat all of this."

"Well, I certainly hope you shall try a little. Careful consideration has gone into the planning of this meal," he said lightly. "I shall be thoroughly put out should you waste away from lack of effort."

"Wish to fatten me up, do you?"

"Mmm." Gray eyes skimmed over her form. "How does the fairy tale go?" He rested an elbow on his chair arm. "Ah yes, I have lured you into my luscious house of candy and gingerbread to tempt you with sugared delights. And when you are nice and plump, I shall gobble you up."

A flush of tangible heat washed like the tide over her skin. There was only light laughter in his tone yet the force of his gaze made her turn away. Stomach fluttering, she tried to look stern. "I suppose you have forgotten that Gretel outwitted the old witch in the end and roasted her alive."

He chuckled, a deep rumbling of thunder before a storm. "How very gruesome."

"Yes, quite," Miranda agreed with a smile. Ah, but he was charming. Unexpected, but decidedly so. "Very well, I shall do my part. Only what of the rest?"

"The servants shall have it." He looked at her with some amusement. "Does that appease you?"

"It does."

The creamy soup, ripe with plump oysters and golden puddles of butter, tasted like heaven on a spoon. She nearly groaned with pleasure and forced herself to eat slowly, aware that Lord Archer watched with rapt interest.

"Wine?" He poured with the deft ease of a seasoned servant.

"Is this how we shall normally dine?" The service was like nothing she'd seen before. While resembling a familiar meal served *a la française,* there were no removes. Everything was simply on the table, including a large platter of fruit, overflowing with velvety figs, glossy pears, and crisp apples, cut open and saturated with rich color.

"No." A touch of humor lifted his voice as his eyes continued their watch. "Call this…"—his hand waved toward the table—"a bit of fancy on my part. I wanted you to have a wedding feast of sorts."

She lowered her wineglass, her gaze catching his, and a strange sensation of longing rushed through her. Perhaps he felt it too, for he looked away and toyed with a silver salt cellar with his long, be-gloved fingers. A footman entered as if by magic, whisked away her bowl, and left while Lord Archer lifted more lids.

"We needn't stand on ceremony," he said. "I've never understood why one must have soup, then fish, then fowl or meat."

She had to laugh. "Or food that isn't too highly spiced. At least not for ladies."

He laughed as well. "Indeed. And all very properly served. Why not eat what we want when we want?" He took her plate. "Although, now that I've had a look, might I suggest the sole? My cook is quite gifted, I have to say."

"Yes, please."

"Food is the one thing I did not miss when I was away from England." He handed her the plate and sat. "I should think I'd find myself much aggrieved should I have to partake in a proper English dinner any time soon."

"Is our cuisine really so awful?"

"When you've sampled what the rest of the world has to offer, yes. Although we do breakfast spectacularly well."

Miranda glanced at her husband. A person's skin, she realized just then, was an indispensable clue as to one's true age. As Lord Archer's attire revealed none of his, she could only guess at his age. His voice was of no help; rich and rumbling, it could belong to a man aged twenty-five to sixty. Her eyes trailed over the lean, muscular body of a man in his prime. With such a physique, he could not be older than forty-five. But the quick, light way in which he moved gave the impression of youth. In his thirties, perhaps? It must be so, as he was too much in command of himself to be a man in his early twenties.

"Have you been abroad all this time, Lord Archer?"

He sat back, resting one arm on his chair. "I haven't lived in England for many years. I returned briefly three years ago and then set back out to travel the world over."

"It sounds exhausting."

"At times. Though I did settle in America for a decade before I began to roam again."

A light came into his eyes that Miranda recognized. "You liked it there, didn't you?"

"I like it here better," he said softly, and Miranda's skin went tight and warm. They stared at each other for a slow moment before he cleared his throat and spoke in a lighter tone. "I like Americans. They do not think as we do. A man is what he makes of himself, and should he make a name for himself, the journey that brought him to his fortune is very admirable to Americans. They praise achievement, not the past. I took the idea to heart."

She eyed him speculatively. "You became a man of industry."

"Of oil and steel," he said.

Food forgotten, she leaned forward, almost afraid to ask, but compelled. "How fortunate were you?"

His eyes flicked to hers. "On last accounting, I am worth fifty-two million dollars." He gave a little laugh. "Ten years in America and I irrevocably think of money in terms of dollars. Hmm...I did not factor in my English revenue. So perhaps it is more to the effect of seventy million..." He looked at her in alarm when she made a strangled gasp. "Are you quite well?"

"God in heaven," she managed at last. The room spun

for a moment. She pressed a palm to her heated cheek. "Yes...I'm all right." She looked up at him. "Seventy million? I cannot begin to fathom."

"It is rather daunting." He poured her some white wine before drawing away. "Though I can assure you, our wealth comes nowhere near that of some of my associates. Mr. Rockefeller and Mr. Carnegie, for example, are much more voracious in their quest for capital."

That he tried to downplay his achievement made her smile.

"At any rate, I have decided to retire from my American activities." He hesitated. "Er, that will increase our holdings a bit when I sell things off," he said wryly.

Her laughter felt unhinged. "A bit, eh? You might as well be Croesus." She looked at him sharply. "*Our* holdings?"

"Of course *ours*. You are my wife." He gave a little bow of his head. "What is mine is yours." His casual stance on the chair shifted to stiffness. "You are making a face," he remarked.

She touched her cheek again. "Was I?"

"The idea of us being so linked does not appeal to you?"

Miranda shook her head to clear it. "To tell you the truth, I find the whole idea rather mercenary on my part. It hardly seems fair that I should gain access to your fortune simply for speaking a few vows in a church." She took a sip of tart wine. "I think you got the short end of the stick in this venture."

He threw his head back and laughed. "I believe you are the first woman in history to think so." He laughed again. "And you are quite wrong."

Their eyes met, and that spark of something hot and

sharp ripped through her again. Awareness. It took a moment to realize, but that was it. She was utterly aware of him. Of the breadth of his shoulders, the deep even way he breathed, the force of his gaze. Bloody hell, but she was beset by the craving to touch him, test the strength in those shoulders.

"Should you continue to be merely half as entertaining as you are tonight," he said with a voice like heated cream, "then I shall have received the greater bargain in this venture, Miranda."

Unaccountably flushed, she set her attention to the lamb. "I think you're cracked, but whatever you wish to believe, Lord Archer."

"I wish you wouldn't call me that." His voice was still soft but there was an edge beneath it.

She looked up to find him glaring down upon the empty place in front of him.

"What? Lord Archer?" she asked, surprised.

"Yes." He moved to touch his brow, but finding the mask upon his face, flung his hand down. "It is too formal. You are my wife, not an acquaintance. Husbands and wives are partners in life, are they not? The one person who will support you when all hope seems lost." He blinked suddenly, as though he hadn't meant to speak such things aloud, then straightened his spine. "Or so one hears."

Emotion clogged her throat. *Partners.* She'd always been alone. Something tender and precious welled up within her chest, and she fought the urge to clutch her hand to her breast to hold onto the feeling.

"Well, in that case," she said when she could speak again, "I suppose I had better think of something more suitable." She worried her lip considering. She ought to call him Benjamin. But it was too intimate, too soft.

"My lord?" she ventured, only half serious.

"Good God, no."

She bit back a smile. "Husband?" She took a sip of wine.

He grunted. "Are we to become Quakers?"

Miranda set her glass down quickly, nearly choking. His eyes crinkled at the corners, a sure sign of him smiling. She sat back in her seat.

"Archer, then." Something queer went through her. A lock had been turned, as though her use of his name had unleashed something untamed inside of her. She wanted to say it again. If only to revel in the odd little thumps it elicited in her heart.

He was quiet for a moment. "Archer sounds well upon your lips."

She took a hasty bite of curried lamb. Perhaps she had drunk too much wine.

Behind him, the fire snapped, the warmth of it heating her bare arms. He must have been positively flushed sitting so close to it, but he didn't seem so. His long frame subtly stretched back toward it, like a cat luxuriating in the heat of the sun.

Fire: her greatest comfort and source of her deepest shame. The great log in the middle suddenly snapped in half, and the fire flared hotter for one brief instant. Immediately, he uttered a nearly soundless sigh, his stiff shoulders easing a touch. Yes, he craved the warmth of the fire. It sparked an odd feeling of kinship.

Indeed, for the first time in memory, she felt...not comfortable, precisely—he affected her too much for her to relax into that emotion—but safe. She felt she might say anything she wished and not be ridiculed for her opinion, nor forced to justify her existence or usefulness. The sensation was a breath of clean air in the deepest of London fogs.

"Does watching me eat entertain you?" she murmured when she felt his eyes upon her.

"Yes. You do so with such hedonistic abandon." His gaze went hot. "It is rather stirring. Perhaps I should bid you to forego the silverware, if only to see how you use your hands."

A breathless laugh escaped her. "I do believe you enjoy unsettling me."

Which she was loath to admit he was rather good at doing.

The corners of his eyes crinkled. "I want to understand your mind. The best recourse is to engage your defenses."

The man had cheek, to be sure. Should she wither under such boldness, he'd have her under his thumb in short order. Miranda's fork clinked against the china as she set it down. "I shall keep that tactic in mind."

Holding his gaze, she reached out to select a thick white section of pear. Soft flesh sank beneath her fingers, the fruit cool and wet against her lips. Archer shifted in his chair, and she took a bite. The fruit burst in her mouth, tasting of warmth and sugar. Giving a little moan of pleasure, she swallowed it down, then slowly licked her lips to catch a bit of juice that ran over.

With the suddenness of a cat leaping upon its prey, he leaned forward and caught up her wrist. "Tread lightly, Miranda Fair." His thumb moved lightly over her fluttering pulse, as she stared with her mouth assuredly hanging open in shock, her heart beating furiously within her breast. "You know, it's never wise to tempt the devil." His gaze lowered to her hand, still locked in his grip, her fingers glistening with pear juice. His rich voice lowered to raw huskiness. "Had I not this mask, I should be of a mind to suck that juice right off your fingers."

Chapter Six

~~~~~⌘~~~~~

Good Lord, what had she done? Miranda cursed herself for such high-handed stupidity as Archer abruptly announced that dinner was over and led her from the room. She had goaded the man into looking at her as a woman. And on her wedding night, of all times. What had she been thinking?

She knew what was to happen on a wedding night; only the enjoyment of sparring with Archer had made her forget all that. Until now. The urge to run the other way was strong. She dared a glance at him, catching a glimpse of one large shoulder, the wide expanse of his chest. She had flirted with him, she realized with chagrin. More than flirted, thrown down the gauntlet, really. Why had she done that? Attraction. Her steps bobbled before she brought herself under control.

Daisy had warned her once that attraction of a physical nature had no rhyme or reason. One might be inexplicably swept off one's feet by a short, bald man of twenty stone and not be able to ignore it. Such things called to the animal inside a person, not the mind. Miranda had laughed and asked Daisy with whom she was keeping company.

Damnation, she wasn't laughing now. True, his frame was attractive, and he was good company, but there was the mask to consider. What was he beneath it? Did it matter?

No, it did not, because they were now before her door, and she had no recourse but to face her fate.

Archer blinked down at her for a moment as though just as unsure.

"I forgot to ask," he said, breaking the heavy silence. "Are your rooms to your liking?"

The tightness in her shoulders relaxed a fraction. "They are utterly lovely." Her large set of rooms included a sitting area by the fire, enormous dressing room, and modern bathing room. Elegant, palatial, yet cozy, they were something out of a dream. "Thank you, Archer."

He nodded slowly. "And the color?"

She smiled, thinking of the golden damask-papered walls, furniture dressed in ivory silk, with ivory cashmere drapes to keep out the cold. "Ivory and gold." She glanced up at him, finding his gaze inscrutable. "I've always longed for a room decorated as such. How did you know?"

"Luck, perhaps." His voice lowered. "Or perhaps I had a vision of you sleeping in a bed of cream and gold..." Archer's gaze traveled over her like a caress. "I would love to see you thus."

Her mouth went dry, and he took a step closer. Miranda gripped the door handle tight enough to feel the skin stretch over her knuckles. His hand closed over hers, heavy and warm, even through the thickness of his glove.

With an unwavering gaze, he slowly turned the handle, and the door's lock snicked open.

Archer bent closer, and her knees bobbled. For a moment they simply stood still, the air between them a palpable thing, buzzing and heated. She stared at the folds of his black cravat, the sound of her life's blood roaring in her ears. His body did not touch hers but she felt the hardened length of it as though the nerve endings along her skin were directly attached to his by little hooks that tugged with sweet pain.

His broad chest lifted in exhalation, and her breath caught it in return. Lord, he was big, and strong, and delicious smelling. It was an ineffable clean scent, yet it consumed her, making her mouth water and her head spin. She took another ragged breath, and a burst of heat flared over her skin and settled between her legs. Her fingers tightened on the handle. Common sense was crumbling like old ruins. Good lord, she was going mad.

A pained sound left him as he came a hair closer. Her inner thighs clenched. Only inches away, he stopped, his body visibly stiffening. Her eyes squeezed shut, and she swayed. Waited.

His deep voice rumbled against her ear. "Good night, Miranda Fair."

Her eyes flew open. He was already halfway to his own door.

Red-hot flames twisted and turned within the grate, undulating and sinuous upon the ashen logs, tiny dancers beckoning him closer. Archer sat before the hearth. Breathe, he ordered of himself once more. In. Out. *Just breathe. Do not think of her.*

Slowly, by agonizing degrees, his heart rate returned to

normal. She had flirted with him. *Hadn't she?* He swiped at his perspiring brow. He was too dizzy with want to think clearly. Too tempted to open that forbidden door, go in and claim her as was his husbandly right. Oh, God.

He looked away from their connecting door. The action brought his attention to the silver salver lying upon the table by his shaking hand. Gilroy had left him the day's correspondence. Resting like an offering upon the various reports and letters was a small paper box wrapped up with a silver bow. The innocuous little box caused his heart to stop and then promptly start up with palpable thuds. Evil had touched that package.

The chair creaked beneath him as he inched forward. The package weighed next to nothing, but that slight weight, the unbalanced feel of it in his hand, chilled his blood. The rotten-sweet stench of death drifted from its edges as he slowly pulled the ribbon free. A thick cream-colored vellum envelope. And something below it. He could feel it, rolling about along the bottom of the box. He lifted the card, his fingers trembling as he did, and he spied what lay beneath. Glossy, despite its yellowed surface, oblong and laced in red, the thing might have been mistaken for a rotting hard-boiled egg—if one overlooked the gore of veins trailing from one end of it. Archer swallowed hard, his fingers turning to ice even as hot fury pounded within his temples. Having sat through more than one autopsy examination, he well knew what the hideous gift was. An eye. A human eye.

The vellum envelope tore under his numb fingers, dread and fury growing in equal measure as he read the note set out in block letters cut and pasted from various newsprint as if part of a child's nursery project: *You should not have done it.*

Only then did he spy the small news article that had fallen from the card onto his lap. Damp with congealing blood and nearly illegible beneath the gore was the announcement of the marriage of Lord Benjamin Aldo Fitzwilliam Wallace Archer, Fifth Baron Archer of Umberslade, to Miss Miranda Rose Ellis.

Pure white light colored his world, biting cold and blinding with its brilliance, like the heart of a blizzard. It pulsed through his hard limbs, strong and true, surging with such force and power that he felt the truth of what he would soon become. For one hateful moment, he welcomed it. The sharp-edged card crumpled in his fist as he stood. He threw it all into the fire. Watched it burn. Heaven help the son of a bitch who'd sent it.

Even as the thought filtered through his brain, damp fingers of dread crawled along his spine to clutch his heart. He sank back into his seat. Who had sent it? And whose eye was it?

An eye for an eye. The phrase hit his mind like the clang of a buoy. It had been a favorite saying of Rossberry's. Archer fingered his jaw in contemplation as he gazed at the roaring fire. Rossberry. A man who had been driven to the brink of madness by fire's cruel kiss. Archer swallowed hard, the heat from the hearth strong enough to warm his outstretched legs. But Rossberry was locked away, had been for years. They had seen to that. A light snort left his lips; they had sent Archer away as well, yet here he was.

He nearly jumped out of his skin when a light rap came from the door. He raked a hand through his hair. "Yes?"

Gilroy opened the door only as far as necessary. "Pardon the intrusion, my lord, but there is a gentleman here to see you."

"Hang it, Gilroy, it is the middle of the night. Why the devil haven't you sent him packing?" Even as he spoke, it occurred to Archer that Gilroy was too proficient a servant to let just anyone in at an ungodly hour. "Who is it, Gilroy?" he asked with growing dread.

The man held himself correctly erect. "Inspector Winston Lane with the Criminal Investigation Department."

Chapter Seven

Miranda's hand glided over the crystal stoppers. Firelight caught in the prisms, sending little rainbows scattering over her skin and upon the bottles. A drink would settle her nerves, then perhaps she could sleep without thinking of masked men, or a certain voice as decadent as dark chocolate. She stopped at the simplest decanter, an elegant thing shaped like a teardrop. Around its neck was a silver plaque engraved with the word "Bourbon." American whiskey. She remembered vaguely hearing her father mention tasting it once long ago.

Out of all the decanters, this one had the least liquor left in it. Archer's favorite, if she had to guess. The stopper came loose with a harmonious ring and released the smoky sweet notes of the liquor.

She poured herself a measure, relaxing at the sound of the decanter letting its treasure loose in a soft *glug-glug-glug*, and the crackle of the ash—not coal—fire within the grate behind her. No wonder men coveted the simple ritual of having a drink and kept such things away from women. To the victor always went the spoils.

Caramel and smoke and heat, the bourbon burned a slow delicious path down her throat. Miranda closed her eyes in pleasure. And then snapped to attention as she heard Archer's voice join with that of another man's out in the hall. Footsteps sounded, heading her way, and she tensed.

Her stomach turned at the notion of facing Archer so soon.

"Let us talk in here, Inspector."

Inspector?

"As you wish, my lord."

Alarm lifted the hairs at her nape. She knew that voice. It was Winston Lane, newly appointed inspector for England's Criminal Investigations Department. Winston Lane, her eldest sister Poppy's very dear husband and Miranda's very dear brother-in-law. She most certainly did not want to face Winston and Archer with her hair down and wearing a ratty old dressing gown, or explain why she felt the need to partake in a man's drink in the middle of the night.

With a wild look around, she considered her options. The door handle turned, and Miranda made her choice. Not a very good choice, she conceded as she all but dove behind the large *chinoiserie* screen in the corner. She was now trapped like a mouse.

From the cracks between the screens, she saw slices of her brother-in-law's face: pale and thin with a long mustache the color of straw embracing his upper lip. His hair, of the same color, was carefully swept back. He had not taken off his tweed overcoat but held his bowler in his hand. Once in the room, he set the hat down upon a small table by one of the armchairs. A bit of boldness on Winston's part as it was an obvious sign that this visit would not be easily rushed.

Miranda tensed and slipped farther into the corner as Winston slowly surveyed the room. He did as she had done, inspecting its contents, looking for clues to what might lie inside the infamous Lord Archer's head.

Then the man himself moved into view. Though Winston inclined his head toward him, Archer was looking at the bar, she realized in cold horror. She could almost feel his eyes upon her discarded glass, still half-full.

"Inspector Lane," he said finally, turning so that only his arm was visible from her hiding spot. "What unfortunate news do you have for me?"

"Lord Archer, I do apologize for the late hour. However, I thought it best to come when I did. I fear by morning my presence here would bring an even greater inconvenience."

For everyone would note it, and tongues would wag.

"Whom should I thank for such a courtesy?" Archer asked dryly.

Winston took a step closer to Archer. "Forgive me, but I have not yet offered my congratulations in your marriage to my good sister, Miranda."

Archer's arm flinched. "Miranda is your sister?"

"She is sister to my wife, Poppy. I am quite fond of Miranda. I was pleased to hear that she had found a husband who could see to her welfare."

Miranda's cheeks colored. She knew what was behind his proper words. He was pleased she had finally left Father. For a cold moment, she wondered whether Winston had heard tales of her less than lawful activities.

"Had I not been away on business this morning, I would have accompanied my wife to the ceremony."

Would he have? Miranda was not so sure. Clearly, he was not altogether pleased at her choice of husband, or he would have said as much.

"Since we are family"—Archer's voice tightened on the word—"let us speak plainly. What do you want?"

Winston nodded. "Shortly after one o'clock this afternoon, Sir Percival Andrew, fifth baronet of Doddington, was found murdered in his bed chamber."

Miranda blinked in surprise as the words fell over the room.

"I am sorry for it," Archer said in a quiet voice.

"Then you admit to knowing Sir Percival."

"Of course. I have known him nearly all my life. Though I haven't seen him in some years."

At that, Winston pulled a small notebook from his pocket to consult it. Miranda knew from Poppy that he did this for show. Winston memorized every fact he collected.

"In eight years, correct?"

"Correct, inspector." Dry amusement laced Archer's voice. "Not since the week I sent his granddaughter's fiancé, one Lord Jonathan Marvel, to hospital after an altercation with him. A fact I am sure you have committed to memory as well."

Winston snapped his notebook closed.

"It is quite a juicy tidbit of gossip that fails to die," Archer said.

"It is said that as a result of that altercation, Lord Marvel broke off his engagement with Sir Percival's granddaughter, causing much stress and heartache between the two families."

"Broken engagements often cause familial strife."

"I believe Sir Percival and quite a few others held you accountable for the mishap."

"As do I."

"Your relations with Sir Percival were not in good standing when last you met."

"My relations with Lord Marvel were not in good standing. Sir Percival and I were of like mind in the matter."

"Which was?"

"Lord Marvel is, and was, a spoiled snot, and I have a foul temper."

Winston's lips curled but his eyes remained shrewd. "Yes, there is much talk of that violent temper, my lord."

"A logical fellow might deduce that a man in possession of a volatile temper would lash out when offended, not wait in cool composure to do the deed eight years later."

"I should like to think myself a logical fellow," said Winston.

"Which means you have something more to go on then mere conjecture."

"Upon questioning of the house servants, some disturbing news was brought to light. Mr. James Marks, Sir Percival's valet, was resting in his room next to Sir Percival's. He swears that he heard his master call out the name 'Archer' as if surprised. A moment later, Sir Percival made an odd sound, and Marks went to investigate." Winston kept his eyes on Archer. "Sir Percival had been sliced across the neck and then eviscerated."

From behind the safety of her screen, Miranda clutched her knees as bile rose in her throat. She did not want it to be him. She liked Archer, almost instantly. And she never took an instant liking to anyone.

"Is that all that was done to him?" Archer's quiet query shocked Miranda back to sensibility.

Winston raised a blond brow. "An odd question, my lord. Do you assume there were more insults done upon his body?"

"You are here because I am suspect. If I am to be accused, I will know the whole of it, Inspector. Now, what was done to him?"

"Sir Percival's face was slashed, his right eye gouged out and missing. His heart taken."

The fire snapped in the grate, and Miranda jumped. Dear God, was she married to a madman? *Please don't let it be so.* She'd gotten her first glimpse of hope. She did not want to recede back into a world where shame and darkness dwelled.

Archer's fingers curled round the back of a chair. "I am sorry for it," he said again, softer this time.

"My lord, that is not all."

"It never is."

Something stirred within her, a churning that came upon a person just before danger caught hold and dragged a soul down.

"A scullery maid, Miss Jennifer Child, reports seeing a man in a black mask running through the stable yard moments later."

Miranda pressed her knees against her chest as if the action would still her pounding heart. For a moment, she considered leaping up and running to Winston. He would take her from here. No one would fault her for seeking an annulment. The thought filled her with a wild sense of freedom. She could do this. She could get away.

Yet she stayed in place. Her heart would not let her move. It could not be Archer. Not the man she had dinner with this very night. He had shown her respect and caring, been protective of her feelings. But what did she really know of him?

"All very damning testimony," Archer said, stopping her running thoughts.

"It appears that way, my lord."

Poor Winston was on dicey ground. One did not question a peer, yet here he was. One certainly did not accuse a peer of murder. Miranda could almost feel Winston's tension. He would not ask Archer for an alibi. But he desperately wanted to hear one. The churning in Miranda's belly grew.

"Inspector Lane, you may question my servants at your leisure. You will find that upon showing my bride her new home, I disappeared from the hours of twelve o'clock noon to shortly before nine in the evening. There will be no one but myself to account for my whereabouts."

Miranda's head fell forward. She had hoped for Archer's reassurance. But the man wouldn't even proclaim his innocence. Surely an innocent man would? Her fingers twitched, digging into the silk weave of her gown. She should go. It was madness to stay. Perhaps he would murder her as well. Slice her throat in the dark of night. Why then could she not move? Silently, she cursed herself for being a fool.

"That is most unfortunate, my lord."

"Yes."

"Yet you can account for your whereabouts." Winston was careful not to phrase it as a question.

"Of course. But I will not. Only that I was alone. I am often alone."

Stubborn man! Her nails sank into the flesh of her knees.

"Do you have a theory as to who might have done this thing, my lord?"

"A coward who likes to play games."

"Murderers generally are cowards," Winston said. "I have one more question, my lord."

"Only one? I cannot believe that. Surely you have dozens to pepper upon me."

Miranda smiled against her knees. Stubborn, charming man. Beguiled by a possible killer. She belonged in Bedlam.

"Questions tend to build upon themselves." Winston moved to pull something from his pocket, the action sending him out of her direct line of sight.

"Do you know what this is, my lord?"

Everything in her screamed to peek between the screens but Archer would surely notice the movement. Her fingers tightened over her knees to keep her in place.

"It is a coin," Archer said plainly.

His deflection was not so easily gained. There was a smile in Winston's voice when he replied. "Do you recognize it?"

Miranda willed her breath to steady. A coin? Her heart skittered to a stop and then picked a frantic pace.

"I believe you expect me to."

"It was found over Sir Percival's eye socket."

"Ritualistic, perhaps." Archer did not move from his position by the chair. Only the line of his arm was visible and might have been made of basalt for all its stillness. "Payment for Charon in order to cross the river Styx."

"Perhaps." Winston's hand came into view but not enough for Miranda to see the coin, only a brief flash of gold. "Sir Percival's valet says that the coin was his master's. Sir Percival has had it since eighteen-fourteen or thereabouts. Called it his guide, though the valet cannot say why."

"An odd way to describe a coin," Archer said idly.

"I agree. But it is an odd piece, is it not? It is not legal tender, not here or in any other country." Winston's blond hair caught the light as he bent his head to inspect the coin. From her corner, Miranda could just see the frown lines about his eyes deepen.

"And the inscription. 'West Moon Club.' I profess, I have never heard of such a club."

The words slammed into Miranda. West Moon Club. Her heart threatened to pound right out of her chest. Though it felt as though the room spun, she forced herself to be still, keep quiet. She did not need to see the coin now. She knew precisely what it looked like.

Oh, Archer. How could she have not seen it? Her breath came in sharp bursts. How many nights had she thought about her dark savior? The man with the haunted voice who would not show his face. Had he wanted to marry her from the start? If so, why did he not claim her then?

Archer's deep voice, so very different from when she first heard it spoken, rumbled over the room. "Had the valet any theory as to the coin's nature?"

"He did not."

"Yet you assume that I have a more intimate knowledge of Percival's belongings than that of his valet?"

Winston and Archer's words faded in and out as her blood rushed through her veins. Did he still have her knife? Was it tucked away somewhere just as his coin was? She pictured the coin, with the pitted face of a full moon fronting it, lying in her jewelry box. She could never bring herself to pawn it. It had been her good luck charm.

"You wish to corroborate the statements of a man who has named you as the prime suspect in this crime, my lord?"

"Sir Percival's valet has given facts. He heard Sir

Percival speak my name. A scullery maid saw a masked man flee across the stable yard. Simple facts. It is you, Inspector Lane, who transmutes those facts into an accusation upon me."

"My humble apologies, my lord. I overstepped when I only meant to question."

"Have you any more questions to lay at my feet?"

She could hear the amusement in Archer's voice now.

Winston could, too. He bowed his head with a wry smile. "Nothing more for the moment."

They moved away.

"You should know," Winston said. "A crime this violent in nature will not go unpunished. Regardless of who committed it."

"I should hope so, Inspector."

"I would ask that you give my regards to Miranda. However, I have no wish to cause her undue alarm by alerting her of my visit."

For the first time in the conversation, Archer sounded truly surprised. "I did wonder if you would ask to see her. If only to offer her a word of warning. That you did not is very trusting of you in your capacity as a brother, Inspector. Do you not fear leaving the lamb in the lion's den, as it were?"

Winston's answer was lost to her as they walked into the hall. She stayed frozen in place. Terror filled Miranda at the thought of Archer coming back into the library and knocking aside the screen to find her. Out in the hall, she heard Winston depart, and Archer tell Gilroy to have his own horse readied. Miranda's iron-tight limbs eased slightly but only when Archer was well and gone from the house did she let herself breathe freely.

Sneaking up to her room, her mind was a whirl. Had

she married a killer? She could not make herself believe
it. Miranda had been a virtual stranger to Archer the night
he had risked his personal safety to protect her. She had
felt a basic kindness in his soul that night. She felt it in
him now. But one did not survive on instinct alone. Facts
were needed.

Chapter Eight

~∞~

With the moon waning and heavy clouds threatening to let loose at any moment, it was gloriously dark. Almost palpable, such darkness. A town house loomed before him, quiet in the dead of the night. Archer went slowly to avoid discovery, scaling the smooth limestone brick wall like a spider. His fingers and toes sank into the mortar as though it was soft butter.

Balancing on a windowsill with his toes, he reached for the *Chatellerault* in his coat. The black enamel hilt felt at home in his palm. A smile pulled at his lips. *Her* blade. Not a day had passed since she gave it to him that he did not hold it and twirl it round his fingers as he thought of her.

He shoved the knife in between the window and casing. With a gentle nudge, the window eased up a fraction, and he slipped his fingers under to lift it.

Nothing stirred as Archer crept inside. A large bed dominated the room, its curtains drawn tight for the night. Very quaint. Archer slowly pulled back the curtain, the knife still in hand. The man within had shrunk with age, the muscles and heft of his once powerful body now withered into a ropy mix of hardness and slack. Soft skin hung around his neck and jowls. But for all that, Maurus Lea, Earl of Leland still held an air of dignity and strength. Archer could barely tolerate the sight of him.

He leaned forward, hovering just over Leland's sleeping form. The man's long bumpy nose whistled as he slept, stirring the white mustache hanging over the corner of his gaping mouth. The smell of camphor and old velvet drifted up. Archer's nostrils pinched against it, but he found himself grinning.

"I say, Lilly, where the devil are my boots?"

Leland surged forward at Archer's shout, his hands grasping for his robe, words of apology falling from his lips. Archer pocketed his knife and took a step back, smiling behind the mask as Leland came to his senses. Leland cursed roundly and fumbled for the clutch of matches tied near his bed.

"Allow me," Archer said, smoothly taking the matches and lighting the lamp.

"Devil take you, Archer," Leland bit out as the light hit his eyes. He blinked hard and swung his feet off the bed to sit up. "You scared the life out of me…" He looked up at Archer, and his long face went slack. "Good God, it *is* you."

Archer set the lamp down on a table and retreated to the armchair by the cold hearth. "So it is."

"I heard you had returned." Leland pulled a silk dressing robe over his bony shoulders and stood. "I would say it was your sick sense of humor that bid you wait until now to hunt me down and bedevil me, but you're too methodical."

Leland went to a small bar and poured himself a

measure of brandy. Archer watched without comment. The man's hand shook badly as he lifted the glass to drink.

"What is it, then?" Leland set his glass down with a thud. "Why have you come back?"

Anger surged. Archer should not have come. Questions he had wanted to ask filled his throat like a blockage. *Why did you turn from me? Was my fate so very distasteful?*

"England is my home," Archer said from the comfort of his seat.

"Bollocks. We had an agreement." Leland studied the glass before him.

"You had a hope," Archer retorted. "And if you thought I was a problem neatly swept away and forgotten then you are a fool." He checked his temper with a deep breath. "The question is—are you foolish enough to challenge me now that I am here?"

A white brow rose high. "And if I were," Leland asked softly, "what then? Would I find myself a bitter end? My body one of the many left to rot in the Thames?"

Archer's voice was equally soft. "Perhaps you would."

The sound of the old man's wheezing filled the darkness, then Leland snorted. "I'm all aquiver." He set his glass down with an inordinately loud thud. "Why are you *here*? I assume you didn't invade my home solely to make assassinations on my character."

"I married."

Leland's face drained of color, his thin lips falling slack. "Have you gone mad?" he managed at last.

Archer flicked a speck of lint off the velvet chair. "Perhaps I have."

"To what purpose?" Leland cried, coming forward in his agitation. "And to what end?"

Archer turned away from Leland's keen blue eyes. He hated those eyes. They missed nothing. "My reasons are my own."

"Who is she?"

"Miranda Ellis—Archer," he corrected. The novelty of hearing his name connected with hers buzzed in his veins like warm champagne.

Leland's shrewd eyes narrowed. "Hector Ellis's youngest daughter, is she?"

He nodded, suddenly feeling exposed in the dimly lit room.

"I see."

"Mmm, I fear you do." It appeared even decrepit nobles had heard of Miranda's beauty.

Leland sighed. "This is madness, Archer. No lady could have possibly done you so great a wrong to warrant such a punishment. I well understand the urge but...". He stopped abruptly as his gaze locked with Archer's.

"I do hope," Archer said as his fingers dug into the arms of the chair, "that you aren't entertaining notions of giving fatherly advice. I should find that laughable in the extreme."

"No, no..." Leland swallowed, backing away a bit. And he ought to. Archer felt capable of just about anything then. He did not miss the photographs lining Leland's mantel. A wife. Children, grandchildren. Leland had them all. Was the great and beloved head of his grand household. Perhaps he would not tell Leland of Percival's death after all. Archer pushed to his feet.

Leland eyed him from under thick, white brows. "Is that the true reason you are here in London?"

"You mean am I motivated by something other than base lust?"

He laughed when Leland glowered. "You know I will not rest until I find a way…" He took a deep breath, and when he spoke, he heard the bitterness in his voice. "Especially now."

"I cannot help you there." Leland spoke with such sorrow that Archer flinched.

"I did not think you could. Just stay out of my way on that account."

Archer turned toward the door. No need for windows now. It irked him that he'd used it in the first place. He'd been hiding in shadows for too long. "My wife will need an introduction into society." *There. That was as good a reason as any for this visit.* "I'll not have her outcast. I realize the season is over. However there are still functions going on. I expect invitations to be forthcoming, Leland. You may tell the others as much."

Leland's mouth worked. "You can't seriously think to go about in society."

"Tell people I'm an eccentric. Our lot has always relished a good oddity at which to thumb their nose. Regardless, no one will be looking at me when Lady Archer is in the room. As I'm sure you can attest."

The man sputtered with irritation, but he could not refuse—nor could the others. They all knew as much. The result of their mad little experiment had hidden away for as long as any of them ought to have hoped. If one of them thought they could scare him away, the fool had made a disastrous mistake.

"Archer."

Archer stopped, but was slow to turn.

"Something has happened," Leland said with a frown.

"Nothing of consequence."

But those eyes saw too much. "If anyone was to take

offense to your return, it would be Rossberry." Leland tilted his head, letting his gaze rake over Archer. "Which you should well know. One wonders why you simply didn't go straight to him."

A trickle of cold crept along Archer's neck. "Rossberry is out?"

Leland's mouth twisted. "Just recently. I suppose they could not cage him indefinitely."

Archer scowled. And yet they all thought *he* should stay away forever.

Leland understood his silence and had the grace to look chagrined. "If you want my help, you only have to ask."

Archer would be damned if he would ask Leland for help ever again. The man had been the first to suggest Archer leave London.

"And what help could an old man possibly provide?" Archer winced inwardly as the words left his lips, but could not bring himself to apologize. "Percival is dead," he said baldly.

Leland went white. "When? How?"

"This night. Murdered. No doubt it will be the scandal of the morning. I am the prime suspect. A servant heard Percival cry out my name. Another thought they saw me at the scene."

Leland nodded once. "Do you know who did it?"

God, Archer had missed his friend. "No"—he cleared his throat—"but I intend to find out."

Chapter Nine

———❦~❦———

"Tell me again why we are going to this party."

In the days after the murder of Sir Percival Andrew, gruesome recounts fell from the lips of newsmen and fruit sellers alike. Everyone was enthralled. Because everyone knew exactly who the killer was: Lord Benjamin Archer.

That he lived right under their very thumb and had not yet been brought to justice only served to titillate. Gossip was a sly foe. Borne on servant's tongues, details of Sir Percival's slaughter slid like fog over London.

Miranda felt the sting of gossip keenly. She remembered when public opinion had turned on her family in the days after her father was ruined. Wagging tongues catalogued every piece of furniture and artwork Father sold off to keep them from the streets.

As for Archer, he said not a word about the murder. Like a dog protecting his bone, he hovered at her side. Although he did not expressly forbid her from going out, he skillfully kept her occupied at home. Might she like a walk in the garden? Perhaps make use of the vast library? On Monday, he sent for a Monsieur Falle, a clever little dressmaker, who plied her with luscious bolts of fabrics to coo over. Each night, she ate delicious meals as he peppered her with various random questions. Did she believe Plato's Utopian Society would work in actual practice? What did she think of the Realism movement in art; should man be represented as he truly was or idealized? What of democracy? Should every man, regardless of birth, have a right to make the most of his life?

She reveled in their easy discourse. It was as if they'd known each other for a lifetime. Oh, they bickered to be sure, save it only served to ignite her curiosity and her need to converse with him further.

How could such a man slaughter another? *Was* she in denial? Or perhaps it was a sign of her own depravity that she identified so easily with him. Whatever Archer might be beneath his mask, she felt safe with him. And it was not just a matter of loneliness. She'd been lonely before; it had not affected her like this, filling her with the need to be near him. She fit within her skin when she was with him. The novelty of such a feeling was seductive.

And so it went. Miranda waited for the moment when his back was turned so that she might go out and discover answers, and Archer watched her as if waiting for her to run away.

Thus it came as a shock to Miranda when Archer strode in the salon earlier in the evening and announced in his imperious way that they were having a night out. So Miranda had donned her battle armor, a silver-satin dress that hugged her body like steel and was very properly put together. This didn't stop her from feeling ill at the prospect of facing the *haute ton*. Staring at the palatial town home looming up before her, trepidation tightened her breast.

Archer hedged a glance in her direction, his grip tightening as if she might flee. *Smart man.* He led them briskly up the marble stairs fronting Lord Cheltenham's stately home. "Have you found fault in my original reasoning?"

She pursed her lips. "'Because we were asked' is an evasion at best, and you well know it."

He chuckled, and her ire increased. Her steps slowed as a gaping footman moved to open the front doors for them.

"Damn it, Archer," she hissed. "Why give them the excuse to gawk?"

She did not want that for him, and felt a surge of protectiveness toward Archer that was as frightening as it was fierce.

Archer bent in until his soft breath touched her neck. "Because, dearest, I refuse to hide any longer." A fleeting caress of his thumb sent a shiver along her gloved wrist. "Courage, Miranda Fair. Never give them an inch or they will stretch it a mile."

Lord Cheltenham's grand hall was not as large as the one in Archer House, but it was elegant, filled with statuary, potted palms, and heavily draped archways. Clusters of men and women congregated in the quiet spots, watching as she and Archer passed. Looks of pity and murmurs followed. Would she be next? Would they read about her in their morning papers? Devour lurid details of Lord Archer's young bride ripped to shreds as they drank their tea and shook their heads at her foolishness?

Irritation rankled, and she held her head up high.

Archer simply walked on as if they were alone. Ahead

of them stood a small group of men by the base of the stairs. They clustered together, looking like a murder of crows with their hunched shoulders and sweeping black coattails. Old age had withered them, cleaving skin to bone, exaggerating the prominence of noses and cheeks. Sharp eyes turned on them, their orbs gleaming in the dim light as they blinked in unison.

"Do you know them?" She hoped not. The men almost quivered with shock and hostility.

Archer's grip tightened a fraction. "Yes."

"Come then, we'll go another way."

Miranda began to shift direction but Archer held her course. "Act as if I am afraid? I think not."

He steered them right into the men's path.

The tallest of them came forward, a man with a white mustache that hung in a frown over his lip. "Archer," he said in the crisp tones of an upper-class man put out, "I am surprised to see you out and about."

Archer inclined his head a mere fraction. "It appears the current rumor is false, Leland. As it turns out, I can leave my fiery throne and walk among honest Christian folk."

The skin around the man's keen blue eyes tightened. "I rather enjoyed that one," he said lightly.

"Stuff and feathers, all of it," said another man. He appeared kind, despite his formidable posture. He glanced at Miranda with soft brown eyes and a gentle smile. "I hear congratulations are in order, Archer."

Archer introduced Miranda to their host, the smiling Lord Cheltenham, then the frowning Lord Leland, and then Lord Merryweather, the last man to approach. Merryweather took Miranda's hand as introductions went around. His deep eyes twinkled slyly up at her as he held on a beat too long. The old devil. "I am enchanted, Lady Archer. Utterly enchanted."

Cheltenham turned to Archer. "We've just concluded a meeting for The Botanical Society today, Archer. I understand you have acquired extensive knowledge on the study of heredity characteristics in...roses, was it?" The man's eyes flashed with an emotion Miranda could not put her finger on but it seemed as though the whole group snapped to attention. She glanced at Archer and could have sworn he was smiling. But the stiffness in his shoulders betrayed little humor.

"I have much in the way of knowledge," Archer said without moving. "But little in the way of success."

The tension within the group increased. More than one set of eyes slid to her and then away.

"Perhaps you would care to join us next weekend and explain your findings?" asked Leland before giving Miranda a polite smile. "A rather dry subject, my lady, but we are enthralled by the process of plant hybridization, for it allows us to create whole new species."

Archer glared, but Leland paid him no notice. "For example, what was once a weak, quick-to-fade rose of ordinary color might be turned into a subject displaying strength, beauty, and longevity." His thick mustache lifted. "The perfect bloom."

"How lovely," she said politely while her mind turned. Archer, a botanist?

Archer leaned toward her. "We are amateurs all, playing with things beyond our ken."

She might have replied, but a disgruntled snarl sounded in hall.

"I wasna aware the society was holdin' a costume ball," came an irate Scottish burr from behind Cheltenham. The men turned at the sound, and Miranda's breath caught. The devil's own blue eyes glared daggers at Archer from lash-less slits. A map of raised scars, silver white and angry red, twisted the man's features into something barely recognizable as human. She clutched Archer's forearm by reflex.

"Rossberry," Archer said tightly as the man stomped over with a younger man in tow. "How nice to see you again."

A small mouth, hidden behind a molted brown beard, twitched with a growl. "If I had known you'd be here, I'd have hid me shame behind a fool's mask as well."

"Ah, but what mask could hide your dulcet tones?" replied Archer lightly. "Unless equipped with a muzzle."

"Mask, muzzle, that this fair face of mine draws less terror than what you hide is the real pity."

Miranda's fingers dug into Archer's coat, but he did not react.

"Really, Father," said the young man next to him. "You are practically begging for a duel with Lord Archer." His cultured tones were nothing like the Highland lilt of his father's, yet there was an air of resemblance between the men, from the shine of their dark auburn hair and the depth of their azure blue eyes. "Having witnessed Archer's cruel efficiency, I don't think you would fare well in the endeavor." He extended his hand to Archer. "Hello, Archer." Wolfish teeth flashed as his eyes raked over Archer's mask. "You haven't aged a bit."

Archer shook the man's hand briefly. "Kind of you to notice, Mckinnon."

Mckinnon laughed lightly. The man moved with a quick grace that spoke of strength and assurance. He turned his attentions to Miranda, and Archer murmured an introduction of Alasdair Ranulf, Earl of Rossberry, and Ian Ranulf, his eldest son and heir apparent, who held the courtesy title of Viscount Mckinnon.

"Enchanted, madam," Lord Mckinnon said, bending over her hand. His gloved thumb caressed her palm as it slipped away, and she bristled. He smiled knowingly. There was something all together animalistic emanating from Mckinnon that made her wary. The look in his eyes said he knew at least a little of her line of thinking and enjoyed the effect.

He had barely let go when Lord Rossberry's fury returned to Archer. "You've got nerve showing yourself, Archer, after what ye did to Marvel. Stay out of my way, an' away from my son, or I'll have your heart on a stake for me supper."

Chapter Ten

Miranda's feet throbbed as she made another turn on the dance floor with yet another partner. The line of young men wanting to dance appeared endless, the exception being her husband, who had disappeared. She begged off when the last young man stepped on her toes. He flushed deeply and apologized profusely.

Limping from the ballroom to the grand upper-foyer, she searched for Archer, only to see his broad back slip past Lord Leland on the way into Cheltenham's private study. Leland caught her eye for one moment, his blue gaze flat and troubled before he closed the door, locking Archer in and Miranda out. She glared at the closed door. *Damnable man.*

"Men can be rather tiresome, can they not?"

Miranda turned to find a dark-haired woman standing by her side. The woman smiled, revealing extremely white teeth from behind painted lips. "I could not help but notice your scowl. Nothing else but a man could produce that look."

Miranda had to laugh, at both the woman's wonderfully forthright nature, and the veracity of the comment. "Quite so," Miranda said with another small laugh.

The woman dimpled. "You are Lady Archer, are you not?"

"Yes. Miranda Archer, Lord Archer's wife."

Miranda studied her anew. That the woman was beautiful there was little doubt, blessed with a heart-shaped face and wide gray eyes. Her exact age was another matter entirely. Perhaps she had a skin ailment, for Miranda could see no reason why such an attractive woman should cover herself with so much rice powder. Her near theatrical application of makeup emphasized the fine lines in her face and gave her the appearance of a much older woman, perhaps well into her forties. Yet the firmness of her flesh belied that assumption, as did her trim figure. She could have been twenty, or twenty years older. It was impossible to tell.

Her style was that of a younger woman's as well. Her dark auburn locks were pulled up high to curl in profusion down her neck. A stylish fringe curled over her brow, a style Miranda admired but hadn't yet gathered the courage to try. The lime-green gown she wore fell in a narrow skirt to the floor before fanning out from the back in a ripple of fuchsia flounces.

She noticed Miranda's study and did not appear insulted, but rather pleased. "Apologies," she said. "I have not introduced myself. I am a kinswoman of yours, though you do not yet know it." Her head lowered in greeting, a smile curling over her dark lips. "Miss Victoria Archer," she said as Miranda's lips turned numb. "I am third cousin to Benjamin."

It was the eyes, Miranda thought, staring. They were the same shade of silver gray. Slowly, Miranda curtsied in turn. "Pardon me," she said, coming out of her fog. "I did not mean to stare. I did not think Archer had any living relatives." She tried to smile. "How nice to meet you."

Miss Archer laughed, a melodic sound as clear as Waterford crystal. "It is quite all right. I am guilty of a little deception. I saw you with Archer and waited for him to leave." She gave a sidelong glance around the ballroom. "I should have had Benjamin introduce us but I admit to wanting a little fun." Her gray eyes tilted at the corners. "My cousin can be somewhat prickly about his private life, no?"

Miranda had to agree. Only, she thought herself a part of his private life. Miranda stared, unable to do less. Did Archer have the same pointed chin? Or wide brow? Did his ears stick out just a bit as Miss Archer's? She hadn't pictured him as such, but could it be? She longed to press Miss Archer about his former life but knew, somehow, that it would be unfaithful to Archer.

"Have you just arrived in town?" she asked instead.

"Mmm…" Miss Archer watched the dancers with interest. She had a strong Gallic nose, aquiline yet proportionate to her face. A hint of French touched her speech. Miranda had been sure Archer was more Italian in heritage. "I have but just arrived."

Behind jeweled-colored fans, the ladies of the ton were buzzing like bees, sending guarded, if not outright hostile, looks in their direction.

Lord Cheltenham appeared, slipping past the ranks of defensive matrons, to stand before them. He bowed shortly. "Lady Archer. Miss?" His narrow face pinked as he grappled.

"Victoria," she offered with a coquettish tilt of the head.

Cheltenham turned red, undoubtedly horrified by such intimacy. "Yes, well...Miss..."—his large Adam's apple bobbed beneath his collar—"Victoria, I wondered if you would care to dance."

That did not appear the case, as he stood stiff and pale before her. But Victoria smiled demurely—if one could look demure wearing smoke-gray eye makeup—and let him lead her away.

Perhaps she was a courtesan, Miranda thought, watching them make a turn. Having never met one, she could not be sure. Aside from the indelicate application of cosmetics, she hardly looked the part. Her gown had sleeves that came to her wrist and a collar up to her chin, though what it lacked in displays of flesh, it made up for in tightness.

Victoria and Cheltenham drifted out of sight as Miranda mused. She fancied following them, but a familiar figure appeared at her side, dark and tall and scowling.

"There you are," she said, frowning up at Archer. "You know you are going to make me quite dizzy coming and going all night long."

He took hold of her elbow and began to guide her out of the ballroom. "Then perhaps I should take you home and let you rest," he murmured, looking around in mild distraction.

"I'd rather we talk." They sidestepped around a rather boisterously reeling couple. "Besides, I just met one of your relations, Miss Victoria Archer—"

He jerked to a halt. "She is not my kin, nor is her name Archer. Why would you think such a thing?"

Miranda blinked in surprise. "Because that is what she claimed."

Archer snarled in disgust.

Miranda frowned. "Why would she say that she was?"

"To amuse herself?" he answered tightly, steering Miranda once more away from the crowd. "Because she is a pervasive liar? I cannot begin to know."

They moved to the edge of the room, and Miranda stopped, not at all liking the hold he had on her elbow, and wrenched free.

"Do stop tugging me all about. I shall bruise." She rubbed the offended elbow and eyed him with distaste. "She seemed perfectly lovely." Archer snorted, and her voice rose. "She displayed more honesty and friendliness than any of the other women I've met here tonight."

Archer's eyes slid round the room behind them as though he wondered if Victoria might appear at any moment through the throng of dancers. "She is a very good actor." He moved closer, and his large frame cut off the noise of the room. "Look, I apologize for being curt with you just now," he said, using the rich, persuasive quality of his voice to its fullest. "You could not have known."

He glanced over his shoulder and then back at Miranda, and she marveled over the effect Victoria appeared to have on him. Until now, Miranda would not have thought him fearful of anyone.

"But you know now," he went on, his gray eyes pleading and soft. "And I should like very much for you not to speak to her again."

Pretty words for a direct order. The spark of irritation grew within her breast. "There is something you are not telling me."

As expected, the corners of his eyes creased slightly. "Such as," he asked blandly.

"Such as why she bothers you so very much. Such as why she chose to use your name." Miranda crowded him lest he back away. "Such as why you share the exact, exceedingly rare eye color yet you are *not* kin in any form."

Archer's eyes narrowed, his chest heaving slightly—all signs that an explosion of temper was imminent. She did not care a whit.

"Must I spell things out for you?" he hissed.

"Yes."

She thought he'd shout, but he leaned in over her like a dark, avenging angel. "She lives in disgrace, with a reputation so low that Cheltenham is asking her to leave as we speak. Association with her can only cause you social harm."

Miranda could only gape. "I should think you of all people would not concern yourself over ill associations and foul reputations."

He flinched as though slapped. His eyes held hers for a terrible moment. "Stay away from her, Miranda," he said flatly, then stalked off, leaving her alone in the corner.

"Blast."

Archer was not in the hall, or on the balcony. A quick circulation of the dining room, salon, and again through the ballroom came up futile. How could such a large man disappear in less than five minutes?

Miranda turned down a dark hall and went up a small landing toward the side of the house where the family rooms lay. Archer might have overstepped social niceties and taken refuge in the Cheltenhams' private spaces—either that or he had left her at the party, an idea that made her chest tighten with hurt. Her step grew light, fear of discovery giving her caution; she had no desire to come upon anyone but Archer.

A set of large double doors lay open near the end of the hall. Yellow light spilled out from the open doorway to lie in rectangles upon the crimson rugs. Voices came from within, little more than an indistinct rise and fall of sound. Her step grew slower, for she recognized one voice in particular.

In keeping with Lady Cheltenham's ornate sense of style, heavy brocade drapery adorned the doorway, with life-sized black marble statues of Hades and Persephone standing guard on either side. Hades' black hand stretched out toward Persephone's turned head, his stone mouth open as if in a plea. Miranda placed a hand upon Persephone's cold marble foot and leaned forward.

A woman's melodious voice rose up. "You have finally come out of hiding, Benji."

"Do not call me that." Archer's voice was so low it was almost inaudible, but filled with raw anger. "You've lost all right to call me anything."

Curiosity screamed for Miranda to stay, but she owed Archer his privacy.

The woman's light laughter tinkled like crystal. "You did not used to object to me calling you Benji, *beloved*."

Beloved? Privacy be damned; she wasn't going anywhere *now*. Miranda risked a look. The pair stood alone before a heavily draped window. Victoria stalked around him slowly, her gloved hand traveling over his shoulder as she surveyed him. Archer stood like timber, his dark head facing forward.

"In fact"—the train of her lime-green gown curled about his ankles—"I remember you being quite fond of me moaning it—"

He grabbed her wrist and wrenched her arm up hard. "What you remember is your own vanity." He bent over her. "If you had any eyes for the world around you, you'd know our time together was better forgotten."

"Bastard!" She moved to strike him. He caught the hand neatly.

"Temper," he warned lightly, though there was little humor in him. He let her go abruptly, and she fumbled back a pace.

Victoria's eyes narrowed to slits. "I should say the same to you. You wouldn't want that mask to come off in a scuffle. People might see what lies beneath." She gave his chin a light flick, her finger clicking loudly against the hard mask.

The cold cruelty of the gesture cut into Miranda, and she bit her lip hard.

"You do not want your sweet bride to run off, no?" Victoria went on, when Archer didn't respond. She tutted sadly. "I ought to have said virgin bride. You cannot have bedded her." She laughed hard, a near mannish sound in all its unfettered glee. "I can just imagine how quickly she'd leave should she gaze upon your horror."

Archer's hand rose high, vibrating with the effort to hold back. "If you weren't a woman," he whispered fiercely.

"Oh yes, you would, Archer." She glared up at him without fear. "We both know you've done that and worse. You ought to have stayed hidden away in darkness where you belong. Why you choose to subject anyone to your presence astonishes me."

Pain radiated from him in palpable waves, and it made Miranda ache for him. His hand lowered.

"You haven't answered my question," he said in a low voice. "Why are you here?"

Victoria made a turn, letting her long train swish

elegantly, and Miranda caught a faint whiff of her heady perfume, thickly sweet like carnations and roses, yet acrid underneath from the overuse of lemon. Victoria's wide mouth turned in a pout.

"I was bored." She cocked her head slightly, her eyes slanting. "Your pretty wife is quite stimulating, no?" Her lips curled into the semblance of a smile. "This must be why you wed her—the *titillating* conversation."

Archer might have been a block of carved basalt.

"Ah, but you guard her well." Her melodious voice was becoming less so.

"Answer the question."

Victoria inclined her head toward the door, just a fraction of an inch, but enough to make Miranda's breath freeze. She eased back behind the statue.

Victoria's voice drifted overloud to her ears. "Do you truly want me to answer you while the mice are at play?"

Miranda felt rather than saw Archer turn toward the door, for by then she had slipped away, her heart pounding, her feet moving as fast as they could without making a sound.

"You bitch!" Archer's hand twitched at his side. Striking her would be useless. "So that was all for her benefit, was it?"

Victoria laughed, throwing her head back with delight. "Of course," she said, snapping round to glare at him with full venom. "Your little chit, as they say, is an amusing distraction. Now then"—she moved to wrap her arms about his neck—"let us kiss and make nice."

He pushed her then, a hard shove that made her fall back a step. God help him, he shouldn't have. But his weakness was already exposed. And it made his heart pound hard.

Her humor died with a snarl. "We had an understanding."

"Based on lies." He brushed by her, and she struck like lightning, grasping hold of his arm so that he jerked back. The thick miasma of her floral perfume filled his nostrils, making his temples throb.

"I love you, Archer."

For a moment, he might have thought her capable of such an emotion, but for the sight of her cold, soulless eyes. "How odd," he said. "The last time we spoke you told me you hated me, never wanted to set eyes upon me again."

She smiled thinly. "You understand nothing of women then." Her fingers bit into his arm. "Have your toy if you must," she said with flat reserve. "But I will not be pushed away again. Only I know what you truly are. We belong together, and it is time you remembered."

He drew her in, vaguely aware that a low growl rumbled in his breast. He would end this now. For too long, he had ignored her mad attachment to him. Victoria's eyes widened, watching him, waiting to see what he would do. A faint sneer curled her red lips. She underestimated him; she always had.

"This way, darling," said a voice from behind them. "Oh, I say..."

Archer turned to see young Mr. Hendren framed in the doorway with his latest mistress clinging to his arm. The pair eyed him with varying levels of distaste and wariness.

"Have we interrupted?" The jeer in Hendren's voice was poorly hidden.

Archer almost told him yes, sod off, but Victoria slid from his grasp and out of the room. He grit his teeth in fury. He'd never catch her now; experience had taught him that well. With a glare at Hendren, he pushed past the couple and went out to control the damage wrought.

He tracked Miranda by instinct, feeling the pull of her lead him through the house. No longer distracted by Victoria, his senses filled with his wife, her scent, the desperate sound of her breathing coming to him over the chatter of revelers and the discordant strains of a waltz.

Outside, the air was cool and fresh, the scent of loam and earth rising from well-tended flowerbeds lining the rear garden. Crushed shells crunched beneath his feet as he strode down the center path, alerting her to his presence. She spun from her position under the willow tree, her glorious hair shining penny bright in the moonlight.

"Miranda." He reached out for her, desperate to hold her, reassure her, and perhaps glean some comfort for himself.

She stopped short at his touch, her eyes wide. "I'm sorry," she said. "I did not mean to..." She bit her lip and looked away ashamed. His heart turned over in his chest. He was at fault here. He'd pulled her into a world of death and depravity. The need to protect her made his arms quake, yet he hesitated. What right had he to hold Miranda when everything Victoria said about him was true?

The wind shifted, pulling strands of red silken hair across her cheek. He could not help but brush them back, his touch lingering on her skin, but something about the breeze gave him pause. He stopped and inhaled. His throat closed tight as the sticky sweet stench of offal flowed over him like sludge. Miranda winced as his hand convulsively clenched on her upper arm.

Clouds scuttled over the moon and then away. Just beyond his bride he saw it, the distorted line of a man sprawled upon the ground, unmoving as dry leaves rustled over him. Miranda read Archer too well and turned to the sight as if called. A scream welled up in her and died as she saw what he did—polished opera slippers tilting drunkenly on the path, thin legs encased in fine trousers, a black stain spread like an oil slick over a white waistcoat, and the throat of Lord Marcus Cheltenham laid open to the night. Archer pulled Miranda hard against his chest, tucking her head into his shoulder as he closed his eyes. But nothing would erase the sight of his friend's bone-white face, blood pouring from his mouth, and the golden shine of a West Moon Club coin resting gently over one eye.

Chapter Eleven

———— ∾ ⌇ ∾ ————

The bookstore was, as the sign said, closed for lunch. Miranda knocked anyway, rapping her knuckles rather hard upon the scarred green door. Eventually, Archer had needed to go out and visit his man of business. Miranda had acted, absconding with the coach and fleeing as soon as Archer was out of sight. Not a very courageous course, but necessary. Her fingers tightened around the coin in her pocket. She had to understand this. And she feared asking Archer.

Poppy answered on the third knock, her quizzical eyes going from Miranda to the waiting town coach on the road behind. "Well, you've managed to arrive at lunch," Poppy said. A fiery red brow slanted. "I don't suppose you'd like to partake of the common man's food?"

"Oh, do shut up, Poppy." Miranda bit back a smile. "Or I'll have to bring up your secret yearning for blue satin knickers."

A brilliant pink flush clashed with Poppy's copper hair. "You and Daisy with your stolen bottle of port. I was sick

for a week." Her stern expression broke, and she gave
Miranda a rare smile. "Come in then, Jezebel."

"Hello to you, too." Miranda kissed her proffered
cheek.

They did not go up to Poppy's flat but into the bookstore, which was really her true home. Eight years older
than Miranda, Poppy had married young, when Father
was flush with funds and inclined to generosity. Thus
she had received a nice dowry upon marriage to her poor
but quick-minded love, Winston Lane. The first thing the
newlyweds had done was purchase the bookshop. When
Winston turned to police work, Poppy took over the
running of the shop, and it soon became her consuming
passion.

They moved farther into the cool, dark place, past rows
of crowded mahogany shelves. The smell of book mold
mingled with the pleasant scent of beeswax and orange
oil. A long, glass-topped mahogany counter sat at the
far end of the store, near enough to the windows to get
a modicum of light. On top of it sat a small lunch upon
brown paper.

"Sit," Poppy ordered, pointing to a stool. She went
round the counter and pulled out two white cups adorned
with blue flowers. Matching saucers and plates followed.
While she set about slicing the brown bread, Miranda
lifted her cup to inspect it. Royal Copenhagen. Mother's
china. Or what was left. Vaguely, she remembered Poppy
stealing out of the house with a large box of undetermined
items one summer day, not long after Father had begun
selling off the housewares. It warmed Miranda's heart to
see the set.

"I've a few more of them," Poppy said while putting
slices of brawn and boiled eggs onto a plate. Her brown

eyes glanced up. "You may have a set if you wish. I hadn't thought to get you a wedding present."

"No." Miranda set her cup down so that Poppy could fill it with tea. "I'm glad you have them."

A pang of nostalgia tightened her breast as she sat hunched over the counter sipping plain tea from Mother's old china cup. Miranda had missed Poppy, more than she'd let herself acknowledge. Missed Daisy too, come to that.

As if summoned, the front bell jangled. Their heads snapped up in unison just as Daisy's familiar voice rang out. "You forgot to lock your door, pet!"

"More's the pity," Poppy murmured as Daisy strolled in looking resplendent in pink satin and crimson bows.

"Miranda, Panda! That cannot be you!" Daisy's sky-blue eyes lifted at the corners as she glided across the room to embrace Miranda.

Her soft cheeks brushed Miranda's, the familiar scent of rosemary blended with jasmine enveloping Miranda like a hug. Daisy stepped back and lifted Miranda's arms to inspect Miranda's sleek new day dress of Prussian blue taffeta. "Surely this is not the plain Jane I knew, nor the be-ruffled peony Father packed off nearly two weeks ago."

"Oh stop," Miranda said with a laugh and broke free of her grip.

"Come for lunch?" Poppy asked. Her brows slanted ominously.

Daisy gave her a quick kiss on the cheek before glancing at the offering upon the counter. "Er, no." Her little nose wrinkled. "Minding my figure, pet." She swept back her undulating train and lowered herself onto a stool with a little plop. "You know what they say. While a man appreciates a feast, too much bounty and he might lose his appetite." Her hand smoothed over the ample swell of her breast. "I'd prefer a man to be hungry when he eats."

Poppy groaned, but Miranda laughed. "I've missed that foul tongue of yours," she said.

Daisy stuck her tongue out, and Poppy cracked a small smile. "Why are you here, dearest? Not that I don't enjoy your company"—her mouth twitched—"only I profess the timing rather coincidental."

Daisy pulled off her silk gloves. "You found me out. I am spying on you." She rolled her eyes. "I was driving by and saw Miranda's coach. Lovely conveyance, by the way, pet. I am insanely jealous. So I ordered the driver to stop. Besides, it keeps me from returning to Craggy, now doesn't it."

Daisy's husband, Mr. Cyril Craigmore, besides being three times Daisy's age, was a bore and had the face of a cragged mountainside—hence "Craggy." That Daisy had found the man revolting meant little to Father when Craigmore had come calling. As Father was newly ruined, Craigmore's wealth held a particular place of import; his seat in the House of Commons had not hurt either. It was only when Craigmore flat-out refused to pass even a farthing in Father's direction that his opinion of Craigmore turned.

"Now then," Daisy said and brushed an errant curl from her brow, "what of your lord and husband? How do you find being married to 'the Bloody Baron, the Dread Lord Archer'? Hasn't murdered you in your sleep, I'll give him that."

Daisy's humor subsided as she caught Miranda's eye. "Oh, pet, I was only having you on." She leaned forward, touching Miranda's knee. "Well, of course, he isn't a killer. I knew that right off."

Poppy did not look as certain but held her tongue.

Miranda pushed away her cup. "And how can you be so sure?" Her voice had gone thick. How close she was to crying.

Daisy cocked her head as she studied Miranda. "Because you didn't go running off into the night, or reduce him to a smoldering pile of ash." The small curl at her brow proved persistent. It fell back against Daisy's cheek, and she batted it away again. "One thing you are not is meek, my angel."

Miranda uttered an unladylike snort. "For all you knew, he might have slaughtered me in my bed that first night, and my poor body was currently drifting down the Thames."

Daisy's answering laugh was the tinkling of bells. "But either way, we'd know what he was about, now wouldn't we?"

Miranda had to laugh. "You're a beast."

"If you need assurance, you could always show him just how capable you are of defending yourself," Daisy offered without quite looking at her.

"No!" Miranda's shout bounced over the quiet store. She took a deep breath. "He will *never* know about that. Nor will I use it upon him." She might have considered it before, but not now.

"No, of course not," murmured Daisy. "I should not have asked."

Heat washed over Miranda, centering on her damp palms. Her sisters pointedly studied their teacups as Miranda fought the swell of panic rising within her. All of their lives had changed because of Miranda's oddity, and not for the better. She tucked her hands against her skirts as if hiding away a lethal weapon. She had only just learned to keep the fire under control. It would not get out again. It could not. *I cannot hurt Archer that way.*

She realized she had spoken aloud when Poppy looked at her thoughtfully. "Then he is kind to you?"

Miranda forced her hands open, thought of cool things, calm things. "I have no complaints in that regard."

Daisy leaned in. "Enough dreary thoughts of death and violence." Her blue eyes went catlike. "Let us get to the heart of the matter. Have you any complaints in regards to the bedroom?"

Poppy snorted in disgust as Miranda licked her lips and wished for more tea.

Daisy grinned saucily. "To be sure, the mask is rather...unsettling, but I must say, the body is"—her light voice dipped to a low purr—"stirring. All broad shouldered and trim of waist." Her voluptuous curves wriggled a bit on the seat. "And tall enough to overpower a lady with ease."

"Daisy," Poppy warned sharply.

Daisy went on with a Cheshire cat grin. "Admit it. Lord Archer cuts quite a delicious figure. I'd overlook the mask to ride such a body. How very wicked to bed a masked man."

"Oh good God, Daisy Margaret!"

Daisy ignored Poppy. "Well, then? Am I wrong?"

Miranda smoothed a pleat on her flounce. M. Falle was really quite good with pleating. Perhaps she'd ask for a bit more on the next dress.

"Miranda..." Daisy's stare would not relent.

"Leave her alone. Not everyone is interested in intercourse."

"Even you don't believe that, pet."

Poppy flushed and she glanced at Miranda. The clatter

of coach traffic on Oxford Street drifted in from outside as Miranda perspired under the harsh glare of their expectant looks.

"Our arrangement is not of that sort," Miranda finally admitted.

Daisy's mouth hung open prettily. "Not of that sort?" she parroted. "Forgive me, dear sister, but when a man who is as rich as sin *and* a baron marries a girl without position or fortune, the only sort of arrangement he could possibly desire is for a nightly tup with his beautiful young wife."

Poppy, for once, looked as if she agreed with Daisy.

"I read to him," Miranda lied in desperation, her cheeks hotter than oven-fresh bread.

Daisy snorted. "Read to him. The very idea. Has he not come to your bed?" she asked as though making a joke.

"No," Miranda snapped rather loudly. She hadn't expected the truth to be so humiliating. "He deposits me at my bedroom door every night and then goes off on his own. Perhaps he takes his needs elsewhere. I really couldn't say."

"That, my dear," Daisy said, "is a *ton* marriage. Be thankful for it."

No, that was loneliness, Miranda thought despondently.

They were silent for a moment, and then Poppy turned to her lunch. As if waiting for that signal, Daisy and Miranda did the same, Daisy delicately sipping tea and Miranda trying to force down a sandwich her stomach no longer wanted.

"Is Winston coming home for lunch?" Miranda asked to fill the awkward silence.

"Not today." Poppy took a large bite of her sandwich and chewed industriously. "The whole department is focused on…" A flush touched her white cheeks. The promotion to C.I.D. had been a crowning achievement for Winston and a source of pride for Poppy. No doubt, Winston leading a high-profile investigation was another triumph.

Miranda set her sandwich down. "Is that why you did not want me here? Did you think the neighbors might see the dreaded Lord Archer's coach outside and inform Winston?"

Poppy's red brows drew together to form a straight line. "If you think I fear my husband then you don't know me at all." Her eyes pinned Miranda to the spot, a rather motherly trick that Miranda had loathed throughout childhood.

Miranda looked away. "I am sorry, Pop. I don't know why…I'm just so…Archer is…he cannot be the murderer. But he is involved." She pulled the coin from her pocket and held it out. "I need your help."

Unfortunately, revelations did not spring forth as Miranda had hoped. West Moon Club was not on any official club register listed. It did not surface in old newspaper articles, history of London books, or any of the other literature that Poppy pulled down from her shelves. Nor was there a West Club, or a Club Moon, for that matter. Checking for old stories or accounts of the two victims did not help. The men in question had lived staid lives as far as society knew. Near the end of the day, all they had to show for their efforts were mountains of books and papers teetering precariously over the entire surface of Poppy's counter.

"Well, I am done in," Daisy finally exclaimed with a fleeting scowl.

Poppy sat back, her rail-thin shoulders bunched and determined beneath her cotton blouse. "I'll have to give this some more thought." She stared in a glazed manner at the books before her.

"I do believe an outside investigation is called for," Miranda said.

Poppy's eyes cut back to Miranda like a scythe. "Absolutely not."

"I'm perfectly capable…"

"You *are*," Poppy interjected, "Lady Archer, society's newest curiosity. You would be instantly recognized."

"I can disguise myself!"

Poppy looked pointedly at Miranda's face before raising one red brow. "Try again."

Miranda could only come up with a baleful glare.

Of which Poppy was immune. "If you are recognized, you would heap scandal and suspicion upon Lord Archer's already overburdened shoulders."

"That is true, pet." Daisy nodded. "It will only add oil to the fire."

Miranda's back teeth met with a click. She would not risk Archer's name to further scandal, no. But she had more confidence in her ability to disguise herself than Poppy and Daisy did.

Poppy smiled and briskly patted her knee. "There. Now that we have that settled, it is time for you to leave. It is nearly supper—or tea time for you lot, I suppose."

They glanced at the windows. The light outside had faded to dark gray, and the lamplighter had come out, his long pole bouncing on his shoulder as he made his way from streetlamp to streetlamp. He stopped by the window, and a muted halo of light illuminated the panes.

"Blast," Miranda muttered, tidying her pile of papers

into a neater stack. "I've got to go before Archer begins to wonder."

Poppy's lips twitched. "Worries over you, now does he?"

She continued to sort the pile. "I don't know if he worries..."

"He ought to. You're incorrigible."

"Or course she is," Daisy said as she smoothed her skirts. "I taught her everything I know."

"Hopefully not everything. Leave the papers, dears. I'll sort them out later."

Poppy duly kissed their cheeks as they parted by the door. "Stay safe."

Something burned inside of Miranda, irritation, dread. She didn't know anymore. "He cannot be a murderer."

"You said that before," Poppy murmured. "Is it what you believe, or what you hope?"

Chapter Twelve

───────────── ❧❧ ─────────────

Having confined all aspects of espionage to skulking behind closed doors or hiding in small spaces, Miranda was uncertain how easy it would be to track Archer as he set out for town the next day. As it turned out, it was quite simple.

A man of uncommon height and breadth of shoulders wearing a black carnival mask while riding astride a gray gelding was not a sight one overlooked. John Coachman—who participated because he had no choice in the matter but wore an exceedingly sullen expression when Miranda told him of her plan—needed only to follow the trail of stunned onlookers like the proverbial breadcrumbs in the forest. Soon they were only four coach lengths behind him. Impatient, she craned her neck, putting her head as far out the window as she dared. Archer's head remained high and forward, his seat light and trained. He cut through the traffic, seeming oblivious of the commotion he caused. Miranda's chest tightened, watching him so. He had too keen an eye not to see the

rudely gawking halfwits who hadn't the decency to let
him pass in peace.

Unfortunately London traffic got the better of them on
Piccadilly, and the crush of omnibuses, carts, and carriages soon swallowed him whole.

"Blast." She punched the seat and sat back in a huff as
the coach creaked to a halt.

From the window came a plaintive bleat as a flock
of sheep waddled by, leaving behind the acrid stench of
urine and lanolin. She muttered again, expecting a cow
to poke its wet nose through the window at any moment.

John Coachman's blond head peeked in as he opened
the box. "S'all right, milady. He's gone to the British
Museum, I'm sure of it."

Miranda perked up. "How can you be sure?"

His brown eyes crinkled. "He's been going there every
Wednesday since as long as he's been here in London."

"Every..." She ground her teeth to keep from shouting. "Then why didn't you simply tell me that when I
endeavored to follow Lord Archer?"

The earnestness of his expression was genuine. "But
my lady, you only asked me to follow Lord Archer, not
tell you his habits." The traffic around them moved, and
John's head snapped up. "Here we go, then," he said
quickly and then closed the box. The coach gave a lurch
and went off at a nice clip.

Her ire died down as they pulled up before the British
Museum. She bade John to wait and entered the cool quiet
of the stately neoclassical front building. A guide took
her mantle and informed her that extraordinary exhibits were currently being held in galleries one and two.
Having never been inside, Miranda hadn't realized the
sheer size of the place. She despaired of finding Archer.

Unfortunately, her quiet word of inquiry to the stout guide yielded nothing more than a raised shaggy, white brow.

"The privacy of our patrons is sacrosanct, madam. I'm sure I would be remiss in my duties if I did not treat it as such." His stern expression broke for a fleeting moment. "However, you may wish to examine the paintings of our Pre-Raphaelites in the Red Salon. I vow you shall find them most enlightening."

She found Archer in the center of the otherwise empty Red Salon.

Miranda stayed back, hiding in the outer corridor just behind the doorway. He stood for several long minutes gazing up at a portrait upon the wall. She dared not move closer to see what it was, but something about the tilt of Archer's head, the way his shoulders hunched, spoke of longing and loneliness.

"Though lovely, that gown is hardly inconspicuous."

Miranda inhaled with a rush, Archer's sudden words causing her heart to promptly stop before starting up again madly. She cursed herself for being seduced by duchess satin the color of new butter and a high-flaring collar of starched bronze organza.

"How did you know I was here?" she said as she moved into the gallery to stand beside him.

Archer chuckled silently but kept his eyes on the painting before him, a voluptuous girl with a yellow rose tucked behind one ear. Her rosebud lips were soft and yielding, her eyes dreamy as she stared off into the distance. Flame red hair parted down the middle, flowing in molten wings down to her shoulders.

"La Bocca Baciata." Archer's rich voice rolled over the Italian like a wave. Perfect diction. Miranda thought of his second name—Aldo. There was Italian in his background, to be sure.

He shifted until he stood just behind her right shoulder, his great height looming over her. "You ought to have hired a hack," he said. "Covered your bright hair with a larger, less beguiling hat, worn heavy perfume to hide your natural scent..."

"Yes, all right. You've gone on quite enough about my lack of prowess as a spy, thank you." Pursing her lips, she kept her eyes on the painting.

He made a sound of amusement, but said nothing more. Miranda hedged a glance at him. Melancholy surrounded him like a shroud. "Why do you come here every Wednesday, Archer?"

For a moment, she thought he hadn't heard her soft query, but then his shoulders moved with a silent sigh. "I would come here with my mother. When I was a boy." Gray eyes cut to hers. "Art brought her peace." He turned his attention back to the portraits. "And now it does me."

They were silent for a moment, then he took her elbow and guided her from the gallery. Although his manner appeared calm, his brisk pace belied his demeanor. Not for the first time, she wished she could see his expression and felt an inordinate surge of hatred toward the hard, full masks he wore. He was so much more than what he chose to show. Curse it, Victoria had seen what lay beneath; why not she?

"Where are you taking me?" Miranda asked.

"I should think it obvious."

She eyed him impatiently, and he made a small bow of acquiescence. "As you are clearly wasting away from boredom, I must make it my duty to keep you entertained."

Her mouth opened, then promptly closed as an

elegantly turned-out couple glided by, their eyes determinedly held away from Archer.

Archer guided her down another corridor and into the zoological collections.

"You have not asked why I was following you," she said when they were alone again.

They paused beside a display case filled with beetles. "To question would imply that I do not know the answer." He glanced at her. "It is because you are the most stubborn, impetuous, overtly curious creature I have ever known."

Something rude passed over her lips, and the corners of his eyes crinkled. She turned away from him and studied a wall of pinned butterflies.

Archer's sigh of resignation broke their stalemate. "All right, I'll play your game. Why are you following me?" Despite his jesting manner, irritation sharpened his voice.

"The peerage murders," she said without thinking.

Until Archer, she hadn't thought of stillness as explosive. The black mask faced her, the eyes behind it flat as pewter as the wide expanse of his chest hardened like mortar. Her heart sank with dread. Why had she prompted this conversation? Curiosity would be the death of her.

"You think I had something to do with them," he said in even, awful tones.

"No!" She gripped the handle of her parasol. "No. But they have all made assumptions based on your appearance, and such skewed logic galls me. Guilt or innocence ought to be established on proof, not hearsay."

His arm brushed hers as he moved past. "So your boundless curiosity bids you to discover my innocence," he said over his shoulder. "Or is it evidence of guilt you seek?"

Miranda quickened her pace to catch up to him. "I'd like to believe you are innocent."

"Why? Don't want to lose the security of my income?"

"*Our* income."

A snort escaped him. "Better to see me hang then and collect all of it, darling."

"Oh for pity's sake!" She thumped her parasol on the floor for emphasis. "I cannot believe it was you."

"Why?"

"I have my reasons."

He stopped abruptly and his eyes pinned her to the spot. "Which are?"

She held his gaze. "I rather thought that my line. Is there a purpose for all this evasiveness, Archer? Or do you simply enjoy driving me to madness?"

His chin jutted forward in a rather pugnacious manner. "I should not have to explain myself to my wife."

"And I should not have to ask for an explanation. Yet here we are."

Laughter rumbled behind his mask. "A fine pickle we are in."

"A fine pickle? An Americanism?"

"Yes. Ten years there and my language is polluted."

She ducked her head, trying not to smile. They turned a corner and walked out into the light-filled main stair. She glanced over to find him watching. "I shall ask it once, Archer. Whatever you say, I will believe it."

His steps slowed to a stop. "Why?" His voice was a ghost in the quiet. "Why give me your trust when you know it is such an easy thing to break?"

"Perhaps the easy giving of it will make it harder to break."

He made a soft sound of disbelief. "Lying is quite easy, Miranda Fair. I can assure you."

"Amusing. But I don't believe that of you." She shifted to face him, the effect of which unfortunately brought her mere inches from his solid frame. She couldn't move away without drawing attention so she went on as if unaffected. "You hide many things, Archer. But you do not lie. Not to a direct question, anyway."

The wide expanse of his chest brushed against hers as he leaned in. "You're collecting pieces of me, aren't you?" His voice turned thick as warm toffee, rolling over her skin, heating it. "A bit here. A bit there. Soon you'll set me out on the table, try to fit me back together."

Ignoring the flurries plaguing her belly, she affected blandness. "I've only got the corners. But it is a start."

A warm breath touched her neck. "I believe you have the centerpiece as well."

Before Miranda could reply, he spoke again. "No. I did not kill them."

Relief eased the tightness in her shoulders. She dared not smile. Not yet. "If you know who did, would you tell me?"

This time Archer did laugh, sudden and sharp. "Not if I can help it." Her ire rose when he suddenly reached out and gave the curl at her neck a gentle tug. "I sense a predilection for trouble coming from you. I've no desire to encourage it."

Chapter Thirteen

———❧❧———

Miranda put the unpleasantness of murder out of her mind. She would enjoy herself with Archer, if not for her sake, then for his. And surprisingly, they did enjoy the day. The museum was enormous, its collection of wonders vast.

When the hour grew late and most patrons made for home, Archer slipped an obscene amount of money to the guard to allow them to stroll the upper floors uninterrupted. Miranda was glad for it. A day spent in public with her husband made her painfully aware of how life was for him. Her heart filled with tenderness when she realized what this day out cost him.

They stopped to study Greek sculptures in one of the upper galleries, and she turned to him, intent upon offering her gratitude.

"Why haven't you left me?" Archer interrupted, scattering her thoughts.

"What do you mean?" But she knew. Her throat went dry and sore. How could she tell him, when she hadn't truly admitted it to herself?

They stood alone in a small alcove facing an ancient frieze. He gestured toward the stairs where the sound of patrons leaving the museum drifted up. "All of them think I am a killer."

He ran a finger along the balustrade at his side, watching the movement. "Morbid fascination compels society to tolerate me. But you..." Archer lifted his head, yet would not turn to face her. "Why haven't you left? Why do you defend me? I...I cannot account for it."

"You cannot account for a person coming to your defense when it is needed?"

"No. Never."

His quiet conviction made her ache.

"I told you, Archer, I will not condemn you based on your appearance alone."

His stillness seemed to affect the air around him, turning their world quiet. "Come now, Miranda. You heard all that Inspector Lane had to say."

Caught, Miranda's breath left in a sharp puff, but he went on.

"Sir Percival called my name moments before he was murdered. Another servant saw someone dressed like me leaving the grounds. All very damning. Why did you not leave then?"

Miranda's heart pounded loudly in her ears. "How did you know I was there?"

He made a soft sound, perhaps a laugh, and fell silent. So then, he would not answer unless she answered first. So be it. She would say it. "It was you. That night. You are the man who saved me in the alleyway."

Stillness consumed him, as if he'd frozen over. "Yes."

She released a soft breath. "Why were you there?"

Archer studied her quietly, a man of stealth waiting to

see which direction she would bolt. "It was as you guessed those years ago. To kill your father."

She knew it, but still the admission shocked her. "But why? What did he do to you?"

"Damage enough."

She bit the inside of her lip to keep from cursing his reticence.

The silence between them stretched tight until Archer spoke, low and controlled and just a bit bemused. "I admit the desire to kill one man, *your* father. Yet you do not question that I might kill another?"

She met his gaze without falter. "Capable, yes. But you did not. Just as you did not kill my father when you had the chance."

He blinked. Surprise? Or guilt? For an endless moment, she waited.

"You have given me your word, Archer, and I will believe it." It was a true answer. But not the whole truth. "I will not run from you."

The wool of his frock coat whispered against marble as he turned to fully face her. She stared back, unguarded for a pained moment. Warmth filled his eyes. He understood. He took a quick breath, and his voice dropped. "You've no notion of the effect you have on me."

The words gave a hard tug to her belly. She closed her eyes and swallowed. "If by effect, you mean finding yourself in uncharted waters, wondering whether you are coming or going…" She stared at his shirt, watching his breath hitch. "Then I fear you have the same effect on me, my lord."

Cool quiet surrounded them, highlighting the soft rush of their mingled breathing. Slow as Sunday, his hand lifted, and a wash of heat flowed over her. But his hand moved to the hard mask at his face. The mask came off with a small creak and a burst of Archer's freed breath. Light hit his features, and Miranda froze.

"Has my face gone blue?" he asked softly when she stood with her mouth hanging open like a haddock.

His lips curled as he enjoyed his joke.

Lips. She stared at them in shock. She could see his lips. Behind the carnival mask, he wore a black half-mask of smooth silk. It molded to his face like a second skin, revealing the lines of a high forehead, a strong nose, and a sharply squared-off jaw. The mask covered almost all of his right side, down along his jaw to wrap fully around his neck. But the left side... The tip of his nose, his left cheek, jaw, chin, and lips were fully exposed.

The shock of seeing all-too-human skin upon his face rendered her nearly senseless. His complexion was olive toned, showing some Mediterranean origin in his background. How on earth the man could have sun-bronzed skin was a mystery to her. He must have shaved before they left, for his cheek was smooth. Grooming his face for a world that would never see it. A pity.

A small cleft divided his square chin. But his lips called her attention once more. They were firmly sculpted; a sturdy bottom lip that almost begged to be bitten. The upper lip was wider than the bottom and flared gently in perpetual humor. Roman lips. She hadn't thought...

"You keep gaping like that, and the flies will come in."

She watched in fascination as the lips moved, amazed to hear his familiar rich voice coming from them. One corner lifted. "Are you going to stare all day? Should I have a self-portrait done for your contemplation?"

She looked up into his eyes, heavily lidded and deeply set, though covered with some sort of black cosmetic, kohl perhaps. Not an inch of his true skin color showed around his eyes. Even so, there was kindness in those end-less gray depths. His eyes drew a person in and kept one wondering.

"Yes," she said.

Archer's jaw twitched. "'Yes,' you are going to stare? Or 'yes,' you would like a portrait?"

Despite his teasing, he was uncommonly still, poised as though she might bite.

"Yes, I am going to stare," she said crisply.

"Why are you cross? You said you didn't like my other masks. I offer you a different view."

"You walked around wearing those terrible masks, filling my head with all sorts of horrible visions and... and..." Her hand flailed in front of his face. "And all along, you could have worn this."

His lips compressed, but they couldn't thin entirely. "What makes you think that there isn't a horror lurking still behind this mask?"

"It isn't the horror," she retorted. "It is the subterfuge." The line of his brows rose beneath the mask. "Those carnival masks must not be comfortable in the least. Blast it, you can't even eat or drink wearing them!"

He crossed his arms over his chest and looked away.

"Why, Archer? Why shut the world out?"

For a moment, she thought he might not answer.

"I don't want pity." He glared at the stern visage of the Greek centaur before them. "I'd rather have fear."

His voice was a phantom, haunted and alone. Miranda's fingers curled into fists to keep from reaching for him. But she understood him. Deep down, she knew she would rather the world see her beauty and overlook the pain. It had stung when he had called her a false front, because he was right.

"And me, Archer?" she whispered. "Would you have me fear you as well?"

"No!" He stopped and stiffened. "I'd rather have you imagine all sorts of horrors than study my face and believe that there is a chance a normal man might be hiding underneath."

She flushed hotly. It was the very thing she'd started to imagine.

Light from a flickering gas lamp caressed the sharp angles of his jaw, the high planes of his cheek as he lifted his chin. "Because there is not. I am not so twisted as to wear this thing if I were whole and untouched."

He glanced at the stairwell as though he'd like nothing more than to flee. "Perhaps we should go. It is getting late."

He moved to put on the mask once more, and her hand flew to clutch his arm.

"Don't," she said gently. The muscles beneath her hand hardened like granite yet he did not pull away. He loomed over her, his newly revealed features inscrutable, all the more because she did not yet know the subtleties of them. Without the warm rumble of his voice, he seemed almost a stranger to her for a moment, but for the scent of him and the familiar lines of his form.

"You startled me, Archer. That is all. I had no right to rail at you." Absently, her thumb caressed the fabric of his coat. She forced it still. "Thank you. It is a gift you gave me, and I am the richer for it."

Flushing and unable to meet his eyes another moment, she let him go. His silence was almost unbearable, but she could not turn from him. She had promised to stay. She gripped the cool balustrade and hoped it might keep her in place.

On a sigh, his stiffness released, and his hand came down to rest next to hers. "I felt you," he whispered. "That is how I knew."

She raised her head, and the world seemed to fade down to a narrow focus of just him, just her.

"I feel you," he said, "whether stalking me through the streets of London, or hiding behind a screen in my library." His words were soft as bunting, buffeting her skin, shivering inside of her.

Her hand opened on the balustrade, fingers stretching toward his. The very tips of their fingers met, the touch sparking between them like a current.

Archer's finger grazed hers. "I feel you. As if you were connected to me by an invisible string." He touched his chest. "I feel you here. In my heart."

She couldn't think past the mad pounding of her blood. She swallowed painfully. "I feel you too."

He sucked in a sharp breath.

Miranda stepped closer, closer to the heat of his body, to the place where her senses came alive—toward him. Her hand trembled as she touched her breast. "I feel you here," she said, both an admission and the true reason she could not leave him.

The corner of his lush mouth quirked. His legs moved into the folds of her skirts, and they were standing but a handbreadth apart. She felt his legs tense, a gather of his resolve. His hand lifted.

She watched it come, his broad shoulders blocking out the light from the windows at his back. The swells of her breasts rose and fell over her bodice with a rapid rhythm. Gently he touched her, his fingertips brushing the upper curve of her left breast, and she gasped.

"Here?" he asked thickly.

A tremulous smile touched her lips as a sudden weightless anticipation filled her, making her head spin. "There."

Smooth leather burned a path to her neck. Archer watched his fingers, the line of his mouth stern, the look in his eyes almost angry. Then, as if in answer to a challenge, he lowered his head. Miranda's breath ratcheted in her chest, became trapped by her corset. Unable to bear it, she closed her eyes.

Soft lips pressed against her breast, barely a touch that sent a bolt of feeling through her heart.

"Archer."

"Miri." His breath steamed against her fragile skin. "*Sono consumato.*"

Slowly, oh so slowly, his lips took the path his fingers made. Up, up, over the curve of her breast to the indent just above her collarbone. Not quite touching her, but skimming the surface. Hot breath ebbed and flowed in waves over her skin as he explored with unhurried languor.

"I am consumed," he whispered against her ear, and she shivered. "By you." Soft lips grazed her jaw in an agonizingly slow trail toward her waiting mouth. Her eyes squeezed tight. She could not bear it. The heat in her was fever bright. No part of him touched her, except that mouth. But oh, that mouth. It destroyed her composure as it moved with steady deliberation toward her lips.

The tip of his nose brushed against her hair as his lips touched the corner of her mouth. A universe of nerves occupied that small corner of her mouth. One touch was enough to leave her dizzy.

Archer held still, trembling as she did. The tips of her breasts brushed against his chest as she struggled to gain equilibrium. Liquid lust surged through her veins like wildfire. She wanted to move, do something rash, crush her lips to his and simply take, press herself against him and ease the heated ache between her legs. She did none of those things, only clutched her skirt like a lifeline as he moved his open lips just above hers.

His breath left in a pained rush that flowed into her. In, out, in. Still he did not kiss her, but let his lips brush against hers as if he knew, just as she, what would happen should their mouths truly merge. She wanted more. She wanted a taste. Her limbs quivered as she let her tongue inch forward, slip out between her parted lips. Of a like mind, Archer did the same. Their tongues touched.

A choked cry broke from her, the silken wet tip of his tongue sending a bolt of heat to her core. Archer made a sound close to pain. For a moment, their tongues retreated. And then.

She flicked her tongue, a small lick. And found his again. The sound of their breathing filled her ears as their tongues caressed, retreated, and met again, learning each other. Every flick, each wet slide of his tongue felt like a direct touch to the center of her sex, until she throbbed there, grew so hot she feared she might combust.

Their lips never melded, only danced with the possibility of it. It was not a kiss. It was something infinitely worse. It was torture. And God help her if she didn't want more.

Their breathing became pants. Her fingers fisted her skirts with near violence. His tongue slipped deeper, lighting across her lips, invading her mouth for one hot moment. Miranda moaned, her knees buckling. Archer's big hand clasped her nape, hard and impatient. Now he would kiss her, take her. *Now*. Her body screamed for that sweet release.

He wrenched his mouth away even as his arm crushed

her against his hard chest. Her heart leapt to her throat, her senses jumbled and confused until she heard the strange thump of something hitting the wall behind her. She froze, panting softly, her nose buried in the black folds of his suit coat for what felt like an eternity but was at most a moment in time.

Archer swore sharply and then moved, leaving her teetering on her feet. She righted quickly and found him glaring around, his frame held tight as a spring. But the long hall behind them was empty. Slowly he turned his attention to the wall before them. The silver hilt of a dagger embedded deep in the plaster still quivered from the impact.

Archer's breath hitched visibly, his eyes narrowing to slits. The force of the throw was unmistakable. Had he not acted quickly, the wicked dagger would have now rested deep within Miranda's back.

"What the devil?" she hissed, disbelief and sheer terror making her voice unsteady and her heart pound.

A mad cackle echoed in the empty corridor behind them, and Miranda started. The voice was neither feminine nor masculine—only evil. Footsteps sounded in the far end of the gallery, near the end of the corridor where shadows dwelled.

Archer squeezed her shoulder. "Stay here."

He took off running. Grabbing her parasol with one hand, and her skirts with the other, she followed. The long corridor veered right, opening to a larger hall and the stairs to the lower exhibits and great court. There the devil stood, paused at the top of the marble stair. He lifted his head, and her heart skittered. Were it not for the man's smaller size, one might have thought him Archer's twin. The villain wore a suit of black and a matching carnival mask that covered his entire face.

"Hell," Archer said.

The man gave a mocking salute and then turned to fly down the stairs. A dash to the high marble balustrade found the stairwell empty; the villain vanished as if by illusion.

"Hell and damn." Archer's hand came down upon her wrist. "Stay here. I will come back for you." His tone brooked no argument, but his touch was gentle. "Stay here."

She hadn't the time to protest before he took hold of the railing and leapt over it, straight down the stairwell.

Chapter Fourteen

Archer!"

Miranda leaned over the rail in time to see him land sure-footed as a cat three stories below and then race off.

"Christ almighty," she breathed. Her heels clattered, echoing off the marble walls as she raced down the stairs, holding her skirts higher than propriety allowed. The only trail left was irate pedestrians glaring in the direction Archer had taken when rushing past.

Outside, the dusky light of new evening colored the streets soft purple and black. She stopped for a breath and scanned the crowds. A hansom swerved wildly, its driver shouting at someone to "watch your soddin' arse!" *Archer.* She ran down the portico steps, weaving past vendors and cabs. But Archer disappeared into the fold.

The black flick of a coattail spied out of the corner of her eye brought her round and down a narrow street that twisted and turned like a crack in old granite.

Hard cobble bruised her soles, her boot heels clicking loudly with every step. Mud and muck splashed her shins, the smell of sewage clogging her nostrils. Pain pinched her side, the boning in her bodice restricting her breath, but she could not falter. Grunts and thuds of fighting sounded beyond the next corner. She rounded the corner, her heels skidding on the wet stones.

Archer and the dark villain exchanged blows so rapidly that for a moment it seemed a vision. It had to be, for their movements were a blur. The two men, covered from head to toe in black, danced their strange dance, coming together and falling apart, their fists flying, legs kicking. Though the attacker was smaller than Archer, he had the strength and speed of a panther.

His slim leg rammed up between Archer's. Archer grunted but threw his shoulder down and slammed the fiend into the brick wall behind him. A snarl tore from the villain's lips. With a cold ringing of steel, he pulled a curved blade from his belt.

The wicked edge of the dagger flashed silver in the dusky light before slicing toward Archer's neck. Archer jumped back, the blade tearing through the side of his coat with a sharp ripping sound. He grunted and then ducked the next attack with neat economy.

Lashing in a wild rage, the villain came at him again and again, Archer narrowly missing the blade each instant. Moving with a blur of speed, he grabbed hold of the villain's arm and brought his fist down hard into the smaller man's gut.

The dark devil staggered, but then spun round and swung his leg out in a wide arcing sidekick. Archer's head snapped back with a sickening crack as the heel connected.

"Archer!" The scream left her mouth in a dry rasp as he dropped.

The villain's arm reared back, his dagger ready to plunge straight into Archer's defenseless chest. Miranda heard herself shout as she charged, her parasol going up and opening into the villain's face. The long blade slashed through thin, bronze silk before hitting the steel frame with a clang. She jerked the umbrella closed and wrenched both it and the knife hard to the side. The masked man's eyes flashed and her heart lurched, but she was ready when he swung his fist toward her face, dropping to the ground, just as Archer growled out a vicious curse and kicked the villain hard in his shin.

The man hurtled sideways, landing with a whoosh of breath, his head knocking with a meaty thwack on the cobbled road.

Archer surged upward, ready to attack. In an instant, the man was on his feet and racing down the lane where shadows claimed him. Miranda expected Archer to give chase but he bent and gently helped her up.

The patter of rapidly retreating footfalls rang out of the gloom, and then the night faded to silence, the swirling eddies of mud-brown fog along the cobbles the last marker of the disturbance.

Archer let go of her arm and stepped back a pace. The black silk mask remained on his head but he had lost his left glove in the exchange. The sight of very human, unmarred flesh compelled her—another chip of his shell had fallen away. She stared at the long, blunt-tipped fingers, oval nail beds, and gentle veining that mapped the back of his naked hand. Fine black hairs began just above the solid bones of his wrist to disappear under his crisp white cuffs. It was his left hand, she realized with sudden irritation. Archer had stated only his right was affected.

Her musings came to a halt when she realized he hadn't

spoken a word but stared at her through narrowed eyes. The knowledge that she'd soon get an earful of Archer's wrath made her knees quake, so she made a pretense of inspecting her gown. A small moan of true self-pity left her lips when she saw the damage. Thick slicks of muck and black water covered the whole right side of the pale yellow satin skirt, most assuredly ruined. She let the train go with a muttered curse and turned to face her silent husband.

He stood breathing lightly, his hands on his slim hips, an unfathomable expression peeking out from behind the silk mask. "Are you injured?"

"I shall be in mourning over this frock for weeks," she quipped, though her chest tightened with wariness. "However, I am unharmed."

He did not smile at the joke but continued to stare, the square line of his jaw hard as granite. A crimson bead of blood welled up from the corner of his mouth before rolling down the side of his jaw. She had almost kissed that mouth.

"You're bleeding," she remarked, unaccountably nervous. A vibrant energy radiated from his broad frame but he held himself so rigid that she feared he might break from within.

Unconcerned, he wiped the blood away with the back of his sleeve. "I told you to wait for me," he said with deceptive calm.

Her hand shook as she smoothed her rumpled satin skirts. "Yes."

"You did not."

"No."

He crossed his arms over his chest and stared.

"You...you aren't angry?"

"Seething," he said lightly. Silver eyes slid over her, and his lips compressed until the muscle at his jaw bunched. Yes, he was at that.

"Y-yet you aren't shouting."

The corner of his mouth lifted. He of all people knew the common response to his anger. "Strange, that."

Exasperated, she turned away and pulled her gloves off to inspect her bruised knuckles. Archer watched without moving, which only served to unsettle her further. Damnable man.

"You insist on following me about," he said with a suddenness that made her jump. "Go into places where only a well-armed man or a person of ill repute would venture. Place yourself in situations that even the best fighter would hesitate to go—"

She rounded on him. "Now, I wouldn't say I *placed* myself in this situation."

His eyes narrowed. "I can either conclude," he went on in a sharper tone, "that you are an astonishingly great fool or . . ."—his voice rose over her gasp of outrage—". . . or you have some reason to believe that you are above danger wherever you go."

A tight smile lifted his lips. "Based on our conversations past, I cannot believe that you are a fool, so I must conclude the latter."

Her hands curled to fists. "Ooh, you are smug! You know the logical course would be to call me a fool—" She flushed hot and snapped her mouth shut.

Archer's brows rose. "Are you calling yourself a fool?"

"No, I am not!" She stamped her foot. "*You* are!"

He threw his head back and laughed. The sound echoed out in the small lane, coming at her from all angles.

Her fists clenched. "You're intolerable!"

"Because I won't shout at you?" he asked through his laughter.

She crossed her arms in front of her chest and looked away. Better to ignore the brute. Oh, why had she admitted to being moved by him? A sound of irritation broke from her lips. Despite herself, she glanced his way, and her traitorous mind chose that unfortunate moment to call forth the memory of his tongue sliding over hers, the hot kiss of his breath against her skin.

He blinked in response, his mouth softening as though remembering too. He was silent for a moment.

"I see..." The silkiness of his voice had a ring to it she did not like—like the chiming of warning bells. He took a step closer. An odd half-smile flittered across his lips.

Wariness crawled up her spine. "Archer..."

"I've abused your feminine notions of how a husband should conduct himself." He took another step. "You *want* me to punish you—"

"No—" The brick wall of the alleyway brushed her skirts. Trapped.

Archer shook his head thoughtfully. "I believe you do."

She read the intention in his eyes an instant before strong hands whirled her round and her cheek was pressed against the cold, damp wall.

"Is this what you want?" His chest crushed into her back, flattening her breasts against the brick. Icy cold seeped into her skin, setting her nipples to harden as an anticipatory thrill lit through her.

"Hmm?" The hard length of his thigh wedged between her own, impudently pushing past thick folds of gathered crinoline and satin flounces.

"Leave off," she said through her teeth. She'd be damned if she'd struggle with him.

His laughter rippled through his chest and into her back. To her horror, heat raced down her belly and between her legs. She closed her eyes and silently cursed.

"I tried that," he huffed against her ear. "You didn't like it."

Her eyes flew open as the cold night air hit her calves.

"Archer, stop!" But his hand continued to wrench up her dress. Gone were cautious, gentle touches, replaced by the firm authority of a man who believed his advances were not entirely unwelcome. The bastard.

"Do not pretend you do not know what becomes of ladies who venture into alleyways on their own."

She struggled in earnest then, but it did no good. He was too big and bearing down on her with his weight. She might as well have been a butterfly pinned to a lepidopterist's board.

"So tell me, Lady Archer..." A large, surprisingly hot hand clamped down on her rump. She squeaked in shock. "What great magic will save you now?"

The other hand joined its mate, one encased in soft leather, one shockingly bare. Even through her drawers, she could tell the difference. She burned in humiliation as Archer held her bottom in his hands, moving them in slow, insolent circles. Her humiliation doubled as she fought against the heat and anticipation that grew within her.

"Do not try me," she gritted out and attempted once more to thrust him away. The action only pushed her bottom into his pelvis.

Archer gave a small groan and pressed harder. "Show me, Lady Archer." Butter-soft lips brushed her neck, his breath a hot caress. "Show me your defenses. I cannot wait forever."

Hands slid from her rump to her hips, threatening

to slip around to the front. A fine shudder ran through Archer's frame, and he went still. "Do it now, or there is no turning back."

She felt the tension gathering in him, his shock at how he touched her, and beneath it, a small tremor of want. She closed her eyes, her cheek pressed against the cold wall, the tips of her fingers slipping on the crumbling mortar. *Oh please.*

The horrifying heat between her legs began to throb, and the cold wall was a refuge for the fire in her skin as the muscles along her belly shivered. Feeling the movement, Archer's body tightened around her. On a breath, his fingers curled, caressing the curve of her hipbones, a delicate fluttering that raised gooseflesh along her limbs. He swallowed audibly, his breath stirring tendrils of her hair. The fingers at her hips trembled as if they sensed the close proximity of their target, and her breath slowed to soft bursts. They tensed together at the edge of a precipice. Miranda licked her lips. She only had to speak. Tell him to stop. She knew it. He knew it. One word.

The silence grew still and thick. Her breasts were heavy, aching against the chilled wall, her nipples hard little points that chafed against her bodice with each rasping breath. Heat suffused her cheeks as lust surged within, taking her to that dark place in her mind that simply *wanted*. One word and he would walk away. She closed her eyes tight, bit her lip, and moved. A small nudge of her bottom that bid him to act.

His breath left on a soundless gasp. Embarrassment burned so hot, it pained Miranda's cheeks. Archer's body grew tighter, his heartbeat a tangible rhythm against her back. And then his hand, trembling with fear or perhaps anticipation, slowly began to move. Down, the tips of his fingers feathered, burning a trail toward the slit in her drawers.

Miranda's teeth sank into her lip. Her corset became iron hands that would not let her breathe. His fingers brushed light as a kiss against her curls, and they both let out a pained gasp. Archer's chest heaved against her, his breathing raw as if he'd run miles.

"Open." His voice was a hot rasp against her ear.

Miranda swallowed hard. One step. Her knees buckled, and she clung to the wall, her eyes still shut tight.

His breath hitched. The blunt tip of his finger touched her flesh, and her head went light. She clung to the wall as that finger moved back and forth, so slow she thought she might scream.

"You're wet." Awe and desire darkened his voice to something almost unrecognizable. A faceless stranger touching her in the black night. "Wet for me."

A strangled cry broke from her lips. It was all she could do.

He slipped deeper, stroking her, learning her. She pressed her aching breasts harder into the bricks, her fingers growing numb where she clutched tight. Unthinking, she moved her hips, rocking them against his touch. The forbidden act sent a fresh burst of heat over her skin.

Archer trembled. His mouth found the exposed skin over her bodice. His tongue snaked out, tasted her. "Faster?"

Miranda panted, tried to find the words. "Yes."

Feather strokes slipped over the wet, taunting. She ground her teeth, and thrust her hips back into him. His cock was a hard weight against her back. His free hand gasped her hips, held them still.

"Harder?" he groaned against her skin before sucking it.

"Yes."

Pleasure boiled within. Her lips parted on a cry. Frantic, she rocked against him, shivering despite the white heat rolling over her. Cruelly, he pressed himself against her, not letting her move as he worked her, faster, harder. Her body tightened like a bow and then she broke, coming apart with small, pained cries.

Archer's teeth sank into her neck. Holding her there as the world fell to pieces and then slowly came back together.

She returned to herself on a shudder, his hand already slipping away to hold her hip gently. His lips brushed her bruised flesh once as if to soothe her. They were silent for a moment, both of them trembling, their chests lifting and falling in unison, then she felt the realization wash over him. He drew in a sharp breath and stepped back, letting her skirts fall as he went.

Miranda sagged against the wall. She could not face him. Not yet. The ghost of her cries hung in the air between them. Her body still throbbed from what they had done. What he had done to her. Her cheeks suffused with fresh heat.

She felt him watching. Regretting? His silence was a cold presence against her back.

"Go on, then," he whispered. A deep breath sounded in the dark, and his voice gathered strength. "I've done you a wrong. Turn me into cheese on toast."

She went utterly cold. Cheese on toast. She'd only used that threat once in her life. In an instant, she spun round. "You mock me?" she hissed at his retreating form.

Archer straightened his ascot with false nonchalance; she saw the tremble in his hand. "Never." He looked down at his bare hand as if he couldn't quite place it. Miranda glanced away from those skilled, long fingers. The sight of them perplexed her as much as it did him.

"I have thought about having you against a wall since the day we met," he said without looking up.

"Oh. I...Oh. Then..." To say any more would expose too much of herself. She turned to face the dark cavern of the alleyway. Goosebumps rose over her skin as she thought of flashing knives and Archer falling. "That man. It almost appeared as if you knew him. Did you know who it was?"

"I rather thought it was our killer."

She opened her mouth to retort but stopped as she saw the sheen of sweat along his cheek. The moonlight cast his skin marble white. For a moment he looked almost ill. Catching the direction of her gaze, he turned abruptly and strode down the alley, leaving her to follow at a trot.

"Where are you going?"

"Home."

A hack rattled before them, stopping at Archer's command. Archer walked through the curling mist kicked up by the coach and opened the door before handling her up like a sack of grain. She landed hard on the leather seat as he swung his bulk inside. As soon as he sat, the coach lurched forward. Her thighs were damp, her flesh tender. The thought of what they had done licked over her like a flame. Well, she would throw reason over it like iced water. *Don't look at him. Speak of something else.*

Archer glanced at her and smirked. "I don't suppose you will tell me just how you intended to turn those young men who attacked you that night into luncheon?"

She sank back into the shadows, away from his keen stare. The weak lamp above their heads swung like a pendulum, moving Archer's dark form in and out of shadow as the coach sped down Great Russell Street toward Piccadilly. "Perhaps when you have told me what Father had done to earn your wrath that night."

Cold and unhinged, she crossed her arms in front of her for warmth. Their cloaks were in the museum.

"What does it matter?" He tried to shrug out of his suit coat but stopped with a marked wince.

"Of course it matters. I—" The cab passed under a streetlight, and she saw the black glimmer of blood that darkened his silver brocade vest. "You're hurt!"

She moved in close, and he shifted as far away from her as he could, which wasn't very, considering the size of the cab and the size of him.

"It is nothing." Despite his protest, he pulled the cravat from round his neck and pressed it hard to his side.

"Good God, you're bleeding like a skinned cat."

"Really, Miranda, you are the most colorful speaker at times." A smile ghosted over his lips. Sparring with her apparently restored his good humor. Or perhaps it was easier for him to brush away what they had done, she thought with a flush. But when she reached for him, he swatted her hand.

She tucked the offending hand beneath her skirts. "This is unfair. You can save my life, assault me in an alleyway—"

"Assault, was it?"

"Just look at you! It's a wonder you are even sitting upright."

"How odd. My definition of 'assault' must be in error."

"You are not made of iron, you know. You should have alerted me of your injury at once. You could have bled to death! What were you thinking?"

His mouth twitched. "I'm going to assume that was a rhetorical question."

Heat burned her cheeks. "After all we have been through," she continued before he could volley any more witticisms, "I cannot tend to your wound?"

He fell silent.

"Don't worry, it is on your *good* side," she sneered. "I won't see anything."

Serpentine slits of silver eyed her with irritation. "You cannot 'tend to my wound' in the coach."

She returned his look with full measure. "Fine. Then I shall attend to it at home."

His jaw flexed as he ground his teeth, and she sat back affecting satisfaction, when really she wanted to hit his stubborn head. They rode in silence for a time, the lights of London moving by in a hazy blur.

Despite her resolve, she found herself looking down at his exposed hand lying limp against his thigh, his skin shifting from gold to silver in the wavering lamplight. He had touched her with those long fingers, made her break apart inside and out. A shiver ran along her thighs. Such intimate things he had done to her. Rather, he had touched her in an intimate place. In truth, he could have been anyone there in the dark for what little of himself he gave to her. But he wasn't a stranger. He was Archer, her avenging angel. Always.

Warmth filled her breast. She pulled her attention upward, to meet his eyes. Unfortunately, her gaze faltered at his mouth. An enticing mouth, curved and firm. Would it be soft? A kiss would tell her. A kiss. That was true intimacy, the conversation of lovers. She had tasted him. Heady flickers of tongue against tongue, but he had yet to truly kiss her. And she found herself craving one. Miranda bit her lip. Speaking was preferable to silence.

"So you came to my home to kill Father," she said conversationally. "On that we can agree."

Archer grunted and continued to look out his window.

"And yet you did not. Why? Was it pity?" She tapped her lip thoughtfully, rather enjoying taunting him. "Exhaustion? I scared you away?" That earned her a snort. "What then? What was the reason?"

He turned to face her with a glare. "Logic compels you to deduce," he said roughly, "that it was I who singled your father out and ruined him, because it was I who wanted more than anything in life to marry you."

Chapter Fifteen

Cagy, rotten blighter. On the inside, Miranda seethed. She knew Archer well enough now to understand that he sought to divert her when he made ridiculous statements or scathing declarations. Moreover, she knew he was lying. Thus, she said nothing in return but let him stew in the knowledge that his plan to unnerve her had failed. She appeared perfectly at ease, as if she did not feel the ghost of his touch upon her skin, did not feel the slickness between her legs with every step. Ignored him when he sent her wary looks. Good, let him squirm. She was not without her own methods of manipulation.

Her theory proved true as he strode into the front hall and headed for the stairs, clearly thinking she'd run for her rooms like a frightened mouse. The man was mad if he thought she'd let him wander off and bleed all over the house before telling her the truth. She followed, lifting her skirts a bit to keep up with his long stride. But when he began to alight the stairs, a small grunt escaped his compressed lips, and his step faltered. She was at his side in a moment.

"Let me help you," she said, taking his arm.

"Go to bed, Miranda."

Her fingers dug into his elbow, and he winced again. A dark patch of blood stained his upper arm as well. She eased her grip but did not let go.

"Shall I make a scene?" She glanced pointedly at one of the footmen who stood at attention in the hall. "Or shall we adjourn to your rooms together?"

A myriad of emotions ran through his eyes, the prevalent one being supreme irritation. "I thought you would never ask," he said through his teeth.

Archer's room. It was much like the library, paneled in mellow woods, with large, comfortable leather chairs and a long leather couch arranged before the hearth. She kept her eyes firmly away from the massive bed hung with silver velvet draping and followed Archer as he stomped over to a sideboard near the window and helped himself to a tumbler of brandy.

Her eyes went to the wide door connecting her room to his. So close. Every night so close, yet he remained the gentleman and kept his distance. That alone filled her with tender gratitude. The ache in her chest *was* gratitude, wasn't it?

He eased off his coat and vest, staying in shirtsleeves and collar, then went to the full-length mirror in the corner. Gently, he pulled apart the torn, blood-soaked linen and inspected his wound.

"Shit." The crisp expletive snapped through the air.

She came closer and pulled in a breath. The wound was a good six inches long and rather deep. Blue-black blood and meaty pink flesh gaped at her. The floor beneath her feet swayed.

"The muscle looks intact—" Archer's head jerked up. "Sit down before you faint."

She backed into a seat and watched as he pulled a stack of white linens from a drawer and pressed one to his side. The cloth bloomed crimson.

"You'll have to excuse me," he said, keeping his eyes on the cloth. "This needs attending and I've no time to..." He swayed and caught himself with a hand to the sideboard.

She jumped up and pulled him none too gently to the couch by the fire. "Then let us proceed."

"No!" His ashen mouth pinched.

She nudged his shoulder, and he fell easily back onto the couch.

"You talk of my stubbornness," she snapped, hauling his heavy legs up so that he lay down. "You're no better than a belligerent ox." A lock of hair fell down over her brow, and she swatted it back.

"How," she asked, glaring at him, "are you to attend a wound that you can't even view without twisting your side and making it gape?"

He simply glared back, his expressive mouth set and firm.

"Well?"

"I don't know!" he shouted, then winced.

"That is enough." Her hands went to his shirtfront. "Let us proceed before you bleed to death."

He caught her wrists in a surprisingly firm grip. "No."

The childish resolve in him irked her to no end. "Is it worth your life?" she asked, still imprisoned by his hands.

Alarm flashed in his eyes, but it was ruthlessly suppressed by determination. "Yes."

A shiver of real fear ran along her limbs. "And where does that leave me?" she asked softly.

His grip eased but the war clearly still raged inside him. She took pity and moved away.

"Here." She took the soft woolen rug from the couch back. "We shall leave the shirt on and cover up your right side."

He watched as she tucked the throw around him.

"I don't deserve you, Miranda."

The softness in his voice made her want to smile but she kept it repressed. "Yes, I know." She straightened. "No matter, I shall soon have my revenge. Now tell me what to do."

"Bring the lamp close. And I need more of the linen cloths."

Miranda did as bidden, and he pressed a large bundle of linen firmly against his side.

"Can you sew?" he asked, looking a bit peaked.

"Yes, but..."

"Good. Go wash your hands. And bring back a bowl of soapy warm water. You'll find a bowl in the cabinet by the washroom door."

When she returned, he lay so still upon the couch that she worried he'd fainted, but his eyes found hers as soon as she drew near and set down the bowl of water.

"Go to the wardrobe over there." He gestured with a jerk of his chin. "There is a black valise on the top shelf. Can you reach it?"

"Just."

She set the things on the table and added the rolls of clean linen she'd found by the valise.

"Take out that length of black velvet—carefully—and the three larger bottles." He rested his head upon the pillow. "Good. We'll tend to the arm first."

"How is it that you have all this," she asked as she

ripped the gaping hole on his sleeve a bit wider. The wound was superficial, a light slash across the large arc of his biceps. Firmly, she told herself that such a display of masculine strength was nothing to gape at like a blushing chit, and set her thoughts to the task at hand.

"I am a surgeon," Archer replied, glancing at the wound. It had already stopped bleeding. "For all intents and purposes. Before...the accident I had completed medical school. I've taken examinations, attended lectures..." He made a sound of weariness. "Though I doubt anyone would let me practice upon them." His wide mouth pulled wryly. "Even without the mask, a noble seeking to work in trade is unsettling to most. And to become a surgeon over a physician"—he *tsk*ed wryly—"it was quite boorish of me."

Gently, she washed and bound the cut with a long length of thick linen cloth, following his precisely put instructions to the letter.

"Now the other wound." His deep voice was rougher now. He took a restorative breath and eased the cloth away from his side. The cut welled but the bleeding had slowed.

He let her pull the shirt farther apart so that she might wash the skin around the wound. "Don't let that water in; we'll clean it with iodine in a moment."

When his skin was reasonably clean, he gestured to the implements on the table. "Unroll that velvet bundle. And watch your fingers. There are knives within."

The rolled velvet revealed its cache of sharp little blades, and three wicked-looking needles that might have been fishing hooks but she knew were not.

Her eyes went to Archer.

"You don't have to do this," he said patiently.

"I do." She took a deep breath and let it out slowly. "What now?"

"The clear bottle is distilled alcohol, the red iodine, and the green laudanum." The corner of his jaw twitched, and he paled a bit. "Hand me the laudanum and dab the wound with the tincture of iodine, in that order please."

Archer uncorked the bottle with his teeth and took a deep pull from it.

"Careful, you can easily overindulge!" The thought of him dying from laudanum poisoning tightened her chest.

A weak smile touched his lips, the drug already glazing his eyes. "I know the proper dosage for myself. I assure you, the effects wear off quickly with me."

He settled back with a sigh and watched her with serpentine eyes as she doused a cloth with the iodine and pressed it to the gaping wound. Archer let out a roar, throwing his head back as his body went taut. "Christ's blood!" he shouted and fell limp against the couch.

Miranda retrieved the dropped cloth with hands that trembled. "I'm sorry," she whispered, feeling close to tears.

Still panting softly, he managed another smile. "It's unavoidable," he rasped. He took another cloth to hold it at his side, lest the blood flow again, then glanced at the row of knives and needles. "Select the smaller of the needles." He licked his dry lips quickly. "There is a spool of black thread in the bag."

Her stomach flipped over as she stared at him in horror.

He held her gaze. "You said you could sew."

"I..." Her lips pursed. She could not very well tell him that she'd stupidly assumed he'd ask her to mend his shirt.

A sound of impatience tore from his throat. "Hand me the needle and thread before I bleed out here on this couch." He reached out, and the wound gaped.

Miranda started. "No." She caught hold of his arm and placed it over his head so that his side lay smooth. "I'll do it. You are in no condition."

He blinked back at her but let the arm stay. "The same could be said of you."

Ignoring that, she set about her task. The sharp little needle curved like a sickle and had a small eye for threading on the blunt end.

"Do not make the thread overlong," Archer instructed. "It might catch in the flesh and cause tearing."

Her grip wobbled. She ground her teeth and cut the thread.

A small pair of tweezers with handles like those on scissors held the needle secure. From short, clear instructions, she learned she was to hold the edges of the wound close together with one hand while piercing his flesh and sewing it shut with the other. She listened intently, focusing on the wound instead of the man. But the needle froze in her hand, refusing to plunge in.

"Miranda…"

She blinked up upon hearing her quietly spoken name.

His skin was ashen. Beads of sweat covered his jaw and ran down from beneath his mask, but his eyes were steady. "It is only a simple handstitch."

"But it is on you," she said with a weak voice.

His hand fell over hers. "I promise not to cry."

The corner of his mouth quirked, and her confidence returned with a rush. She bit back a smile and bent her head close to his side.

"Remember, ninety degree angle going in, a quarter of

an inch depth. Hook through, then ninety degree out." He took another long drink of the laudanum.

His flesh resisted and then gave with a silent pop. Archer went rigid but made no sound as she set to work. Once the first stitch was made, her hand grew steadier, the stitch more sure. The sound of Archer's light breathing filled her ears.

"Do you really believe that you ruined my father?" she asked, pulling the thread gently through his flesh. His side twitched then stilled.

"No," he admitted in a low voice. "That is one sin that I do not carry on my conscience."

She adjusted her hold, taking care not to push the flesh too tight or slack. Gentle firmness was needed. "No," she averred. "That sin is mine."

Archer was silent but Miranda could feel his eyes upon her. "I thought," he said after a moment, "Ellis's fortune was lost at sea."

"Mmm…" The needle pierced through the red, weeping flesh and then out again. "But had he not already lost more than half his fortune in a warehouse fire, he would have been able to recover from that setback."

The muscles along her neck and shoulders ached. Archer's stare did not help matters.

"It happened when I was ten," she said. The wound was almost closed, just a few stitches more. "I often stole into the warehouse. I called it my treasure chest." The final stitch pulled through. She tied it with a small knot and then took the iodine-laced cloth and dabbed the length entirely.

"I…I was showing a trick I'd learned to my friend…"—*like an utter pompous fool*—"I didn't mean to start a fire." *Rather, she hadn't meant for it to get out of control.* Her hands fell to her lap where they lay like leaden weights. She dared a glance at Archer and found his gaze inscrutable.

"You were only ten," he said, reading her as usual.

"I know that now."

He held her eyes with his. "Good."

It was that simple. One small word and a weight lifted from deep within her breast. She surveyed her handiwork. It looked awful, lumpy and red, with ugly black stitches marring the flesh.

Archer lifted his head and looked down the length of his nose to see the wound. One corner of his lips lifted. "Good," he said, surprise mixing with admiration. He glanced up and his smile deepened. "Very good, Miranda Fair."

She made a small face. "It looks horrid."

Archer rested his head again as she packed up the materials. "It always does in the beginning. The swelling will ease. Clean the needle with alcohol," he added with a glance at her progress.

A comfortable silence settled warmly over them as she cared for his instruments.

"You remind me of her, you know."

Archer's sudden yet detached observation gave her pause. She looked up to find him frowning as though he hadn't meant to speak those words.

"Of whom?" she asked in a low voice. The stillness in him made her wary, as if she ought to whisper.

His lips curled in a sad smile. "One of my sisters. I had four of them. Beautiful girls with shining black hair, soft gray eyes. Claire was the baby, nearly ten, then Karina, who was eighteen and preparing to come out to society, Rachel, who had her first season the year before and was a beautiful nineteen-year-old fighting off ardent suitors at every turn." He smiled thinly. "I had a devil of a time with her. She liked attention and received more than her share.

"I loved them all. I was twenty-six when my father died. The running of the family fell to me. I took to the task without resentment. It was the role I had been born to play. Until that spring.

"There was a duel, fought in Rachel's honor. A young fortune hunter had thought to ruin her reputation by stealing a kiss during a spring fete. I did not kill him, but my mother thought it best I stay out of town for a bit. She sent me to Italy." He sighed lightly. "Mother always knows best, hmm? I loved it there. I might have stayed indefinitely."

He blinked up at the ceiling. "Three years later, influenza hit London. Mama, the girls, they fell ill." The thick column of his throat worked. "I came as soon as I heard. It was too late for Mama, Claire…They were gone and buried by the time I arrived. Rachel soon after."

Only the flutter of his lashes betrayed any movement. Miranda felt his pain in her own heart. A thought occurred to her. "You said you had four sisters, save you named only three…" She trailed off as his eyes lifted, and the anguish in them drove the breath from her body.

"Elizabeth…" It was a dry husk of an answer. "My twin." Archer closed his eyes. "Her mind was my mind. We never needed to use words between us. I knew her thoughts as my own. Mother said we used to turn at the precise moment when sleeping in our cots, though we did not share one. She was…I could not…" He broke off with a choked sound and then stared listlessly into the distance.

"She died in my arms. At times, I feel as though I am missing a limb...something..." A shimmer of tears pooled over his eyes before he blinked them away. "Her loss was a pain not easily endured," he said softly. "After that, the thought of death terrorized me. I dreamed of being trapped in moldering tombs with only her body to keep me company." He glanced down at his stitched side. "I am shamed at what I've become. That she should have to see this horror..." He snapped his mouth shut with a wince.

Miranda moved without thinking and knelt before him to clutch his dry ungloved hand. "Don't keep this burden to yourself. Take off the mask and let me see what troubles you so."

He looked at her, his great body stiff. "I don't want your pity."

"Do you believe that is why I ask?" she whispered.

A sad smile ghosted over his lips. "No," he said after a moment. "But I cannot. Not even for you, Miranda Fair." The tired resolve in his voice made her heart ache.

"But why?"

His long fingers curled over her. "You look at me. *Me.*"

She knew now what that meant to him. No one looked at Archer. They saw only the mask. To the world, he was an effigy, not a man.

The gray depths of his eyes reflected the painful truth as he spoke with weary regret. "That would not continue should I indulge you."

"Do you think so little of me?"

The fire snapped and crackled behind the grate. Orange light flickered over his golden skin, highlighting the fine grains of black stubble that covered his jaw and the red gash upon his lip. "It is not you who falls short of the mark; it is me. I am a coward," he whispered thickly, then looked away, his chin set and stubborn.

"You are no coward. You are so very brave—"

"Everyone promises to stand by me—" His jaw clenched, pain flashing in his eyes. "Always in the beginning. But none of them do." He swallowed hard, arranging his expression into dispassion with force of will. "I cannot risk it with you. Not you. None of the pretty words your sweet mouth weaves will change that so please don't try."

Chastised, she drew back. Though she understood him, his refusal did not hurt less. Archer lay prone, his skin gray and sweating, and she found herself wanting to fuss over him, wipe his brow, tuck him into bed. But he would not allow those things, she knew. She settled for covering him fully with the rug and adjusting the pillow under his head. He watched her sleepily through the thick fan of his black lashes. The boyish vulnerability in his unguarded look made her want to curl up alongside him.

"I should not have manhandled you the way I did." His lashes fluttered and then lifted. "It was uncalled for."

She sat back on her heels by the couch. The memory of his big hands upon her returned and with it a heated ache. How shocked he would be to know how close she had come to turning around and begging him to push up her skirts, to push into her. It shocked *her* more than she cared to admit. She tried to find her voice.

"It was not an assault, Archer." She flushed but forced herself to look at him. "We both know that."

His gaze warmed. "I meant before," he said thickly. "Shoving you against the wall..."

"You were angry."

His smile was lopsided. "I was angry," he repeated,

mocking himself. "I was terrified. And it is no excuse." A soft gaze traveled over her hair. "You saved my life."

Her smile was tremulous. "You saved mine first."

He made a noise of derision but an answering smile played at his lips. The smile faded as he caught sight of his bound wound. A grave stillness settled over him. One that grew as his eyes lifted to hers. They were frozen, flat. Winter lakes that chilled her to the bone.

"I've been a fool," he said in the same frozen tone.

"What do you mean?" Dread crept along her spine.

His expressive mouth flattened as if tasting bitters. "For tonight. For bringing you into this life." His chest lifted on a breath. "Miranda..." Weakly, he tried to touch her hand. She drew away. "You shouldn't be here."

Miranda straightened, ignoring the painful rhythm of her heart, and the way her hands shook. "Yes, of course. You should sleep."

But Archer would not be so easily evaded. Pain and wariness bracketed his mouth as he spoke. "You shouldn't be with me," he corrected softly. "I—annulments are easy enough gained. Considering we have never..." He bit down on his lip hard enough to whiten it. "Well...as is the case, it can be done. Pick a house, wherever you want, in another country if it pleases you, and I shall set it up."

A small chuff of air left her as she fell back on her rump. "Why?" she asked. "Why offer for me?" Her strength returned on the waves of anger. "Why bring me here, make me *care*, if you didn't want me?"

"Not want you?" He lifted his head off the pillow. "Not want you?" His eyes flared in the firelight. "Christ, Miri, murder and knife-wielding assassins aside, you are the greatest adventure of my life."

Archer's words raced like wine through her veins, leaving her flushed and just a bit dizzy. *As are you.*

He leaned forward, wincing as he bent. "If ever a man wanted...I'm trying to keep you safe. Being my wife is not safe. And I was a fool to think it ever would be."

They stared at each other in the resounding silence, then his head fell weakly back on the pillow. Frowning, he blinked up at the ceiling as if it contained some great secret.

"As for why," he said slowly, "I was lonely." His deep voice fell to something above a whisper. "I saw you in that alley, facing down two thugs with nothing save those little fists, and I thought, here is a girl who fears nothing."

His eyes flicked to hers, and Miranda's heart flipped over. "How I admired that," he said. "So much so I did not want to leave. Later, when the loneliness got so great"— he sighed—"I thought of you again. Thought, this is a woman who won't fear me." He flicked a piece of lint off of the rug. "Who won't run away."

Miranda's throat worked as she fought to speak. "How perfectly ironic," she managed at last.

Archer's eyes shot to hers, a frown pulling his lips.

"I was engaged to be married," she said. "A little over a year ago. Did you know?" Of course he would not know; why would he?

He stayed silent, waiting. But something in his eyes flickered with unease.

Idly, she toyed with the fringe of the rug that covered him. "His name was Martin Evans."

"The boy with whom you sparred that night."

"Yes. Not that it matters, really." Martin had long since stopped being that boy. She licked her dry lips quickly. "He left me. In the vestry of my family church on the day of our marriage. He said he'd rather live alone than pretend to live a life in love with me." One hot tear ran over the bridge of her nose before she blinked the rest furiously away. She would not cry for Martin again.

She felt Archer move and turned enough to see his black fingers curling into the rug. "Any man who would leave you is an idiot," he said.

Miranda gave him an admonishing look, and he had the grace to grimace.

"Was," she corrected, after a moment. "Despite our dissolution, Father gave him command of a small ship for which he managed to find backers. They were to go to America to purchase tobacco. It was our family's last chance at fortune. The ship never made land."

Archer made a vague noise of condolence, but it did not sound like sorrow.

Her lips curled a bit. "I suppose fate knew better. He wasn't meant for me."

"No," Archer agreed with conviction. They both looked away and were silent.

"In the vestry," he repeated as though thinking back on her words. "Where we were married."

She glanced up and found him studying her. "Yes," she said.

He sighed. "And so you married me."

She took a shallow breath. "You see, when I met you in the vestry that day, I too thought this is a man who is fearless. Who won't run away from things..." She bit her lip.

"Who won't leave you," he finished for her.

Stiffly, she nodded, unable to look him in the eye for fear that she would fall upon him and tell him how very much he was coming to mean to her. Her emotions felt too raw, and her pride too tender, for such needy protestations.

For a moment, he seemed almost afraid, then his body steeled as if in defiance, toward her or someone else, she couldn't know. His eyes burned into her. "Then I will not."

Chapter Sixteen

O h! Isn't it simply darling?"

Poppy's eyes narrowed over the elaborate lime silk hat poised in Daisy's hand. "Rather, the most hideous thing in creation."

Daisy set the hat down with a little sniff. "What you know of fashion, I could fit in a snuff box. Is that a snood you're wearing in your hair?" Daisy glanced at Miranda with blue eyes that twinkled. "Good lord, I haven't worn one of those since we were in pinafores."

"And what you know about the rest of the world, Dandelion," Poppy cut in sharply, "could fit in my—"

Miranda lifted a bolt of India silk high for inspection, cutting off her line of fire. "Look at this cloth," she said brightly. "Didn't Mama have a dress made from this exact pattern when we were girls?"

Daisy ran a gloved finger down the shimmering saffron length. "I do believe she did." She shrugged. "I suppose old is new again."

Poppy muttered something about how Daisy ought to

know as much firsthand. At the time, Miranda thought it a good idea to take her sisters shopping, believing an outing with Daisy and Poppy might be a fine distraction to the dilemma of Archer.

For days now, the man moved through the house like twilight shadows, there yet shifting away from her should she come too near. Though if she were absolutely truthful with herself, they had been avoiding each other, neither of them feeling so inclined as to discuss what had occurred that night. What did one say? *You have touched me, brought me indescribable pleasure. I want more. I want you.* Miranda fought off a blush.

No, she would not be the first to succumb. It was too humiliating. She sighed as she opened her mouth to break up yet another squabble when a familiar face flashed among the throngs of shoppers who milled about Liberty & Co.: the slanting gray eyes and dark curling hair of Victoria.

"Do you know her?"

Daisy's idle question made Miranda jump within her skin.

Miranda smoothed a hand over the silk, feeling the cool through her glove. "Only by introduction." She glanced sharply at Daisy. "Do you?" She had quite forgotten that Daisy was a veritable walking *Debrett's Peerage.*

"Of course." She tilted her head as Poppy drew near to listen. "Victoria Allernon."

"Allernon?" It was a jolt to Miranda's middle. "She told me her name was Archer."

"As in your husband, Archer?" Poppy's fine nostrils flared as if catching wind of the hunt.

"She claims to be a cousin to Archer," Miranda said in a low voice, the three of them tracking Victoria with their eyes while trying, somewhat badly, to look absorbed in the cloth before them.

"A fine thing to say," said Daisy. "And hardly likely. Though she does know Archer." Her golden curls swung low as she leaned farther in, the gleam of gossip animating her eyes. "Eight years back, she was heavily involved with a young Lord Marvel..."

The pit of Miranda's stomach pitched and rolled. She clutched the fabric to steady herself.

"Apparently, Archer objected. Whether it was because he had formed an attachment to Miss Allernon himself or because he had a strong dislike for Marvel in general is unclear." Daisy took the bunched cloth from Miranda's stiff hands and folded it. "No one had ever seen Lord Archer in Miss Allernon's company so the whole reason for the argument remains shrouded in mystery. At any rate, the two men came to blows. Poor Lord Marvel was left a babbling shell of a man, and Archer quick-footed it out of town."

"Daisy Margaret Ellis Craigmore!" Poppy's eyes flashed under censorious brows. "I cannot believe you refrained from giving Miranda this bit of information before she married Lord Archer!"

Daisy's mouth fell open into a little round O as she glanced from Poppy to Miranda. "Well, I would have, had I not forgotten entirely about it."

Poppy's straight brows tilted. "Even when Father told us the name of Miranda's intended? It isn't a thing I'd likely forget."

Daisy went beet red, and Miranda put a calming hand upon her arm. "It's all right, Daisy. I knew of Archer's fight with Marvel." She looked pointedly at Poppy, who seemed inclined to interject. "I simply didn't know it was over Victoria."

Miranda's eyes followed the little blood-red satin top hat tilted upon Victoria's raven locks as it bobbed about in the fine china department. "And what of Victoria," she murmured. "Did she stay with Marvel?"

Daisy absently toyed with the cloth beneath her fingers, her blue eyes tracking Victoria. "No. She returned to the Continent and hasn't been heard from since."

"The question is," Poppy said, her brows slanting severely under her red fringe, "why is she using Archer's name?"

"I have to believe that she would like to renew her dalliance with Archer," Miranda said.

Her sisters erupted into twin volleys of outrage, hissing about what they'd do to Victoria should she come near.

"You might have your chance," Miranda muttered. "She is coming this way...no wait." She clutched Poppy's elbow. Another option suddenly appeared much more agreeable. If she wanted information on Archer and Victoria, she might as well get it from the horse's mouth.

"Let me handle this, please. After all," she said, letting her voice drop to a whisper, "you know what they say."

"What?" Poppy asked darkly as Victoria drew near.

"Keep your friends close and your enemies closer... Victoria"—Miranda stepped round the table and inclined her head—"I thought I recognized you."

"It is a shame we could not persuade your sisters to come along," Victoria said as they stepped into the small yet bustling teahouse of Victoria's suggestion. It catered to mainly middle-class women, physicians and barrister's wives who fancied a bit of refreshment after a hard day of shopping.

"On the contrary," Miranda said. "I must thank you for

rescuing me from an afternoon of bickering. My sisters, I fear, are far too divergent in their opinions to get along well."

Victoria smiled. "Quite understandable."

They settled into a private table. As soon as the maitre d' left the little nook, Victoria turned to Miranda, and the lamplight flickered over her unnaturally white features, giving them the appearance of a mask. "It pleases me that we are having tea. I thought of inviting you before, but I got the impression that you might object."

Miranda held her gaze. "Because of what I saw that night." There was little use dancing around the subject.

Victoria's painted lips curled slightly. "You must not think too badly of me, *mon ami*. Archer broke my heart once. And I'm afraid I've never forgiven him for it. I acted badly," She shrugged. "I express myself too passionately, I suppose."

Even with Miranda's limited knowledge of love, she knew Congreve to be correct: Heaven has no rage like love to hatred turned, nor hell a fury like a woman scorned. "I did not mean to pry," she said, hoping that the apology would ease Victoria into a talkative mood.

The woman's smile turned genuine. "La, I expect no less. It is what I would have done." She leaned in. "Only, I do not think we should tell Benjamin of our *tête-à-tête*. For if anyone was to object to our meeting, it would be he."

Benjamin. Miranda's stays pinched as she reached for her serviette. "Archer is . . ."

"Most protective?" Victoria finished with a light laugh. "I know this well." She placed her napkin across her lap with an elegant flick. "He used to have this little saying, our Archer. Keep the ignorant ignorant, and the innocent out of the way."

Tea arrived, sparing Miranda the trouble of a reply. White-liveried waiters laid out the service with sharp precision. A fragrant pot of tea in delicate bone china, meaty little tarts, flaky fruit pastries topped with crimson jam and saffron-yellow custard, and snow white dollops of clotted cream for their hot scones. Miranda had been famished before. Now all of it looked as appetizing as a still-life study.

"And you?" Miranda asked when the waiters had gone, and she began to pour her tea with care. Its fragrance released in a soft cloud of steam, mixing with that of hot milk and lemons. "Do you believe the ignorant should remain so?"

Victoria regarded her with eyes so gray and luminous that, for a moment, she could think of nothing but Archer. Miranda looked away.

"What is it that you wish to ask?" Victoria's voice, low and rich, rolled over Miranda.

She set the cream pot down with a clink. "What do you know of the West Moon Club?"

She could have cursed aloud. The words were out. There was no taking them back. Save they were the wrong words. She had meant to ask her about Lord Marvel and Archer. She could not account for the slip.

Victoria's smooth brow wrinkled as though she too were expecting another question entirely. "That is a name I did not expect to hear," she said slowly. "And you, *cher,* what do you know of this club?"

Miranda fiddled with her napkin and then let it drop. "You knew him before his accident. His disfigurement occurred as a result of the club's…activities." She was unwilling to say more, yet knew she had already said too much.

"You think that what happened to Archer is the reason why its members are dying?"

"I cannot assume otherwise," Miranda said stiffly.

Victoria shrugged. "I am no more enlightened than you. Is it the work of madness? Or cold revenge? I know not. Only that their secrets go back years. Their masks older than Archer's."

Victoria took a slow sip of tea, her gray eyes studying Miranda over the golden rim. She set her cup down with care before folding her slender arms before her. "But that is not what you truly want to know."

"It isn't?" Miranda challenged blandly, her heart slamming madly against her ribs.

Victoria's slight weight fell onto her forearms. "You wonder if I have seen what lies beneath the mask."

"I know that you have. I…how…" The line of Miranda's jaw ached. She could not, would not, ask it of Victoria.

"Poor dear, he has not shown you then."

It was not a question. Miranda looked away, to the small sliver of window peeking beyond the dining curtains where the dark shadows of carriages passed by as they rumbled down the street. "It does not matter."

"But of course it does," Victoria whispered, the smell of silk mingling with old flowers. "He is the man you lie down with at night. Rise up with to greet the sun. Where lies trust, if not in your husband's arms?"

Miranda would die before she admitted this was not precisely the truth of the situation. The little dining nook wavered before her eyes, magnified to monstrous proportions as though viewed through a reading glass. She blinked back unshed tears, refusing to let them fall.

Victoria's voice drifted across her skin, soothing and dark. "What if I told you it is something wondrous and beautiful he hides?"

The breath left Miranda in a pained gasp. The cruelty of it. Victoria's smile merely grew.

"Infinite beauty. Not the hideous disfigurement he claims. Would it assuage your fears? Make it easier to bear, that you do not live with a monster?"

The thickness of Miranda's tongue pushed past her dry lips. "I would say that you were a liar."

Victoria studied her face for a moment and then laughed, like silver sleigh bells in the snow. "Ah, but it would be such a nice dream to dream, no?"

Miranda's fingers dug into the slick silk of her aquamarine skirts. "It matters not to me what he looks like beneath the mask."

"Yet here you sit, asking the questions you ask because your curiosity overwhelms your pride. How can you not want to know?"

"I asked you about West Moon Club because I want to help Archer. Not unmask him." A lie. And they both knew it.

Victoria's thoughtful expression did not change, and the silence grew. From beyond came the gentle murmur of the main dining room, the kiss of silver to china, then Victoria's chair creaked as she shifted to rest her temple upon her knuckles. "Then, what is it you wish to know?"

"Why do you know so much about West Moon Club?"

"Not as much as you think." The small curve of her bottom lip quivered. "My love was a member."

The floor beneath Miranda tilted. "Who was he?"

"I..." Her eyes grew bright. "He was lost to me long ago."

The genuine sorrow in Victoria's eyes moved Miranda to touch her hand, but she stopped short, inexplicably unwilling to make contact. "They say time heals all wounds, but I don't believe it."

Victoria met Miranda's eyes, and her tears threatened to spill. She gave a little laugh and brushed them away with a flick of her gloved hand. "Ah, well, it is a pity I have so much time on my hands."

They were quiet for a moment.

"So it was not Lord Marvel, then?" *Or Archer?*

Victoria's little smile returned, knowing and sure. "You are referring to the quarrel between Marvel and Archer." She stirred her tea once more. Tiny clinks that hit Miranda's nerves like an anvil. "Archer did not like the idea of Marvel taking his place."

The cooled tea within Miranda's cup began to steam. She let it go quickly. "Taking his place?"

Victoria's cheeks plumped, her eyes gleaming as though she knew precisely how she tormented Miranda. "Of course, we were no longer together." She tapped the rim of her cup thoughtfully. "Nevertheless, there was a modicum of jealousy involved as Archer does not like being replaced. In any capacity. So they discussed the matter." Victoria's brow lifted. "I assume you've heard the outcome of that discussion?"

Woodenly, Miranda nodded, and Victoria's little teeth flashed like seed pearls beneath red-painted lips. "And did you, then, learn of how the elder members sent him away?"

When Miranda shook her head like an automaton, Victoria continued. "He was an embarrassment, a living testament to their failure. And one not easily controlled. Poor Archer never was able to govern his temper." Her dark head tilted as she sipped her tea. "Quite the motive for revenge, is it not?"

Miranda could not argue the fact. So she sat as stone, her stays pinching her ribs, the cold length of silk encasing her torso tightening with each breath.

Victoria seemed to understand Miranda's struggle between loyalty and logic. "Miranda, *cher*, I do not think it is he who does these things. Murder in secret is not his style. Archer in a temper is a glorious and vocal spectacle."

She looked off fondly as though remembering something altogether intimate, and the collar about Miranda's neck suddenly felt too tight. She swallowed hard, forcing a cooling breath as the room began to grow warm.

"Though you cannot deny," Victoria went on, "he makes a most excellent target, should one want to make him appear guilt—"

"Do you still love him, Victoria?" She no longer cared to hear Victoria's theories. Only to know where they stood.

Victoria tilted her head. The image of a great spider wrapping its victim up with silken threads to suck its life's blood came to mind. And Miranda thought Archer had been quite correct in his desire to warn her away from Victoria.

"I believe you know that answer," Victoria said in a voice like the gathering of a storm.

Cold sweat broke out over Miranda's skin as her temper rose. The room heated, the gas lamps above their heads flaring white-hot. Victoria glanced at the lamps, her brow knitting. Miranda took a breath. Then another, pushing down that familiar feeling of *need*. The need to let go of her temper, and with it, the painful coil wound within her. *Control, Miranda. Do not become that monster.*

"Do you mean to try to win him back?" she asked.

Victoria's lips pulled as if to offer the merest hint of apology. "And if that is my intent?"

The lamp about Victoria's head wavered wildly as Miranda spoke. "Then you shall have to go through me."

Victoria reached with shocking quickness, enfolding Miranda's wrist in a grip like iron. "I find that I like you, Miranda. Despite myself, I do. So I shall give you a small piece of advice. If you intend to keep your husband, believe nothing you hear. Everyone lies. Most especially your husband. If he thinks it will protect you, Archer will not hesitate to employ the simplest equivocation to keep you in the dark. Do not let him, or risk losing him entirely."

Chapter Seventeen

———❦❦———

Everybody lies. Miranda could not stop Victoria's warning from echoing in her head in a constant refrain. What were Archer's lies? Why did he feel the need to tell them?

The muted song of a fiddle drifted through the din of caterwauls and raucous laughter. Despite the late hour, street urchins wove underfoot, brushing their little fingers light as spider silk over the pockets of the unwary. With any luck, they'd steal enough to keep them alive. Some were no older than three—little *snakesmen* and *goniffs* in the making.

Blue darkness cloaked Miranda, the scant lamplight saved for taverns. Her booted feet crunched over something that felt and sounded unnervingly like bones, and she decided that the darkness was a blessing. In more ways than one. With a bowler crammed down low and her shoddy coat collar pulled up high, most of her face was hidden. Dirt covered her skin, hastily smeared on as she'd crept through the garden after Archer had ridden off into the night.

Experience told her Archer would be gone for

hours—doing what she couldn't begin to fathom, though she suspected it was as clandestine as her mission tonight. Cheltenham's murder, and the attack at the museum, lay heavy on him. Since then, he had gone out every night, when he thought her long abed. She knew he was in search of the killer. Even though he tried to hide it, she could see the frustration and rage in his eyes burning just below the surface. And it ignited a wild urge in Miranda to protect him and find out what she could, where she could.

Cold air, heavy with icy shavings of soot, filled her lungs. She resisted the urge to tuck her head farther into her collar. One walked with purpose here, or one would be quickly singled out. But the smell brought tears to her eyes. Onions, piss, shit, rotted meat... The thick stench of rot was the worst, working its way into mouth and throat, a promise of one's future: death and decay. She pressed her lips tight and forged on.

Her mark stood beneath one of the few working lampposts. Nearly a head taller than the rest, he was as lanky as a garden ladder, his shaggy brown hair dull in the flickering light. He was older, just as she. Fine lines fanned out from his cheerful brown eyes. But the grin. That gap-toothed grin remained the same, an equal mix of ready humor and malice. A group of younger men and boys surrounded him, watching his every move, modeling their behavior to his. He was boss now to this small group, after having worked his way up through the ranks. His velvet green bowler and mustard-colored sack suit were a bit less shabby than the clothes of his mates. Perhaps one day he would run the whole area.

Her steps slowed. How to get him alone? It wouldn't do to come upon him with his gang hanging about. Willing to wait, she leaned against an abandoned lamppost. The lamplighter had passed it by. Passed by most of the street lamps here. This neighborhood wasn't deemed fit to have good light, or fresh water for that matter.

A sudden anger sparked hot in her breast, and with it an idea. Perhaps she alone could smell the acrid sweet tang of gas that had leaked out of the unused lamps to pool in the thin, trash-filled gutter running down West Street. It was enough to burn. One small spark would do the trick. Her loins tightened with a throb of excitement, and a familiar power ignited within. She shoved her hands deep into her pockets to hide their trembling, and her fingers curled around the cool coin hidden there. She held onto it like a lifeline. Should the task be done incorrectly, the whole of West Street could ignite like a lamp. In truth, the very fog-fouled air of London was an incendiary bomb waiting to go off. Nothing too grand, she promised herself as a cold sweat broke out over her skin. Only a small spark, directed with precision at the gutters.

An organ grinder and his monkey danced by. Then she acted. A shiver of pleasure pulsed through her limbs, and the gutter along West Street flared to life with a sudden hiss. Gasps rushed through the night as a yellow river of fire ran between the throngs of people. Among the laughter of surprise and the general mayhem, Billy Finger lifted his head. His brown eyes glared round before catching hers. They narrowed for one cool moment. Miranda touched her brim, and the familiar gap-toothed smile curled in response. She was, as they say, all in it now.

"'Ello there, darlin'," he said as he came near. "Know how to make an entrance, you do." The overpowering scent of grease, sweat, and bay rum—most likely lifted from a recent house job—followed him. "An' how's me favorite mot on this fine night?"

"Don't call me that," she hissed in a low voice.

His feathery brows rose. "Wha? Mot?"

" 'Mot,' 'darling.' " She stiffened her shoulders to make them appear broader. "I'm a man, remember."

The gap-toothed grin appeared again. "Right. An' a very convincing cove you are." He snorted, blowing stale breath over her. "Only a blind codger would happ'n upon you and not want to put his old *nebuchadnezzar* to the grass."

"Don't be disgusting." She shifted down farther into her collar where the air was fresher. "I'm not planning on showing my face—"

"Eh, Billy, who's the fancy bloke?"

Billy turned with a snarl to the younger rough that had come upon them. "He ain't no bloke! This 'ere's Pan, a regular brick and me pal, so I'd watch me mouth if I was you."

The rough, who was no older than sixteen, backed up. "No need to raise your dander."

Billy gave a sharp jerk of his head. "Eh, hook it. An' keep an eye on Meg. Lazy toffer's been treatin' her corner like a doss."

The youth ambled off.

"Turned to the skin trade, have you?" Miranda asked. The idea of Billy as a pimp soured her stomach.

Billy gave a twisted smile. "A man's got to make his livin', hadn't he?" He picked at something between his teeth and then spat. "An' you're getting too old to blend here, Pan."

Which was more than likely true. Versed as she was in blending on these streets, she was now too tall to pass as a youth and too slender to look like a man, despite her bulky attire.

"We made a fair bit o' tin together," he went on, "but it ain't safe. Even for you." The hardness in his eyes would never truly fade, but for a moment, they softened in concern.

Looking at him, she felt the same sense of oddness as always in his presence. That he, the youth who would have raped her in an alleyway some three years ago, should be something close to a friend these many years later. Their paths had crossed for the second time when Father had lost his fortune and forced Miranda into a life of petty crime. Only Billy Finger, who'd been nipping palms, among other unsavory activities, found out one day, spying on her as she lifted a wallet from a nob walking down Bond Street.

He followed and, once again, cornered her in a dank alley. With no mysterious stranger to come to her aid, Miranda had been forced to show him just how unfriendly she could be. Only she'd become carried away, and the entire alley became engulfed in flames. His piteous screams tore into her conscience. Horrified by the damage she wrought, she stamped out the flames consuming his ragged clothes and took him home to wrap him up in cool cloths soaked in milk Miranda had filched from the market.

From that day on, Miranda had a partner. It was Billy who taught her how to be a bouncer, to pretend to be an honest customer in a shop, flaunting her beauty, distracting the clerk while Billy, as palmer, pinched his goods. The most miserable days of her life.

Yet they had become something of friends. He taught her more than any respectable lady could imagine. And when he was caught on the job, he held his tongue, and did not rat her out, but did his time. No longer was he her partner, but still an invaluable resource for information should she need him. She needed him now. No stone could be left unturned.

The fire in the gutters flickered then died, and the crowds surged in, an occasional nervous laugh the only sign that anything untoward had occurred.

"What do you make of this?" Miranda handed him Archer's coin. He turned it over with his stubby fingers, and she caught a glimpse of the tight, shining skin rippling over his left wrist. Scars that had earned him the esteemed new moniker of Burnt Bill. Her fingers went numb.

"An odd sinker, this. Lookin' for bit fakers, eh? I know a few . . ."

"No," she said. "I don't need counterfeit money." The idea was laughable. "I thought perhaps it might be a marker for an address."

"Might be. I've 'eard tell of fancy blokes usin' such rubbish for their lil' societies." Billy's blunt nose, crooked from too many breaks, twitched. "Right glockey, if you're askin' me."

She smiled but only just; should Billy realize he had made her laugh, he'd wax comical to distraction. "It was just a thought," she said with a shrug. A sinking realization that she might be spinning her wheels made her insides burn.

Billy shifted closer. Behind him, the laughter of street doxies seemed to swell before settling down into the din of West Street. "This isn' about them peerage slayin's, is it now? I 'eard your new cove is in the thick of it. *Lord* Archer, is it?"

Shock pounded against her temples. "How did you know?"

He rocked back on his heels, gripping the green-and-yellow plaid satin lapels of his coat. Really such attire should be outlawed. "Me 'ead isn' stuck up me arse. I 'eard you got hammered for life to one Lord Archer. A right canny fellow, if them news rags is to be believed." Keen eyes bore into her. "Wotcha doin' g'ttin' involved with that lot, anyways?"

"I had no idea you read," she said in true surprise.

His scanty brows rose. "'Course I don't bleedin' read. Meg's the one with the learnin'. Don't listen to her go on normally, 'cept for this here..." He reached into his inside coat pocket and pulled out a folded piece of newsprint.

The corners were battered and a spot of grease marred one edge, but it had been carefully wrapped in a length of wax paper to protect it from further harm. She unfolded the paper with a trembling hand. There—along with a story proclaiming Archer as a person of high interest in the peerage slayings—was a line sketching of Miranda, named as Archer's mysterious and exotic new bride. Her lips had been drawn into a rather smug-looking smirk, but the artist had captured the essence of her quite well.

Billy bent over the paper, bringing along a fresh wash of ripe onion to her nose. "A right fair doodle, if I say so."

"Quite," she rasped. Such salacious news stories had ceased to bother her. But that Billy kept a drawing of her on his person...Guilt clawed at her throat with wretched, hard fingers. She hadn't given him a passing thought in a year.

Eyes carefully averted, she handed him the drawing. "Have you heard of a West Club? Or Moon Club?"

Billy shook his head. "Only club 'ere is 'Eaven an' 'Ell." He jerked a thumb toward a solid structure three houses down whose doors were opened wide to allow for the steady stream of London dandies and roughs coming in and out. The small sign above the door read HEAVEN on top with a pair of angel's wings and a blue arrow pointing up and HELL with a distinctive red pitchfork pointing the way down.

"Fancy a romp with a judy an' it's up to 'eaven you go."

She ducked her head as a group of gentlemen got out of a newly arrived carriage. Some of them looked vaguely familiar, and no doubt counted themselves among those who frequented the same parties that she did. "And what do you do in Hell?" she asked, eyeing the men from under her brim.

"'Ell's for darker stuff, love. A bit o' this an' that…" A gleam of mischief lit his eyes as he flipped Archer's coin through his fingers with ease. "Fancy a look?"

"Thank you, no." She took the coin midflip. "Is there a Moon Street in London, perhaps?"

"Not that I've 'eard." He scratched beneath his hat, sending it further askew. "Look 'ere, if anyone's 'eard of this West Moon Club, I'll find 'em, right?"

"Thank you, Billy." She handed him a wad of pound notes.

"Keep your chink." He shoved her hand away. "It ain't like that wi' us." A shocking wash of pink crossed his wide cheeks. They both looked the other way in awkward silence, and she noticed an older man headed in their direction. He moved with a presence that rippled down the whole of West Street.

The man wasn't very tall, probably as high as Miranda's shoulder, and wore an unassuming suit of black under his thick dark cloak, but the crowd parted for him with a deference that spelled trouble. Billy cast his eye that way and paled. He made to grip her elbow but stopped, realizing that the gesture would mark her as a woman.

"Let's make scarce." He kept his stance casual, not looking toward the man, but he remained aware of the man with all his senses.

"Who is he?" she murmured as they walked toward a small alley.

"Black Tom. He runs the Dial's. Knows who belongs an' who don't. He ain't keen on outsiders unless they're 'ere to pay. Come on."

They turned a corner, almost making it to the safety of the alleyway, when they ran into a wall of men. The motley crew eyed them with various levels of humor and malice.

"Goin' so soon there, Billy?" came a musical voice from behind.

A foul oath passed Billy's lips as he slowly turned, taking her with him.

Black eyes gleamed like onyx beneath thick brows as the man Billy had called Black Tom regarded them. A wide brim top hat lay cocked upon his head, leaving greasy locks of raven hair to fall about his large ears and into his high collar.

"I should be offended, not gettin' an introduction," Tom said lightly.

Billy shifted his feet. "Blimey, Tom, didn't think you'd want to bother wi' such riffraff."

"Thought wrong, boyo."

A soft chuckle went through the group as though they were one entity.

Stiffed-backed, her pulse throbbing, Miranda could only stand and wait. The black eyes of the boss hadn't left hers for a moment.

"Tis me kinsman from the East End," said Billy through white lips. "A simple lad, really. Right nickey in the noggin', he is."

A scant brow rose. "Get on wif you, Billy. Havn' a laugh at our expense? Why, it'd take a flat not to know toff from a toffer. Even in cove's clothes."

Strong hands wrenched her from Billy's side. Her head hit the iron lamppost as two roughs pinned her against it for Tom's inspection. At that, the small man doffed his cap and offered an eloquent bow. "'Ello, there, darlin'."

Resignation pulled down Billy's long features as two others took hold of him. The boss stepped in close, the smell of gin and unwashed male hitting her nostrils like a brick.

"Wha's your name, then, luv?"

"Meg," she mumbled, trying to sound as simple as Billy claimed. A useless endeavor. A simpleton would only be easier sport.

A dirty finger traced her cheek, his long nail scraping flesh as he licked his wet lips. "But you're a fine bit o' stuff, aren't you now." A smile split his cragged features. "This 'ere's my bit of dirt you're standin' on." He took a step closer, and the men held firm, their hard fingers bruising her flesh. "Wha' come on my turf is mine. An' I takes wha's mine."

Male arousal hung thick in the air, a palpable excitement that turned her stomach. Crowds of people milled about, not one of them looking, not one of them foolish enough to do so. She closed her eyes and swallowed hard, their laughter penetrating the weak veil of darkness. She was as good as raped and dead if she did not act. Yet a cold sweat broke over her skin at the thought. She shivered, sickness and rage gaining purchase with equal speed. The sounds of the night came in from all sides. A street filled with people. Witnesses all. And innocents as well.

A thumb caressed her bottom lip. Blood thundered in

her ears and with it the gathering storm. *Do it. I cannot.*
Quite suddenly she wished for Archer so desperately that
tears threatened. *Don't think of him.*

The sound of laughter and joviality rang out down the
street. Yet here... Hot breath hit her cheek, hot as the air
that gathered around her. "Fancy a toss, luv?"

She felt rather than heard Billy move, and the resulting
scuffle. Her eyes flew open to see her friend held fast with
a knife at his throat. His eyes bulged, fear making him
quiver.

"You workin' me, Billy Finger?" Tom said without
taking his eyes from Miranda. "Denyin' me my piece?"
The man spoke lightly but the evil flatness in his eyes
betrayed his tone. He'd gut Billy and enjoy every second.

Billy's Adam's apple bobbed. "Don't—" The knife at
his throat cut him short.

Black Tom cocked a thick brow. "Don't, wha? Hurt
your littl' toffer?" Rotted teeth flashed. "She mean that
much ta ye, then?"

Billy licked his lips quickly. His skin took on a grayish
hue as sweat seeded over his high brow. "Don't piss 'er
off," he managed.

The stovepipe hat on Tom's head tilted back as the man
gaped. "You bammin' me?" His laughter cracked out,
joined by the rest.

"'Ere now, lad," he said through chortles, "'as no man
ever taught ye how to 'andle a haybag?" Tom's cold black
eyes snapped to Miranda, hatred and pleasure burning in
them as he took another step forward. Sick dread over-
flowed in her belly, leaking down her limbs and setting
them to shaking.

"You need a toss, sweetin'." A blow to her head
knocked her hat free, sending half of her hair awkwardly

over her cheek. A throb of heat went down her spine, and with it, the urge to hurt. *No. Too many people.*

"Don't." She did not want to do this. The face before her wavered as her control was overwhelmed by need.

A warped smile winked at her. "Too late for beggin'."

White-hot heat stretched her skin tight and crackled through her hair. Dimly, she heard Billy moan, saw him strain to pull away from his captor, away from her. But the coarse hands of Black Tom kept reaching for her. The laughing eyes of his crew looked on as he ripped her coat open. Cold air blew through her thin lawn shirt. A small child ran between the legs of the men, chasing a broken bottle. Too many innocents. Blood throbbed in her ears.

"Very nice, indeed," he muttered a moment before he grabbed her breasts and squeezed.

A roar lit through her ears. She could not think; the thing had her. It broke in a terrible wave of heat. The gas lantern above her head exploded in a volley of fire and pelting glass.

Tom flew back, blazing with yellow flames. His scream mingled with the loud pops of the lamps down West Street exploding like cannon fire.

Chaos erupted, men and women screaming as the hapless onlookers scrambled to get away. A stream of rushing men and women caught her up and carried her along as the fire danced toward the ramshackle building behind. The aged timber and empty rooms acted like a tinderbox to the fire's greed, and the structure roared to life with a burst of scorching air.

"Billy!"

Screams of mass panic swallowed up her dry shout. Black Tom rolled upon the ground, an inhuman sound vibrating from him as the fire ate him.

"Billy!" Her knees cracked against the hard cobble and the red leviathan grew higher. It looked her in the face, kissing her cheeks with a hot blast. For one blessed moment, she spied the familiar outline of her friend against the flames as he ran off into the wild night, then a hard blow from behind brought her down.

Smothered by the foul stench of fish and wet wool of a lady's skirt, she struggled to get free of the woman lying on top of her. Arms tangled with limbs as they both tried to rise.

"Get off!" shouted the frantic woman. A sharp kick to Miranda's ribs sent her flying back, and the woman scurried away. A foot crushed her hand, and she sobbed. Blinded by fleeing bodies and thick smoke, she could not tell up from down.

Suddenly hands had her, strong and sure. She surged upward, pulled into a hard embrace. Black smoked burned down her throat as they hurtled forward, knocking people down like pins, crashing through an old wooden door and into the cool quiet of an abandoned brick building.

Panting in the dark, she tried to move. Her rescuer kept her crushed in his embrace, pressing her tight against the wall. Heated breath touched her ear as he turned his head. She reared, flailing her limbs in useless protest. A large hand clamped over her mouth, the arm about her a vise.

"Stop," he hissed. "Stop, I say!"

She kicked out, finding a shin, and a grunt wrung from the man's lips before his embrace tightened.

"I saved your life, you."

Her struggles slowed as the vague familiarity of the voice seeped through her panic.

"There now," Lord Ian Mckinnon breathed, letting his

hand fall. "Easy. I don't want to receive the same treatment as that poor prig did back there, I can tell you."

As usual, letting the fire out had drained her physically. She sagged against a cold, damp wall and took a deep breath of air. It was dank and smelled of decay, but was blessedly free of smoke. In the distance, the clanging of the fire brigade bell rang. Mckinnon eased back, but he did not break his embrace. Miranda blinked up to find his strong features arranged in a grin.

"That is quite the trick, lass."

"I don't know what you mean."

Sharp canines showed beneath his thin mustache. "You know precisely what I mean. I saw it all." He leaned in until their breath mingled. "Even the moment when it broke free."

Her stomach lurched, but she affected calm. "You watched me get attacked," she said, ignoring the obvious. "And did nothing?"

The caress of his voice at her ear sent little prickles of unease down her spine. "I watched you defend yourself. I saw the look in your eyes. You were never truly afraid." He edged back to look into her eyes. "That interests me."

"What do you want?"

With slow ease, he studied her. "What are you doing here?" he asked after a moment. "Don't tell me it's to play dress up. I won't believe you."

She shoved at his bulk but he did not budge. Rather, he settled in comfortably, letting his length nestle along hers. A tight knot claimed her stomach. His embrace might have been intimate, yet it left her cold and irritated.

"Get off, will you?" She shoved again.

"Not until you tell me."

"I owe you nothing."

He laughed shortly as she struggled again to free herself. "I saved your life."

Which was precisely the reason she couldn't feel the burning anger toward him that she felt for Black Tom. It did not stop her from wanting to smack the smug look off of his face, however.

Mckinnon laughed again. "Never mind," he murmured against her ear. "I know." His hand plunged into her pants.

Screeching, she bucked, the heat rising once more. But suddenly he was off, dancing back with haste.

"Easy now," he said lightly. "Cool yourself. I was simply looking for this."

He lifted his hand high, and a golden flash caught the weak light. Archer's coin. Inwardly, she groaned.

Mckinnon gave it a glance and then raised a questioning brow. "You're trying to clear his name, aren't you?" He smiled. "If you think learning West Moon Club's secrets will absolve Archer, you are wrong."

She fell against the wall with a small gasp. "You know of West Moon Club?"

He flicked the coin high and then caught it neatly. "My father is a member, aye?" Mckinnon tossed her the coin. "I know more than I care to know."

"Then will you—" She stopped, and he grinned.

"It's never that easy, is it?" he said.

A pregnant silence ran between them as his gaze held.

"I'm leaving." She moved to go but he stepped forward, not touching her, but pinning her to the spot just as effectively.

"You're right to worry. Archer's back is to the wall, and he knows it."

Her shoulders hit the cold brick behind her as she edged

away from McKinnon's advancing form. He stopped, seeing the movement, and regarded her with shrewd eyes.

"You'd do anything to protect him, wouldn't you,
lass?" Soft wonder filled his voice.

She pressed her hands into the wall. "I believe you are
overreaching."

Mckinnon shook his head slowly, a feral grin creeping
over his shoulders. "I don't believe so." He took a small
step closer. "Shall we find out?"

Chapter Eighteen

⟡

The Rusty Spanner was located in the middle of a crooked narrow street two blocks off of the London Docks. The scent of tar rising from the sail maker's shop next door overrode everything: the thick perfume of tea, the briny sharpness of sea water and dried fish, the sulfuric smell of the tanneries, and the general stench of too many people and goods forced into one small area.

Archer tried to ignore the burning in his nose as he walked down the street, the low-lying buildings leaning this way and that like a set of jumbled bottom teeth in an overcrowded mouth. It was dark here, save for the golden light spilling from the tavern windows and the sound of merriment within. Someone had procured an accordion, and from the sound of the boisterous singing that accompanied the instrument, the patrons within were already well in their cups. Not well enough. The music stopped the moment Archer came through the door, the dying wheeze of the accordion punctuating his entrance. Through the thick, gray haze of tobacco smoke, a multitude of glassy eyes stared at him. But only for a moment. The song started up once more, the singer's voice unsteady at first, and then the accordionist began to play. The patrons returned to their fun but Archer knew better than to feel safe from attack. Hard stares bore into his back as he made his way toward the bar. He kept his head bent, the rough-hewn beams overhead so low he might brush them should he stand in full.

He could only imagine the scene if he'd come dressed in his usual fashion; the black top hat, mask, and cloak would have caused an outright revolt. He'd dressed like one of them, donning a heavy peacoat—the collar turned up high, thick woolen skull cap pulled low—then wrapped his face with linen. Even so, sailors were a superstitious lot. At best, they thought him a victim of a tragic accident, which made him bad luck. He couldn't blame them. He remembered his days of sailing and that feeling of helplessness mixed with excitement. It took some nerve to put your life in the hands of that tempestuous mistress, the sea.

He did not feel fear now, only a sick knot of hope mixed with fury. Fury for Cheltenham. His fists ached to strike something when he thought of the elderly man slaughtered like a pig. And hope. That coil of emotion stuck like soggy pudding to his gut ever since Leland had sent him a note telling him of Dover Rye, Hector Ellis's old manager and sea captain. Apparently Dover had been stealing out from under Ellis all this time, a bit of larceny among thieves. Dover had been the captain of *The Rose* when it had pirated Archer's ship. Only Dover lived. All this time, he'd been hidden away in some forgotten taproom.

The man behind the bar watched Archer come forward. He was a big fellow, chest like a full sail, masts for arms, ginger-haired and skin reddened by the sun. He set down the mug he'd been wiping.

"An' what can I be getting you then?" There was a fair amount of accusation in the man's voice. That, along with an odd mix of Scottish and Cockney.

Archer sat on a high stool. "Ale."

He set down his coin, and a large tankard of thick ale appeared. Archer drank for a moment, well aware that the barkeep had not wandered off but continued to study him with a jaundiced eye—a keen eye that knew Archer wasn't there for ale or company.

He set the tankard down and met the pale gaze. "I'm looking for a man," he said without preamble.

"Aye?" The barkeep grinned, revealing deep dimples. "There's a doxy house down that street that caters to man-drakes. Best you be asking there."

Archer chuckled low, knowing it irritated the barkeep. "And you know this from personal experience, do you?"

Dark promise glinted in the barkeep's eyes. "I also know how to make a man disappear if I was of a mind."

A large man knocked against Archer's shoulder. When Archer glanced that way, a set of brown eyes beneath bushy white brows stared back at him for a moment before the man set to his drink. Archer suppressed a sigh. He didn't want to hurt these men. Most especially not the man sitting next to him; the burly fellow had to be near sixty years of age.

He took a slow slip of ale. "I'm looking for Dover Rye."

There was only a moment of hesitation from the bar-keep, but it was enough. "Never heard of him."

"Oh?" Archer sat back a little. "For I've heard tell that this establishment is run by one Tucker Rye, son of Dover Rye."

The man barely blinked. "You've been misinformed."

"Tucker!" The shout made more than one man flinch.

A short but ample woman clambered up the crooked stairs near the back. "Tucker Rye!"

The barkeep turned two shades of red. "Leave off, Mabel! Can you no' see I'm right before ye?" His blue eyes flicked to Archer in wariness as he shouted.

Mabel was undeterred. "I've been waitin' a bleedin' hour for you to take down them casks. If you can' get off yer lazy arse—"

"Hush now, woman!"

Tucker Rye kept his eyes on Archer. As the shouting woman drew near, she too spied Archer and grew hushed and stood open-mouthed and wide-eyed. Rye's overlarge fists curled, defiance blazing in his pale eyes. "You best be goin' before I'm of a mind to call in me mates."

"I've faced worse than a bar full of men such as these," Archer said. The man stiffened, lifting his head, ready to fight. Archer merely smiled. "You won't come near to harming me, I can assure you. And I'll only haunt the place until I get what I want."

He glanced to the corner of the room where a dark booth sat unoccupied. "Why don't we sit a moment?"

Rye slapped the bar in irritation. "Fine then."

"What do you want with me da?" Rye asked as soon as they sat.

"He was the dock manager and captain for Hector Ellis."

Rye's gaze narrowed. "Aye. A bad lot, Ellis was. We've no' dealt with him for years."

"We? You worked with him as well, then?"

The man's expression hardened, angry over the slip. "Aye."

Archer sat back. "Then you might have sailed on *The Rose*."

Rye's round nostrils flared, and Archer leaned forward, letting the weak light of the table lamp show full on his gauze-wrapped face. "Forgive me," Archer said. "I forgot. *The Rose* sank off the coast of Georgia. You'd be dead. Unless *The Rose* made a stop elsewhere. Perhaps lightening its load of men and cargo before going back out to sink in the Atlantic."

Frustrated rage almost made Archer punch the table, or Rye. He'd been a fool to not to have considered the possibility until now.

"Who are you?" It was not Rye who spoke but the old sea dog who'd sat next to him at the bar. He stood now by the table, towering above them and fixing a stern look on Archer, although it was not entirely hostile.

Archer considered not replying but something niggled at the back of his mind, and he chose honesty. "Lord Benjamin Archer. And you are Dover Rye."

"It'll be something Hector Ellis has done," Dover said, sitting next to Tucker Rye. His weathered hands were swollen with work, so much so that they appeared more wood than flesh. "Are ye wanting justice, then? For I'll tell ye now, husband of Pan or no', you'll no' be walkin' out of here if you aim to take us."

Archer looked at the men for a long moment. "I'm more interested in *The Rose*. Were you on that ship?"

At this, Dover pulled a scrimshaw pipe from his pocket and slowly set to lighting it. Thick whorls of smoke ghosted in the air before being swallowed up in the blue haze that hung over the room. Behind them, men began singing again, stamping their feet to the beat. "We stole from you," Dover said finally, his dark eyes squinting through the smoke. "I know that well. As I know of your agreement with Ellis. If ye can call it that."

Archer sat back. "Then you know of what I am capable."

"Aye." Dover took a deep draw off his pipe. "I believe ye got a fair trade for your loss. More than fair by my measure." He lowered his pipe. "I trust yer treatin' Miss Miranda kindly."

Miranda. He didn't want to think of her now. He dreamed of her with the constancy of breathing. Waking dreams. He had only to let his mind wander, and it went to her. The silken, slick feel of her skin, the way her lithe body felt pressed against his, fitting like hand to glove. He had gone too far in the alley. The rush of the fight, his fear and anger—it had overwhelmed him and pushed him over the edge. He would not repeat the mistake. Nor would he regret it, however.

Archer forced a light tone. "Do you think Miranda capable of demanding anything less?"

Dover laughed loud, and his son smiled. Yes, they both knew Miranda well.

Mabel set down three tankards and then bustled away. Dover took a sip of ale, and Archer did the same.

"What is it yer lookin' for, then?" the seaman asked.

"A box. Black lacquered. The size of a cigar holder." He ought to approach the thing delicately but impatience got the better of him.

Tucker Rye took a deep drink and gave an appreciative smile. Archer did not blame him. It was stifling in the tavern, and the ale was cool. Archer took another long drink.

Dover set his pipe down and moved under the smoky light of an untrimmed gas lamp. His weathered features flickered in and out of shadows. "The box was taken off in

Leith, along with everything else. We found the Madeira hidden in the hold right quick. Sold that an' the saffron in Amsterdam. Only later did we find the crate, filled with straw and naught but that simple box within. The pearl necklace it held was fine, fetched a good price later."

Archer's teeth unclenched as he made himself speak. "And the box?"

Dover's bushy brows lifted before he shrugged lightly. "Gave it to me lad." He gestured toward Tucker. "He asked for it."

"Is it the box you'd be wanting?" Tucker Rye asked. "Or the ring inside of it?"

Both men turned to him in surprise. Tucker Rye shrugged. "Found the hidden slot and the ring that very night. Kept that bit o' knowledge to meself," he said with an apologetic wink to his father.

Dover grinned. "Aye, an' what sort of son would you be if you gave up such a treasure with ease?"

Father and son laughed comfortably.

Soft warmth spread over Archer as he sat with the men sipping ale. He hadn't shared a drink in years and had forgotten the feeling of it. Strangely it was comforting, as was the sound of frivolity around him. Miranda would like it here. He wished she were sitting next to him. *Don't think of her.*

"Being a right tosser," Tucker went on after a moment, "I bragged about it in the tavern." He gave a humorless laugh. "A man bet me for it. Three rolls of the dice, and it was his."

"A just penance for gamblin'," Old Dover retorted with a snort.

Archer set his heavy hand upon the table. "Who has the ring?"

"Don't know for sure. Could be anywhere now. Seamen aren't apt to keep treasures such as that overlong."

Weariness settled over Archer, pulling at his eyes until he felt as though he must close them. "Give me a name."

Tucker's smile warped, blurring at the edges, and as he leaned forward, the light hit the faded tattoo upon his forearm—a black wolf with DEI DONO SUM QUOD SUM inscribed around it. Rye saw the direction of Archer's gaze and grinned. "Figuring it out, are you?"

From deep within the stores of Archer's mind, information rose up. DEI DONO SUM QUOD SUM—*By the grace of God I am what I am.* "Clan Ranulf..."

"Aye, mate. Lord Alasdair Ranulf, Earl of Rossberry."

Dover's laughter wheezed out as Archer's hands curled into fists. "Didn't know Ellis was in his pocket the whole time, did you?" He laughed again, his wrinkled face leering through the smoke. "Ellis hasn't the brains, nor balls, for piracy. We was under orders to hunt your ship down from the first."

Archer sat back with a thud. "I'll..."

Tucker shook his head, knowing the direction of Archer's weak threat. "Won't do you any good, mate."

Archer pulled in a breath, the sound of the singing growing muffled. "Oh?"

A twinkle of malice lit the man's eye. "We 'eard you might be coming for us. Said we was to take real good care of you, should you show."

Too late, Archer realized the feeling coming over him. By then, the sound of a footfall was behind him. He surged forward, sending his empty tankard flying and the bench beneath him clattering. *Too late*. The sack was over his head, the men falling on him before he could turn. His chin cracked against the table. Down he went, the drug turning his legs to water, his mind a fog, and the men tied him up tight. A sharp kick to his left side took his breath, and as darkness seeped in he heard old Dover, his words muffled through the heavy cloth now wrenched tight around Archer's head.

"Make sure no piece of him's found."

Archer came to with a gasp as though suddenly doused with ice water. He hadn't been out long. Men were carrying him. Four of them, by the feel of hands upon his body.

"Lord, he's heavier than a cannon, he is!"

"Just as solid too," said the one holding his legs.

Archer hung limp as they bumped along with him. His head was heavy, his mind a fog. Whatever it was they gave him would have killed an ordinary man. As it was, however, he only needed a moment or two. A breath of fresh air would have helped, but the shroud over his head was too tight.

"Shut it, both of you. We're nearly there."

And then he smelled it. Burning. The acrid scent of burned goods, wood, rubber, metal; everything and anything. The distant clang of buoys and the mournful wail of a foghorn told him they were still at the docks. There was only one place near the docks that smelled pervasively of smoke—the Queen's Pipe, a massive kiln set up to destroy condemned goods. They meant to burn him. Terror skidded through him, an altogether unfamiliar and unpleasant sensation. He moved then, thrusting his arms and legs wide. The thick bonds that held him snapped as he fell.

"Christ! He's alive!"

He landed hard on the ground and in an instant was up, tearing the cloth from his head.

"Get him!"

Archer caught a glimpse of a dark alleyway and wet dock boards, and then they were upon him. Archer grinned wide as he went down under a heap of arms, fists, feet, and legs. The blows landed on him like rain. He let them tire, and then he used his fist, the right one. The time for mercy had past. He swung hard and felt the satisfying crunch of bone as a man's jaw connected with his fist. His foot went into yet another's gut, sending the thug flying back into a heap of rubbish. Still two came at him, both holding knives.

He whirled, catching one by the arm, snapping the man's wrist, slamming his forehead into a tender nose. Snap. Crunch. Something took over. A white mist of fury that made his blood sing, his heart pump. Light. Strength. It surged through him.

It took a moment to realize that the blows upon him had stopped, and the only sound was that of gurgling, like water eking down a clogged drain. Archer blinked, his vision clearing, and he found himself holding onto a neck, his fingers still in the act of crushing the man's windpipe. The fellow in question was a big one, nearly as tall as he was. Archer held him aloft, high off the ground as he choked the life from him. *Stop!* Clawing helplessly at Archer's gloved hand, the man's eyes bulged, his mouth agape. With a last gurgle, his struggles stopped. Still Archer held him, his hand locked around that meaty throat, unable to let go. Archer's chest heaved.

The fellow went limp, hanging there in his hand. *Stop!* The man fell with a thud. Archer stared down at his hand. He'd killed with the strength of his left hand alone. His human hand. Shaking, he pulled off his glove, convinced he'd find his skin altered. The sight of normal flesh sent a flood of relief through him, and he sank to his knees, flexing his fingers experimentally. Not yet changed. But stronger.

Around him lay the broken bodies of the men he'd slain. He'd killed them all. A diamond-dust sky lay overhead, broken only by black flumes of smoke drifting by in the breeze. He gazed up at it, breathing deep. The blood lust, the white haze—he'd felt the pull like never before. Shame swept over him. He ought to have walked away, left these men to the night. He did so then, his feet sounding dully on the old wood as he left the broken mess of bodies behind.

Emptiness pressed upon him as he made his way home. He wanted to collapse, crumple into a helpless ball against the pain of it. Murder tainted his skin and pounded through his veins like a drug, whispering for more; he was losing the battle.

Despite a firm resolve to keep his distance, Archer found himself standing before the glossy white door to Miranda's room, his fist poised before it, caught in indecision. He was certain he had heard a soft sob break from behind her door as he crept past to his room.

His fingers curled tighter. Perhaps he had misheard. There was nothing now save the sound of the hall clock steadily ticking and the subtle creaks and groans of a house settling down for the night. He eased back to go and...there! Another muffled sound. Miranda crying. Into her pillow, if he had to guess. Swallowing past the thumping of his pulse, he braced himself and knocked. Immediately all was silent, stunted. And then...

"Yes?" Her voice came husky and afraid.

It sent a pulse of agitation through him. "Miranda," he said. "Are you well?"

More thick silence greeted him. Archer pressed his palm against the cool wood, contemplating whether to leave or push his way in and assuage his worry.

"Come in," said a wobbly voice.

Her room was warmer than the hall, the banked fire and her body giving off heat. And the scent of her permeated everything. Wild grass and something fresh and sweet, like spring peonies. Although it was utterly dark, he walked with ease, seeing as well as if it were day.

She sat up, her ruby-gold hair spilling around her shoulders, down her back. A prim white nightgown covered her from neck to wrists. *Even so.* He took a step, and his knees buckled. Sweet Lord, a woman should not look so appetizing swathed in innocence.

Miranda fumbled around, looking for her bag of matches.

"No," he said, coming closer. "Don't bother with the light."

She hesitated, that lovely frown of hers wrinkling the smooth space between her brows, but she sat back against the pillows. "I didn't want you to stumble."

"It's all right." He came alongside the bed and she gave a start, realizing he was so near. "I know the layout."

A weak smile touched her lips as she looked toward the direction of his voice, her gaze missing him by inches. Silver tracks of tears mapped her curving cheeks.

"Why are you crying?"

She bit her bottom lip. "Will you sit with me?"

He was no match against her wide eyes and the tremor that took her plump mouth. Carefully, he sat on the bed. It seemed a dangerous thing to do. Her sweet scent enveloped him, leaving him lightheaded, his heart pounding. He took a breath to calm himself. It was that or put his head on her lap and beg her to hold him.

"Archer?" she said in the silence. "Would you...?" She bit her lip again and shook her head violently. "Never mind."

"Tell me," he coaxed softly.

"Would you..." A lovely blush of rose touched her cheeks. "Stay with me?"

Her strangled request drove the air from his lungs. He struggled to find more, his heart a panicked rabbit in the cage of his ribs.

Hearing his disquiet, Miranda blushed deeper. "It is simply..." A shudder caught her with violent hands. "Oh, God...Never mind. It was ridiculous to—"

"Of course," he said.

After a moment, she eased back against the pillows. Yet embarrassment kept its pink kiss upon her cheeks. Slowly, Archer removed his coat and boots, tripped up by the shaking of his hands. And then his gloves. He could not tolerate them a moment longer. Already his skin itched to distraction. He left the bandages covering his face. Though she could not see him, a storm brewed outside, and one bright bolt of lightning might reveal all.

A cold sweat broke out over him as he eased into the bed next to her. He did not trust himself to get under the covers. Hell, he barely trusted himself to lie beside her. And yet, it was heaven. The tight, jittery feeling in his gut unfurled as he lay back and felt the warmth of her body so close to his.

Miranda scooted over to give him more room and a free pillow. They lay stiff upon the soft bed and stared up at the ceiling. She was two feet away from him. It felt like two inches. His cock took in that fact and began to stir. Archer willed it down. Begged, really. The little bastard would not listen.

"Now," he whispered, not trusting his voice, "why were you crying?"

Her lower lip disappeared between her teeth. "I went to bed...upset. I had a nightmare." She blinked rapidly as a tremor lit through her. "I dreamed of a tomb. And of you lying like ice upon the floor. You had died."

He wanted to kiss her cheek for letting him in, yet her words were an icy draft that made his gut clench with foreboding. He turned to face her. "You and I are haunted by the same dreams."

She turned too, her slender hand a pale shadow resting on the bed between them. "I would not like it if you died, Archer."

His heart stopped, his throat closing tight. Slowly, he reached out. She made a little sound of shock when his bare fingers touched hers. He didn't care. His fingers laced with hers as he clasped her hand. Something within him settled as if holding her hand had somehow anchored him. The rightness of it was a sigh from his soul.

"I would not it like either." He meant to speak lightly, only it came as a rasp.

Her pulse thrummed against his wrist as they held onto each other in the dark. Unable to resist, he caressed the silken skin along the backs of her fingers with his thumb. The faint smell of smoke drifted from her like a match just snuffed. Perhaps she had stoked the fire earlier. She shifted, and the scent faded, leaving only the natural fresh sweetness of her. The heat of her breath touched his cold skin. Mirroring his movements, she let her thumb drift over the back of his hand. Archer felt the touch along the whole of his body. He held himself still, breathing light and fast from the effort.

"Your hand," she whispered.

He knew what she meant and smiled. "Don't get excited. It is my left hand." His smile grew when he saw her frown of disappointment. His Miranda Fair loved a good mystery. That she had a little puzzle piece snatched away irked her, undoubtedly.

"You're an awful tease, Archer," she murmured.

He chuckled. God, but it felt good to be with her. The horrors of the night melted away, receding to some shadowed place, remembered but no longer as real. "Yes," he whispered. "But you like that about me."

The heavy fan of her lashes brushed the tops of her cheeks. "Mmm…" Her mouth curled. "Just don't hold it against me in the morning."

"Never," he promised. Warmth spread through him, contentment tempered by a sweet ache that made him yearn to hold her close against him. He swallowed thickly. With his free hand, he touched her hair and tucked an errant lock behind her ear. The movement was quick and light, not enough for her to truly feel the skin on his right hand. His need to kiss her made him tremble. But he would not. One kiss and he would be making love to her. He could do that. Here in the darkness she wouldn't see. Only his Miranda would not be content with just that. She would want to know what he hid. He would not be able to bear it.

Unbidden, he thought of another woman. Marissa, Archer's former fiancée. Theirs was an arranged match. Yet she had been a lifelong friend and a confidante. Until he had told her of what he'd done, and shown her his hand, which had begun to change. Her look of disgust and horror, the resentful anger over his "depraved and utter foolishness" burned through him still. *"You've become the stuff of nightmares, Benjamin."* She'd left him without a backward glance. And now she was dead and gone. Like so many others.

Miranda's lids lifted, and she looked at him with tender concern. "You're shivering, Archer. Get under the covers."

He closed his eyes against temptation. "I'm getting warmed by the minute. I promise." Still holding onto her hand, he drew it a little closer, next to his heart. "Sleep now. I'm here."

She closed her eyes on a sigh, her hand relaxing in his. The sounds of the night flowed around him for a moment before her low voice broke over it. "I was a thief."

Archer tensed in surprise. She had told him. He knew what she had been, of course. It had enraged him when his man of business relayed how Ellis, having squandered the money Archer gave him, had forced Miranda to steal. How Ellis had hidden his misdeeds from him for so long Archer could only marvel, but the news had firmed Archer's resolve to claim his bride upon returning to London.

"Father taught me. He's from the streets originally, the Seven Dials. Taught me to talk like one of them, how to act, blend." She let out a short laugh. "A lifetime of Mother trying to make me a lady destroyed in a fortnight." He tightened his grip, and her answering smile wobbled. "I started out as a dipper, picking nobs' pockets while giving them a pretty smile." Her accent changed when she spoke the language she'd learned to survive. The warmth in her voice turned thicker, yet harder. "Then as a bouncer marking ignorant clerks in jewel shops." She swallowed hard. "They never thought to look below my bosom to see how busy my hands were."

Slowly the pad of her thumb ran over his knuckles, and

his attention divided between her words and the wonder of her touch. One might think years of wearing gloves would have dampened his nerves to sensation. It only served to awaken those receptors, making every caress, every fleeting pass pure torture. He felt the very moment she tensed, but she only clung tighter as if finding his hand a lifeline.

"In the beginning, I reveled in it," she said. "Because they were stupid enough to fall victim, not see past a pretty face." Her brows drew tight. "I hated them as much as I hated myself."

"If you are asking me to hate you as well, I fear I cannot comply."

A reluctant smile touched her lips. "No?"

He squeezed her hand. "Never."

Her smile faded. "That is twice now that I have told you a shameful story of my past. And twice you have reacted without the censure I expected."

His thumb played along the soft crease of skin between her thumb and forefinger. "And why should I judge you," he said quietly, "when I have surely done worse."

"Have you?" she asked in the same tone.

Her eyes were gleaming rounds in the shadows as he spoke. "I have broken just about every commandment, save . . . five and nine, if memory serves. I've always honored my father and mother," he said with mock solemnity. "And I don't recall bearing false witness against anyone."

A smile touched her lips before slipping away. "And murder?"

Settled and quiet on a soft bed with his wife, he saw with cold clarity the faces of the men he had killed. A chill touched his heart. Despite his vocal temper, he had never been a violent man. His parents had taught him the value of life. But that had been before. Victoria's voice filled his head. *Only I know what you truly are.* He swallowed, feeling ill. God save him.

"Yes." And what right did he have being near Miranda? His conscience bid him to flee; his heart held him still. "Though I can say that each time was in self-defense, it does not lessen the fact that I have stolen lives."

Pearly white teeth gripped the plump swell of her lip as a shiver lit through her. Thunder drummed in the distance, low and rumbling. An age-old, childish fear ran down his spine, tempting him to huddle beneath the covers, and he tried to draw away, but she would not let him.

"That an innate sense of self-preservation bid you to act does not lessen the guilt, does it." She spoke with a confidence borne of experience. He vowed then she would never know that guilt again. Never have to steal or fear. Even if he was no longer living, his money would keep her secure.

He forced himself to speak. "No, it doesn't."

She nodded, her silken hair a red spill over her pillow. The rain came tapping upon the window and then a violent gust of wind rattled and demanded entrance.

"I have never told anyone that story," she said after a moment.

The pillow beneath his head rustled as he lay watching her. "Why did you tell me?"

Her small hand clasped his tighter, drawing him near. "The whole of my life I have relied on beauty first, brains second. It was expected, even requested. But you saw right through me from the start. You are the only man I've ever known who has looked beyond my face and wanted to know me for me. And I find myself wanting you to know the whole of me."

I love you. For one agonized moment, he feared he

had said it aloud. His soul fairly shouted it. Three long
years and not a day had passed when he hadn't thought
about her. She'd filled his mind until she'd become the
quintessence of womanly perfection, so much so that
when he had come for her, he feared she might not live up
to his impossible expectations. And she didn't. Yes, the
real Miranda was brave, loyal, and pragmatic. She was
also meddling, quarrelsome, and opinionated. The real
Miranda was human, and by God, she took his breath
away. He knew he would love her until the end of time.
What was he to do?

Thunder rumbled over the house as their breath mingled. "And you?" he managed past the tightness in his
throat. "Have you not given me the same gift? Not in all
the years since I've donned this miserable mask has anyone dared bother."

The air between them grew heavy, languid. He would
not kiss her. He would not. His heart thumped a wild
rhythm against his ribs. But he could hold her. Only that.
Slowly, as a man approaching a skittish colt, he reached
out. She lowered her lids as his hand curled around her
tiny waist. The feel of her body melting against his left
him breathless for one dizzy moment. Gently, he tucked
her head beneath his chin. He wanted to bury his face in
her hair and breathe her in, linger there for days just holding her. Did the rest of the world not realize what excruci-
ating pleasure simply holding a woman could inflict upon
a man?

He was ten types of fool for bringing her into his life.
And selfish. So very selfish for doing it when he knew full
well there was no hope for him. He knew this. Only logic
was desire's bitch. It never stood a chance. And from the
moment he saw her, neither did he. *Find the ring.* Daoud

had been certain that the ring had the answer to his cure. Find the ring and then he would claim her.

Her slender hand rested over his heart as she sighed. "I hate being afraid, Archer."

Carefully, he smoothed her hair and tried to remain relaxed. That she was afraid, in danger, because of him made him want to scream. "I do too." He kissed the top of her head and closed his eyes against the rush of helplessness and rage. "Sleep, Miranda Fair. I'm with you now."

Chapter Nineteen

───❦───

"Shall I get rid of this person, my lady?"

It was past six, a highly unfashionable time for callers, which was confirmed by the set pinch of Gilroy's nose. Furthermore, the caller was a gentleman. And alone. Quite boorish, said Gilroy's twitching nostrils.

The tip of Miranda's finger pressed into the edge of the caller's card. The name upon it mocked her. Time to pay the piper. Just what his price might be put a bitter taste in her mouth.

"No." She smoothed her skirts with an unsteady hand. "I shall see him." Her voice did not sound quite right, she knew. She had awakened alone and remained that way all day. Archer was avoiding her. She knew it in her bones, and it made her want to strike something. Or perhaps someone.

She put the card down. As her husband was missing, her caller was an ideal target. Besides, she needed answers. Billy had sent word through one of his urchins. Not even a whisper of West Moon Club, or any variant thereof existed on the streets. Given the way information ran through the veins of London's street rats, this was odd.

The gentleman's back was to the door as he stood in the salon with his top hat tucked under his arm, taking a detailed study of the room's objects. He turned at her entrance, and his vivid blue eyes sparkled with mischief. "Ah, Lady Archer. Time only enhances your beauty."

"It is rather late for a call, sir," she said as Gilroy shut the door.

The corners of Mckinnon's eyes crinkled. "Would you rather I called when Lord Archer was in residence?"

She moved to stand by the mantel, with its close proximity to handy weapons such as andirons and scuttles. "Been watching the house, have you?"

He smiled readily. "Nothing so sinister as that." The crisp line of his frock coat broke as he seated himself comfortably on the settee. "I happened to see Archer riding down Shaftsbury. He causes quite a stir, you know." Mckinnon let out a relaxed sigh and put an arm along the seat-back. "I do believe one lady actually swooned."

Pea-brained nitwits. She studied the ormolu clock upon the mantel and waited.

Blue eyes studied her with growing humor. "Come now, madam. Would you not be more comfortable sitting down?"

There was no use standing like an uncommunicative statue; Mckinnon would never leave that way. Stiffly, she moved to the chair closest to her, but Mckinnon frowned. "And leave me sitting all alone?" The mocking in his voice worked upon her nerves like nails on slate. She leveled him a hate-filled glare and then stomped with ill grace over to the settee.

"There," he said when she plopped down on the far end of the couch. "Much better."

He angled himself toward her, drawing a knee within touching range of her thigh. She twitched as the gentle brush of his fingertips moved the cap-puffed sleeve of her evening dress.

"Understand me." Miranda glared into his smiling eyes. "My patience only stretches so far. I agreed to meet with you, nothing further. As I said before, no enticements of Archer's secrets shall induce me into letting you touch me."

Absently, Mckinnon caressed his left cheek as though feeling the spot she'd slapped the other night. "And as I said, I'd no intention of taking what isn't freely offered. But what of the little question of *your* secret, Lady Archer?"

"Will remain so if you're a pile of ash on my floor."

A burst of shocked laughter left his lips. "Touché." The self-satisfied smile he'd been wearing returned. "Fortunately for me, we both know that won't happen." He leaned in, his hot breath wafting across her neck. "How about we come up with an arrangement? I shall answer a question from you, and in return, you shall give me something I want."

She wrenched away, ready to flee, and he held up his hands. "Hold! Hold! I believe you suffer under a misunderstanding, Lady Archer." Sharp teeth flashed beneath his trim mustache. "I've no interest in blackmailing a woman into bed. It offends my pride."

"Despite all evidence to the contrary," she snapped. Her skin crawled with the desire to move away from him.

Mckinnon's eyes skimmed over her form, lingering at the low edge of her bodice. "You keep jumping to conclusions and I'll wonder if you like the chase."

When she glared, he smiled. "Oh, I want you, to be sure. But I'd rather you see the error of your ways. You've aligned yourself with the wrong man. And I fear it will get you hurt."

"Do tell me, sir, how is it that I've got the wrong man?"

He crossed one long leg over the other. "Is that your first question?"

"No. It was rhetorical, you boor. What is West Moon Club? And I will not accept one-word answers."

His teeth flashed. "Very well. They were a society of scholars, noblemen all who had one common goal—use science and medicine to discover ways to enhance men, to cure them of *disease*." He choked over the word as though it was distasteful to him. "And ultimately, find a way to end death itself."

She could see how Archer, who dreamed of tombs and death, would find such a mission appealing. It would bring him a sense of purpose. But how had it gone so very wrong?

"What precisely were they trying to discover?"

"That is, you realize, another question. But as I am feeling generous..." His expression grew utterly impassive. "Immortality."

"Immortality?" Shock prickled over her cheeks. "But how? Did they find it? Of course they must have believed so...Does Archer believe—"

"Barring the repetitive nature of the first question," Mckinnon drawled, "I believe that was three more questions. You owe me one first."

"Very well," she said through her teeth.

His gaze was a caress as he rested his temple against his fist. "Do you feel pleasure when you let it free?"

Heat flamed instantly over her skin. She swallowed

repetitively, tasting bile. The fire in the grate roared with merry contentment as she stared into it. *Of all the questions.*

"Have you ever been burned?" she asked. "Your father has. Has he ever spoken of it? Of the unending pain of having one's flesh seared? I've only burned my fingers, accidents of cooking. I can tell you that was enough to bring a sweat to my skin at the thought of fire consuming me."

She glanced at him to find his countenance pale. "I roasted that man. Yes, he intended to defile me, just as most men of the streets would without a second's thought. And I burned him alive. I've caused agony beyond endurance, destroyed fortunes. And you think I derive pleasure from such knowledge?"

Mckinnon ducked his head to study the brocade settee with undue interest. "I am sorry, Miranda. I did not think."

Unexpected guilt punched into her. The ugly truth was that she did feel pleasure when the fire broke free. It coursed through her veins like lust. But she would rather die than have someone know it. Such darkness went beyond understanding.

"You may not believe me," he said, "but I understand what it is to lose control to disastrous consequence." When she would not look at him, his voice softened further. "You have the next question."

"You know my questions."

Mckinnon's voice rolled over the divide between them. "They found what they thought was key to life everlasting. I do not know how it was achieved. Father refuses to say. Archer drew the short straw, as it were. Unfortunately, the results were not what they intended. Whatever happened to Archer was horrific enough to disband the club and send the members scurrying for cover."

Her disjointed breath was a rustling in her ears. "Immortality."

"Stranger things, my dear." Mckinnon smiled sadly. "The experiment transformed Archer. Irrevocably. Fits of rages, obvious physical deformation. He is unstable, perhaps mad."

She jumped to her feet. "Bollocks. You're saying this to turn me against Archer."

He watched her pace. "Florid language aside, you know that is not true. Well, yes, true that I want to turn you against him. But this is not a falsehood. Have you never heard the rumors? Of him beating Lord Marvel to a pulp? I assure you, there are other stories…"

"Rumors. Such as the one that claims I came straight from a bawdy house?" His mouth opened but she rushed on. "I live with the man. He is not mad. Has a temper, yes, but it is not madness."

"Then you don't believe that he sought immortality?"

She paused. Stranger things. Her skirts pooled in a wash of burgundy as she sank back next to him. "I don't know what to believe." Miranda worried her bottom lip; everything about this business confused her. "An odd name, West Moon Club."

"Quite." Mckinnon settled farther into the couch. "It is in reference to the Norwegian fairy tale, *East of the Sun and West of the Moon*."

"I know this story," she said, the long-forgotten memory making her smile. "One of father's sailors once told it to me while the men unloaded cargo. A great polar bear takes a young woman as his bride and, in return for her obedience, he gives her great riches. Only she discovers that he is really a prince caught in a sorceress's spell."

"Mmm…" said Mckinnon, the corner of his mouth

lifting. "Thus you will remember that when the nosy young lady ignores the bear's request for privacy and discovers his secret, he is whisked off to a place east of the sun, west of the moon, destined to marry a troll princess."

She plucked at a stray strand of her hair that had drifted to her skirts. "Yes, well... But she did save him in the end, did she not?"

Mckinnon looked at her askance before going on blandly. "East of the sun and west of the moon is essentially nowhere. The club existed nowhere, the meeting place to constantly change."

Miranda sighed and blinked up at the ceiling. "I shouldn't believe any of this." Scorn laced her voice, yet part of her whispered to listen well. "Why... why is someone killing these men?" She glanced at him. "Does he want the secret? Is he trying to torture it out of the victims?"

"And risk the same end as Archer?" Mckinnon frowned. "But there is another way—one that even the club considered, although it was ultimately deemed too horrific even for them." He shifted and watched her carefully. "There are those who believe that by imbibing a man's flesh, one absorbs the victim's power and his soul. I didn't say I believed it," he protested, catching her skeptical look. "But it is an accepted practice, performed as far back as ancient Egypt. I happen to know that Archer himself translated several hieroglyphs on the subject."

"Ridiculous." It was a strangled gasp. "Eating flesh simply makes one a cannibal. You're trying to frighten me. Immortality is a myth."

"Does it matter?" Bright blue eyes held hers. "Whether or not Archer became an immortal isn't the point. Those men believed they'd found immortality—unequivocally. Forgive me, my dear, but you have no notion how powerful an inducement belief can be for one who is desperate for a cure—" He stopped and took a deep breath. "To evade death, cure disease, whatever the motivator may be, someone out there is hacking these members up and taking their hearts—the known house of the soul. Personally, I think it is quite clear. Someone is hell-bent to gain immortality any way he can."

He leaned forward, and his warm breath caressed the curve of her cheek. "If that is the case then he really ought to leave the rest alone and dine on Archer."

Incensed, she reached out and grabbed his wrist. His skin was shockingly warm, as though fevered, yet he appeared in perfect health.

"Know this," she said in harsh tones, "if anyone should find my husband"—she swallowed past a lump of nausea—"appetizing, should one hair on Archer's head be harmed, I shall leave little more than ash of that unfortunate fellow."

To make her point, she turned her gaze to the hearth. The densely packed coals, burning a steady orange, appeared to swell, going vermilion and then white hot before exploding within the grate.

A trickle of sweat rolled along Mckinnon's brow, but he smiled. "How very protective of you." He turned toward the parlor windows where the setting sun had painted the sky purple with streaks of gold. "It appears Lord Archer has returned."

All was quiet, then the soft clips of hooves sounded on the gravel drive. Mckinnon set his eyes upon her. "Shall I stay and discuss things further?" A devilish grin pulled at his cheeks as his thumb moved to caress her wrist where they were still joined.

She released his wrist with a jerk and was composed

when the front door opened. Mckinnon, however, got to his feet with practiced insolence. And as Archer strolled into the parlor, dreadfully unaware of his presence, Mckinnon made great show of straightening his clothes.

Blood drained from Miranda's face. She knew how it must look and hated that she had put Archer in a position of vulnerability in his own home. He stopped, framed in the open doorway with his feet planted wide, his large hands curled into tight fists as his broad chest heaved.

"Ah, and the man behind the mask gives us a tantalizing peek." Mckinnon's smug barb cut through the silence, and she winced at the realization that Archer had left off his outer mask, a further humiliation in his eyes.

For a moment, simply seeing him again caused her heart to flip, then she noticed his expression. Rage, rage like nothing she'd ever seen colored his flesh, made his eyes blaze. The tip of his nose and lips stood out bone white.

"Archer..." She trailed off as his eyes flicked to her. And the rage yielded to such unmitigated hurt that her heart squeezed tight.

"Get out."

His words were a knife in her heart. But his eyes looked past her.

"Get out of my house," he said again to Mckinnon.

Mckinnon gathered his gloves and top hat from the side table. "I shall take my leave here." His eyes took on a sudden twinkle, making Miranda wonder if irritating Archer had been Mckinnon's true purpose all along.

Mckinnon caught her hand before she could move. The weight of Archer's eyes bore into her as the devil leaned over her hand and kissed it. It snapped her out of her shock, and she wrenched her hand free. "Oh, do get out!"

He laughed lightly as he sauntered by Archer, who stood

like granite in the doorway. Mckinnon paused before him, and the men stared at each other for an agonizing moment, while her blood rushed like wildfire. Archer's eyes trailed over Mckinnon, pausing at his hands as though he would like nothing better than to rip Mckinnon's gloves from his grasp and hit the man with them. Something wild gleamed in Archer's eyes for a moment before it was snuffed out, and his gaze returned to Mckinnon's face. A dead calm went over the men, and she tensed, ready to push between them, saving Archer from having to act, but Mckinnon put on his hat and slipped past.

"Good evening then," he called lightly in the hall.

The door slammed shut with a reverberating crack, and then there was silence.

"Archer." It came from her lips in a rasp.

He looked at her for one long moment, his face devoid of emotion, his eyes blazing like stars, then he turned and quietly walked away.

Archer had disappeared as if made of ether. Facing empty rooms, Miranda headed toward the stairs when Eula's voice stopped her.

"The Prince of Darkness is in the greenhouse."

Miranda paused, her hand upon the newel post. Greenhouse? In all her wanderings, she'd never happened upon a greenhouse. The housekeeper saw her confusion and snorted. "Take the back stairs to the top. You'll find it."

"Eula," Miranda fought a smile, "you're helping me? I'm touched."

"Pish." Eula stomped off, waving Miranda away as if she were an insect. "It's either that or have you run amok messing up my house."

The narrow back stairs wound up four stories, the air

growing more dense and heated as she ascended. At the top, a black door stood closed against her. Slowly, she turned the knob and pushed into a world of green and the warmth of summer.

Above her, the black hand of night was stayed by sheets of glass held together by a grid of white-painted iron. The greenhouse itself ran the length of the house, a cavernous jungle of languid ferns, fragrant orange and lemon trees, and clusters of velvety roses. Roses everywhere, a kaleidoscope of color.

Gaslights hissed in the quiet, reflected off the panes of glass. Humid air enveloped her in a rose-scented kiss as she moved forward, past an iron chaise and into the thick quiet. A scuff of a shoe brought her round a corner.

He stood before a marble-topped work counter, his capable hands busy filling a large pot with soil. Just under the graceful sweep of his jaw, his pulse beat visibly. That sign of life, the column of his neck working as he swallowed, sent a shiver along her skin.

The way he breathed, the singular angle of his head when he bent it—they were as familiar to her now as her own reflection. More so because she could not grow tired of watching him. Was this an immortal man who stood before her? It could not be. It was the stuff of legend. A cold shudder took her. And if by some mad reasoning it were true, he would leave her behind. Because she was most assuredly mortal.

She took a step toward him but stopped short at the sight of the potted rose on the counter. "Oh my." Her breath caught. It was utterly lovely, so white that it was luminescent in the dim light. Silver veining laced its petals, caressing its edges. The enormous bloom stood erect and alone in its little pot. "It's gorgeous," she said.

Archer inclined his head slightly. "You'd think differently were you a rose. Should I pot it with the others, it would take all of their nutrients. Within hours, they would wither on the vine. Wasted to give the silver rose its strength."

Miranda moved to touch it but a sudden wariness stayed her hand. "If it is so deadly to the others, why do you keep it?"

Braver than she, Archer reached out and gently touched the glinting silver edge of a petal. "Sentimentality, I suppose." Something in his voice made her heart squeeze.

"Only one bloom?" Deep-green leaves sheltered the single flower like a mantle.

"It cannot produce more than one bloom at a time. New buds compete for the light and only the strongest remains."

He said no more, but ripped open a sack of rich black soil. "What did he want?" The quietness of his query did not fool her. The trowel in his hand shook under his tight grip as he filled the bottom of a larger pot with soil. A soft snort came from his lips. "Never mind. I know."

The trowel hit the counter with a clang, and she flinched, the stays at her waist cinching tight as she waited for the imminent explosion.

It did not come. He simply stared down at the scattered soil as though trying to make sense of the mess. And a queer feeling tilted her insides, watching him retreat instead of turning to fight. Shame washed over her. Mckinnon and his blasted horror stories. She was no better than a calf-eyed fool for listening to him. Perhaps the club sought immortality. Perhaps not. But Archer was her husband. The man who protected her with his life. He did not deserve wild speculations.

"He told me about—"

"West Moon Club?" Archer's mouth curled in a bitter smile when she started in surprise. "You have my coin. You are a busybody of the first order. It doesn't take a mystic to know that you'd have discovered all you could about West Moon Club." He stabbed at a pile of soil with his trowel. "You might have asked me, instead of him."

She drew herself up. "And you are cagey and evasive at best. Am I now to believe you would have answered?"

A small, humorless laugh escaped him. "Ask me now and see."

Heart in her throat, she forced herself to speak. "McKinnon believes you were looking for the secret to immortality." It sounded ridiculous to her ears, yet he did not start in surprise. Instead, he merely glanced down at the soil, unseeing.

When he finally spoke, his voice was hollow, detached. "Immortality was not the goal, though I suppose by prolonging life, one is evading death." Carefully, he lifted the exposed ball of soil that held the rose and settled it into its new pot. "This rose you see here is our most successful endeavor."

Miranda blinked at the silver rose trembling delicately as Archer filled soil around its roots. "You expect me to believe these murders are about a rose?"

"No." A wry smile touched his mouth. "However, knowing you will march headlong into danger, do you expect me to tell you whom I think responsible?"

A breath of frustration left her. "Thus you force me to seek answers elsewhere."

Archer tensed but would not face her. "You already have, though, haven't you?" A clump of soil flew into the pot with a thud. "I hope your time with Mckinnon was worth the knowledge gained. The question is, what did you exchange for his stories?" The trowel scraped over the counter, hacking through the pile of soil. "I know that dog well enough to understand he would not give away anything for free."

"It appears you know both of us quite well," she said without thinking.

The trowel clattered to the slate floor. Archer took a bracing breath, then clenched the sides of the counter. "I've work to do, Miranda. Please go."

Slowly she went to him, conscious of her feet on the floor and the hammering of her heart. He did not move nor turn as she came up behind him, close enough to feel the tense energy that surrounded him. "You've no reason to be jealous."

His head remained bent over the pot. "Is that what I am?"

Her breath hitched, but she could not move away. She knew the feel of his body now. The hardness and the power it held when he'd pressed up against her in the alleyway. And she craved it. Her head fell forward, coming just short of touching the space between his shoulder blades. She stared at the black suitcoat before her and the gentle rise and fall of his back.

"His endeavor failed." Her pulse tattooed against her throat in a painful staccato.

He stirred, a tiny shift of movement away from her. "Not for lack of trying."

"No." She took a breath. "But as a woman, I thought it easier—quicker—to let him ask…" The be-gloved hand upon the table curled into a tight fist, and she spoke firmly. "Then send him on his way."

He grunted with indifference. Her hand hovered at his

shoulder, the need to touch him warring with caution. He tensed as though preparing to shrug off her touch, and her hand fell to her side. She closed her eyes and shifted forward so that they were closer still. Just to be near him. They stood in silence, breathing the same rhythm, slow and deep and steady. The heat of his body mingled with hers, the space between them as small as a change in breath. A quiet trembling took hold of her limbs.

"You've no reason to be jealous," she whispered again.

The soft wool of his coat brushed her lips when he turned. Gray eyes gleamed like moonstones as he stared down at her, his breath coming in sudden disjointed draws.

"Archer..."

The look in his eyes vanished at the sound of her voice, and he dipped his head as though suddenly unable to keep it up. "It is as you said," he answered quietly. "There is no reason for my jealousy. I've no claim—" The line of his jaw tightened.

A rush of feeling akin to anger, yet softer, ignited in her breast. His jutting upper lip was set hard, the fan of his dark lashes hiding his eyes.

"Don't you?" she whispered, scarcely able to speak. "For even if you don't, I certainly do."

They radiated through him slowly, her words. His eyes lifted to her, the line of his brows tilting slightly. Their gazes locked as they stood quietly studying one another, the things they'd left unsaid hanging in the air.

He took a quick breath, and his voice dropped thick and unsteady. "Miri..." His hand lifted as though he might touch her but suddenly he was stepping away, moving to the far end of the counter to make a pretense of organizing his gardening tools.

"You misunderstand me," he said with false casualness. "I simply meant that I have no right to object to your choice of callers."

Blood rushed in her ears as she stared at him. Every line of his body betrayed the lie in his words. "Why do you turn away from me?"

The corner of his mouth lifted, but there was little humor in his eyes as he blinked down at the desk. "I rather thought we've been avoiding each other."

"Yes." She took a step closer. "It's been a smashing success."

A parody of a laugh broke from his lips, but he did not reply. His fists rested on the marble as he stared off. "I only wanted to be near you," he whispered, so low she wondered if he was even speaking to her. "To live in the shadow of your light. That you would want—" His lips pulled in as he bit down on them. "I cannot think when you are near."

He was pulling away when she needed him to catch her. *She'd killed a man the other night.* He had killed. Did it haunt him, too? Did he strive every day to control his anger? Questions pounded like a pulse in her throat.

"Do you ever find yourself tired of all this secrecy?" she whispered in the thick silence.

Archer sucked in a deep breath and turned his head. It seemed that he might reach out to her. The illusion faded with the hardening of his long body. "Always," he whispered back.

He fell silent, staring at her as though he longed to say more. But he was as incapable of taking that first step as she, and he went back to his potting. The lines around his mouth deepened, and her resentment melted. Perhaps trust did not work that way. She couldn't know; she had never fully trusted another soul in her life.

Her heels clicked on the slate as she drew close. He inhaled sharply and turned to face her. Archer's lids lowered as if meeting her gaze would be his undoing. His chest heaved like a bellows as she slowly leaned forward and let the warmth of his body envelop her. The fine grain of stubble tickled her lips as she pressed a gentle kiss upon his cheek, lingering over the subtle scent of him, and his eyes closed almost as if he were pained. He swallowed audibly, his broad chest hitching as they regarded each other from across the small distance that separated them.

"If you want to be near, why deny me?" Her lips grazed his chin. "Deny yourself?"

He blinked back at her, frozen to the spot. Slowly, his gaze traveled over her before resting upon her lips, and the frozen expression on his face melted. He could not shutter the yearning that burned hotly in his eyes.

Slowly, she cupped his cheek. The air grew heavy, her chest tightening with each draw of breath. Archer closed his eyes, seeming to steel himself, and she knew he meant to pull away again. The idea of it slashed at her breast. Suddenly everything became quite simple.

Her hand slid to his neck as she closed the gap that she could no longer tolerate. Archer's eyes snapped open, and a tremble ripped through him. "Don't..." The protest died as her mouth fitted to his.

A shock of feeling coursed through her limbs at the touch. His breath caught sharply as though he too felt the shock. His body grew taut as a bow, quivering with barely held restraint. And she knew then that as much as he desired it, he feared touching her. Lifting to her toes, she angled her head and kissed him again, a slow searching kiss that parted his lips. Her teeth caught the delectable curve of his upper lip, delighting in the feel and taste of it, desire coursing through her veins like molten honey. A noise tore from Archer's throat—part whimper, part plea—and he pulled back slightly.

"It was never about denial," he said, even as his arms tightened around her waist to crush her hard against him—where she'd wanted to be all along.

"What was it, then?" she said on a breath.

"Preservation," he rasped before he kissed her deep and sure.

Like a brand to dry tinder, her insides ignited. She swayed as his lips moved over hers to learn the shape and feel of them by touch. The warm wet slide of his tongue over hers caught her like a fish on a hook, tugging sharp and sweet and deep within her belly. Her world became him. Archer. The fresh scent of his linen shirt, the tickle of his lashes against her temple. Silence thundered in her ears, tempered by soft murmurs and the rustle of clothes. His tongue sliding, searching, taking. The silk of his lapels crumpled under her fingers, her breasts shifting against the hard wall of his chest as she pulled him closer. One kiss built upon another until her mind went dark and quiet. Heat pooled in her belly, swirling and volcanic, rising up to play over her skin. She sighed and a question drifted over his kiss, causing her breath to quicken painfully.

Yes. Oh, yes. And now.

Archer replied, and the intensity of it knocked the strength from her knees. She sagged in his arms with a whimper. He swallowed it down, his kiss delving deeper. Licks of pure pleasure ran over her skin, beneath the tight confines of her heavy clothes. He muttered something coarse and possessive and fisted the loose knot of her hair. Pots rattled as he fell against the counter, taking her with him.

*   *   *

He'd lost his mind. He didn't care. He was somewhere hot and delicious. And he was surrounded by Miranda, her supple warmth, her luscious, plump mouth. He sank into the kiss, learned her flavor.

God, he was hot. His skin burned. Burned where she touched him, where her small hands caressed the expanse of his chest. His blood roared through his ears as he came at her mouth again and again. Soft, hard, he suckled the thick pillow of her bottom lip. Light kisses, then deep. Searing need took his thoughts down dark roads.

Groaning, he turned, pushed her onto the work counter and stepped between her endless legs. He wanted to taste her skin, lick his way down her long neck, over the sweet swell of her breasts. But not yet; he couldn't leave her mouth. Didn't want to. Kissing her was better than any of his imaginings. And he had imagined a lot. Her mouth was maddening, firm, soft, slick, smooth—an agony. Skirts rustled as he gathered them, bunches of silk filling his hand. He caught a flash of smooth creamy flesh. *Take her, tunnel into her tight, wet, heat.* Miranda's tongue snaked over his, and his knees almost buckled, for she was kissing him with the same desperation.

Trying to gain control, he grabbed the marble edge of the counter. His free hand would not let her go. It slid down her slim back to that tight little bottom. He wrenched her closer, and she arched into him, her hands falling back for support. Soft breasts crushed against his chest. He thrust his hips between her legs, grinding against the place where he wanted, *needed* to be. Heat washed over him. His clothes weighed him down, smothered him. Sweat bloomed over his skin, yet he shivered.

The stone beneath his hand burned. He gripped it

tighter. She suckled his upper lip, and he groaned, consumed by heat and the elusive taste of her. Good God, he was going to die. An apoplexy due to lust. Tension and pleasure coiled so tight in his gut he feared he would spill right there and then. His arm shook, his grip on the worktop painful.

A sharp crack rent the air, and Archer pitched to the side as the worktop gave out from under his arm. He stumbled back as Miranda gave a shocked cry. Even as he fell, his arm stayed locked around her, trying to protect her. Archer righted, and standing on unsteady feet, he studied Miranda.

Golden red hair tilted drunkenly from her topknot, strands falling about her shoulders, but she appeared unharmed. Her mouth was swollen and red and so bloody gorgeous he found himself leaning toward her before the fog completely lifted from his brain. Archer blinked, and he shook his head a bit to clear it. He stepped back, suddenly aware of the chunk of marble he still grasped in his right hand. Cold shock slapped his skin as he looked behind Miranda to the ruin that was his work counter. Black scorch marks flared over the white marble top, now broken into two jagged pieces.

He had bloody well torn the thing apart, had set it aflame somehow. Nausea swelled up from his gut. "Jesus Christ!"

Miranda turned and went the color of curdled cream.

"Christ," Archer said again, backing away from her. He might have killed her, crushed the life out of her in his zeal. Terror knifed through him at the thought.

Miranda gaped up at him, her expression echoing his. She swallowed hard, no doubt coming to the same horrific conclusion. His brain froze, unable to come up with a word of explanation. He needed to get out. Get away from her. Tears welled in Miri's eyes before she wrenched around, turning her back on him. His heart stuttered.

"I'm sorry," she whispered. "I have to..." She didn't finish but ran from the greenhouse as though the fires from hell were upon her.

He wanted her to go. Be safe from him. But the sight of her fleeing tore through his heart.

Chapter Twenty

———∙◦∙———

Ian Mckinnon entertained his whore for half the night.

Three floors below, in the quiet dark of Mckinnon's library, Archer pulled his watch from his pocket. Nearly two in the morning. He rolled his eyes and snapped the watch shut. It galled him to wait. In his current mood, he wanted to kill anyone lucky enough to get sexual satisfaction. Most especially McKinnon.

But surprise was key when invading Mckinnon's lair. As it was, Rossberry had slid away upon learning of Archer's interest. Now the bulk of Mckinnon's staff had disappeared overnight, either having been let go or sent on elsewhere, disbanding with the same ghostly efficiency as Rossberry's staff. Archer could ill afford to let Mckinnon slip through his fingers. Not after what he'd seen tonight—his golden ring upon the man's finger, glinting in the light. So real it was a shock to see it. It had taken all of his control not to rip it from Mckinnon's hand then and there. But Miranda would have seen and asked questions.

A loud thump and a disjointed groan came from above,

drawing Archer's gaze to the carved flower medallion upon the ceiling. If the cur didn't finish soon, he'd drag him from his bed. Archer finished his single malt with an impatient swallow. At least the man stocked a proper bar.

Laughter rang out, the whore's nasal titters tempered by Mckinnon's deep rumble. Archer suppressed an oath. Even when he'd been whole, he hadn't been able to bring himself to pay for pleasure. The pair scampered drunkenly down the last set of stairs, coming into view as they paused in the hall. Light from the flickering wall sconces fell upon the woman, and the lingering taste of peaty scotch turned sour in Archer's mouth. Ginger-haired, green-eyed, and uncommonly tall, she possessed nauseatingly obvious qualifications for Mckinnon's selection. Her fine clothes and good skin marked her as quality goods. Archer repressed a snort. One might as well try to pass off chalk-water for cream.

Archer waited in silence while Mckinnon paid his doxy and sent her on her way with a loud slap to her rump. Humming a satisfied tune, he sauntered into the library moments later, headed for the drinks table.

"A rather pathetic imitation for the real thing," Archer said, shattering the peaceful silence.

Mckinnon started, his fine slippers scuffing on the parquet. A low growl sounded in his throat as he whipped around, puzzlement over how he had missed an intruder knitting his brows.

Yellow flashed in Mckinnon's blue eyes as Archer lit the lamp.

"Even for you, Mckinnon."

Realization came quickly to Mckinnon. "Of course," he said lightly. "You smell like nothing." He straightened his dressing gown and helped himself to a tumbler of scotch. His throat bobbed against his open collar as he swallowed it down in one gulp. The glass landed hard upon the wood. The smoky lamplight cast shadows over Mckinnon's lean features as he glanced at Archer. "Well, perhaps like frozen death."

Archer smiled blandly. "And you smell like wet fur."

Mckinnon laughed. "Aye, well." His eyes gleamed in the dull lamplight. "You haven't come for my irresistible charms, I see. Then what? Eavesdropping give you a cheap thrill? I'd have to guess you're still repressed by that juvenile fear of bedding whores."

"Is that what you call it?" Archer flashed his teeth. "Here I thought it was an aversion to paying someone to want me. I'll get my pleasure for free, thanks."

Mckinnon grinned. "But are you? I suspect your presence here rather screams your fear of where your wife's affections lie."

Archer smoothed a wrinkle in his trousers, his hand shaking but a little. He was fairly certain where her affections lay. The thought of it coursed hot through his blood.

The man's keen eyes took in what was certainly smugness dwelling on Archer's lips, and he snorted in disgust. "I may be sick."

"I'd mind your shoes, then."

Mckinnon displayed a set of sharp canines in a parody of a smile. "Are you going to tell her you're responsible for this? For all of them?"

Archer's hands settled comfortably in his lap. "For Rossberry too, I suppose."

A low growl, little more than a rumble, came from Mckinnon's throat.

Archer forced a laugh he did not feel. "My, but you are an impressionable pup. More so than my wife."

Mckinnon's silky voice drifted across the dark. "But she's thinking about things now?" His eyes crinkled in mirth. "Isn't she?"

Archer simply stared, his heart thundering in his ears, the urge to crack Mckinnon's spine making his fists clench.

Mckinnon's smile faltered, but he straightened with bravado. Glass clinked as he fiddled with the crystal stopper on a decanter. "Why are you here then?"

Feeding on Mckinnon's disquiet, Archer regarded him for a minute more and then spoke. "The ring."

A dark brow quirked as Mckinnon glanced down at his hand and the slash of gold upon it. "Foolish to take my gloves off, wasn't it?" He flashed his teeth. "I'd become too comfortable, I suppose."

Confident or not, base jealousy pushed through Archer's insides. Mckinnon's smile grew. He poured himself another drink. The faint movement brought the musky tang of sex into the air. Archer breathed through his mouth and waited.

"You know," said Mckinnon finally, "I don't believe I shall part with the ring. It was a gift from my father, you see. And it holds such fond memories of seeing you suffer, and all that."

It wouldn't take much to snap the mutt's neck.

Unaware of the danger, Mckinnon turned and leaned a hip upon the console. "I am, however, willing to consider a trade. A dip in your wife's luscious—"

Mckinnon flew across the room, the blow from Archer's fist slamming him into the wall, in a spray of plaster and flopping limbs. A painting of the Thames teetered on the wall above him as he fell in a heap on the floor. Mckinnon sucked in a ragged breath and then launched upward.

The impact caught Archer around the middle as Mckinnon tackled him. They fell back with a thud, sliding across the floor to crash into a writing desk. Wood splintered, paper fell like leaves about them. Archer felt the sharp prick of a broken table leg against his back and then he spun, throwing Mckinnon off him in one move. The man tumbled several feet then leapt up, just as Archer did.

"You're stronger now," Mckinnon observed with a breathless laugh. Archer rather had the same thought about Mckinnon but kept it to himself. Blood colored Mckinnon's teeth red as he snarled and came at Archer again.

Archer slid past, catching Mckinnon's outstretched arm. He swung the man around and tossed him like a rag into the far wall. Mckinnon collided with a curio cabinet in an explosion of glass.

"Faster too," retorted Archer as shards of glass pinged upon the floor. He straightened his lapels, and when Mckinnon rushed him, he swung low, catching the man in the gut. Mckinnon roared and whirled round, his fist connecting with surprising force to Archer's temple. Archer saw stars. He blinked them back and lashed out, hearing the satisfying crunch of bone as his fist sunk into Mckinnon's face.

Mckinnon fell like a broken mainmast. Archer pressed his foot into his neck to keep him from rising. "I think you've had enough, young pup."

Mckinnon's eyes narrowed to blue slits. "Bastard." He spat, blood gushing from his skewed nose and split lip. "If the moon was brighter..."

Archer pressed down. "Unfortunately for you, it isn't."

Mckinnon flailed against him. His blows upon Archer's legs grew weak and ineffective. When he took on a bluish hue and blood began to bubble from his nose like froth, Archer eased his step a fraction.

"Now," Archer said, bending over the snarling, coughing man, "you've begun to bore me." He reached down and yanked the ring from Mckinnon's finger, far more cruelly than necessary, then stepped away.

Mckinnon wheezed and rubbed his neck tenderly. "Ye bloody frozen bastard." He hauled himself to sitting and spat a large glob of something foul upon the floor, but made no move to get up. He knew better than to challenge Archer now. "Ye best start runnin' now. The moment that moon waxes..."

"Yes, I've heard it all before." Archer strolled toward the door, stepping lightly over broken bits of a chair. "From your *father*."

"Cocksucker."

Archer stopped and glanced at him. Already the blood was easing its flow from Mckinnon's nose, the puffed flesh about the man's face regaining its natural color.

"Careful," Archer said. "You wouldn't want that to heal before you reset it."

Mckinnon let lose a volley of curses as he set his nose straight with nary a flinch. Archer laughed lightly but his humor faded as he clutched the ring in his palm. "Stay away from her, Ian."

He was almost through the door when Mckinnon's call stopped him.

"Benjamin."

He did not turn, but waited.

"Why did you bring her into this nightmare?"

Guilt slashed at Archer, unexpected and raw. He closed his eyes for a brief moment. "Asks the man who'd take her from me if he could."

Mckinnon made a bleak sound. "I suppose I understand you better than I thought."

Archer's head suddenly felt too heavy to hold up. "Then we've come full circle, you and I."

"Aye, and yet damn if ye aren't making the same fool mistakes ye've witnessed in me," Mckinnon retorted sharply, the misery in his voice bringing forth the Scottish accent he tried so hard to eradicate. "If ye have any love for her, show her what you are before it's too late for her to flee."

Chapter Twenty-one

———❧❧———

Archer did not allow himself a moment's rest until he was locked in his library. Curtains drawn, the lamp turned up high, he hunkered down at his desk and forced his hand to uncurl. The golden ring against his black palm was real enough; still he drew a deep breath and studied it to convince himself it was truly in his grasp.

Yes, it was. He picked the ring up and felt a pang deep in his breast. The familiarity of it. Some nicks were new but others he remembered well. Even the weight felt like home. Three quarters of an inch wide, the golden ring had a stylized engraving of the sun merging with the moon at it center.

Archer smiled and ran the tip of his finger over the engraving. His mother had given it to him on the day he'd left for Cambridge. A sun for her son. He had always been her *sun*, the child born as the rays of the setting sun passed over her bed. And Elizabeth, her moon, born a full hour after Archer as the moon appeared in the darkening sky. As children, he and Elizabeth had often curled up in her lap, listening with rapt attention to the story of their birth. Mama had been proud of delivering such strong, healthy twins.

His smile wavered thinking of them, and the pang in his chest intensified. Too long parted from this ring. He thought of Elizabeth's ring, *la luna*. Mama had given her the moon, a glorious moonstone ring that Elizabeth had cherished.

"Keep it safe for me," she had said with her dying breath, using what little strength she had to pull it off her finger and force it into his hand. He had cried then, desperate sobs that he ought to have held in for her sake but couldn't. The one and only time he remembered crying as a man. He'd begged Elizabeth to keep it on, if only to give her strength. But she'd been adamant. "I'm at peace with death. Don't let this ring follow me to the grave, *fratello*."

It had been his most precious possession from then on. And now it rested safely on Miri's slim finger. To see it on Miri often made him smile. Archer pulled himself out of his sentimental reverie with a deep breath. There were more important matters at hand.

Archer remembered well the day he had pressed the ring into Daoud's hand as they stood on the docks at Cairo, the scent of spices mixed with the dankness of the Nile still sharp in his memory. "Send word through this," he'd told his steward and the one man he trusted with his life. "You know how it works?"

Daoud's black eyes had been deadly serious as he nodded. "You may count on me, my lord."

There had been little time then. Archer's past had caught up with him once again. He dared not stay in Cairo a moment longer, lest all his work be discovered. And they'd been so close to finding a cure. Daoud had been the clear choice to stay behind; his knowledge of ancient languages was beyond even Archer's.

Daoud had embraced him, kissing both cheeks with solemn dignity. "Go with God, my lord."

"And you."

His friend's lonely figure, lined silver in the moonlight, had faded into the darkness as Archer sailed away.

Weeks later, Archer had received word; Daoud had been found at the foot of the Great Pyramid—killed by thieves, the magistrate had said. But by then, the man's final message was already in Archer's hand: *"Have care, my lord. I fear someone does not want this uncovered."*

Archer knew then that Daoud had been aware his life would soon be over.

The knowledge that he'd led death to his good friend brought bitterness to his mouth. But now he would finally know if Daoud had been successful.

Breath stilled with anticipation, Archer pushed his pinky nail deep into the crescent moon and, hearing a familiar click, turned his finger counterclockwise. The hidden mechanism moved, and the ring slid apart, revealing an inner compartment that Archer had installed. Archer's breath caught sharply. A small length of paper was wrapped around the inner ring. No, not paper but cloth, two thin rectangles of cloth inscribed with blood, he realized, as he gently eased the tightly rolled package open and held one, then the other, carefully beneath the lamplight.

Archer could only marvel at Daoud's skill as his eyes traveled over the tiny print, so neat and clear. It was in code but easily read since Archer knew the cipher. The weight on his shoulders did not lift as expected but crushed him as he read. He drew an unsteady breath, the cloth before his eyes blurring. He blinked hard. No cure, but a solution—if one could call it that. Mckinnon had been correct. No cure. Only despair. In all these years, he never thought the cure would be his own destruction. Christ, he had been so certain.

His chest ached. He longed to put his head to his desk and give in to self-pity. Ruthlessly, he pushed away the image of Miri. Not now. He'd never make it through the night if he thought of her. His lips pursed tight as he read the missive once again.

"Hidden away in Cavern Hall all these years," he muttered. The irony was not lost on Archer. The scene of his downfall was the last place he would have looked for the answer.

The edges of the ring cut into his palm. He had thought his curse derived from ancient Egyptian magic but it appeared he was wrong. Druids. Archer knew nothing of their myths or ways. To his knowledge only one man did, and he was damned put out at the idea of approaching him. He could not stomach pulling another into danger, yet he had to be sure it would work. Then catch the monster before it struck again.

Two men stood over the body, one tall and thin, his fair hair like old hay in the pale morning light. The other was thicker, shorter, his shock of red hair too bright to be cowed by dreary atmosphere. Their voices floated in the mists, mingling with the lapping of water and the low gong of a distant buoy. Quite easy for the killer to hear them from behind the pile of abandoned crates at the edge of the pier. Normally, staying behind to observe the aftermath of a kill held no interest. But as the body had been found so quickly, watching the police arrive at the wrong conclusions was as good an amusement as any.

"A foul business, this," said the ginger lad. Carefully, he wrapped the gold coin he had collected from the victim in a cloth and pocketed it.

The blond man nodded absently, his attention on the dead man's head, where twin holes marked the absence of ears. It had been a pleasure to divest Lord Merryweather of them, the killer thought. "And getting fouler by the day."

Ginger adjusted his brown cap, angling it against the weak sunlight. "You realize this here is Lord Archer's property." He inclined his head toward the warehouse behind them before squinting at the taller man. "You still question whether the bastard is guilty?"

"Careful, Sheridan." The blond knelt down beside the body to study it. "You are speaking of my brother-in-law. And a peer of the realm."

"Thousand pardons, Inspector, but let's be reasonable, eh? Every victim we find is connected to Archer in some way. Witnesses have seen a masked man lurking about at odd hours. They say—they're saying he's the devil in disguise." The young man quickly crossed himself.

"Hysteria," said the inspector. "We've got claims of Lord Archer appearing in five different places. Simultaneously. Young Jack trailed him to Lord Mckinnon's home last night, then straight home, no detours. We must step carefully and not succumb to hearsay or fairy tales." He glanced up at Sheridan. "Now, let us return to the facts before us. What do you see? What is the pattern?"

"A bloody mess." Sheridan coughed hastily. "All right. Heart taken each time, the sick bastard. This one's missing his ears. Cheltenham lost his tongue—bloody gruesome—and Sir Percival his eyes."

The inspector rubbed the end of his mustache with his thumb. "See no evil, speak no evil, hear no evil."

"Portentous devil, our killer."

"Hmm..."

Portentous devil, how very amusing. So, the inspector liked to think there was a pattern, did he? Really it didn't matter what those old fools had seen, heard, or spoken. They simply had to be punished; they had shunned Archer, forced him to withdraw. And he had disappeared for too long. Now that he was back, he would suffer before he was destroyed. Killing his friends, and making London society believe Archer was responsible, was too much fun to resist. The only problem remaining was the woman. *She* had brought him back to London, and so she would live. For now. That didn't mean one couldn't toy with her a bit first.

Chapter Twenty-two

—❦—

Everybody lies. Miranda stood before the dressing room mirror, waiting in dull silence as a maid hooked up her party dress for the Blackwoods' masquerade ball. She blinked at her wavering reflection.

Victoria's warning had come back to haunt Miranda. Without doubt, Archer kept things from her. He still was. Lying. But then, so was she.

The maid's small form blocked the mirror as she gently smoothed Miranda's bodice, then turned to collect white satin gloves and a fan. Miranda's reflection returned, the lamplight above her catching red glints in her hair, giving it the appearance of live coals. The image of fire and destruction burned bright in her mind's eye. She had scorched that marble worktop, and it had broken in half like a piece of burned toast.

There were lies, and there were lies. Was a secret a lie? If one wanted to protect another?

She could not fault Archer for his protectiveness. The killer's frustrated rage was growing; he would strike again, and soon. Miranda felt it on some level of intuition she could not fully understand. Archer would try to protect her, wrap her up in ignorance like cotton wool. But who would protect him? Miranda could, and she would. If she had to call upon the fire she would, exposure be damned.

She glided down the stairs to meet Archer. She held tighter to the banister as he came into view, his feet planted slightly apart as he stood in the center of the hall, his eyes on her. He looked like a highwayman, standing there with his silken mask and long black opera cloak, a scarlet vest the only slash of color in his inky attire.

Yes, there were lies. But there was also truth. The truth of feeling. Deep down, she knew this man. Archer. Beyond the mask. She knew his soul, his heart. Perhaps that was enough.

"That does not look much like a costume," he observed as she came near.

She might have said a number of things, demand they talk, or spill her soul. She simply held up her mask. "That is because I have not finished putting it on."

Archer snorted softly. "And who shall you be once you don your grand disguise?" Calling it a disguise was to use the term in its weakest form. The small, silver lace mask, shaped like a butterfly and set with crystal beads, concealed only the area about her eyes.

"La luna," she said with a smile.

"Then I shall be *la notte* to your moon." Archer lifted the hard black mask he held and slipped it over his thinner silk one. Donning the full mask changed his identity from the man who smiled at her with ease to the unyielding face of Lord Archer. It was several moments before she realized she stared at him.

He took a step closer, his lovely mouth and sculpted jaw hidden away once more. "Which is really only lip service since everyone shall know I haven't a costume."

"Nonsense," she replied a bit thickly, for he was very near. "It will be the first party in which no one gapes at you like a mindless fish. And I, for one, am glad of it."

A smile came to his eyes. "You are very protective of my feelings, Lady Archer. It is sweet."

Heat flared on her cheeks. "La," she said, fumbling to put her mask on. "I simply find ignorance intolerable. Stare the first time, fine, but the second, or th—"

Archer lifted his hands to her face. And it was she who gaped like a fish as he gently took the mask and eased it into place. "How strange you look hidden beneath that mask."

It occurred to her that he might have just then understood her frustration a bit better. But she didn't press him.

"I missed you, Miranda Fair," he said with sudden tenderness.

"Archer." When he went still, she forced herself to say the words. But they were not the right words. "I apologize for the other night, for leaving you the way that I did, I mean." She would not blush, not think of his mouth, his taste.

Gently, he pulled away. "The fault is mine. It . . . it is for the best, I think."

A dull weight settled in her belly at his softly spoken words but she forced herself to nod. He wanted the distance, and so she would give it to him. "Pax, then?" she said.

The corners of his eyes crinkled. "Pax."

His hand on her elbow stopped her walking on. "Whatever may come, Miri . . ." He stepped closer, his grip tightening, "Whatever mistakes I make, you are the most important person in the world to me."

The words ought to have warmed her heart. Instead, she felt like crying.

There were so many black masks, dominos, and cloaked men that Archer fit right in for once. Still, she could not persuade the real Archer to dance.

"I do not dance, Miranda," Archer said when she pleaded once more.

"I don't believe you." Irritation burned in her breast. Marie Antoinette and King Louis twirled past in a rousing polka. "You move better than that when fighting, blast it."

Archer's eyes cut to her. "Then perhaps I should have brought swords. Still fence, do you?"

Her foot stamped from frustration but she held herself still. "Beast," she hissed.

She could feel his evil smile. Miranda bit back her own smile. Perhaps it was perverse, but sparring with Archer was better fun than a full-crush ball. She wondered suddenly if he felt the same.

He put one big hand upon her back as if to pacify her. "Let me get you some champagne, and then you can tell me what mask is your favorite." Mirth sparked in his eyes. "Perhaps I can buy one for my own."

Miranda refrained from rolling her eyes. *Cheeky bastard.*

She might have been comfortably abed. That they were here to socialize was laughable. Archer had obstinately put down his name on all the slots of her dance card, a socially unforgivable tactic but effective in keeping her by his side.

Archer stalked off to get the champagne and had barely left her sight when Lord Mckinnon glided up to claim the first waltz with a mischievous smile, knowing Miranda could do little more than accept.

"And what are you supposed to be?" she asked as they began to dance. "A wolf?" Mckinnon wore a half-mask shaped like that of a wolf, but his uncommon blue eyes and feral grin slanting beneath the pointed snout had given his identity away immediately.

A grin pulled in his dimple. "A werewolf." He dipped his head near to hers. "A far more terrifying being, I should think. And you, Lady Archer?" he prompted when she did not reply. "What is this enchanting costume to represent?"

She turned her head slightly, moving her mouth away from the close proximity of his. His breath smelled of meat. Like the bloody prime rib Father favored.

"La luna," she said.

He chuckled deep within his chest, the effect of which sounded oddly like a growl. "No wonder I am enthralled."

"How very predictable a retort," she said blandly. His hand upon her waist felt uncommonly warm and too possessive. When she edged away, Lord Mckinnon smiled and adjusted his grip, bringing her subtly back.

"I'm here to warn you," he said during a turn, "my father means to ruin your husband."

He glanced toward the corner of the room, where his father stood glowering at them with an ill-concealed irritation that made his scarred face appear twisted as a tree's roots. Caught by their gaze, Rossberry turned abruptly and stalked off.

Mckinnon leaned in. "You realize, he believes Lord Archer somehow responsible for the explosion that scarred him." The look in Mckinnon's eyes said he felt the same.

"Quite the stunning turnaround in your concerns, sir. One might think you actually cared for Archer's safety. But then, we know that is not true."

Mckinnon's lips twitched. "If it were simply Archer's neck, I should not care in the least. His recklessness is his own doing. But I fear you might be hurt in the crossfire." Behind the brown mask, his blue eyes grew serious. "You care for Archer, that is clear."

Woodenly, she nodded.

"Then listen to what I am saying, and hang my motives. I thought I had convinced Da to return to Scotland and let sleeping dogs lie, but he maintains a single-minded determination." They spun past less graceful dancers. "My father is not well. He possesses a volatile nature."

She slowed. "Are you suggesting that he would resort to violence?"

Lord Rossberry was an elderly gentleman but he was of the height and build of the villain. And she could not discount anyone. Had Mckinnon known the truth all along and now suffered some delayed conscience?

"I am saying that the clan Ranulf has a long history of eradicating those they view as threats."

Ice slid down her spine. She stepped out of his embrace as the last notes faded. "Then perhaps you should warn my husband."

Something flashed in his eyes—reluctance, hesitation— she couldn't be sure. He pushed it away with a forced, flirtatious smile. "I prefer dancing with you."

"The dance is over." She turned, leaving him standing in the middle of the dance floor as she collided with Marie Antoinette.

Silver eyes flashed behind a lace mask. "A thousand pardons."

The scent of lemons and flowers touched Miranda's noise so faint that she might have dreamt it. She gave a start. Victoria? The woman slid through the crowd. Miranda tried to follow, only to be swept into the fold. The Blackwoods must have invited every family of quality in London. A miasma of smoke coming from the gas lamps and candles thickened the air, the laughter buzzing around her causing her head to spin. She could not tell which way was which, surrounded as she was by leering masks and deceased persons of notoriety. She was headed toward the rear of the main hall when a hand grabbed her arm and whirled her around like a top. Her shoulder hit the wall as the twisted veneer of Lord Alasdair Rossberry loomed before her.

She stared down at the hand that held her, then up to his face, still unable to believe he'd physically accosted her.

"Lord Rossberry! What is the meaning—"

He wrenched her arm hard and slammed her into the nearby wall with enough force to rattle her bones and send a large section of her hair tumbling down. "What did my son say to you?"

Her senses settled, and she pulled up straight. "Take your hand off me, sir, or lose it."

Old though he may be, the man was strong as an ox and would not let go. He yanked her closer. Blue eyes blazed from reddened slits of skin. "Heartless wench, bewitching hapless men with your wicked beauty. You'll no' snare young Ian as well."

She tore free, most likely bruising herself in the process. "Have care, sir." The terrible burning within her pushed to get out. "We are in a room full of observers, and I should not like to think of what would occur should Lord Archer see you manhandling me."

"Oh, I can well guess, ye besom. Why not find out now?" He made to grab her again but stopped as the air between them flared hot like the blast from a bake oven. Rossberry felt the change and stepped back a pace, a shadow of fear clouding his eyes.

"I would not advise it," she said in even tones that she did not feel.

They stood silently taking each other's measure, when a soft voice caught her attention.

"Lady Archer?" Lady Blackwood, dressed as a regal Queen Elizabeth, glided up to them, concern marring her smooth brow.

Rossberry flinched as though yanked from a trance.

"Is everything all right?" A touch of warning deepened Lady Blackwood's soft voice as she looked pointedly at the elderly earl.

Rossberry's twisted lips were wet and trembling as if he might start shouting. Finally, he snarled in irritation and stepped back.

"You are a fool to cast your lot with that man," he hissed, pointing a clawed finger at Miranda. "And now you'll pay for it, just like the others have." Spinning around, he stalked off, leaving her alone with an equally stunned Lady Blackwood.

"I must apologize for my uncle," she said with a flush. "He is a cantankerous, paranoid man. Though quite kind to his kin."

"Your uncle?" The serene woman before her seemed a world apart from Rossberry.

Her lips lifted wryly. "Great uncle, actually. He gave my husband and me this house as a wedding gift."

"How generous." What more could she say? That he should be in Bedlam seemed indelicate.

Lady Blackwood shook her head slowly, rustling the large Elizabethan-style ruff around her slender throat. "I fear he has been holed up in the wilds of Scotland for too long." Lady Blackwood's small hand touched Miranda's elbow. "Really, he is quite harmless."

To whom, Miranda wanted to ask, but held her tongue. Lady Blackwood's blue eyes were wide and pleading for understanding.

"It is quite all right," Miranda said. "There is a mad aunt lurking in my family closet. We let her out, of course. But only at Christmastime."

They both smiled. The pained smile of repressing ugliness for the sake of propriety.

"I shall think no more of it," Miranda said with false lightness. "Nor shall I mention it to Lord Archer."

Lady Blackwood eased visibly, but then eyed Miranda's hair. "Oh, dear. Your coiffure has fallen." Her cheeks pinked. "I really do apologize for the incident. Let me have a maid see to your hair. Shall I escort you to the lady's retiring room?"

Miranda hesitated. The unruly state of her hair would surely cause gossip and speculation as a lady's hair did not come undone without a struggle. While she'd like to think the catty gossips wouldn't assume Archer was the brute who accosted her, Miranda knew that's exactly the conclusion they would settle on.

"It is an easy fix, Lady Blackwood," Miranda said. "One that I can see to myself. If there is a room I could use to freshen up, I would be most grateful."

Thankfully, Lady Blackwood seemed to understand the implications of Miranda's dishevelment as well. Further, Miranda did not think the lady wanted it to get out that her mad uncle had accosted a guest. "At the top of the stairs there is a small guest room," Lady Blackwood said. "Feel free to use it for as long as you wish."

As Miranda climbed the stairs to the guest room, she resolved to push the incident with Rossberry out of her mind. Unfortunately, it did not stop her from feeling like the fox in the wood.

Miranda had called him something foul when he'd left. An expletive so low and quick, Archer wondered if she was aware that it had escaped her lips. The word was quite apropos—he felt more like one at this moment than she would ever know. Normally, he enjoyed sparring with her, waiting to see what she'd throw back at him. But he could see that he'd disappointed her with his rejection. In truth, he had wanted to dance with her, badly. But feared if he'd taken her in his arms, he'd never let her go. He had to smile at her foul little mouth, however. It made her all the more delectable. Perhaps it was the Italian in him but every "damn" that sprung from her plump lips, every "bloody hell" uttered with her smoke-and-honey voice sent a lick of fire over his cock. Every time.

The polka moved into a waltz as he wove through the crowd while trying to keep from spilling the glass of champagne he held. It was too hot in this crush of people. His mask itched; sweat trickled down the side of his face with no hope of wiping it away. Each day it felt more like a prison. It was becoming harder to keep the world out altogether. Because of her. *Miranda.*

Archer's head jerked up with a snap. That voice. He knew that voice. His chest tightened so quickly the breath left him. He sought the voice out over the buzzing of laughter and music.

"Miranda . . ."

Archer's vision clouded with a red haze. The tightness in his chest turned to pain. *God damned bloody hell*. His knees buckled as rage flooded through him. The glass fell to the floor and splintered into a thousand shards. He was halfway to the stairs before he realized he'd taken a step.

Someone cried out as he shoved a hapless man out of his way. He quickened his pace. Miranda's perfume lingered in the stairwell from when she'd ascended it earlier. Archer heard that foul laugh, deepened now to a low chuckle, and then the sound of Miranda's voice calling out. Archer convulsed. Miranda was up there, meant to hear just as he had been. She was up there, walking into that thing's trap. Fear for Miri nearly crippled him for one awful moment, then he raced up the stairs.

Chapter Twenty-three

———❧❦❧———

With her hair properly pinned, Miranda emerged from the guest room feeling refreshed and more than a little foolish for letting Rossberry get the better of her. Her confidence faded, however, as she faced the gloomy darkness of the hall and realized that all of the lights had been snuffed out.

"Miranda."

Startled, Miranda braced a hand against the wall. The voice had no direction, only intent.

"Miranda."

"Hello?" she called.

No one responded. Logic cried out to run. But she could not. And when the door at the end of the hall creaked slowly open, she could only stare, the panting of her breath like thunder in the resounding silence.

Icy drafts of night air flowed over her heated cheeks as the door swayed back and forth. Only the wind. The French windows fronting the drive were open, the white lace curtains floating and swirling. Blue moonlight ghosted over the parquet toward the rug. She wrenched off her mask and moved forward as though entranced. Something was waiting for her.

She was going to scream. She felt it rise in her throat, trapped only by the fear that tightened all her muscles. Miranda took a step closer. And suddenly a presence was rushing up behind her. Intent upon claiming her.

She turned in mindless terror, colliding bodily with something large and dark. The thing caught her by the arms, and her scream broke free. She lashed out only to be drawn against it.

Her body knew him before her mind did. *Archer.* Her hands clawed at his lapels as Archer's arms wrapped around her.

"Archer." When she could breathe, she gave his chest an unsteady thump with her fist. "Good Lord, you gave me a fright." But when she tried to pull away, he held her tight, his big hand cupping the back of her head.

"I apologize," he said. It was then she felt the rapid tattoo of his heart against her cheek. "I thought I heard…" He eased back to glance at her, but his body stayed tense, alert to any threat. "Something here is amiss. I can feel it."

She glanced at the open door, and a chill crawled down her spine. "I do, too," she whispered.

"We are leaving," Archer said. "Now." He did not give her a chance to protest but tugged her down the stairs. Miranda was more than willing to go. With each step, she felt the burn of unseen eyes upon her back.

He took her down the back door and out the service entrance. Their four-in-hand landau waited in the drive with the hood up, the dark bays gleaming blue in the bright moonlight. Archer offered her a hand up to the coach. A sable rug and hot water bottle lay in wait upon the seat, and she tucked herself in, glad for the warmth. Archer was just about to follow when a loud crash echoed through the courtyard. They jumped, but a nearby footman was quickest to recover.

"That would be Henrietta," the footman said with a glance at a small woman bent over a fallen crate of glasses near the kitchen door. "One of the maids. She's a bit soft in the head."

Muffled sobs reached Miranda's ears as the poor woman tried to adjust her heavy load.

Archer jumped down from the coach step. "I'll be just a moment."

The footman, caught in the position of looking less than chivalrous, followed at a reluctant pace. Miranda watched Archer go, soaking in the prowling way he walked.

The violent crack of a whip and a shrill shout from above made her jump. The coach lurched forward, throwing her back in the seat as the frightened horses took off. She fumbled to right herself, dimly hearing Archer shout her name, but another, far worse sound from the driver's seat cut his cry short—the cackle of the same fiend who had tried to kill her at the museum.

Her fingers turned to ice but a spark of familiar heat ignited in her belly. *I'll kill him*, she thought with clarity. *Char his bones for what he did to poor Cheltenham.* But she couldn't bloody do it while in the coach.

"Miranda!"

She turned to the back window. Archer raced down the drive after her. Hopeless, the strength of four strong bays nearing full gallop pulled the coach farther out of reach. He flung off his outer mask and did not abate. Her hopelessness turned to astonishment as she watched him surge forward, his long stride moving at speeds no man ought to possess. Archer gained. Closer. The fiendish coach-man lashed his whip, urging the horses on, and the coach pulled ahead.

Archer's speed increased and, in a magnificent bound, he landed on the running board with a thud that rocked the coach. Archer jumped onto the roof and threw himself upon the fiend with a grunt. The hard leather coach top dented beneath them.

Unmanned, the coach lurched dangerously, and Miranda fell to the floor. The sight of a large black object falling by her window drew her to the back window as Archer and the villain hit the hard gravel road and tumbled head over heels to land in a twisted heap upon the ground.

"Archer!" The coach hit a rut, and she fell back. "Bloody hell!"

The terrified horses did not break stride but seemed to gain purchase. There was only one avenue of escape, and she was not about to attempt it in a gown. Tossing about like a cork in a sea, she tore at her skirts until free. How far she'd traveled she could not tell but a clear memory of a narrow bridge and winding forest road prickled her skin. She had to be nearing those pitfalls, and a speeding coach would not make it through.

The latch to the hood lay overhead. She fell once, then twice trying to reach it. The ride grew rougher, the lamps swaying recklessly. Placing her feet on either side of the seats, she leapt upward and knocked the latch open. The front half of the hood fell down with a crash.

The cutting wind brought tears to her eyes, the clatter-ing of the coach and pounding of hooves near deafening. Blinking fiercely, she concentrated on the four bobbing heads of the horses, blue black in the moonlight. In dismay, she saw the long reins dragging along the ground. She could never reach them.

Ahead a dark shadow cut across the moonlit road. The crick in her neck remembered that particular ditch well when they'd gone over it on the ride to the party. *Too deep a rut.*

The coach careened toward it, and she dove back into the cab, hitting her knees and head hard as she landed upon the floor. In the same instant, the coach crashed over the ditch with the deafening sound of squealing horses. She braced her feet and hands as the coach spun sideways, slowing down, then gaining momentum as it began to tip to the side.

From outside herself, she heard her screams, felt her body lift into the air. Wind rushed over her. By sheer will, she curled inward and hit the ground with such tumbling speed that the world blurred, the sound of breaking wood and shattering glass a roar. The weight of the tumbling carriage bore down on her, and then everything went black.

Archer's head hit the ground with a meaty thunk. Stars lit behind his lids as he rolled, his limbs tangling with another's, dirt spraying his eyes. For a moment, he lost all thought of who or what he was. Then he swung blindly, knowing that his opponent would soon do the same. His fist connected with a jaw harder than bedrock. Pain vibrated down his arm. He swung again and missed. A faint cry echoed down the road. Archer scrambled to his feet. *Miri!* Miri on the coach.

A hand clamped like a manacle over his ankle. Archer spun through the air, whipped around by the unholy force upon his leg, the light of the moon a blur before he hit the hard earth. A knee crushed into his elbow. He wrenched to the side, and another knee followed, trapping him in the dirt. He roared, bucking up, but the body sitting upon him pinned him down as easily as if he were a child.

"You're quick. But not as quick as I."

Like lightning, the hand struck, catching Archer across the left temple. Brilliant white exploded before his eyes and then the faint outline of a black mask appeared, hovering above him. From far off came the sound of wood splintering and horses squealing. Archer's heart stopped, terror strangling him. *Miri*. A roar died in his throat as a cold length of steel pressed against his jugular.

"Want to save her, do you?" Again the laugh. Softer this time. The edge of the knife pricked Archer's skin. "I have all the time in the world. You, unfortunately, do not." The masked face above his tilted, catching the blue rays of moonlight gleaming down. "We have played enough games. Time to decide."

The knife snagged over his cravat and down his thin linen shirt, burning a trail to his heart. Sweat tickled his brow as the needle-sharp point stopped at the place where his heart thumped against his chest. "Your heart or hers." The eyes behind the mask flashed. "If hers is still beating after tonight, that is."

Archer's fingers twitched, his heels digging uselessly into the earth. Crushed beneath the coach? Despite the knife, he bucked again, felt the sting on his chest. The knees upon his arms pushed down harder. Red rage blinded him. "Do it, then." His teeth ground into each other. "Take mine, and let us end this now."

Laughter rang out. "So you'd rather die than save her?"

He blanched and the laughter turned chilling. "I didn't think you would. And let me assure you, if you deny me, I will cut her into very small pieces when you are gone."

Suddenly the knife was gone. Icy breath touched Archer's nose as the masked face drew near. "The new moon and the winter solstice occur on the same night this year. Four days from now. Change under such powerful forces will make that romantic heart of yours incalculably strong. So I'll grant you a reprieve." Teeth flashed in the night. "To show how caring I can be, I give you until then. If you do not comply…"—a hand lashed out, smacking Archer lightly, highlighting his feebleness—"not only will I cut out her heart and eyes, I will keep her alive as I do it."

Archer thrust his head forward, ready to smash the vile thing's nose in, doing whatever it took to kill it. He met with air, lurched up into nothingness. Laughter echoed in the void, and then he was alone, sitting like a child on the dark road.

Chapter Twenty-four

———— ❧ ❧ ————

Darkness. Quiet. Miranda reveled in it for a moment, breathing hard, holding the earth as though an anchor. Dirt crumbled beneath her fingers, and dead winter grass prickled her nose. She sneezed and the back of her head slammed into something hard. The carriage was on top of her, she realized with a start of terror. She flopped about, desperate to be free of her prison. It would not budge. Her chest squeezed painfully, her throat closing. *Breathe!* She took a slow breath, and another.

Tentatively, she wriggled her toes, fingers...all working. Everything ached, but there were no sharp pains that she could detect. Other than the horrible pounding in her head and a slight throbbing on her elbows and knees, she felt perfectly fine.

She had room, not much of it, but enough. No sound of horses. Which was all fine save there was no one around for miles, and she was assuredly out of sight of the main road. The image of bugs and vermin crawling in to taste her flesh loomed high in her mind, and she started violently. Then the ominous sound of strained timber creaked overhead. She froze, the pounding of her heart filling her ears, when another sound broke through the muffled silence of her tomb—a man shouting. She pressed an ear toward the carriage body. Another desperate roar of terror, the sound of which went straight to her core.

"Miranda!"

"Archer," she whispered, tears blurring her eyes. A whimpering sob broke from her lips. He'd come. He was alive.

"Miranda!" His shout was clearer now. He was by the carriage, obviously looking around for her and failing.

"I'm here." Her voice sounded pathetically small and weak in the dark space. He wouldn't hear.

"Archer!" she called louder, filling the space with her voice.

Pounding footsteps reverberated through the dirt, then came a jostling of the carriage above. The wooden body of the carriage sunk down an inch and pressed into her bottom.

"Stop!" she screeched. "You'll bloody crush me."

Odd, she thought as the pressure instantly ceased, one could always tell when another was cursing violently, even when the words were unclear. The thought of Archer in a temper rallied her more than anything. He'd find help and get her free.

She could only gape in a stupor when a loud groan ran through the wooden carriage frame and the pressure upon her back began to ease. Surely he did not mean to lift the bloody thing himself?

Surely he did. The carriage slowly rose, pale moonlight seeping in as it ascended. The toes of muddy boots came into view. Another groan shot through the night, this one altogether human and strained. A cacophony of splintering wood, squeaking springs, and Archer's shout rang in her ears as the carriage toppled back onto its broken wheels to land in a rattling heap next to her. Cool fresh air filled her lungs.

"Thank God. Miri...ah, stop!"

Archer jumped to her side the instant she began to wobble to her knees.

"Don't bloody try to rise! Damn fool, woman...Your spine may have been injured," he lectured as he knelt before her. "Not to mention..." His words faded from her hearing as she drank up the sight of him—alive and whole.

His usually gentle upper lip was set firm, a sure sign of irritation. The squared-off line of his cheek and jaw was pale blue in the moonlight but unmarred.

"Your ankles appear unharmed..."

Dimly, she felt the gentle touch of fingers running up her calf. He'd retained his silk mask, but a large rent ran along the shoulder seam of his fine suit coat, and a lapel was gone. On the whole, however, he did not look like a man who'd gone head first off a speeding coach.

"Can you turn your head? I say, can you turn your head!"

"Pardon?" She blinked and found his eyes narrowed on her.

"Can you turn your head?" he asked with forced patience. "Slowly."

She turned her head from side to side.

"Good." He went on with his examination. "Lift your arms?"

She did as asked, only half listening. The skeletal form

of the carriage's wreckage had caught her eye when she turned right. Black scars of turned-up earth and grass marked the carriage's trip down the slope. It had landed on a streambed. Only luck and dry weather had made it possible for her to fall within the deepest crevice of the dried-up bed, with the carriage landing on its side above her. A shiver of gratitude rent through her.

Such a blessing brought her back to her senses and, with it, the realization that Archer's big hands roamed over her hips, scarcely covered by her thin drawers.

"Hold on!" She slapped at his hands.

His lips curled grimly, but he did not look up from his work and brushed her hands aside. "Be still. Of all the stubborn..." He broke off into mumbled Italian, which she could not follow, her Italian being limited to fencing terms.

His large hands moved up to her ribs, his touch light yet assured. The same could not be said for her breathing, which rapidly became unsteady as he put a hand on either side of her rib cage and gently felt along each bone with his fingers.

One thumb brushed the soft underside of her breast, and she froze. And so did he. Archer lifted his eyes to hers, focusing on them with such frowning intensity that she could only stare back wordlessly. His eyes narrowed further, the hands at her sides unmoving. Then his stern mouth broke into a lopsided smile.

"You're unharmed," he said thickly.

"Well, of course I am," she said rather sharply, fearful that the slightest movement would cause his hand to slide upward. "I could have told you as much if you'd have let me."

"You're unharmed," he said again and then closed his eyes with a sigh of relief.

Chapter Twenty-five

─────────~∾◦∾~─────────

Maurus Robert Lea, Seventh Earl of Leland, rarely slept anymore. If he were lucky, four or perhaps five hours of sweet oblivion would claim him. Lately, however, the god Hypnos rarely granted him a visit. He began to wonder if such sleeplessness was the work of his mind striving to keep itself useful until the day that final sleep would claim him. Surely it would arrive sooner than later.

Thus he was very much awake, sitting before his coal fire hearth, listening to the storm that was brewing up and taking stock of his overlong life, when the clock struck three in the morning and blows began to rain down upon his front door.

"Leland!"

Startled, he tripped over his dressing robe as he scrambled to his feet. Wilkinson met him in the hall looking alarmed yet impeccably groomed, his snow-white hair neatly combed, his collar points high as Dover cliffs. Leland doubted he looked as well.

"My lord?" the butler inquired with a hasty glance at the door. The blasted pounding had not abated.

"Open up, Leland!"

"All is well, Wilkinson. Go to bed, will you. I'm far too old to be mollycoddled."

"Yes, my lord."

Leland knew the man would stay in his butler's closet until his master went to bed. He pushed the thought out of his mind and wrenched open the door to face the wily bastard whose voice he knew so well.

Archer did not appear wily just then. Only lost. Rain bounced on his shoulders as he stood drenched in the doorway. He wore only the half mask tonight. It stuck to him like sealskin, outlining the weariness and utter defeat carved on his face.

His massive chest lifted as he pulled in a deep breath. The plea came out a rasp, as though he wished to pull it back in with every word. "I need your help, Lilly."

For one angry moment, Archer thought Leland might slam the door in his face. The man stood frozen before him, his ridiculous peacock-printed dressing robe hanging askew over his nightgown, his thin legs like birch sticks trembling above worn velvet house slippers. He might have been Ebenezer Scrooge standing there with such a sour scowl upon his face. But then he moved, stepping aside to bid Archer entrance.

"Come," he said, keeping his eyes on Archer.

Archer brushed past him, feeling very much the specimen pinned to a dissector's board. But the time for humility had come. He'd made sure Miri was in bed and then slipped out. Even though it struck terror in him to do so, plans had to be made.

He followed the old man into a library nearly identical to his own. A coal fire glowed in the hearth—warmer than wood but foul smelling.

"Drink?" Leland was already pouring himself one.

"Have you bourbon?"

A thin smile lifted the man's mustache. "No. Can't say I've developed a taste for that Yank swill."

"Snob. Scotch, then."

Leland handed Archer a glass, and he took a grateful swallow, then moved closer to the hearth. Little hisses and black smoke puffed out of the grate as water dripped from Archer's back and shoulders.

"You'll put my fire out," Leland admonished.

"I didn't know where else to stand." Or to go.

"Why on earth didn't you put on a cloak, or hat, for that matter?"

"I was distracted."

The man was beginning to sound like his mother. Then again, Leland always chastised. Leland, the pinnacle of common sense and order—until West Moon Club.

"Let me get you a dressing gown."

Archer snorted. "Thank you, no." Yet he could hardly stand freezing his stones off and conduct a proper conversation. He clenched his jaw, absolutely refusing to let his teeth chatter.

Leland took a long drink of his Scotch. "I insist. I'll never hear the end of Wilkinson's grousing should you soak the carpet or, God forbid, mar the upholstery."

"And the ruling class runs in fear of their chiding servants." Archer smiled and took another sip.

"Quite." Leland reached for the bellpull.

The stiff-faced butler soon returned with an equally

ridiculous dressing gown imprinted with saffron-yellow butterflies. Archer scowled down at it. "Your wife's?"

"A present from, I'm afraid." Leland's expression wilted a bit. "All of them are. Can't bear to replace them."

The skin along Archer's neck tightened. "When did she pass?" Had Leland loved her? He certainly had not when he married her; Leland had confessed as much to Archer long ago. Archer's fingers curled into the worn silk.

"Sixty-nine. Hurry up, you're still dripping." Leland snorted. "Or are you going to act like a virgin and change in another room?"

Archer's hand hesitated at his collar. "You're sure you want to see?"

Leland's mustache drooped. "Sorry. I'd forgotten, if you can believe it. If it bothers you, I shall step out."

Archer pulled off his cravat. "It does not bother me." Part of him wanted Leland to see. See what he'd shunned. To understand what Archer was facing. He pulled at his sodden mask first. The swollen ties snapped, and the mask slid off.

"Christ's blood," Leland gasped. He sat heavily in his chair and tried to take a drink. His shaking hand proved useless in the endeavor.

"I did warn you." Archer spoke lightly yet his chest had tightened. Despite himself, he felt exposed, as though turned soul-side out.

"Yes. You did." Leland managed a drink as Archer divested himself of his shirt and slipped into the dressing gown. But not before he'd seen Leland's eyes go to his bare chest and quickly away. A fine shudder passed over the old man's frame.

They had all seen the beginning of his change, but that had been confined to his right hand. And now, solid, dependable Leland was shaken to the core. How then would Miri have reacted? He swallowed hard, wanting to put the mask back on, but pride stayed his hand.

"Don't despair," he said, taking the empty seat by the fire. "It isn't on you."

"Might as well have been." Leland's gnarled hand passed stiffly over his eyes. "Had I not been such a coward." Leland lifted weary eyes to him. Again, a wince convulsed his face but he held firm. "Both of us were chosen. Only you had the courage to try."

Archer's throat burned. "And look where it has left me."

"I am." Leland took a deep breath and set his drink down. "With what do you need my help?"

This was easier. Archer pulled his gloves off, grateful to be rid of the fleshy wet leather. He could tell Leland recognized the ring he wore. He worked it from his finger and took Daoud's notes from their hiding spot. "I need you to read these. Here is the cipher."

Leland fumbled in his breast pocket for his spectacles. "If you would turn up the lamps. I'm afraid my eyes are not what they once were."

The man's mouth moved as he read, his head tilted toward the light, thick half-moon spectacles at the end of his long nose. Unable to keep still, Archer left his chair and paced.

Leland studied Daoud's notes, and a deep frown worked across his brow. "You cannot mean to do this. You are no more responsible for this madness than any of us! You needn't be a sacrificial lamb. Especially now..." He trailed off with a swallow.

"Now that I have married?" Archer supplied softly. He forced a shrug. "I might try...Hell, I have tried." He touched the altered side of his face. "The situation has changed. That thing wants Miranda." His hand curled into a fist. "I cannot leave her unprotected."

Leland's frown remained. "I understand the sentiment. But surely if anyone can stop this, it is you, Archer." Leland bit his lip, an action Archer hadn't seen since Eton. "I thought you wished to save your soul."

Archer rubbed his hand hard across his face as if it could ease the restlessness inside. "I've had my hands about that wretch's neck twice. Twice and I cannot...I cannot destroy it."

The color drained from Leland's flat cheeks. "By God."

"Not by God," Archer said wryly. "Most assuredly from hell. And hell is where it will return. But I cannot send it there as I am." He lifted his left hand. Strong though it was, it was still made of flesh and blood. "I am no match now, a fact used against me to great advantage."

He broke from Leland's gaze, and the pity residing in it. "I must change. For all our sakes." He touched his glass then let his hand fall. "Even changed, we are evenly matched at best."

He heard Leland's sharp intake of breath and looked up to find him gaping.

"This is why you need my help." Leland lifted the paper in his hand. "Because of this new revelation?"

"Yes. There can be no doubt as to my success. To fail would bring disaster. On all of you." Archer gripped the mantel hard. "Do you think it can be done?"

"I'm not quite certain." Leland studied the note. "Ah, the Druids." He glanced at him above his spectacles. "I take it that is why you came to me."

Archer gritted his teeth, and Leland snorted. "You always were transparent..." He blanched. "I say, Arch...

Had I come across this sort of thing before...That is to say, it never occurred to me the curse might have come from the Druids."

"It never occurred to me that you might have withheld information. If that's what you're on about."

"I ought to have looked." Leland's long fingers clutched the soft cloth in his shaking hands. "Druid priests knew of magic that we are only beginning to understand. Such blundering is inexcusable of me."

A remorseful Leland was near intolerable. "You are looking now," Archer said brusquely.

Leland nodded, and resumed studying the note. "It shall take some time. A few days to consult some old texts."

"Understood. Just find what you can. Will it work...?"

Helplessness brought a rage upon Archer. To find Miri slaughtered...Archer would rather be dead himself.

Leland's eyes bore into him but Archer refused to turn around. "I am not afraid to die," he said, staring at the red coals in the grate.

"Then why—"

"Haven't I ended my life long ago? When I knew myself cursed?" He turned. Leland had put down the notes. His long hands lay limp in his lap, bone white against the peacock-blue silk.

"The ironic thing is, I rather like life," Archer said. "As odd as mine is. Losing my soul is another issue entirely. I should not like it..." His voice trailed off, awkward in the heavy silence.

"Certainly not," Leland agreed softly. He sighed and moved to his bookshelf, and after a bit of searching, he pulled down a large tome covered in thick, embossed leather. "I shall start now. I never sleep these days, anyway. A good riddle will be a boon." His worn slippers shuffled over the oriental carpet. "Have another drink. Or shall I set you up with a room?"

Archer shook his head slowly. It felt heavy as a ballast stone. "I am going to retrieve that sword." He pointed to Daoud's letter for emphasis. "Now."

The book in Leland's hand closed with a decisive thump. "If you think you are going to leave me behind, think again."

Archer's lips twitched "Can you keep up?" he countered softly.

"Such effrontery," Leland answered with a snort of irritation.

Archer reached for his damp clothes. "Then we had better get moving."

They rode horses. And despite Leland's protestations, Archer worried over him. His frail frame wobbled a bit as they cantered up a small incline. The man held on. The storm had ended and the fog returned, icy and thick. Darkness was nearly complete, and they might have gotten thoroughly lost were it not for Archer's extraordinary vision. He led the way to the outskirts of town and those desolate caves that had seen the origin of his destruction.

His breath came out as white mist, eaten up by the muddy dark. Silently, they wove through a copse of trees and came to a stop by a growth of thickets.

"Looks abandoned," Leland said from behind him.

"It was meant to." Archer leapt from his horse and pushed away the thick overgrowth. Heavy timbers barred the entrance. They lifted easily in his hands and landed in a muffled crash in the undergrowth behind him. Yes, abandoned. Thank God for small mercies.

He heard Leland dismount as he worked on clearing the entrance. He remembered it well, knocking the boulders down over it and pushing the great tree trunks in front of them. Barring this place from any further mischief.

His blood pumped. The iron door came into sight. He glanced back at Leland and then gave the heavy door a shove with his shoulder. It gave with a great groan and a small puff of red iron dust. One more shove and the door teetered back and then landed with an earthshaking thud upon the soft ground.

"Torch." He held his hand out waiting for Leland to light it and hand it over. Thick cobwebs and swirling dust motes colored the mouth of the cave gray. He brushed a clump of cobwebs aside and then went forward, stepping back in time.

No torches burned now in the narrow passage, yet in his mind's eye he saw them, lining the walls, leading the way. The irritating scent of patchouli hanging in the air, and the chants of men echoing somewhere deep beyond. At the time, it had given him a morbid thrill. He'd gone willingly. Afraid of nothing, and everything. A grim smile touched his lips. That, at least, had not changed. The memory faded, and he faced the dark, moldering passage once more.

Leland stumbled behind him, and Archer held out a steadying hand.

"You remember the way?" Archer asked. He did not want to turn round and find his friend lost.

"How could I not?" came the dry reply.

"Good. Let's get on with it."

They moved slowly, Archer brushing aside cobwebs or kicking errant debris out of the way. The path twisted hard right, and Archer felt his breath coming quick.

Cavern Hall was only steps away. It opened before them, a perfectly round cavern of rough limestone walls. Empty torch rings, twelve in all, hung from the walls, and above, suspended on a heavy iron chain, the great chandelier was still filled with stumps of thick candles. On nights of the full moon, the cavern used to glow like orange fire from the hundreds of lit candles. But long before West Moon Club had discovered the cave, it had been used for ancient rituals. A millennium of torch smoke had painted the ceiling black, and the shuffle of men's feet had trampled the floor to a smooth surface.

The men stood for a moment, both of them silent as memories assaulted them. Archer knew Leland thought of the same night. The chanting, the excitement. That cup, filled with a silver liquid that might have been mercury. Archer closed his eyes. The white-hot pain as the icy liquid had slid down his throat had brought him to his knees before his friends. And then Leland, turning away in shame and horror, had refused to finish his drink.

Archer moved to the large semicircular niche carved into the far wall where a sacrificial altar lay in wait. Resting on a large, rectangular block of granite lay a thick slab of basalt. An evil-looking black stone. The same stone bed on which Archer had been destined to lie upon and finish the process—had he not fled into the night, too terrified of the viscous pain that pulsed through his veins after he'd swallowed down that vile brew. For a moment, he thought he heard laughter.

Archer and Leland slipped their torches into the holders that hung on either side of the altar so that a dim halo of wavering light illuminated the niche.

"The note says it's under the altar." Leland's thin voice echoed softly in the empty space.

Fancy that, Archer thought. He would have never thought the altar hollow. He reached out with shaking hands, afraid to touch the stone but forced to do so. Icy cold seeped through his leather gloves. A chill ran over him. Gritting his teeth, he slowly began to push the stone from its base. It pivoted, the sound of stone grinding against stone filling the air. Archer dug in his heels and pushed harder. The stone slipped farther until a small crack of dark appeared. A whoosh of dry air burst from the stone's base, sounding like a woman's gasp in the silence. Archer jumped back. Leland too. But nothing more occurred.

Archer ground his teeth and finished pivoting the stone. The great square base proved hollow as promised. Archer grabbed a torch and bent forward. A long brown bundle lay nestled like a babe deep within the dark well of the table.

Leland eased the torch from his hand and held it aloft as Archer reached down. His fingers made contact, and every inch of his changed self screamed in protest. His muscles hardened painfully. He took a breath and forced his fingers to curl over the thing. And when they did, his left side seemed to sigh with ease. Divided, his body was. Part shrinking in fear, part craving release. He made quick work of taking the bundle out and placing it on the altar top. Nothing more lay within the hole.

"Undo it," he said to Leland. He was sweating profusely, which almost never happened, and he doubted his trembling hands could manage.

Leland seemed to understand. He set the torch back and carefully examined the bundle. It was made of leather, so old that the small ride from its bed to the table was more than enough to start its disintegration. As no markings or adornment covered the leather, Leland simply cut through it with a penknife and peeled it away, much as he would have done when inspecting a mummy. Archer had a vivid memory of them in Cairo, long ago when they had fancied themselves archaeologists.

The image was reinforced as the brittle leather crumbled, revealing fine linen wrappings. Leland's white head bent closer. "A coin." He handed it up to Archer.

"Greek inscription," Archer said. "It is from Claudius the First. A tetradrachm."

Leland's hands shook nearly as badly as Archer's had done moments before. The linen unraveled to give up another prize—a small collection of papyri held in a leather folder. "The roman soldier's writings."

Daoud's note had been specific. Two letters sent home in the time of Claudius by a young soldier named Marcus Augustus revealed that he had stumbled upon a most horrific spell. The first letter explained his findings, a way to conjure a demon of light, a creature of immense power who could judge innocent from dammed, and in so doing, destroy the evildoer. The second letter was of a different tone. He begged his dear sister to burn the first letter. That he would hide away his discovery where it would never be found, in the place of worship of the newly slaughtered Druid priests. Fortunately for Archer's purposes, the sister had not burned the letters but kept them both. Only to be discovered by Daoud more than a millennium later. More research by Daoud had uncovered where the soldier had been stationed. Another account from one of his fellow soldiers stated that a small dispatch of men had found a cave and, within it, a sacrificial altar made of granite and basalt. The description and location of the cave matched Cavern Hall exactly.

Archer could well appreciate the amount of work Daoud had done to verify the far-flung story. He missed his friend just then. *For you, dear friend. For all of my slaughtered friends.*

Leland's fingertips barely touched the papyri as he looked them over. "Greek as well. I shall study it in a moment."

Archer nodded, and the elder man put the tome aside in favor of further unwrapping the bundle. A strange hum emanated from it. Archer doubted Leland heard it, but Archer felt it with every cell. His skin twitched as the last vestiges of the linen fell away. A wide leather scabbard was embossed with symbols. The ornate hilt was bronze. Bronze that oddly gleamed like new. That was all he saw before he had to step away and get a breath.

"Easy," Leland murmured. "It cannot harm you now."

"So say you," Archer choked out with a bit of humor. He passed a shaking hand over his exposed jaw.

Leland turned the ancient sword, still safely tucked in its sheath. "Fascinating. See the inscriptions on the hilt?"

Archer inched a bit closer. "Egyptian glyphs?" It was all he could say before backing away.

"Yes. How very interesting. Not Druids, then..."

Leland's scholarly detachment began to grate on Archer. "Is it what we seek?" he asked with a bit of impatience.

Leland's bushy brow cocked. "Need you ask? You feel the power in it, yes?"

"Assuredly." That and more. A sense of his mortality. Strange that. The sensation of being in mortal danger was almost foreign to him now.

"It makes one wonder," Leland mused. "Is this why Cavern Hall was chosen for the ritual?"

The members of West Moon Club hadn't picked Cavern Hall; they'd been led there and were told it was a place of great power. Suitable for those fool enough to try their hand at playing God, Archer thought bitterly. He paced away. "Why choose the very place that houses the sole object capable of one's destruction?"

"I am thinking it was more a matter of being drawn to this place because of the power the sword emanates. One needn't know about the sword to feel its pull."

"I suppose that could be it," Archer said as Leland carefully set the sword down.

"Let me see..." Leland had picked up the papyri and was now reading over them. "It appears Daoud misread the situation. According to the solider, Augustus, a secret sect of Egyptian priests was tasked with the creation and care of beings they called *Children of Light*, but whom Augustus calls *Lux Daemons*, or *Anima Comedentis*. Augustus came upon them when his legion destroyed their temple in the name of the Empire. If there were any light demons left by then, Augustus did not come upon them. Augustus stole both the sword and the secret for creating the light demons.... By God..." He fell back on his rump.

"What, for God's sake?" Archer snapped.

"He tried it!" Leland's eyes reflected like wading pools in the flickering light. "He became one. But unlike you, he knew how to end it. Only he chose not to."

The room seemed to go dim. *Another one. Out in the world.*

"Being a thoughtful fellow," Leland went on, reading in abstraction, "he kept the sword with him. Should he grow weary of life, he would use it well." He thumbed through the pages. "Apparently, the Egyptians had a way to control the light demons, the sword. They claimed it is the sword of Ammit, The Devourer."

"The Eater of Hearts," Archer said. They shared a look, then Archer laughed without humor. "Son of a bitch."

"Apparently, Ammit is the mother of the first light demon," Leland said.

Ammit, an ancient Egyptian demoness, was said to devour the hearts of those found unworthy by the Underworld God Anubis. God, he hoped that bit was allegorical. The idea that his friends' stolen hearts were actually being consumed turned his insides. That he might one day crave a similar meal nearly made him cast up his accounts.

Thankfully oblivious to Archer's shaky constitution, Leland read on. "The priests claimed that the sword was forged in the lake of fire in Duat, the Egyptian Underworld."

The lake of fire was said to both destroy and purify. The undeserving would be consumed, their souls doomed to become forever restless, thus dying a second death. Those judged true of heart would be spared. " 'The water thereof shall be yours, but to you it shall not be boiling, and the heat thereof shall not be upon your bodies,' " Archer quoted.

"So says the Book of Gates," Leland finished with a familiar gleam in his eyes before returning to the text. "The rest is in the usual vein...the sword can only be wielded by one of true heart and courage; the light demon cannot be destroyed by any other means..." He trailed off and looked at Archer. "Read it. You know ancient Greek better than I."

Archer's hand shook as he took the ancient text. Leland was right. Save Archer found himself utterly weary and surprisingly timid. He did not want to plan his death. He wanted to go home to his wife.

He knelt close to the torches and read through the entire story. A glimmer of hope, so small as to be laughable, flickered within his heart as he reached the end of the tale. A small smile tugged at his lips.

He stood then, careful not to harm the papyri. "We have what we came for." He would not take the sword. "I ask that you keep everything until I am ready."

Leland got up more slowly, his old knees audibly creaking, but Archer did not help him; his friend would not want it. "There is much to plan. And texts to consult."

Chapter Twenty-six

———— ❦ ❦ ————

The Blackwoods' staff found John Coachman's body in their stables, his throat cut and his heart taken. The news sent Miranda to her rooms for half the day, leaving Archer helpless to comfort her. In the cold light of morning, they buried him in the family plot behind Archer House, near an old birch tree. A gentle breeze passed over, and ghostly white limbs swayed like the skeleton of a hand reaching down to grasp at the newly turned earth. Archer took comfort in knowing this death, and the others, would soon be avenged.

"How do we go about catching this killer?" Miranda asked when they'd settled down in the library.

Archer, who'd been in the process of handing her a glass of bourbon, paused. A dark fear twisted his insides. "We?"

God help him, no matter how much he desired to confide in Miri, he would sooner die than do so, for the impetuous woman would not think twice about going forth to seek her own vengeance.

"Yes, 'we.'" She took the glass from his stiff hand. Caramel sweet perfume danced in the air. "*We* have already established that the killer is after me. Thus *we* must find him first."

He straightened to his full height. "*You* are going to stay here at Archer House," he retorted crisply. "And *I* shall remain by your side to protect you."

"Of all the ridiculous plans." She took a sip of bourbon as if needing to restore herself. "We might as well lie down like dogs!"

Archer drained his glass and stalked away. "Your confidence in me is heartening, Miranda," he said from the far side of the room.

"Well, then, what is your plan?" she asked. "Other than acting the jailer."

A knock on the library door kept Archer from answering. Inspector Lane was calling, informed Gilroy. Normally, Archer hated being interrupted, especially when he was with Miranda. On this occasion, however, Winston Lane's arrival was more than welcome. Archer quickly bid Gilroy to allow Lane entry.

Miranda muttered an oath as he gave her a grin and slipped on his full mask. Lane soon strode into the room, his bony frame lost among a brown sack suit and billowing blue Crispin cloak, his bowler hat tucked under his arm.

"Miranda." He came near, bringing with him the acerbic scent of the damp London air tinged with an unnerving hint of blood. "Are you well, sister?"

Miranda gave him a strained smile. "Well enough. Hello, Winston."

"My lord." He inclined his head to Archer. "I heard you had a coach accident last night. Nothing too dire, I hope."

"The horses spooked," Archer said. "It was a nuisance, but we are unharmed."

Lane's mustache twitched slightly at the ridiculous understatement. "I am glad." He cleared his throat. "The CID thought it best, given the delicacy of the situation, that I handle this matter."

"I'm glad it is you," Miranda said in earnest.

"I must ask you both some questions. That is, if you agree, my lord."

Archer gave a nod. "You are Miranda's family. I should not think you capable of upsetting her." Or he'd throw the good inspector out on his ear.

"It would grieve me to do so." Lane folded himself into the nearest chair and pulled a small notebook from his coat pocket, and with it, a stubby pencil. "Now then," he said, "I am to understand this last victim was your coachman, was he not?"

"Unfortunately," Archer said. John was a good lad who deserved far better.

"Rather odd as the other victims were all older, titled, and apparently members of a club of which we can find no record, though we know it exists."

Masks were good for some things, and Lane proved no match for Archer's silent stare. The inspector looked away and went to the door to call Gilroy. Lane returned with an object in his hand. A dark discoloration marred part of it, and Archer realized with a sick lurch that it was Miranda's mantle, covered in blood. Lane set it down on a chair, and the scent of her perfume lifted from it, so thick just then that it seemed as though the cloth had been doused with it.

A muscle along his jaw twitched. A woman's perfume was as good as a fingerprint. Miranda clearly thought so and turned pale as cold cream.

"We found this near the body of your coachman." Lane peered at Miranda. "Can you tell me when you last had it in your possession?"

"When I entered the Blackwoods' home last night. I gave it to a footman, but I didn't remember to retrieve it when we left."

A small frown worked its way between Lane's brows. "You didn't think to collect your cloak upon leaving?"

Miranda colored. "I was feeling ill. I only thought about getting home."

When Lane merely looked her over thoughtfully, her green eyes narrowed. "You don't think..." She could not finish.

But Archer could. "You think perhaps Lady Archer had an amorous encounter with our coachman, and I happened upon them?"

"Archer!" she hissed, turning to glare at him. He blinked back, unmoved.

"After all," he went on, "all of the victims are in close connection with me."

"Archer, stop! That is ridiculous. We did not even know John was dead when we left the party."

"I believe, my lady, that Lord Archer would rather place himself as the suspect than have us look to you." He glanced from her to Archer and his mustache lifted. "Very admirable. However, we have gone over those scenarios and found them unwarranted. More likely, that is what the killer wants us to think. He took Miranda's cloak, perhaps even killed your coachman, in an effort to place her at the crime scene. But why?"

That Miranda had been brought into it...the sofa back caught in Archer's grip creaked in protest. "I don't know," he said stiffly.

"Hmm…" Lane draped the cloak over the chair. "I am wondering if perhaps the killer approached your coachman disguised as Lady Archer."

Miranda's head snapped up. "Rather odd for a man to do."

"It is at that. And perhaps I am mistaken. However, I cannot think it was you, dear sister, who murdered your coachman."

"Well, that is gracious of you, Winston."

Lane gave Miranda a small, apologetic smile. "No stone can remain unturned. Even if it means checking the alibi of one's sister-in-law."

Lane snapped his notebook shut and then stood. "This has been a trying time for all. I should let you get your rest." He gave Miranda a kind look before addressing Archer. "Just one more thing, my lord." He reached into his coat pocket and pulled out a West Moon Club coin. "Another coin was found with the body." World-weary eyes pinned him. "Care to speculate as to its meaning?"

Archer faced Lane head on. "No." Speculation wasn't needed. It was another invitation to Cavern Hall. And his doom.

As soon as Winston left, Archer went to the window to stare out of it. Sunshine lit over his broad shoulders and caught the rounded curves of his mask, making it gleam. It shut Miranda out most effectively.

She rose and stood beside him. "You knew we could not be considered suspects in this crime."

He kept his eyes on the window. Tension crackled about him like a storm. "Yes."

"So you purposely laid blame at your feet to force Winston to reveal what the police thought."

He turned to look at her. "Is there a point to this line of inquiry?"

"Not really. Only that I find your tactics without conscience and...admirable. Well played."

He twitched in surprise. "I am shocked, Lady Archer," he teased in a low voice. "Winston Lane is, after all, your brother-in-law."

"He is also CID. I cannot think them our friends in this. Not quite yet. That Winston was here to question us tells me as much."

Beside her, Archer sighed and wrenched off his mask as though wearing it was getting more intolerable by the moment. She turned to survey him.

"Sir Percival's valet said Percival called the coin a guide. Why?"

Archer's head fell to the window as he sighed. "Because it is. We each received one. Each set of bumps upon the moon face makes up symbols that work with a cipher, thus revealing the location of the meeting place." He glanced at her. "It doesn't mean anything, Miranda. Only another breadcrumb to lead your good brother to my door."

"But why you?" When he did not answer, her hand curled into a fist. "Evading CID is one thing. Hiding from me is another, Archer."

He made a sound of annoyance. "Hiding...how very dramatic."

Miranda's fist thumped on the windowpane. "Moon's members are being systematically killed." The truth was lurking in his eyes, though he did an admirable job of trying to hide it. "But you remain untouched. Why?"

He glared at her. "I wouldn't say untouched."

Miranda waved her hand in irritation. "I remember that day in the museum quite clearly—"

"As do I." Archer set his hands on his trim hips and glared at her. "One tends to remember when one's wife is nearly murdered."

Wife. The word gave her pause. At times she nearly forgot what they were to each other. Partners until death. But she could not let sentimentality rule the moment.

"My point being," she said, "that you did not appear at all surprised when you first laid eyes on the fiend. On the contrary, you appeared to recognize him."

"What I recognized," he retorted rather nastily, "was myself. I knew then that the killer meant to appear as me."

"He could have killed you at the museum, but he did not. It was an easy kill."

"I am not so easily dispatched," Archer muttered, turning his head slightly away. Her line of thinking must have been hitting near the mark because no pithy remarks were forthcoming.

"You are quite remarkably strong and agile," she admitted, eyeing his impressive frame. The speed she'd seen last night was magnificent. "But not indestructible."

"No." He spread his arms wide. "One of your little verbal barbs would do me in, I'm sure." He glanced as his chest at though checking for injury.

"Jest all you like," she said, strolling around him, caging him in; she'd have the truth from him yet. "It won't do you any good."

He paced as well, his boots thudding over the carpet, until they circled each other like two great cats taking the other's measure. "I am positively shivering with fear," he said with a smile.

"Aren't you," she murmured, and Archer scowled. "What is your true affliction, Archer? How did you survive that tumble from the coach with nary a scratch?"

His mouth thinned. "I could ask the same of you. Your fall was infinitely worse, yet here you are..."—his eyes raked over her and a small shiver took hold of her belly—"unmarred."

"Pure luck."

"Luck," he repeated. "You see? Not so mysterious." His voice was a caress. She swallowed with difficulty.

"How...how did he get away the second time?"

"I failed to give chase." His attention was on her lips now. She did not like the look at all, for she knew he aimed to distract her. That he was doing an excellent job only aggravated her further.

"Why?"

"You were stuck in a runaway coach." He did not lift his eyes from her lips. "I thought it more pressing to save you."

His dark head seemed to move ever closer. "Have I told you that your mouth is quite lovely?" His lids lowered a fraction. "Lovely and plump."

Most assuredly trying to distract her. A wash of warmth invaded her limbs. "Perhaps you can write a sonnet about it later. But there is the one question that puts it all into place." Her eyes held his as she leaned in, crowding him. "Are you immortal?"

The air in the room seemed to vanish with his sharp inhalation. Archer stared at her, shock and horror mingling in his eyes. After a pregnant silence he spoke, his voice thick and rusty. "That's what Mckinnon told you?"

She refused to be shamed. "The valet said Sir Percival had the coin since 1814. All the other members are old men. No more deflections, Archer. Is it true?"

He whirled away and stalked to the tall windows overlooking the south lawn.

Tears clogged her throat and burned her eyes, but she would not let them fall. "I thought I could accept the distance our secrets put between us. But not if doing so threatens our very lives. This is too important." Her heart ached as she watched his shoulders move under the force of his unsteady breath. "Let me in, Archer," she whispered.

Slowly, he turned to gaze at her with troubled eyes. "Miri..."

Something in his eyes turned her cold. Suddenly it all seemed clear, his strength, his speed. Stranger things... *And if it is true, was there someone out there intent upon cannibalizing him?*

Her stomach rolled as her mind spun with images of Archer cut open, his flesh devoured by an unseen monster, and she pressed her middle, holding down her panic. "It is a nightmare," she whispered, fingers numb and cold.

Archer straightened with a sharp breath. An odd smile pulled at his lips. "Does this look like the work of immortality?" He gestured casually toward the bruises blooming yellow and blue along his jaw and cheekbone. "Or the torn flesh that you yourself stitched together?"

The mocking in his tone was unmistakable. Nor did she blame him. She could scarcely wrap her head around the idea. She steeled herself as he walked with purpose to her side. "Come." He took her arm in hand. "You like stories? I have a grand one."

They marched through the house, her skirts rustling loudly as she struggled to keep up. Expectation and anxiety had her pulse pounding. They did not slow until they were well away from the house, headed back to the graveyard.

Archer led her to a set of weathered headstones, not

far from where John's fresh earthen grave lay. "Benjamin Archer, Third Baron Archer of Umberslade, died in eighteen fifteen," Archer said, pointing to the grave that bore his ancestor's name. "I am not that man." He took a breath, and his body grew stiffer. "Simply a fool who ignored certain destruction and survived."

Dead leaves danced underfoot as they stood in silence. Goose bumps lifted on her skin where the cold wind hit it.

Archer stirred. "You are chilled." He touched her elbow.

"I don't believe you." Miranda's words flicked through the air like a whip, and he flinched.

"They searched to eradicate death," she pressed. "Perhaps your grandfather failed, Archer. But you are here, a man who is now deformed by some grand experiment. And the worst of it is you won't tell me what it was." She stepped away from his explosive silence. "If you will not let me in to help, then I will find someone who will."

Archer caught her wrist and wrenched her against him so fast her head spun. "Mckinnon, you mean?"

"If I must."

"You'll see me dead first!"

She slapped at him with her free arm. "I believe that is someone's point, you ape!"

He snatched her flailing arm, as his other arm cinched about her waist. When she stilled, he let one hand go. The wide expanse of his palm flattened against her back, hedging her closer, until her breasts flattened against him. "Feel my heart," he prompted thickly. Beneath her clenched fist, it pounded a fierce rhythm. "Believe me when I say that it is all too human, and just as weak."

He clasped her neck and brought her near until their noses touched. "You may choose to believe what you want." His lips brushed against hers as he spoke. "But if you think discovering these secrets and unmasking a killer will stop this madness, then you are a fool."

She closed her eyes. The rough grain along his chin grazed her jaw, his hot breath drowning her senses. "You have one option left to you." His voice dropped to a whisper as the arms about her squeezed tight, quashing her resistance. "That is to trust your lying ape of a husband to see you safe."

It would be so easy to relent, to melt into him and be coddled. Part of her wanted to, with the desperation of a child. Yet where would that leave him? She wrenched her head back to glare at him. "You cannot expect me to—"

His lips crushed hers, a bruising force that pushed tender flesh against hard teeth. She whimpered as his hands clutched her head with unmoving strength, and his lips nipped and sucked for one sharp moment. Then she was free, stumbling back without an anchor to steady her.

Archer's chest heaved as he glared in dark fury. "I cannot see you die!" he shouted. Startled crows scattered from the trees in a flurry of wings and wild caws.

He spun round with a flap of coattails and strode over the lawn, boot heels crunching upon the freezing soil. She flinched as his final words boomed out like cannon fire over the emptiness.

"I will not!"

Chapter Twenty-seven

—————❧❧—————

M y lord?"

Archer started with a sharp breath. He hadn't heard Gilroy enter the library. The man stood slightly away from the desk, the silver mail tray in his hand.

"Mail, is it?" he asked, surprised at how weary his voice sounded as he took the letters.

The butler hesitated. His eyes were rheumy nowadays. Archer looked away from them. He did not think he could watch Gilroy fade as well.

"Is there something you wanted, Gilroy?"

Gilroy's thin mouth compressed. Yes, there was something he wanted very badly to say. That was obvious. Only years of training prevented the man from speaking plainly. Gilroy drew himself up full.

"Lady Archer has declined dinner," he said without a hint of reproach. Which only made Archer's transgression more clear. "Shall I set up for one? Or perhaps bring a tray in here?"

The leaden weight in Archer's stomach intensified.

Miri no longer wanted to eat with him. He ached. In every muscle, in his heart, it hurt to breathe now. Yet she still inflamed him. Her honeyed scent, the way she lifted that one amber brow when he said something she did not agree with, made him *want*.

Archer scrubbed a hand over his jaw. Gilroy was still waiting for a reply.

"I find myself not entirely hungry either. Let the staff have it."

"Very well, my lord."

Archer did not look up from his desk as Gilroy left but slowly thumbed through his mail, if only for something to keep his hands occupied. A thin missive stopped him. Although it had been years, he knew that handwriting quite well.

His fingers were clumsy, tearing open the envelope in haste. Something inside him already knew what the note would say.

It can be done.

–L

His eyes went to the lunar calendar lying on the desk. Two days left until the new moon met the winter solstice. This night and one day, really. All that he had left to spend with Miranda. He raised his head, listening intently. Miri. He could just hear the soft steady sound of her breathing, the faint rustle of her dress when she moved. Archer rose from his desk. It was cowardly and selfish, but he needed her like he needed air.

She was in the salon, sitting unseeing before the backgammon board. A pang grasped Archer's heart at the sight. Candlelight highlighted the creamy curves of her cheeks, setting her rosy hair aglow. For one precious moment, he could not breathe. His vision blurred, and he blinked hard.

"Miri."

She turned, stiffening at his unexpected appearance. "Yes, Archer?"

He swallowed past the thickness in his throat and nodded toward the board. "Play a game with me?"

He was letting her beat him, Miranda was sure. The man barely paid mind to the game but sat in silence, gray eyes glittering from behind the black silk mask, watching her every move.

She looked up from the game board to find him watching still.

"You're staring," she murmured and moved her piece along the board.

"Yes. You look beautiful."

Heat rose in her cheeks. She could only be thankful for the mellowing glow of candlelight to hide it. "You told me you cared not for how I looked."

Archer leaned slightly forward in his chair. "I am an ass, Miri. You well know it. A boorish, unpardonable ass."

She had to smile. "So long as *you* know it." Her voice did not work properly. She offered him the cup and dice but he did not take them. He moved an inch closer, and his large frame enveloped the small gaming table.

"I know that your beauty renders me senseless." Archer's well-formed mouth broke into a smile. "I look upon you, and pure stupidity flies from my mouth. The sight of you in that golden dress makes my toes numb. I want to send Monsieur Falle roses, I'm so grateful."

She laughed, and he did too, a rich unguarded laugh

that made her insides flip. "You see?" he said. "Pure, unmitigated stupidity."

The corners of his eyes crinkled in mirth, and she laughed again. "Then I shall save you from yourself," she said. "I am appeased. Speak no more of my beauty and spare yourself further humiliation."

She touched his hand lightly. The smile on his lips wavered and fell. His eyes went to her hand on his, and a shuddering sigh passed over his long frame. Miranda drew back as though burned, but he continued to blink down at his hand resting upon the game board.

"Archer, what is it?" Her fingers curled closed. "Are you ill?" she whispered as the flat planes of his chest rose and fell.

"Ill?" he choked out with a sudden laugh. His gaze reached as far as her lips before he froze again, and his mouth trembled. He looked off into the fire. "Is need an illness?" he muttered as though to himself. "I suppose it is."

"Archer," she said sharply, for his strange attitude began to nettle her. Her insides fluttered, sensing the coming of a storm.

As though breaking from a tether, his head snapped up, and the breath left her body as she saw what was laid bare in his eyes.

"Miri."

One word, only her name, and yet it told her all she need know, of his pain, his desire. Of what he was asking. She pushed away from the table, not knowing where she was going, only that she needed to move.

"We've both done so well at keeping our distance, haven't we?" she said as he stood and stalked her. But she wanted him, so much so that her arms shook with the need to hold him.

He tried to touch her cheek, and she shifted away. "And are you happy?" he asked softly.

Happy? Perhaps. Satisfied? No. Tears burned behind her eyes, and she took an unsteady breath. "Why *now*, Archer?"

Need tightened his mouth and left his expression raw. "Because today I truly realized that I could lose you in an instant." He took a small step toward her. "That life was not a long road that stretched before me, but here and now. And the thought of spending one more day, one more breath without knowing the feel of you in my arms has become too much to bear."

Suddenly his hand was cupping the back of her neck, pulling her to him, his mouth soft and warm upon hers. She nearly groaned from the pleasure of it.

"I want you, Miri," he whispered into her mouth. He pushed her against the door, the starched linen of his shirt crushing into her bodice as his tongue delved between her lips.

She moaned and clutched his lapels as he kissed her with deep, slow kisses that made her knees weaken.

"Beyond reason, I want you . . ." His free hand skimmed her waist, easing down to her hip. "You want me too."

"Yes." *Beyond reason.*

Again he stroked her, softening his kiss, and she sighed and tugged at his jacket to feel the hard muscles shifting beneath.

He pulled away a fraction. "The lights."

Miranda broke the kiss, and he looked back, pleading for understanding. A spark of anger ignited in her breast. "You want me," she whispered, a lump rising in her throat. "Yet you will not reveal yourself to me."

He flinched and averted his eyes. "No."

"No," she repeated. She moved to go.

He grabbed hold of her shoulder and pressed his forehead to hers. They were still for a moment, his breath fanning her face. "Please, Miri. I've lived a lifetime of regrets. If I could have this any other way...I need you." As if unable to stop himself, he kissed her again, tender kisses that melted her defenses. "Miri..."

His kisses consumed her. She tore her mouth away to clear her head, and Archer went still.

Each tick of the mantel clock sounded like a gong within her ears. The desolation in his expression cut into her. In truth, she needed him too. She was damned tired of denying her wants. But there were other things to consider. Fire, destruction, loss. "I'm afraid."

The corners of his eyes tightened. "Of me."

"No!" Miranda's fingers curled over his lapels to keep him close. "Of myself. Of losing control." It hurt to say, hurt to meet his eyes. She found only tenderness lingering in their gray depths.

"And I'm afraid of wasting my life always being in control," he whispered. "But no matter what direction I take, all roads lead to you." Gently, he rested his forehead to hers once more. "Let me come home, Miri. If only for one night."

Home. She'd been searching for it the whole of her life. And found it in a man more elusive than shadows. "Home is not where one visits. It is where one returns to at the end of each day."

A sigh whispered over him, and he cupped her cheek. "For all my days, Miri."

She closed his eyes briefly then whisked open the door. "Come to me at midnight."

"Leave the lights off," he said as she walked from the room.

Chapter Twenty-eight

A tomb. It was a fitting description. Miranda shifted irritably beneath the heavy weight of her bedding. The darkness was complete. She blinked, waiting for her eyes to adjust to some light, but there was none. Archer had chosen a cloud-filled night to voice his request.

The reason for such utter darkness started mad thoughts racing. He'd called himself a horror. She shuddered, despite the warmth of the covers. What was beneath the mask? Was he scarred? Worse? She couldn't imagine worse.

She turned to lie flat on her back, and the skirts of her peignoir slid over her thighs. The sound of her breathing and heartbeat grew overly loud in the silence. In truth, she could not dissect Archer into parts. She saw him as a whole. She thought of Archer not in pictures but with feeling. Archer was warmth, laughter, kindness, and excitement. Her eyes prickled with unshed tears. She wanted him to come to her. She wanted to hold him, ease his pain. Above all, she wanted him to show her what it was that caused him such agony.

Something in the room changed. Miranda realized with a start that he was here. The soft sound of his tread upon the carpet filled the silence. Without sight, she could only hear, and wait. The idea suddenly terrified her.

There was a pause. She closed her eyes and prayed for strength. The covers lifted gently, and her breath hitched. The featherbed dipped as he eased down onto it.

She turned her head and tried to make out his form. There was nothing to see. Nothing but the scent of the silk dressing gown he wore, and beneath it, the delicious yet ephemeral smell of *him*. He might have been a ghost.

His breath fanned her face in soft bursts and she knew he was unsettled. "I will not harm you," he finally whispered in a voice raw with both fear and anticipation. "Never."

No, Archer would never harm her. But what was to stop her from accidentally harming him? He had only to touch her, and she wanted to ignite. Unable to speak, she nodded even though he could not see. The bed dipped further as he leaned into her, and the faint warmth of his body caressed her. She inhaled in a rush. The brush of his lips upon her jaw set her pulse pounding, loud enough for him to surely hear it.

Her thoughts spun. Archer in her bed, Archer touching her, Archer making love to her. Her breath stuttered, and Archer pulled back. "It's still me, Miri." Gently, he brushed her hair from her temple. "Only me."

And that was the problem. He was everything. He was her sunrise, sunset, and everything in between. Sweet pain wrenched her breast, and she found herself blinking back tears. "I cannot think of *only* in terms of you, Archer," she whispered.

In the dark, his hand found hers, and their fingers

linked. "That is where we differ," he said. "For me, there is only Miri. And nothing else." Soft lips trailed over her earlobe and down her neck. His mouth brushed over her skin, nuzzling and tasting, down to her collarbone. Pleasant warmth spread along her limbs, and she closed her eyes with a sigh.

The hard line of his muscular length pressed against her. She fought the urge to turn into him and rest her cheek against his chest. He made no move to kiss her. She started to speak but stopped as she felt, with unmistakable clarity, his fingers grasp hold of the topmost satin ribbon that held her bodice in place. Her belly tightened painfully as he pulled with infinite slowness on the end of the ribbon. The bow came undone with a gentle tug, and the silky bodice slipped a fraction. A wave of heat washed down her limbs.

Archer's breath released with a sigh. His hand went to the next bow. In a haze, she wondered over the accuracy of his touch. Surely he could not see.

Slowly, the long ribbon traveled through its tight loop, moving by inches until she bit her lip in anticipation. It caught at the end, holding a moment as though teasing her, then released. The bodice slid open with a whisper of silk. Her breasts lay exposed, her nipples hardening against the cool air. She took a shallow breath, acutely aware of her breasts trembling from the movement. Archer groaned deep within his chest. Her belly quivered as he bent over her.

The space between her legs softly throbbed, the urge to lift her breast to his mouth enough to make her shake. Her fingers dug into the pillow beneath her head. She would not be the first to...Firm lips grazed the tender peak of her breast, and then his hot, wet tongue slid over her nipple. She gasped, and he licked again, long and lazy as a cat. Heat washed over her skin and down into her belly as he continued to lick her nipple, swirling and flicking the hardened nub with unhurried languor. Whimpering, she arched up greedily, wanting a stronger touch.

Archer complied, pulling the nipple into his warm mouth to suck it gently, so that she felt the heat and wetness of his mouth, the press of his tongue. She groaned, tiny wisps of flame licking up her thighs, and reached for him. Deftly, he caught her wrist and pinned it high above her head.

His lips released her nipple with a soft, wet pop before traveling to the full underside of her breast. Little mewling noises escaped her as he nuzzled her breast, sucking and nibbling on it before returning to its peak with a sigh of pleasure. His big hand skimmed over her ribs to palm her neglected breast, kneading it gently, brushing his thumb over the throbbing tip until she did not know which sweet torture was greater, his mouth or his hand. He tweaked her nipple, and she rose off the bed.

Miranda pressed her thighs together, trying to ease the ache between her legs. But Archer knew. Something near a chuckle rumbled in his chest, and his hand caressed down her hip to inch the thin lace skirt up with his fingers. The peignoir pooled about her waist, and with it came the cool kiss of air upon her legs.

"Archer..."

He had both of her hands now pinned high above her head as he feasted on her breasts, while his sly fingers tickled her thighs, coaxing them open until they spread like wings for him. He trembled then stilled. His lips grazed over her neck to her earlobe to nip it.

In the darkness, she felt the curve of his lips smiling

against her ear, then the deep rumble of his voice as he whispered, "Do you want me to touch you..." The tip of his finger slid between her legs and gently pressed against a spot that made her gasp. "Here?"

She shivered at the unexpected thrill of Archer speaking such things to her, and the feel of his finger playing wickedly with her body. "Yes." It was little more than a sigh, but he heard.

He smiled again. "God, you're lovely." He exhaled with a shudder and softly kissed below her ear. The smile returned, the rough grain of his cheek caressing her jaw. "And mine."

His thumb made a slow, tortuous circle, and her abdomen clenched. She lifted her hips, turning toward him, searching for his mouth, but he moved his lips to her neck. His smooth chest pressed against her torso, his strong fingers moving slowly against her sex, delving into the slickness. Madness. She wanted him on her. In her. She could not think. She wanted his mouth. That tempting mouth she'd stared at for an eternity.

"Archer..." she panted. "Kiss me."

A strangled sound of need tore from him, and he surged upward. His lips met hers, open and fierce. She drank him up, her mind reeling with heady intoxication. His tongue slid over hers, tasting of brandy and cream, as he pulled her close and the hard length of his sex pressed into her belly.

"Let me," he groaned against her open mouth. His fingers plunged into her hair, holding her head immobile as he fed off her lips. "Only, let me and I'll never stop."

She wrapped her legs about his, her hand sliding beneath his silken dressing robe to stroke the flesh too long denied to her, and he groaned again. The feel of his skin, the smooth dip in his lower back. A window opened in her mind. She was holding him. There were no scars rippling over his back, no mangled flesh, only smooth, cool skin. Only Archer. Archer's bare hands on her, the hard plane of his cheek, the gentle press of his brow against hers. Unmasked. It was unforgivable to do it but she had to know. But then *he* would know. He would know her secret—and what would he say?

Anger surged over her skin, hot and sure. Toward him. And herself. Would she be any different than he if she hid her secret? His large palm slid up to cover her breast in possession. No, she would not. There would be no more secrets between them. The decision barely settled in her mind before the familiar burn leapt free of her skin.

Light blazed all at once, the sconces and hearth flaring to life in an instant. Miranda's eyes squeezed tight against the blinding brilliance as a mighty roar of outrage rang in her ears.

He leapt as though burned, flinging the coverlet over her in one swift move. Still half-blind from the sudden light, she struggled with the covers, kicking them back and swinging her tangled legs free. Black spots danced before her eyes as she righted herself. She blinked again, and the room drew into focus. He was gone. She gazed around in a panic and caught a sudden movement. In the farthest corner of the room, between the curtained window and the large wardrobe, he pressed deep into the shadows like a frightened animal.

And she stalked him as such, coming as near as she dared. With his back to the corner, his hands flat against the walls, he stiffened as she drew close.

Miranda's steps slowed as she gazed up at the man she called her husband. He could only gaze back, his eyes wide and slightly panicked. They stared at each other for a moment before his eyes drifted downward to her breasts. The line of his throat convulsed. Hastily, she drew the edges of her bodice together and tied it.

"Thank you." The familiar sound of his warm, rich voice made her twitch. "After tasting such delights, the sight of your lovely breasts at this moment just might do me in."

She could only gape at him.

"How did you do it?" Soft gray eyes moved over her and then away. "The lamps?"

"I—I...it is complicated." How could it be? She stared, unable to comprehend what she saw.

"Your cheese and toast solution?"

She stepped forward, and he took a sharp breath, his fine nostrils flaring. "Archer, please...don't jest with me."

"What am I to do?" he whispered. "Any moment now, you'll come to your senses and order me from your room." Agony broke over his face. "And I will not be able to bear it."

He was right to fear. The irrational part of her wanted to scream in confusion. She had expected scars, horrible burns perhaps—or maybe disfigurement. But the man before her was smooth. Smooth yet damaged all the same. The whole of his right side was altered somehow. It was as though half of his body had turned into living ice. His flesh was clear, nearly translucent, like quartz. The hair on the right side of his head was silver. He wore it shorn close to his head, short silvery hairs meeting with black. Half man, half statue. The oddity of seeing healthy golden flesh merge with clear marble in a jagged line down the center of his body seemed unreal, as if a dream.

"What has happened to you?"

"*Lux Daemon*," he said with a wince. "Light Demon. Or, if you want to use the more apropos term, *Anima Comedentis,* a Soul Eater. That is what I am becoming. I drank an elixir, the liquid form of the demon, actually. At the time, we thought it a cure, a vaccination that would make man immune from disease. Fools. It has preserved my body while it slowly transforms me into a monster. A thing that feeds off the light of souls, craves that light more than air."

"You're ... possessed?" she asked through cold lips.

"This demon, it isn't a higher being of intelligence with thoughts such as ours, more like a virus. It infects the host and changes it to suit its purposes." He raked his fingers through his hair. "Nothing I've tried can reverse it. Only sheer will slows its tide." A desolate laugh escaped him. "Something to be grateful for, I suppose." He closed his eyes as if pained. "Once it reaches my heart, takes over my brain, I will turn. For they are the house and window of my soul."

"There must be a way—"

"It is indestructible, Miri. I cannot be physically injured where I've changed. Not in any obvious way, at least. Knives, swords, bullets are unable to pierce this flesh. The only recourse I have not tried is setting myself on fire." He snorted softly. "I find the notion vastly unappealing."

She could well understand that, though the thought of him considering the action made her heart ache.

He gazed down at his fists. "I am a nightmare. Just as you said."

Her mouth turned to sand. Stupid, unforgivable words she'd uttered. "You are not." She reached out to touch his cheek, and he jerked back, his head hitting the wall with a thud.

"Don't."

He was weak as a kitten under her gaze, and she took advantage ruthlessly. The tips of her fingers grazed his translucent cheek, and he shuddered. Her fingers curled, recoiling from the foreign flesh, so very smooth. Just like marble.

His eyes, now that she could view them fully, were beautifully formed, deep-set with friendly crinkles at the corners. Thick, dark brows curved gently upward as though he were in a constant state of ironic inquiry and found the world amusing, if not a bit ridiculous. The skin around the right eye was silvery blue, making the gray of his iris all the more startling. A smudge of black remained in one of the tender grooves around his eyes.

"Kohl," he said, watching her as she rubbed her thumb over the smudge. "Vegetable dye on my right lashes and brow. Eula said I'd blind myself but I really didn't see any other recourse..." His helpless babble trailed off as Miranda continued to stare without speaking.

The line of change ran from beneath the hairline of his left brow in a diagonal slant to the right, down across the high bridge of his nose and toward his right jaw. Most of his neck was healthy flesh but the wicked line of blue-crystalline skin divided his torso from collarbone to navel where it moved toward his left hip and disappeared under his dressing robe.

The left side of his body glowed with healthful vigor. Fine black hairs dusted his chest and abdomen. His breath quickened as her fingers brushed over the hairs, but he did not move to stop her. The stitches had healed clean, the scar from the knife fight now a thin smooth line. The sight of it gave proof that it was truly Archer before her and not a vision.

His right side was just as beautifully sculpted with hard, flat muscles, but entirely hairless and clear as quartz—moonstone, she realized, catching a glimpse of her wedding ring. A body of sculpted moonstone with nothing inside, no sight of bones or blood. Nothing a living, breathing man might need to survive.

"It wasn't fair for me to claim you." He held himself as still as a soldier. "I've behaved abominably. I am sorry," he said, not meeting her eyes. "Sorry to have brought you into a life filled with such horrors." His head bowed, exposing the tender column of his neck.

How could he think himself a horror? He was beautiful. The sculpted lines of his face were strong and sure. Without the mask, he appeared younger than she'd thought, perhaps just thirty.

His hair lay thick on his well-shaped head, and she ran her hand over the shorn locks bristly as a boar brush, before resting it on the back of his warm neck. " 'I might call him a thing divine,' " she quoted. " 'For nothing natural I ever saw so noble.' "

He winced, and she knew he was more comfortable with being reviled. She'd seen enough looks of revulsion cast his way to bruise her heart for a lifetime.

His dressing robe gaped at the chest but held fast at his waist with a silken cord.

"Show me all of it," she said quietly.

His expressive brows lifted but the cord gave way with a pull of his silver hand. The robe slipped apart and then fell. Narrow hips, long and well-formed legs of translucent flesh shone in the light; even the proud length of his sex had turned.

"Oh, Archer." Her hand slid along the milky silver of his skin, down his neck and to his chest, moving along the ridges of muscle, outlined like sculpted crystal. It was ironic that he likened her to a Michelangelo, for his was a body the master would have admired. He shivered delicately but held still. His body was not as warm as it ought to be, nor was it cold. It was cool, as though he'd been out on a crisp autumn day. Not ice and marble but satin skin.

His hand touched hers, stopping its exploration. "Neither man nor beast," he croaked.

She met his gray eyes—silver, she realized. A flash of silver like ice took over his gaze when he felt great emotion. It was part of the change.

"I ache for your touch," he said thickly. "Yet to look upon you fills me with despair. I cannot have you as I want you. And I despair."

She pressed her palm into his chest. "Oh, Archer, you have me. I am yours."

He shook his head woodenly, the corners of his eyes creasing as though he were at war inside himself.

She wrapped her arms about his trim waist and pressed her lips to the cool expanse of his chest. "You have no choice in the matter, Benjamin Archer. I love you. Nothing you say will change that."

Something in him broke. Miranda felt the tremor against her arms before a great sob tore from him. His arms curled round her as he began to cry, and his strength gave out. She fell with him, landing upon his lap to cradle his head on her shoulder.

He clutched her tightly as though she might slip away, sobs wracking his body as the loneliness he'd held within unleashed in a torrent. The sound of his anguish pulled tears to her eyes. He cried like a babe unbidden as she murmured unintelligible words of comfort, stroking his soft hair.

After a time, he quieted and the shaking ended. She dried his tears with his dressing gown and then held him, their arms and legs akimbo, the flickering light of the wall sconce above and the quiet of the house surrounding them. She loved him. It had always been so. His arms relaxed, and he turned his face into the crook of her neck.

"I love you too," he whispered tenderly. "So very much."

Miranda closed her eyes with a sigh and let her head fall against his.

"Say my name again," he pleaded against her skin.

A smile ghosted over her lips. "Benjamin."

He nuzzled the sensitive hollow of her throat, creating little shivers down her back. "Again."

"Benjamin."

His lips found hers.

"Benjamin," she said between soft, gentle kisses. "Ben." She caught his face in her hands, one cheek warm, the other cool.

His beautiful gray eyes locked onto hers, and his lips curled into a smile. "I have not been Ben to anyone," he said, his voice rough with emotion.

She brushed a kiss over his high, clean cheekbone and then on the corner of his mouth. "That is because Ben belongs to me." Her lips fitted over his, opening his soft mouth with her own, and he sighed. "*You* are mine."

He pulled her closer. "I have always been yours, Miranda Fair. Just as you have been the only one for me. Only you. Always."

The hard swells of his shoulders quivered beneath her touch but he put a staying hand upon her when she moved to kiss him. "Miri…" He cupped her face in his hands, and his eyes grew haunted. "I admit not being able to reason where you are concerned. I see you, and I want you. I love you to distraction." His forehead rested against hers. "Miri, if we had only one night together"—he swallowed hard—"would you still want this?"

His words slid cold down her back. "What are you saying, Archer?"

Archer ran his thumb over her lip. "The killer is still out there. There isn't a cure for me. I . . ." His eyes closed. "I wish the situation were different."

She clenched his wrists, as if they could anchor her. A tremor went through him, and his long fingers slipped into her hair.

"What did you say before?" she whispered. "That life is here and now?" Her hand went to his cheek. "We shall take the here and now." Miranda swallowed past the lump in her throat. Slowly, her hand went to the ribbon at her breast and pulled the tie loose. The peignoir slipped from her shoulders. "I've been your bride long enough; now make me your wife."

Archer studied her with an expression that was almost fierce. The avid heat and want in his eyes sent a bolt of heat straight through her. Tenderly, he cupped her cheek, holding his gaze with hers as he slowly bent forward, giving her time. Time to move away, time to change her mind. Miri met him halfway, her lips melting against his, their sighs mingling. His kiss was deep and sure as if they had all the time in the world. She murmured her pleasure as he pulled her farther onto his lap to straddle him.

God, he was strong. Muscles shifted and bunched beneath her questioning hands. Smooth, cool marble became heated stone as his kiss deepened and became insistent. He trembled, and the strong arms that bracketed her tightened. "Don't stop." It was part plea, part demand.

"I'd forgotten," he whispered, "how it felt to be touched. To have hands upon my skin."

Then she would never stop. Tremulously, she caressed the smooth slope of his back to the rounded curves of his shoulders. Archer sighed, his long body moving against her hand like a contented cat. "And kisses?" she murmured and placed a kiss on one corner of his mouth. Then the other. "More of those?"

His eyes drifted closed. "If you must." His breath hitched as she kissed the tender spot at the juncture of his neck and shoulder. The skin was satin there, cool and strong. She moved to the other side, where the scent of him was heady and warm, and his pulse jumped beneath her lips. Silence lay thick around them, highlighting the lazy crackle of the fire in the grate. She pressed each soft kiss along his shoulder, increasing the cadence of Archer's breathing.

Firelight flickered over his skin, setting it aglow like sunshine on winter ice. Down her hand went, over hard, flat pectorals, along the little ravine that divided his abdominal muscles. His navel was a small half-moon and ticklish, she discovered as taut muscles around it twitched at her touch. The thick length of his sex lay almost flat against his stomach, reaching toward his navel. It was changed, the color of ice. Fascinated, she wrapped her hand around it.

Archer hissed sharply. His hand locked on her wrist. "You will kill me," he rasped. His grip on her tightened as if to pull her away, but then he stilled, and his fingers settled over hers, holding her there, urging her on. Enthralled, she stroked down. A weak curse tore from his lips, and his head fell against her shoulder. Heat swelled over her as she stroked, watching him shiver, his muscles tensing. He was hard as marble, yet pulsing with life. She squeezed and a choked sound rumbled in his throat.

"Harder?" she whispered. Vividly, she remembered him pushing her into a cold wall, his long fingers probing her. The helplessness and urgency, the luscious heat. Her insides tightened.

His brows knitted, a look of agony darkening his features yet his mouth was slack with pleasure. "Yes... God, yes."

She complied, and he convulsed, his narrow hips thrusting up to meet her as if compelled. Her core pulsed in response. She wanted to bite his neck, lick his skin, drive him over the edge. Groaning, Archer burrowed his face into her neck, his hands weakly clutching her upper arms.

"Faster?" He swelled within her hand.

"Yes."

A strangled sound died on his lips as she moved faster, watching his large frame shake. Heat throbbed between her legs; the empty void there wanting to be filled. Archer's fingers bit into her skin, his breath coming in shallow gasps. Unable to help herself, she leaned forward and sank her teeth into the hard muscle of his shoulder. The response was immediate. Archer's hand clasped hers, yanking it away, as his other cupped her nape and pulled her down to his mouth.

The kiss was deep and hard and frantic. She wrapped her legs around his waist as his tongue plumbed her mouth in deep strokes, and he tweaked her nipples, tender little tugs that pulled mewling cries from her lips. Red lust sent her head spinning. Her arms wrapped about his damp neck, and she rocked against his sex, her breasts heavy and aching, her skin tight and hot. "Archer," she whimpered against his mouth.

Soft carpet met her back, his hard flesh and untapped strength surging over her, pressing her down, his mouth never leaving hers. "I will try to be gentle, Miri," he promised against her lips. The tip of his sex bunted up against hers, so big that she convulsed. "I swear," he said breathlessly. "I'll try."

And then she understood.

"It is all right." Her hand curled around his neck. "I've done this before—" She broke off in horror, and their gazed locked. The tips of her breasts trembled against the smooth contours of his chest as he froze. Archer's expression shifted, warring with jealousy and something deeper. His clear eyes gleamed, and she realized it was the masculine thrill of possession.

"But not with me." And with those calm words, he entered, thick and hot and parting her swollen flesh so slowly that the whole of her senses focused on it. Lord, it was not like her first time. He was bigger. Almost too much for her. She felt stretched and invaded, yet a tight ache quivered in her belly, demanding that she be taken. And taken thoroughly. Heat crested over her skin at the thought, and she arched up into him, her legs parting on a breath, but he stopped, the line of his throat moving as he swallowed.

He hovered over her, his arms shaking with effort, the sinews along his shoulders and chest standing out in fine relief. "God." He pushed a little deeper and then stilled again. "Too good," he croaked.

"Too . . ." She cleared her throat. Desire steamed in her veins. "Too good?"

His muscles twitched, his breath ratcheting. "Jesus, yes." Brows furrowed, eyes shut, he held a look of intense pain, but for the way his lips opened, panting and soft. So utterly delicious looking that she licked the tender column of his throat.

"*Miri.*" A bead of sweat trickled along his temple as he gave her a helpless look. "I'm a lit cannon about to go off." He swallowed hard. "It's been years and you're . . . you."

That he was all but undone by her sent a possessive thrill coursing through her veins. She wrapped her arms about him, wanting to bring him closer. Unhinge him the way he unhinged her.

"Don't move," he rasped. "For the love of God."

Smiling, she smoothed her hands over the taut swells of his buttocks and gripped them. Her legs slid up his thighs to wrap around his waist, and he groaned hard, nudging a bit deeper. Pleasure scattered through her center. Poor Archer, he didn't stand a chance. "Think of England, darling."

A choked laugh burst from his lips. "Witch." His eyes opened, and the pained expression broke into something so tender and hot her heart kicked. "God, I love you," he whispered, then thrust in with a deep glide that made her moan.

His nostrils flared before the tight hold he had on himself broke. His mouth took hers, open and wanting. Their fingers twined, and he lifted her hands high above her head, holding them there as he pumped into her with hard, deep strokes. Liquid heat, thick and viscous like lamp oil, flowed through her limbs. She writhed against it, pain blurring with pleasure. So this was need. Little grunts rumbled in his throat as he took her harder.

More. More. And more. It was not enough. And too much. Her breasts trembled with each thrust, the silk carpet at her back abrading her skin. The floorboards squeaked as his rhythm increased. His tongue plunged into her mouth, tangling with hers, stealing her breath. A dark, swirling thing—*need*—gripped hot and strong. She moved against him, straining, reckless with it. Her nails scored his back to spur him on. He grunted and slipped a hand between them, finding the slick nub of sensitive flesh between her legs, and tweaked it. Her body tightened in white-hot pleasure, and her heels dug into the floor as sensation punched into her.

He watched her as she came apart. Pushed deep within her, he ground himself against that sensitive spot that fractured her, set her body on fire. Gasping, she gazed up at him, and those silver eyes held hers. For one sharp moment, he was whole and unchanged with golden skin, tousled black curls falling over his brow. A picture of the man he truly was inside. *Mine.* Tenderness, lust, and love crushed her chest, so brutal and sharp that she sobbed.

"Archer." She touched his cheek. And like that he came. Hard. His shout reverberated through the room as he bucked above her, the tendons in his neck standing out like vines, his cock pulsing within her. Another wave of blinding heat took her. She clutched him as if she could pull him inside of her skin. They strained against each other for one tense moment before her hands fell weakly to the floor.

On a sigh, he settled over her, cocooning her within his arms, their sweat-slicked bodies sliding a bit as they lay panting. Slowly she came back to herself. Archer eased onto his side, taking her with him, his lips tickling her damp brow as his long fingers threaded through her hair.

"Oh my," she whispered breathlessly.

A puff of warm air hit her cheek. "Quite."

His lashes curled like black fans around deep gray eyes. With a wobbling smile, he kissed her, a gentle touch meant to soothe, yet his lips clung, then nipped. A surge of warmth washed thorough her. His tongue touched hers, and his cock, still deep and hard inside her, twitched. Anticipation fluttered. Flushing, she rocked her hips in question. He smiled against her lips and nudged back. *Oh my.* Warmth turned to heat, the tight ache returning to her belly. *Again?* His eyes met hers, and she saw the heat there, languid yet sure.

"Stamina," he whispered against her mouth. A wolfish grin lit his features as he rolled back over her and gently but firmly proceeded to give her an in-depth lesson on the very subject.

A figure stood alone in the empty rooms of a grand town house. From outside came the gentle clatter of a hansom, and farther off the soft chime of bells. Unending darkness, both outside and in, made the cold room an inky well. One more day and everything would fall into place.

Soft clicks sounded as the killer paced in slow meditation. The watch called the hours, a gentle song that announced the ebbing of time. Archer's movements used to be as predictable as the tides. And now, one could never be sure. A grunt of agitation rang out. Archer's reprieve had been too long. Foolish. Another reminder was needed.

Chapter Twenty-nine

Wonderful, beautiful, blissful, gorgeous, lovely. Adjectives floated around in Archer's head like cherry blossoms falling in late spring. He wanted to laugh, shout, and run amok, singing at the top of his voice. Snatches of romantic poetry learned in his salad days came to mind. *She walks in beauty like the night; shall I compare thee to a summer's day?* He smiled then, looking up at the ceiling above his bed. He certainly did not possess the talent to fit into words what he felt. Too bad Byron was dead. He'd have hunted him down and introduced him to Miri. The master poet would have found words to do her justice.

He glanced at his glorious, beautiful, wonderful wife lying asleep at his side. The deep curve of her narrow back glowed like Egyptian alabaster in the sunlight. The silken tumble of her hair, golden with glints of fire, fell over her pillow and onto his shoulder. As always his breath came in little stabs of sweet pain when he looked at her. Miri, his miracle, his little fire starter. Laughter bubbled up within him. He ought to have known she would possess some extraordinary power; she was too sensible to have such little fear in dangerous situations. Cheese on toast, indeed.

A small sound escaped her lips, and she shifted in her sleep, lifting her arm a bit. The curve of her breast came into view, plump and pressed against the bedding. Archer's cock twitched impatiently. He wanted to see her nipples. Nipples that had fulfilled his lewd imagination, deep rose and entirely suckable. He grinned, remembering how she liked that, how she nearly came undone whenever he touched them. That she gave herself fully to him should not have surprised him—Miri never did anything by half—but it did. The tightness in his chest expanded. She was his. Every cell in his body knew her, sang her name, and throbbed with the same thoughts over and over: *mine, want, need.*

He ought to be satiated. He'd come to her again, and again. It merely had the same effect as throwing brandy on fire. He simply burned hotter. A heat nearly frenetic in its intensity.

His fevered brain drifted back to the early hours of the morning, of sliding against her silky skin, his cock pushing into her tight heat, gently, oh so gently, for she had been swollen and tender. Yet ready. *"Now, Archer. Now..."* His loins tightened at the memory of the stiff tips of her breasts brushing against his chest. His mouth against hers, lips and tongue slip sliding as that tight, slicked heat slowly milked him.

She had been so hot, a living brand in his arms, and the very air around them heated with her, warming the cold within him until he too grew flushed and feverish. Hot lust coursed through his limbs, throbbing in his cock. Her trembling little hands roamed over his back, one long finger tracing a path of fire down his spine, and then lower to slip between his buttocks and explore there as well. The molten shock of it. He'd come undone then, plowed her softness without finesse or thought. Simple need that made him come in her like a brushfire.

Afterward, she'd burrowed closer, wrapping her elegant limbs about his. Yet there was a touch of fear in her eyes. "The sheets are steaming."

Heat surrounded them, a caress of balmy air that caused the little red tendrils about her temples to curl in riotous profusion, as they lay damp and limp in each other's arms.

"The air as well." He wasn't capable of saying more. His heart raced, his breath still coming in quick pants.

Her great eyes had gazed up at him, misted and green like sea glass. "And if the fire within me should break free and consume us both?" she whispered, a tiny line forming between her arched brows.

Then I'd die complete. His fingers sifted through her silken hair. "Then it would have consumed us long before." He'd smiled then, a tremble of lips for all his exhaustion, and touched her face, his fingers weak yet sure as he traced her succulent mouth and felt her shiver. He understood then. Pleasure, fire, guilt, and destruction, they were inextricably woven together for her. To feel pleasure in the midst of releasing such terrible power, how very well he understood that particular dilemma.

His brow rested against hers. "You think I don't feel that same thrill when I use what gifts I have?"

Her warm voice cracked like a crust on honey. "You're not afraid? Of what I am?"

Had she not been so earnestly worried, he would have laughed at the irony. Instead, he looked at her solemnly. "You are getting a good look at me, are you not?"

"That isn't the same. You're cursed."

He'd laughed then, his heart as light as air. "Funny, I don't feel cursed at the moment."

A weak smile broke over her lips, fighting with a frown. She was not completely convinced. He kissed her eyelids, her cheeks.

"The fire is your strength, what protects you when I cannot. Do not fear it, but embrace it, for it is part of your soul. You know how to use this gift, Miranda. Inside, you know." When she released a shuddering sigh and gave a short nod, his hand tightened on the back of her neck and drew her near, need and lust rekindled just by holding her close. "Kiss me." *Set me afire again. And again.*

Next to him, Miri gave another soft sigh. Pure lust shot through him as he watched her elegant back lift and fall. Even now, should he roll over and slip his hand down that sweeping curve, over the rounded tightness of her bottom, she would turn to him, her slim arms open, that luscious mouth soft in invitation.

Despite his personal vow to give her some rest, he found himself moving to touch her as he craved when the image of a young urchin knocking on his front door came sharply to mind. *The boy handed Gilroy a small white box tied with a silver ribbon. For Lord Archer, guvnor.* Cold, dark dread sucked Archer away from Miranda. He swung out of bed and headed for his dressing room, aware of each instance that his feet struck the floor, and of every hard beat of his heart. The world had caught up to them.

Gilroy greeted him with some surprise as Archer trotted down the stairs, his dressing robe snapping around his ankles. From somewhere to his right, he heard a sucked-in breath. One of the footmen. Archer had left off his mask, forgotten it entirely in his haste. Did it even matter anymore?

The innocent-looking box lay in Gilroy's white-gloved hand. A silver ribbon wrapped round it. *Christ.*

His pulse pounded at the base of his neck as he drew near. "The box, if you please, Gilroy."

His stomach lurched at the light weight of it, and the faint feeling of something sliding about within. A smell drifted up. Death and rot. Archer thought he might be sick.

He headed for his library, only vaguely aware that Gilroy followed. The ribbon slipped from his fingers twice. Finally, the lid lifted, and with it, the floor seemed to slide beneath him. Miranda's fragile butterfly mask, spotted with dark blood, fluttered in his hand as he lifted it from the box, and then he spied what lay beneath. Shriveled and brown, one might think it a withered bloom. Merryweather's ear. Pain sliced through him, white-hot like a brand to his heart. He stood for several moments simply trying to breathe through it, Gilroy's knobby hand upon his shoulder, holding him steady. But the pain would not abate, nor the terror that made him want to scream. Because his time was up. He'd have to part from her. *Miri.* He sank to his knees, away from the box, and the card that fluttered to the floor, its message written in a simple scrawl.

—*Cavern Hall. On the new moon.*

Chapter Thirty

———— ❧❧ ————

Tender and sore and very nearly exhausted, Miranda
stretched luxuriantly along Archer's bedroom couch with
a sigh. She'd never felt better. Her skin tingled, her chest
felt both tight and filled with a sense of largess, as though
the world might fit inside her. Like a girl she giggled,
turning her head toward the leather backing to feel its
cool smoothness.

Archer had gone out with a newly hired security spe-
cialist. They were to survey the grounds for points of
possible weakness, he claimed. Rather a bit of overkill
at any rate, Miranda thought, as she and Archer were
a far greater threat than any fence. For the first time in
memory, she felt truly grateful for her power—her gift, as
Archer called it. Her strength would protect them, and the
rest they would solve together.

"It will be only a short while," he had promised with
a kiss.

"Well, this is a fine kettle of fish," said a familiar, sharp
voice.

Miranda whirled around to find Eula scowling at her.

"Here you are, stretched out like the cat that ate the cream, and His Majesty is sauntering about the house mask-less and *whistling* like a kettle." Her mouth puckered as though filled with lemons.

"That is quite the number of eloquent metaphors, Eula," Miranda retorted, too happy to spar even with her. "Have you more to heap upon my head? Or may I help you with something?"

Eula's wrinkled face turned puce. "I have been taking care of him for the whole of my life. The *whole* of it. Seen the suffering that curse has caused him. And you two think one night of passion will solve everything." Miranda sat up, surprise and outrage warring within her, but Eula's puckered mouth broke into a wide grin, and she spoke over Miranda's sputtered protest. "Package for you, *madam.*"

A rectangular package sailed from Eula's hand and slapped lightly upon Miranda's thighs. The knowing look upon Eula's face as she left the room caused Miranda's heart to trip as she curled her legs up before her and ripped open the box.

A calling card slipped out. One that she recognized with a flush of irritation. He'd left a note on the back, scrawled in his slanted hand.

> *Every woman deserves to enter a marriage fully armed. One day Archer will thank me. Even if he'll never admit it.*
>
> —*I*

That Mckinnon seemed oddly concerned for Archer's welfare left her cold and confused. With a shaking hand, she tossed the card aside and reached inside the box. A gilt frame slipped onto her palm. She pulled the tissues back and her ears began to buzz. There, in precise and masterful brushstrokes, lay a face well-loved and unmistakable. The same ironic brows, gently curved tip of the nose, fine gray eyes full of humor. Archer. A mad snort left her lips as she spied a tiny dot of black just above his left eyebrow. Archer's beauty mark—mole, rather. Men, he had insisted, do not have marks of beauty. Debatable issues aside, it was he. Unmistakably. And dressed in a double-breasted waistcoat, frock coat with tails, and a high, swaddling collar. A man of an earlier time.

Even if she could invent a reason for his antiquated dress, she could not overlook the painted date upon the portrait: 1810. Nor the engraved plaque that read, LORD BENJAMIN ARCHER, THIRD BARON ARCHER OF UMBERSLADE. It might all be tricks. But her heart knew it was not. She had let herself be lied to. Because it was easier.

More papers drifted from the box, her eyes picking up the relevant details as though pinpoints of light touched upon them in illumination: BENJAMIN ARCHER, BROTHER OF RACHEL, KARINA, CLAIRE, AND ELIZABETH. SON OF KATORINA AND WILLIAM. LORD BENJAMIN ARCHER TO RETURN FROM ITALY. LORD ARCHER TO ATTEND SISTER ELIZABETH'S FUNERAL. And the final nail: LORD BENJAMIN ARCHER, DEPARTING FOR AMERICA, OCTOBER 20, 1815.

Archer's family. Archer's loss. Archer's lie. Of course it was.

Numbly, she picked up the papers, tucking them away. One thought revolved sickly around in her head. Benjamin Archer had drifted through life, unchanged, since

1815. She knew him too well not to know that he'd been searching for a cure all that time—and had failed. Even more distressing—what did it mean to Archer physically should he find a cure?

He came home shortly after three. She heard his light greeting to Gilroy in the hall, followed by the rapid tread of his boots up the stairs. Her heart pounded overloud in her breast at the thought of confronting him. She had sat like a statue for the rest of the day, barely able to think or to breathe, only to wait. Now he was here.

Sliding to the foot of the bed, she set her feet on the floor. Determination to have her say steeled her spine. The connecting door to their rooms opened a moment later. His eyes went immediately to her, and a smile broke over his face. "That," he said shutting the door behind him, "took inordinately long."

He tore the silk mask from his head as he came near. Miranda's resolve softened as she saw the joy in his eyes in doing so. It was the first time he'd taken the mask off in front of her. Black kohl encircled his eyes, and her lips twitched.

"You look like a bandit," she said as he bent to kiss her.

Archer paused, caught between a grin and a grimace. "Right." He brushed a kiss over her nose and then strode toward her bathing room, impatiently pulling off his suit coat as he went. Her heart stayed locked in her throat as she stared after him.

He emerged not a minute later, freshly scrubbed and wearing only his drawers and shirtsleeves. "Is it unmanly to say that I prefer your face cream to mine?" he asked, unbuttoning his shirt with a deftness and speed that entranced her.

"No." Nothing about him could ever be considered unmanly. Again the flash came, of him not changed but whole and unaffected. Golden skinned. His hair not shorn but with glossy raven locks. *Ben.*

The shirt fell to the floor, and her breath hitched. He was simply beautiful. From the corded muscles of his shoulders and arms, to the little hollow between his collarbones, and the flat, matched ridges running down his abdomen like paving bricks, all of it was beautiful, and enough to make words fail her.

He read her look and grinned wide enough for small lines to dimple his cheeks. "Hello," he whispered before catching her up. She could not think. It was like a drug taking hold of her when they kissed. She pressed against him, her lips throbbing under his ministrations. Could a man be an addiction?

His quick fingers made short work of her laces. Her bodice fell free, and his thumb ran under the curve of her breast. Hot shivers fanned out along her belly. She pulled away, her hands going to his shoulders to hold him off. "No," she said. "Stop."

Her tone froze him. Slowly he moved off the bed and sat back on his heels. His gray eyes searched her face and, reading what was so plainly there, he set his chin firm—a fully guilt-ridden gesture if ever Miranda saw one.

"Were you going to tell me?" she asked.

"I don't know." The pulse at the base of his throat throbbed as he sat watching her, his body still as stone, and the ache in Miranda's chest turned to pain.

"Well, that *is* heartening," she snapped, her fingers digging into the covers. "Honesty above all, is it?"

"Who was it?" he said, still frozen in place. "Eula?

Mckinnon?" A hot wash of color rose up over his left cheek, and he jumped to his feet. "Son of a bitch."

Miranda jumped up too. "What does it matter who told me? It should have been you!"

"Tell you?" he snapped, his color rising. "You, who professed the possibility of what I was a nightmare?"

She winced at that, but her anger flared higher. "God! How stupid I've been." She paced in a helpless fury. "I asked you flat out. And what do you say to me? 'Lord Benjamin Archer died in eighteen-fifteen!'" Her voice rose as she punched the air. "When really it was you all along! Lord Benjamin Aldo Fitzwilliam Wallace Archer, third Baron Archer of Umberslade."

Ben watched her rant, his arms crossed over his chest, his jaw tight. "Yes, I am the third Baron Archer of Umberslade," he said tightly. "Does it really change who I am?"

"Of course it does!" She spun round. "It makes you a liar. When I have given you all of my truths."

He took a step forward, the flat muscles along his abdomen bunching. "By degrees," he said, flinging his arm wide. "Doled out like pieces of Sunday cake. And I understood that. It is what we all do."

"That is not at all the same thing! There is a difference between refraining from divulging the truth and outright lying."

Archer snorted. "Which appears to be knowing what questions to ask."

Her fists balled at her sides in an effort to hold still. "You ought to have believed in me. Believed in us. And those men, those poor old men. You're as old as they are!" She pressed her hands to her face, wanting to scream but unable to. "God."

"And what should I have said?" His dark brows rose in

inquiry. " 'I'm sorry, darling, but even if I do get better, I might turn into a withered husk and most likely die within months.' Would that have eased the way?"

Hearing it come from him hit like a slap. The floor tilted beneath Miranda. She could not stay and watch him be destroyed. "I'm leaving," she said through numb lips.

She turned for the door.

He was in front of her in an instant, slamming the door shut with his fist. "No." He grabbed her shoulders, spinning her round, shoving her back against the wall. "No," he said again, his voice breaking. His lips crushed against her, his fingers biting into her flesh.

She yielded to the pressure, and his tongue dove into her mouth. Miranda sucked it hard, needing to taste him, and he groaned. His fist pressed into her back, holding her tight enough to take her breath away.

"You can't leave me." He took her lower lip between his teeth. "I won't let you go."

She nipped back, her legs clenching his hard thigh. Shaking, his hand tore at her chemise and the fabric ripped.

"No." She wrenched her head to the side, away from his seeking mouth. "No!"

"Miri." It was a whimper of pain.

Suddenly she was hitting him, striking his hard chest with her fists. "You should have told me!"

He took her assault without flinching, and her hands fell to her sides. Hurting him only hurt her more.

He gazed at her sorrowfully but made no move to touch her. "My only excuse is fear," he whispered thickly.

"A sorry excuse," she sobbed, breathless from her spent fury. "When have you ever felt fear? The dauntless

Lord Archer. When I think of how you looked upon Cheltenham's body...you didn't even flinch. It was as if you
felt nothing."

"Felt nothing?" he hissed. His brow wrinkled as he
stepped back. "Felt nothing!" He moved with a blur of
speed and struck the side of the wardrobe. The thick
wood tore like paper under the impact of his fist.

He spun back to face her, the fine muscles along
his shoulders and chest tensing as a milky light pulsed
through his changed flesh—the sight of which alarmed
Miranda more than his fury.

"It was all I could do not to scream when we found
Chelt." He grasped the short hairs upon his head as though
he'd tear them out. Words poured from him like a purga-
tive. "Cheltenham and I visited each other in the nursery.
Merryweather and I roomed together in Cambridge. And
Leland...Leland was my best mate. He brought me into
West Club, then helped cast me out of London."

His large frame began to shake as if he'd soon break
apart. Miranda moved toward him, the pain of seeing him
suffer stronger than her anger, but he glared at her fiercely.
"Do you have any idea..." His breath hitched. "I've had
to watch them age, turn gray. I couldn't stand it. I had to
get away. That is the true reason I left, not because they
told me to go. And when I came back they were old, withered. A reminder of what I should be."

He took a shuddering breath, and his shoulders fell.
"I've watched *you* age. From a lovely young creature to
this woman who is so achingly beautiful...God!"

He spread his arms wide in entreaty before letting
them fall. "I lied. I lied when I said your beauty does not
affect me. I look at you, and I'm breathless, dizzy from it.
I want to kneel at your feet and worship you. While the

baser part of me wants to fling up your skirts and stick my cock in you until we forget our names." His nostrils flared as he glared at her, accusation and pain mingling within his eyes.

"But none of that matters," he said, trembling before her, "because every day that I am with you, I am more convinced that God made you just for me. For in ninety years on this earth, no one has made me feel the way you do, as if every day is an adventure. You make me laugh. And I never laugh. I go around smiling like a witless fool. So yes, I kept it from you, because I am so desperately in love with you that the knowledge that you might love me too was irresistible. And I was afraid it would turn to dust should I take off that mask."

A sound tore from his throat, and he turned away to lean against the wardrobe, resting his forearms over his head. The silver lines of his body glimmered in the afternoon sun that slanted through the lacy curtains. His voice drifted out, rough and choked. "How am I to resist the one thing I've ever truly wanted?"

His forehead hit the wood with a thud. "I am sorry, Miri," he finished weakly.

Miranda's vision blurred. There were lies, and there were lies. She went to him, sliding between his strong body and the wardrobe. Despite his distress, his arm automatically reached out to cocoon her against him as he breathed raggedly. "I'm sorry, Miri," he whispered against her hair. "I'm sorry..."

She smoothed his back. "Hush." Her lips brushed across his collarbone. She looked up at him through her tears and found his eyes red, his thick lashes clumping like spikes. "Do you think it is any different for me? I want you so much it is a constant ache."

He made a sound, and his lips found her temple. Soft kisses to ease her tears, yet her heart grew cold. She was losing him. He was retreating. Behind thick walls where feelings could not hurt him. She felt it as surely as the lips upon her brow. Miranda had lived in that cold dark place for most of her life.

She turned toward him, her cheek caressing his chin. "I need to hear your voice every day or I despair. You are the balance of my soul. I cannot lose you, Ben. I would not live through it."

The very idea caused her to sob, and he caught her mouth with his. "Don't cry," he whispered against her lips, his big hand cupping her cheek. "I can't bear it." He kissed her tears as she kissed his cheeks, eyes, and beloved jaw line.

She closed her eyes and let her forehead rest against his as they breathed together. Sick dread slid down her belly. She could sense the wild desperation filling him. She would lose him to this madness.

"We can solve this together." She kissed him softly, desperately. The taste of him broke her heart anew. "We will find a cure. And this killer...It takes only a thought for me to finish him. Do you understand?"

Suddenly he went utterly cold. "Yes." He closed his eyes and released a deep sigh. The fight in him seemed to drain. "I understand you perfectly."

When she moved to kiss him, he cupped her face in his hands, and his gray eyes searched her face as if to commit it to memory. "Know this, there is only one truth left to me." His trembling fingertips caressed her jaw. "That I love you." He said it again, his voice broken, his arms pulling her tightly against him. "I love you. The rest is darkness."

Her fingers curled around the smooth swells of his biceps. "Then let me be your light."

Archer shuddered, dragging an open-mouthed kiss across her cheek to claim her lips. "Always, Miri." He grew tighter, colder in her arms. "All that I am, all that I become, is for you."

Chapter Thirty-one

———— ❧ ❧ ————

No!" Miranda lurched out of bed, her heart pounding painfully. Shaking, she buried her face in her hands until little prickles of awareness set in. She whipped round, knowing she was alone, but needing to see. The bedding at her side was rumpled and empty. *Archer.* On his pillow lay the silver rose and a note. Pain spread through her middle, doubling her over, and she grabbed the note, seeing Archer's heavy scrawl, more slanted than usual.

—Forgive me.

Her knees knocked as she fell from the bed and scrambled to reach the water closet in time. She retched until she had no more to give, then fell upon the smooth, hard floor. *Why? Why, Ben?*

That he meant to face the killer alone was clear. Forgiveness meant only one thing—he did not mean to survive this confrontation.

Miranda curled into a tight ball, pressing her knees

hard into her aching chest. But the pain did not abate.
Cursing roundly, she climbed to her feet and washed her
face and mouth. Wallowing would help no one. *That God
damned sneaky bastard.*

Her fencing clothes, long unused but never forgotten,
flew from her wardrobe as she heaped more curses upon
her errant husband. If he thought she'd sit at home and let
him go off to die he was sorely mistaken.

"Eula! Gilroy!" Her shouts rang out shrilly as she
strode down the upper hall not two minutes later. Miranda
swallowed down her panic. She needed to think. The bun
secured at the nape of her neck was tight enough to pull
her scalp, and her head pounded rather dreadfully.

The hall remained empty. Miranda's boot heels clattered on the steps as she raced down them. "Eula!"

Finally, the cheeky woman appeared, shuffling with a
gait worthy of Methuselah.

"Trying to wake the dead, are you? What's amiss? You
and Lord Rapturous run out of fresh beds?"

"He's gone, Eula." Her lip trembled, and she bit it hard.
"For good."

Eula drew herself up with purpose. "Where?"

"I-I don't know. I thought you might." *Damn and hell.
I will not cry.*

She gaped at Miranda. Eula at a loss for words nearly
undid her. Miranda turned from her and headed for the
library, almost colliding into Gilroy. The stately butler
stumbled along, hastily dressed and rubbing the back of
his neck in a most unusual outward display of discomfort.

"Apologies, my lady." He made an effort to straighten.
"I was abed when you called. I do not know what came
over me."

Miranda eyed him carefully, taking note of his glazed

expression. "Lord Archer is gone. Do you know where he is?" She rather thought Gilroy did not.

"No, my lady." He blinked several times. "I've not seen him since he gave me a tisane for my aching joints last night."

Miranda ground her teeth together to keep from shouting. Poor Gilroy did not deserve her censure. "Tisane," she bit out at last. "The bloody man gave you a sleeping draught so you wouldn't wake when he left."

Gilroy's lean face went white. "You mean he has gone to face that fiend?"

Despite her resolve to stay calm, she grabbed his frail arm. "Do you know who it is? Where he could have gone?"

His shook his head wildly. "On my honor, I do not."

She closed her eyes for one precious moment. "Thank you, Gilroy. Have my horse saddled. Make sure to tell them I shall be riding astride. And find me a riding cloak."

His scandalized expression might have been laughable. "But my lady—"

"Blast it, Gilroy! I can't very well go out in a silken mantle." She gestured to her trousers and linen shirt. "Just find a damned cloak that will fit me and be quick about it. I don't care whose it is," she shouted at his rapidly retreating form.

Eula eyes gleamed. "Well, if yer up for screaming like a harpy then I expect you've enough mettle to bring him back."

Miranda tasted blood. "Find me a sword. Archer surely has one lying about." Her insides quaked. She hadn't practiced the sword in years, but the yearning and the need to wield it now stirred her blood, making her muscles twitch. "And Archer's spare pistol as well. Loaded, Eula," she said over her shoulder before she shut herself up in the library.

The room lay still and cool. It might have been waiting for him. She went to his desk. The cluttered chaos over it appeared untouched. She tore through it, searching for something, any clue. There was nothing.

Defeated, she dropped her head upon the desk. Tears would not come, no matter her frustration. She sat for a long moment, simply breathing. The killer's identity drifted just beyond her grasp, as ephemeral as smoke in the wind. She cast aside Lord Mckinnon. She rather thought Mckinnon flirted with her mainly to antagonize Archer. Irritating but not viscous. These murders had nothing to do with her and Archer, but with Archer and West Moon Club. Then there was the fact that Archer knew who the killer was. While Archer wanted her away from Mckinnon, he did so out of possessiveness, not from a genuine fear for her safety. Lord Rossberry then? But these murders were calculated, coolly done. With rage, yes, but the killer was a planner. Rossberry struck her as all rage and impulse. Then who?

Every conversation, every fight she'd had with Archer played in her mind, until the small tableaus of her life with him spun in a flash of colors like the inside of a kaleidoscope.

A thing that feeds off the light of souls...I am not so easily dispatched...What if I told you it is something wondrous and beautiful he hides...immortal.

Miranda reared up, her heart pounding in her throat. The spinning wheel stopped. What was once a blur suddenly came into sharp focus. Archer bending over Victoria. *Why are you here?*

Slowly, she pushed back from the desk. For every

father there is a mother. And every creation, a creator. *Stay away from her, Miranda*. Victoria, with her silver eyes and flashing white teeth. The makeup covering skin that surely gleamed like moonstone. *Archer broke my heart once. And I'm afraid I've never forgiven him for it.* Heaven has no rage like love to hatred turned, nor hell a fury like a woman scorned.

A mad cackle broke from Miranda's lips. He knew. He'd known all along. Only one thing could have escaped a man as strong as Archer: another immortal.

What I recognized was myself.

And now he'd gone to Victoria. Save she was whole, and he still part human. A final battle that he would not win. Unless...

"Bastard!"

Chapter Thirty-two

❧❧❧

Too bloody long. It took too bloody long to track down the home of Lord Maurus Robert Lea, Seventh damned Earl of Leland. Leland was Archer's best mate, was he? Brought him into this folly? Then he damned well better know where Archer was.

She rapped the knocker hard enough to draw stares from a smartly dressed couple headed out. One did not pound upon doors in Belgravia. Miranda glared in kind and resumed her assault on Leland's door.

It was yanked open by an affronted-looking butler who quivered with restrained irritation.

"Lady Archer to see Lord Leland," she snapped. "In short order, if you will."

He narrowed his eyes, no doubt seeing only her mannish costume. "He is not in. Here, here!"

She ignored this protest as she pushed past him. "Pardon me if I see for myself. Lord Leland!"

The sputtering butler was hot on her heels but skidded

to a stop as Lord Leland flew out of his library. Leland made a polite bow, drawing near.

"Lady Archer—"

Miranda pulled the sword from her belt and pinned Leland to the wall with it.

"You will forgive me, my lord, but let us get straight to the point." She nudged the uncapped sword against his cravat. "Tell me, where is my husband?"

Beside her, the butler moved to grab her arm. She pulled the gun from her waistcoat and aimed it at his heart. The hammer cocked with a loud click in the cavernous hall. "I'm quite a good shot as well," she said, keeping her eyes upon Leland. "Your master might be injured during a scuffle."

Leland swallowed hard but his sharp blue eyes stayed on Miranda. "Go on, Wilkinson," he managed at last. "Lady Archer and I have need of privacy."

The butler ran off, most likely to find reinforcements, and Miranda pocketed the pistol.

Leland looked down his crooked nose at the sword still hovering before him. "If you wouldn't mind, Lady Archer. I shall need my throat if I am to talk."

She lowered the sword and stepped back a pace.

He smiled thinly. "You know you might have simply asked."

She laughed without humor as she sheathed her sword. "I might have done," she said. "Save I am damned angry. And damned tired of high-handed men at the moment."

He gave a small bow of his head. "Understood."

"Do you know where he is?" Now that she was there, her fear surged forward once more, leaving her trembling.

"I do." He sighed then, looking very much his advanced age. "I am afraid you shall not like it."

Her lips quivered before she got hold of herself. "Where Archer and revelations are involved, I never do."

"Then you know him well." He extended his hand toward the open library door. "Come. We have some time left. And there is much to discuss."

She prowled the room like a wild lioness, the gold-red cap of her severely pulled-back hair glowing in the sunlight that slanted through the open windows. Leland watched her as he made his way to the drinks table. Her legs, encased in buff trousers, were long and supple, the firm thighs muscular but feminine. He'd seen firsthand the deftness with which she wielded her sword. Power, grace, a fencer's body. He cut his eyes away from the curved arc of her bottom. For God's sake, he was old enough to be her grandfather, great-grandfather in some families. Still, that hadn't stopped Archer.

"Would you like a drink?" he offered, keeping his gaze resolutely on her face, and not anywhere near her fetching and quite pert bosom.

She gave him a small smile of gratitude, and his old heart skittered a bit. Hers was not the dainty, sweet beauty of fashion. It was a sculptor's dream, precise, unearthly. She was Nefertiti, Helen of Troy. Beauty such as hers stunned. He blinked hard. Why hadn't he noticed before?

"Have you any bourbon?"

"Not you as well?" Leland shook his head. "Perhaps I ought to buy a cask."

She laughed, all warmth and huskiness. And Leland understood why Archer had lost his head over her.

"Perhaps you ought to," she said. "It is really quite good. As you are bereft, I should like a whiskey, then. Neat, please."

He poured her drink and watched, his breath catching, as she glided over to take it. The curve of her hips, the dip in her waist; she was a Stradivarius. Damn his eyes, he felt like a man of thirty inside. A small shard of envy toward Archer cut him then promptly brought him round. Hard enough to bring him shame. He bowed formally and handed her the glass.

"You are very much alike, you and Archer."

She quirked a burnished brow. "Our taste in drinks?"

"Yes, that. And in temperament as well." He gave her a tight smile. It hurt too much to do any more. His oldest friend had gone off to destroy himself. And left him to pick up the pieces. "He too would have stormed in to hold me at sword point should he be in a temper."

Eyes the color of Chinese celadon glaze ran over him in appraisal. "I suspect you are a man of action as well, sir. Though perhaps you prefer to skewer with words rather than swords?"

He laughed. "You are quite right, madam. Touché."

Her sculpted cheeks plumped then promptly fell. Her eyes misted. "Where is he, Lord Leland?"

Leland set down his glass. "Please be seated, Lady Archer, and I shall tell you all."

She complied, folding her lithe body gracefully into the same chair Archer had occupied not long ago.

"Promise me one thing," he said as he sat across from her. "Let me finish what I must say, and then you may do as you wish."

Her shapely mouth curled into a lopsided grin. "I do not have a history of keeping such promises, sir. But I shall try."

So like Archer with her forthright nature.

"What has Archer told you of all this?" he asked.

As Leland listened, awe filled him over her capacity to take all the horror in and still love Archer. For all he was.

"So it was Victoria, then," she finished, "who created him?"

"Yes." He ran his fingers over the base of his glass. "I shall be forthright with you now. For you have to understand the allure she held for us. All of us within West Moon Club were scholars. And through our collective effort, we learned much about the ancient world. Archer and I went to Egypt to excavate ancient tombs, immersed ourselves in the pharaoh's world. It was all for naught. True, there were hints, allusions to life everlasting. Does not our own Christian Bible speak of men living well beyond the pale? Is Noah himself not said to have lived past nine hundred years?"

He curled his hand into a fist, remembering those years of frustration. "We could not find a true solution. Until she came."

For a moment, he simply remembered the day Victoria had walked into their meeting as though it were not a secret society at all. A goddess, silver and light. Exquisitely beautiful. "You can well imagine the effect her appearance had upon us," he said to Lady Archer. "You've seen Archer. And she was fully transformed. We did not doubt a word she said. Or her claims that she was an angel of light." His laugh was bitter. "Not an angel. No, we would learn that when it was too late."

What Lady Archer thought, he could not know. She held herself in complete control.

"We would not all be given the gift, however. She was to choose the most worthy." He shifted uncomfortably in his seat. "She settled on Archer and me. We became her lovers."

A soft blush stole up Lady Archer's cheeks but she

remained silent. Nor could Leland blame her for blushing. Even now he could see Victoria, her nubile body writhing beneath his. Pert breasts. Nipples translucent as glass yet succulent, they drove him mad. *Take me, Maurus.* The heat of her body. The light pulsing through him as he bedded her. He'd felt invincible. And later, when she had wanted more.

"I desire you and Archer in my bed. Together. Come to me, my heathen men."

By God, he had been willing. So shameful. But there it was. The hold she had on him was madness. And Archer's wrathful expression. His dark brows scowling. He had stormed out, shoving past her bed in disgust, even as Leland had been crawling into it, all but tearing his clothes from his body in his lust-filled haste. Her sick laughter filled his ears even now.

"It was a test," he said to a stone-faced Lady Archer, realizing that he'd said the whole shameful tale aloud. "Archer was stronger. Possessed the willfulness that she desired. I was merely a secondary diversion."

"You resented him for it," Lady Archer said softly.

"Yes."

Her sculpted face remained impassive. "All of you did, because Archer was the favorite."

"I cannot deny it," he said wearily. "Not one of us realized how lucky we were not to be favored. Until that night. There was a ceremony at Cavern Hall, a place she told us held great power. All of us drank from a silver chalice, filled with a silver liquid. One sip only for the rest of the members. A taste to keep them enthralled and do her bidding. But Archer and I . . . we would drink a cupful. The liquid took time to work. We were to drink and then she would bestow her kiss. The Kiss of Light. Victoria would push her energy into us, thus completing the transformation. We would then fall into a deep sleep for one day and one night. When dawn broke on the next morning, we would be full-fledged Angels of Light in body and in soul.

"On the night of the ceremony, Rossberry came to us. He was frantic. He'd found an ancient text. We would not become Angels of Light, benevolent beings who lived forever off the light of the sun, but demons who drew their power from the light of souls. And in doing so, we would lose our own souls."

He took a steadying drink. "We were fools. Too blinded by her thrall to believe. Or at least I was. Archer had doubts, but the moment was all but upon us.

"Every vein in his body stood out silver against his skin when he drank that brew," he whispered. "Then his eyes. Viscous silver ran over them before he blinked it away, and the gray irises turned to mercury. Victoria simply laughed. Time to pay the piper, she said.

"Archer regained his strength, and with it he ran, not into her arms as she had expected. But away from her. Out of the hellish cavern. Victoria had merely smiled."

"She wasn't angry?"

Leland glanced at Lady Archer. "Irritated, perhaps. She thought he would come back. He was her true mate, she declared. I knew then that she was in love with him. I was nothing. So I ran too. One sip was all I tasted."

"It did not affect you?"

Leland smiled wryly. "I am ninety-two years old, my dear. An age most men do not reach. And should they do so, are usually quite useless. Yet I can ride a horse, read my books, walk to my club and back. I am not immortal, but my life has been altered from its human course. I age slowly."

"When I met you, I thought your age closer to sixty."

"Precisely." His lip trembled. "I've outlived one wife, three children, and one grandchild." The coals in the grate settled with a hiss as he stared into his glass, watching the honeyed liquid swirl. "That is why I've avoided Archer all these years. Guilt. All of us got what we truly wanted that night, a chance to live beyond our years, without fear of sickness or sudden death. All of us save Archer. And Rossberry."

"What happened to Rossberry?"

"Victoria. She found out what he had told Archer and set him on fire. Left him to die. By some miracle, the man survived."

Lady Archer shuddered. "How horrible. Although it is a wonder she didn't simply kill him."

"She might have cut him apart or taken his soul. However, something about fire disturbed Victoria—she would shy away from it. So I suppose she considered it the worst sort of punishment. I cannot help but agree. Rossberry suffered horribly."

"Why does he hate Archer?"

"Rossberry believes Archer told Victoria of his defection. Archer would never betray another man's confidence. That deed was Sir Percival's doing." He took a small sip of his whiskey and welcomed the burn. "There is no arguing with Rossberry. He is not... There is something extraordinary about him. About all members of his family, for that matter. It would serve you well to stay far away from him—and Lord Mckinnon, as well. There have been mysterious disappearances connected to their lot over the years."

"Mckinnon knows Archer very well, doesn't he?" she asked.

"They studied medicine together. And were good friends. Archer went to him for help in the beginning. But Rossberry soon turned his son against him."

Her clear green eyes lifted to his. "Then Mckinnon is..."

"As old as the rest of us, and never had a drop of the elixir. Why he doesn't age, I cannot say. As for Rossberry, he must be one hundred and thirty by now." Leland held up a hand when she leaned forward intently. "I don't know what secrets they keep. We didn't understand until later that Rossberry and his son were never fully human. In truth, I believe Rossberry wasn't looking for immortality but a cure for whatever it is that haunts his family."

Her ripe mouth puckered but she nodded in acceptance. "And the rest of them? Was it simple jealousy that caused them to dislike Archer? Or the incident with Marvel?"

He felt a small jolt. "You know of that?"

"Only that Archer and Marvel quarreled over her."

Leland snorted. "Archer was trying to save Marvel. Victoria had come back and seduced Marvel. She urged Marvel to make the change. Archer was incensed. He knew firsthand what would happen to the youth." Leland took another sip of his drink. "Marvel was just another pawn. I believe Victoria thought if she roused Archer's passion, got him jealous, that he would realize the depth of his love for her and return. Instead, Archer got his first true taste of the monster he would become when he beat Marvel within an inch of his life. He agreed then to the members' ridiculous banishment to keep them, and others, safe."

"Ever the protector," she murmured, her brow furrowing. The frown increased. "I still do not understand why Victoria has waited all these years to return. Why did she not go after Archer from the first?"

"The woman is well over three hundred years old. What is sixty years to an immortal? The equivalent of a few months, perhaps?" He shrugged, enjoying the feeling of such a crude gesture. "I believe she truly thought he would return to her, that Archer was merely in a mood. Unfortunately for all of us, he proved he was very much over her wiles."

"By marrying me."

"No, my dear," he said softly. "By falling in love with you."

She took an unsteady breath. "Hell hath no fury..."

"Indeed."

Lady Archer rose from her chair in one fluid movement. "So he had to change to stop her."

"You cannot begin to understand the power she has."

"Believe me, Lord Leland, I can." Her hips swayed as she paced. "If Archer possesses even one-tenth of her strength, I can imagine." Her bitter laugh cut off abruptly, and she rounded on him. "You said he would lose his soul..." She paled, beginning to see the inevitable conclusion.

"Yes," he said slowly. "When he changes, he shall crave the light of other souls the way you and I crave air. The very first life he takes shall damn him for eternity. And with each life thereafter, a bit of his humanity will go."

She swayed and grabbed hold of the mantel.

"That is why he fought this curse with everything he had," he said. "The kiss is an act of consent. Without it, the elixir must work on its own, slowly. For a short time, Archer thought he'd found a cure. There was a ring."

Her green eyes sharpened. "A ring?"

"The ring hid a note from his old valet, Daoud. Victoria killed him long ago, but not before he sent a message containing the true nature of the demon curse to Archer."

"And he found the ring?" The hopefulness in her voice crushed him.

"Yes. Just recently. There wasn't a cure, my dear. Only a way to end it." He forced himself up and crossed the room to his desk, all the while aware of her trembling lips and shimmering eyes.

"This is the Sword of Light." He lifted the ancient weapon out of his drawer. "The only thing that can pierce a light demon's flesh. Archer must thrust this sword into Victoria's heart and destroy her."

"And then?" It was the barest whisper.

Leland's strength wavered. "Then he must turn it upon himself."

He watched her fall apart, press her hand to her middle, curl into herself, yet remain standing. Agony slashed at her features. But she did not cry. She took a deep breath but her resolve failed. A keening wail slipped through her lips. He went to her only to have her lift her hand and warn him off. She got hold of herself and straightened.

"Why—why do you have the sword?"

"We must not risk her finding it until Archer's change is done. I am to take it tonight. Leave it outside the cavern where they have gone."

She paced again, holding her middle as though holding on to her sanity.

"All is not lost," he said desperately. "Archer need not lose his soul…"

"Only his life! Forgive me for being selfish but it is a small consolation to me." She whipped round before stalking back to the fire. "How?"

"Should he be destroyed before he takes a life, his soul will remain intact."

"And just how is he to avoid that?" she snapped. "When he must first destroy Victoria?"

Leland blanched. "I . . ."

She snorted. "You did not consider it, did you? Neither of you did."

His hand shook as it ran through his hair, sending limp strands over his brow. "The legend was quite clear; those who take up the light without thought of personal greed shall find redemption. Only a savior true of heart shall wield the Sword of Light, and out of fire that comes not from man but the gods the blade shall come alive and meet its destiny."

Lady Archer stopped her restless pacing and stared at him. "Fire?"

"Yes. Such artifacts usually come with fanciful riddles. Most likely it is allegorical. However, the Egyptians, who crafted this sword, believed that the lake of fire, from which this sword was forged, had the power to both purify and destroy. The innocent would be redeemed by fire, and the guilty annihilated. Perhaps piercing her with the blade shall turn her to flame," he mused.

"Thought this out, have you?" She sighed. "Forgive me. I am unsettled."

"Quite understandable, my dear."

She took a deep breath and then steeled her spine. "There is only one recourse." Emerald fire lit her eyes. "I shall have to destroy Victoria. And then . . ." Her lips trembled violently. "And then Archer as well."

"Out of the question!"

Lord Leland's shout cracked through the air like a shot.

"I was not asking for your permission, sir." Miranda's heart felt as though it were truly in danger of failing, so great was the pain, but she looked at the elderly man with resolve. "There is little choice in the matter. Archer cannot kill her, or he will lose his soul. You cannot do it because you are too frail."

His mouth opened in outrage, yet he could hardly deny the truth of her statement.

"Archer forfeited his life to change," he said with heat. "Because that is the only way to defeat her. She is too strong otherwise!"

"That is where you men have failed to understand," she said. "Should you have thought it through, you would have realized your error. Archer believed he must engage in a physical battle. He thought only of his previous battles with her. Like a man, he sought to solve this problem with brawn."

Were Archer here, Miranda would have hit him with something very large and very hard. *Damnable man. Why did you have to shut me out?* Black fingers of panic crawled across her field of vision. She took another deep breath.

"And in his blind haste, he overlooked his true weapon. The sword." She went to Leland's desk. The sword lay upon it, a seemingly simple weapon. Nothing so dazzling as to decry it the ultimate threat against an immortal demon. Her hand closed around the bronze hilt, and a sizzle of power coursed against her palm. She nearly dropped it, then adjusted her hold. Another shot of power surged through her, and deep down, the fire inside of her seemed to answer it, flaring hot in her veins for an instant. She pulled the sword from its sheath.

"Careful," Leland warned unnecessarily.

It was an evil-looking thing. The leaf-shaped blade was pure black, made of a metal she could not place.

Light coming through the windows caught its edge with a gleam. Frightfully sharp. Her hand wavered. She would plunge this into Archer's breast. *I cannot!*

Victoria. Think of her.

"He needed only to use the element of surprise," she said.

"My dear Lady Archer, you cannot think that you shall take Victoria by surprise." His white brows touched his hairline. "It is folly. I will not allow it, I say."

Miranda sheathed the sword and attached it to her belt with the hook on the back of the scabbard. "As I said, Lord Leland, I have not asked for your permission. I shall do this thing."

He moved to stop her, and her temper broke. "If anyone is to end Archer's life, it is to be me. If I cannot have him back, I can save his soul, damn you!"

He eased away. "I understand your pain—"

"You do not! Nor do you understand my strength. You see only a helpless female. Why is it, do you think, that Archer hid this from me?"

"To spare you the pain of knowing beforehand," he said with equanimity.

"No. He hid this from me because he knew I am well capable of facing Victoria, and if I had found out about her, I would have tried to kill her myself."

"Then he is well-justified in his precaution. The very idea horrifies me." Leland drew himself up. "If I must protect you from yourself, I will."

"I do not need your protection. If anything, you need protection from me." And with that she let the fire free.

Flame from candles and lamps in the room burst from their glass houses with an angry hiss. Leland let out a strangled sound, like that of a man choking upon his soup. "Impossible."

Her laugh was bitter as she reached for her cloak. "You of all people should understand that all things are possible." She slipped her arms into her cloak and headed for the door. "We leave now."

Chapter Thirty-three

Night came quickly and with it an icy wind that cut at the skin. Leland faltered, his thin frame buffeted by the wind. Miranda pulled her horse near and handed him the small lantern she carried. The light was little more than a pinprick of yellow on a dark mantle.

"Let me..." She took his hands, feeling the cold through his fine leather riding gloves. He twitched in surprise but she held tight. *Warmth.* Heat coursed from her middle and into her palms. Leland gasped as the heat traveled into him. She leaned forward, taking his neck in her hand. Softly, she blew over his face. *Heat.* The air steamed, hot and strong, and he closed his eyes with a sigh.

When Leland revived, she let him go and set a strong pace once more.

"What is it that you do?" Leland asked after a moment.

They had not spoken since he'd explained Archer's plans for her. Should Archer fail to kill Victoria, or himself, he would crave souls with all his being. Loving Miranda as he did, he would crave hers above all others.

Leland would take her away and hide her where Archer could not find her. The high-handed way in which Archer had deceived her had Miranda seething for a good hour, but it was hardly Leland's fault.

"I can create fire," she said as her horse picked its way up a sharp incline. She could not help the beast. She could barely see. They were out of London now, traveling into an ancient forest of oaks and beech trees. "Control it on a whim. So long as there is something to burn."

"What you did just now, that was not fire."

His observation hit Miranda. He was correct. What she had done to him was new. And yet she had done it without thought. She'd simply *known* she could warm him.

"The principle is the same," she said with hesitation. *Was it?* "I thought of heat, warmth, and thus it came."

"Fascinating."

The silence of the forest pressed in, cut only by the lonely jangle of their horses' bridles as they ascended the small rise. Boundless darkness stretched out on all sides. Had she been alone, the emptiness would have unnerved her. But she was not alone.

"The others all thought him a monster." Cold air burned her throat. "Why didn't you shun him when he returned? You and Cheltenham?"

Leland kept his eyes on the road ahead. His pale face wavered like a phantom in the light of the lantern hanging on his pommel. "Because we knew he was simply a man, with weakness and frailties. Who yearned for the same things all of us do—to love and be loved." He glanced at the reins in his hands, then away. "That he should find it after all these years, only to have to give it away with both hands." He shook his head slowly. "It is a little thing to stand by him."

They spoke no more and headed farther into the cold gloom.

By the time Leland called softly to halt, Miranda's hands were stiff claws on the reins.

"We leave the horses here." He turned down the light and dismounted with a stifled groan. "I cannot stress enough the danger we are in." His eyes were glowing orbs in the starlight that eked through the ancient tree canopy. "Her senses are excellent. Hearing uncanny—"

"Then I suggest," she cut in softly, "that we refrain from speaking any further."

Grimacing, Leland offered a short nod and then took her elbow in hand. Half a mile they crept along, their feet sifting through brittle leaves to find the hard ground beneath so as not to make a sound. Sweat trickled down her back; her thighs burned under the slow movement.

They headed west, the forest before them no more than shapes of black and gray. Ahead, a black bulk appeared to be a steep hillside. A tiny flicker of orange light announced the opening to a cave.

Leland's soft lips trembled against her ear. "The torches are lit. Like Archer, she will be resting. We must go to Cavern Hall. That is where he will be."

The scent of incense hung heavy as smoke, clogging her throat. Archer was here. She could feel him. The sense of him plucked at her skin and pushed her heart to beat fiercely. She kept pace with Leland and then outdistanced him. She knew where to go. Archer pulled her along. Down the dark, winding passage toward the orange glow of firelight.

Around a sharp corner, a large cavern opened up before her. In the center of the cavern, bathed within the flickering light of the torches, lay Archer, sprawled on his side in a naked tumble of limbs, his head thrown back and twisted away from her. His beautiful body now completely silver and glowing, he lay unmoving like an icy Icarus fallen from the sky.

Miranda tore free of Leland's sudden grip and ran to him, heedless of the danger. His frozen shoulder bumped hard against her knee as she fell upon him. Moonstone flesh. A sob escaped, bouncing off the rough walls.

So cold. Her fingers burned against the contact of his skin as she lifted his heavy head into her lap. His classical profile lay stark and silver against the black of her cloak, utterly beautiful and horrific all at once.

"Ben." Her trembling hands moved over his jaw, through the brittle strands of his silver hair. Completely transformed. Lost to her. Pain clawed at her throat. The smooth expanse of his chest like moonstone against her fingertips. *I cannot do this.* "Ben, what have you done?"

"He has chosen me," said a girlish voice.

Framed by the dark hollow of a cave passage, Victoria stood like a silver angel. Free of makeup and her wig, her skin gleamed, swirling with pulsing light. Silver hair streamed like moonbeams down her back and over her gown. Such a lovely image for something so foul.

"Ben, is it? How sweet." Her white teeth flashed, nearly blinding. "Does it upset you that you have lost? How sad. I knew all along that he was mine."

As if to answer, Miranda's fingers curled around Archer's neck, drawing him protectively into her lap. "You know nothing, you frozen bitch."

Victoria laughed. Ice tinkling into a crystal glass. "My, but your tongue is most foul. Had we met otherwise, how tempted I would have been to turn you." Her smiled faded, a mere dropping of her cheeks. "As it is, however, I shall take great enjoyment in watching him feed off of you."

Leland's boots scuffed against stone as he moved behind Miranda. Victoria's eerie silver eyes flicked to him and the reflective gleam in them dulled. "You, on the other hand, I shall keep for myself." Her wide, thin mouth lifted into a feral sneer. "You need to be taught a lesson."

"Leland," Miranda said, not taking her eyes from Victoria. "Leave us, please. Victoria and I have much to discuss."

"Yes," agreed Victoria. "Let us ladies have our *tête-à-tête*." She licked her lips. "I shall come and find you later. My last meal was not nearly enough." She stepped to the side and bile rose in Miranda's throat as she saw the gray husk of a lifeless body lying in the dirt.

"Good Christ," gasped Leland. "It is Rossberry."

"Yes," said Victoria. "He was becoming a nuisance to my Benji. I saved him for last to heighten his fear. And I must say, although his heart was tough and bitter tasting, his soul was most interesting to consume."

Miranda's fingers dug into Archer's cold neck. How much longer did they have before Archer became like this? Was the sun nearly up? An eternity seemed to have passed since they had started their weary journey. "Leland"—she dared not look at him—"go now. I shall see to this."

He moved back a few paces, remembering perhaps his vow to her, and Victoria laughed again, clapping her hands together in delight. "Such authority, Miranda. I do like you."

"I wish I could say the same."

Silver eyebrows lifted but Victoria merely smoothed the folds of her silver satin gown. Her choice of dress was in the empire style popular when Archer had been young. Perhaps she had selected it for him. The idea left a bitter taste in Miranda's mouth.

"Ah, but it is simple, feminine jealousy that brings us

to strife," the witch said with a light sigh. "How petty it is, hmm?" Her pleasant smile twisted. "He was always mine. He pledged himself to me. He may have forgotten for a time." She shrugged. "In the end, he remembered. He came of his own free will."

"Free will had nothing to do with it," Miranda snapped. "You've been toying with him all this time."

Victoria gave her a bored look, like a child who dreams of sweets while receiving a dressing down. "What fun do I have otherwise? Besides, all of them had to pay. I loved them all. And they worshiped me. For a time." Anger tightened her mouth to a bud. "Then they turned from me, and banished my Benji, and he was lost to me."

Her cold anger flared in the air for a sharp moment and then deflated just as quickly. "For that, they must pay. But the moment had to be right. It was better for me to kill them when Benji returned."

"You did it to push Archer into a corner," Miranda said. "To turn them all against him once again and leave him little chance of remaining in society."

"*Exactement!*" Victoria clapped her hands together with a smile. "Ah, but it is satisfying to face a woman of intelligence."

"You might have simply killed me," Miranda found herself saying. She wanted the fight now. Wanted Victoria to come at her so that the bitch might die. "I am your true threat, after all."

Victoria's silver brows rose delicately. "I might have," she admitted softly. She glanced at Archer. "But men are like children, no? Take away their favorite toy too soon, and they throw the greatest temper." Her eyes snapped back to Miranda. "That is what you are. A toy. One that has lost its luster."

Victoria took a small, sauntering step into the open cavern, and the firelight flashed over her skin like diamonds in the sun. "Now that we speak of toys. Did you like the present I left you?"

John Coachman. Something much like a snarl flew past Miranda's lips.

Triumph flashed in Victoria's eyes. "He was most amusing. Such a strapping youth. Ah, but the look of surprise on his face when I came to him in the stable yard wearing a mask and your cloak, begging him to bed me. He resisted. Until I knelt down and pleasured him."

Miranda's fingers twitched over Archer's skin. When she said nothing, Victoria's brows drew together in annoyance.

"The boy was in love with you. Did you know? He whispered it in my ear just before he took me." Victoria's wide mouth curled. "I must say he was an excellent lover, so very common and forceful. I was almost sorry about having to hurt him." The corners of her catlike eyes creased, the silver irises reflecting like a mirror, utterly soulless. How could Miranda have ever compared them to Archer's?

"But then, he thought it was you who killed him. I saw it, the pain and shock in those big, dumb eyes—"

"Enough!" Miranda's shout echoed off the cold walls. "I will kill you. For John Coachman, Cheltenham. And Archer. I will send you to hell for Archer."

"Such confidence!" A peal of delight rang out. "This shall be a most amusing night." Her head snapped up, the look in her eyes vicious. "You need not be whole for my Benji to feed. Tell me, what shall I tear out first? An arm? Your eyes?"

Slowly, Miranda eased Archer's head to the ground.

The lack of contact with him broke a tether deep in her soul. *Ben.* She could not lose him. Victoria's silver eyes bore into her, triumphant, gleaming. *She did this to him.* Heat whirled up in Miranda's belly like a vortex.

She rose to her feet, the heat coursing through her limbs like power. *The fire is your gift.* She flipped the ends of her cloak over her shoulders, revealing the sword belted at her hips. Slowly she rounded Archer's prone form. Victoria watched her come, a patronizing smile pulling at her frozen lips. Miranda's innards knotted in terror. It had been so long since she had used a sword. And never, never with the intent to kill. Sweat rolled down her back and made her palms damp. She kept walking until they stood not twenty paces from each other in the large cavern.

Miranda ignored the frantic beat of her heart that pleaded for her to flee. *You know how to use this gift.* She planted her feet wide. "You should be running," she said, pulling the sword free with a ring of metal and purpose. Around them, the torches flared as if sensing its power.

Victoria threw her head back and laughed, but her eyes cut into Miranda like shards of glass. "Silly child. I can kill you with one touch. You should be begging."

Pulsing liquid heat flowed down Miranda's arm into the brass hilt of the ancient sword. *Burn.* Blistering heat coursed over her palm, turning the weapon into a brand. The wicked length of the black blade hissed in the cold air. *Knives, swords, bullets are unable to pierce this flesh.* It would be a very short fight. It would have to be. Miranda had known it from the moment Leland had told her what she faced. One strike from Victoria would kill Miranda. Her breath hitched wildly, her belly pitching and rolling. Failure was a heartbeat away. The cloak lay heavy on her shoulders, a sure hindrance to any sword fight. Her hand trembled, the pain of holding the fire and heat within her nearly intolerable.

Miranda let Victoria see it all, the vulnerability and her pathetic weakness in comparison to Victoria's strength and speed.

Miranda gripped the hilt tighter, securing it against the slickness of her palm. "Come and get me then, bitch."

Victoria snarled and lunged, faster than wind. Miranda stepped hard left, slashing downward as she came. The force of the swing threw Miranda backward. A piercing cry of rage mixed with pain reverberated through the hall. The room spun, and Miranda's heart locked in her throat, fear buzzing in her ears. An arm, broken like fractured glass, lay in the dirt. Miranda blinked at it, her boots crushing silver fingers underfoot, the sword burning hot in her trembling hand.

Victoria's eyes bulged at the sight of her severed limb. "*Petite pute!* I shall rip you apart!"

A silver blur of light crossed Miranda's vision as Victoria lashed out. Miranda jumped back. Too slow. The blow caught her shoulder with enough strength to send her tumbling. Her head and shoulders smashed into the unforgiving earth, a whirl of dust and torchlight blinding her eyes. Miranda clutched the sword like a lifeline as she rolled along the ground. *Do not fail.* Dizzy and breathless, she hopped to her feet, falling against the rock wall for support.

A scream bubbled up as she heard Victoria advance. Miranda's hand flew to her collar. Victoria was upon her, ready for the kill. Miranda tore the cloak from her neck and spun to the side as Victoria bore down. With a guttural cry, Miranda flung her cloak over Victoria's hurtling body. *Burn!*

White flames burst over Victoria. She shrieked, consumed by the burning cloak wrapped tight about her. *Burn.* Her translucent arm tore at the cloak even as her silver skin split and peeled.

Miranda roared, the red-hot sword in her hand arching high before plunging into Victoria's chest. The meaty thud of the impact sounded, and Miranda grunted, pain radiating into her arm. Victoria reared, trying to break free, but the ancient sword did its magic and held fast.

The heavy wool of the cloak tore away from Victoria's face. Screeching in agony, she careened toward Miranda. Miranda's boot heels dug into the shallow earth, her thigh muscles straining as she held Victoria back with the strength of the sword and the flame. *Burn.* The sword sunk deeper, Victoria's bones crunching.

Miranda's knees buckled. Victoria's strength was too much. Miranda's feet skidded over the ground. Victoria pushed against the sword, bearing down despite her agony. Cold stone bit into Miranda's back as Victoria pinned her to the wall, coming closer. The heat of the flames tightened the skin on her face and drew tears to her eyes.

A scream burned her throat as Victoria's curled claw, blackened by fire, raked toward her face. Knifelike nails sliced across Miranda's brow. Pain and blood flooded over her eye, half-blinding her. Weakened, her arms wobbled, and victory flared in Victoria's hellish face.

Then Miranda saw him, just beyond the burning flames surrounding Victoria's body. A length of silver, his sculptural beauty sprawled on the dirt. *Archer.* The fire within Miranda roared in defiance. Its power surged through her limbs, straight down the sword into Victoria's heart.

Her blackened mouth rounded into a wide O. Silver

from Victoria's skin began to drip, like paint from a brush or blood from a wound. Around the blackened skin, pale blue eyes looked back at Miranda in helpless horror, before the hard body beneath the cloak convulsed and, like a log burned from the inside out, it turned gray and crumbled, falling about Miranda's feet in thick clumps of black and orange embers.

Miranda hissed and jumped back from the remains. The hilt in her hand fell free to shatter upon the ground in so many sharp fragments—the sword itself was gone, destroyed along with Victoria. Only then did she allow herself to breathe, panting in exhilaration and horror. She had killed again, and she almost screamed from the knowledge.

"Lady Archer?"

The soft query nearly brought Miranda out of her skin. She whirled and faced Leland, who stood a few feet off. His long face was pale, reflecting the horror that had just occurred, but his eyes were filled with something that looked much like pride.

"Are you well?" he asked, keeping his distance, but concerned nonetheless.

Blood dripped from her brow and ran along her cheek. She pressed a hand to her head and winced. The skin on her palm was angry red and blistering—the strange symbols from the sword's hilt branded into her flesh. She let her arm fall. "It is done."

Weariness pulled like heavy bonds upon her limbs. Leland hovered. She walked past him to Archer. So still. His expression was relaxed, the lush curve of his mouth soft. Her beautiful man. If only she could let him go.

Leland's knees cricked as he knelt beside her. "The sword is gone."

Cold dread seeped like ice water through her veins. "Yes." And no. No. There was no way to spare him now.

Leland's knobby hand ran over his face, dragging his white mustache down. "We must get you away." Leland glanced at Archer and he frowned. "Archer will soon wake."

Miranda clasped Leland's hand, the skin beneath hers as fragile as old linen. "Dear man, don't you see..." Ruthlessly, she bit her trembling lip. "I never meant to leave. Without Archer, I have no soul anyway. It is best he take it into him. That's where it belongs—with him."

His grip was hard. "No! You will be damned. And Archer as well." Spittle flew from his dry lips. "I gave my word, and by God, I shall keep it!"

"What do I care of damnation?" Miranda's throat closed. "I don't even know if I believe..."

"In God?" Leland squeezed her hand. "With what you have seen tonight? Can you not see divine justice at work?" He blanched. "Please, if you do not believe, then have care for the soul that Archer sought to protect."

"If there is an afterlife then surely Archer and I will find it together. Now—" she pushed a small smile—"don't make me force you to leave."

He flinched, clearly remembering the fire.

And she did too. Her heart gave a lurch. *Not all fire destroys.* She looked down at the man she loved. The tender curve of his neck showed no sign of a pulse. But soon. Soon the sun would come, and he'd awaken. And be nothing but a soulless demon. *The innocent are redeemed by fire, and the guilty annihilated.* The vivid image of what she'd done to Victoria loomed large in her mind, and it occurred to Miranda that she did believe. She looked down at her husband. She would save him. Save herself as well. Gently, she lifted him as much as she could and eased behind him, winding her legs around his torso. Ben's heavy head fell against her breast.

"Leave us," she said to Leland.

"Lady Archer—"

"Go now."

Her eyes stayed on her husband and the way his silver lashes cast shadows upon his cheeks. God, how she wished to see him smiling at her and hear his rich voice once more.

"Go," she said when Leland did not stir. "Or be consumed with us."

Leland hesitated for a moment, perhaps more. She curled herself over Archer. "It's all right," she whispered against his cool ear. "I am here now. You aren't alone." Her tears pattered onto his sculpted cheek, rolling into his closed eyes. She blinked hard. "You'll never be alone again."

Leland's heavy footfall echoed in the emptiness and then there was quiet. Miranda's arms came around Archer's broad shoulders. "I never told you, but that day you asked me why I was following you...do you remember it?"

She wiped her nose with the back of her sleeve and then held on tighter. "I thought I was so sly, trying to goad you into revealing your secrets, but you knew what I was doing. You always saw right through me." A weak laugh broke free. "There was a moment...you looked at me and our eyes met and I thought...I thought, 'I love this man—' "

A sob ripped from her throat. She pressed her cheek against the top of his head. No breath came from his lips. "It didn't matter that I hadn't seen your face. I knew—I knew I would love you until I died. But I was afraid. And I pushed it out of my head. For too long. Stupid of me, really. Because I'd been waiting for you too, Archer. My whole life." A keening wail escaped her. She swallowed the rest down, clinging to Archer like a buoy in a storm.

His lips yielded against hers, unmoving but soft.

"It will only hurt for a short while," she whispered against them. "And then we will be free."

Torchlight flickered like the rays of the setting sun over his long, silver body. Miranda inhaled deeply and then opened his lips with hers. *Let us be judged.* Her breath exhaled in a rush of heat, flowing into him. *My soul and his.*

Once more, heat surged up from within, wrapping itself around her, around Archer. *Purify.*

Pain. It cut into Miranda. The heat and the pain. She held on, thinking of the flame. *My soul and his. With all that I am.*

Her lips trembled against Archer's, the scorching heat in her throat nearly unbearable.

Distantly, she heard a hiss, like the sizzling of a fry pan. More heat. Her eyes flew open, dazzled by pain. Blue-white tongues of flame danced over them. Strange blue flame, nearly cold in its intensity. She could only stare helplessly; she was caught up in it now. No turning back. Her linen shirt burned away. Brown flakes of charred clothes whirled up into the air, caught in the flames.

She forced another surge. *Purify.*

A deep groan ripped out of Archer, and she almost lost her grip. His sinewy body convulsed, bucking hard against her aching thighs. She curled over him, wrapping her ankles round his legs, holding him down. *Forgive me.*

White-hot fire tore over them, pulling her hair from its bun. Red-gold strands lifted high, whipping round her face. From outside herself, she heard her piteous screams. So like Victoria's. *More*. Archer flopped within her arms, groaning, his lips parting in a gasp. A maelstrom had them, fire and wind scouring her skin. And yet she did not burn. She could see that, but was mindless as to why. The pain was real enough.

Suddenly Archer lurched up, tight as a bow, tearing from her arms before falling back into them. His smooth skin pebbled with perspiration, then began to weep like a flower in the morning dew. Rivulets of silver rolled like mercury over the swells of his muscles. Blue tongues of flame licked it away as Archer writhed against her, his eyes shut tight as if against the pain. Something near joy touched Miranda's heart as she saw the poison bleed out of him, revealing golden skin as it went, but then the foul silver substance touched her skin, and she screamed.

Bursts of white colored her vision. Razor-sharp pain tore at her skin as silver seeped from Archer and onto her. She curled over him like a shell, her breasts crushing into his shoulder blades. They convulsed together until a pulse of heat and pressure shot out from his center. Miranda fell back, her head cracking against the ground. The heat of the room left with a loud whoosh of air.

Darkness ebbed and flowed at the edges of her vision.

Ben. She sucked in a draught of air and forced her body to rise.

He lay on his side once more, one arm hanging limply over his broad chest. Shadows played over skin, as golden as honey, as his arm softly rose and fell in cadence with his breathing. Steam rose from the ground around him, a silver mist that dissipated against the cold air. A soft groan came from his mouth, and he flopped onto his back, revealing whorls of black hair over his sculpted chest. *Ben*.

She scrambled to his side, trembling so badly that she could nary get a grip on his shoulders. Warmth. His skin radiated it. Black shorn hair brushed softly over her bare thighs as his head lolled toward her. High color was on his sharp cheeks.

"Ben." Her voice came out in a croak.

The tension in his expression eased but still he would not awaken. Frantically, she brushed her lips over his brow. "Ben. Please." Her hair fell about them like a veil, pooling onto his bare chest and shoulders. "I love you, Benjamin Archer," she whispered against his ear. "More than my life."

A tremor rippled through him, and then his eyes flicked open, soft gray and fringed with sooty lashes. They locked onto her, and she forgot to breathe.

"Miri…"

Chapter Thirty-four

❦

Darkness. And cold. They surrounded him, unending and weighty. A frozen womb he could not escape. Deep within himself, he heard his cries, terrified, like a child's. *End this. Set me free.* Dread clawed at his soul. He would run if he could. Soft hands were at his neck. Soothing. He strained toward the touch. Useless. He could not move. The hands slipped away, leaving him alone.

And then the pain. A hot brand forced down his throat. *God help me.* Colors—red, white, and orange—burst before him. Razor claws flayed him inside out. He fought against the heat and the agony. He could not endure. *No more. Please.*

And then warmth. He fell back with a sigh. Beautiful warmth, flowing like a dream. The scent of roses. Silken strands caressing his aching skin.

"I love you, Benjamin Archer." Angel wings against his ear. "More than my life."

Love. Miranda. *Miri.* It surged through him like a

cooling wave. His eyes flew open to the light. A fiery nimbus of hair and grape-green eyes glimmering with tears.

"Miri."

She sobbed. His love. Her creamy white skin was blotched with red, her eyes and nose swollen and seeping, a gash marred one fine brow. Never had she looked more beautiful.

"Ben." Her slender arms flew around his neck, and he leaned into her with a sigh. Her plump bare breast pressed into his shoulder. Miranda naked? She curled up against him, the satin warmth of her thighs smooth against his tender skin.

He lifted his arm to hold her, his body sluggish as though moving through thick mud. The world around him was dim, almost grainy, like a photograph.

"Oh God, Ben." Miri cried harder, her delicate frame shuddering against him.

"I'm here." His throat burned, razors against raw skin. Where was here? Rough stone walls. Hard dirt beneath him. Memory threatened to suck him down.

A black cloak fell gently round Miri's shoulders. She took no notice. He looked up. His dearest friend stood behind her. Leland. His face withered with age. His deep-set eyes wet. "Hello, Arch. Good to see you again."

Suddenly dizzy, Archer closed his eyes tight. He could not look at Leland without thinking of blood, bones, Cheltenham...the others. Victoria's mercury eyes boring into his, her dead lips opening his mouth, the smell of the grave in her kiss. *I knew you would come back to me, Archer. May you burn in hell, Victoria.* Gray light had filled him. Ice cold and final. He'd changed.

Panic grasped him with heavy hands. He surged

upward, knocking Miri off balance. *Victoria. Where was she? He had to get Miri away.*

Miranda righted herself and shoved her arms into the cloak, pulling it closed. "She's gone."

He must have said the name aloud. He turned his head to his wife. Her eyes were flat. "She is destroyed."

Impossible. He blinked in a daze and then saw...his legs, the long golden skin and curling black hairs dusted over them. His breath came out in a pant, his eyes traveling upward. His ruddy penis lay against his thigh, the dark sac of his balls nestled against black hairs. *Christ. Unchanged.* Whole again.

Miri's warm hand curled over his shoulder. He whipped around. Her beautiful lips trembled, her glorious green eyes shining. "Archer." It was a breath. "The curse is gone."

He moved, catching her up and crushing her slim body to him. All at once, she began to sob again, great wrenching cries that showed the depth of her anguish. His name left her lips as though a plea. He sank his fingers into the cool silk of her hair. *More than my life.* Gratitude washed over him like a benediction.

"I'm here," he whispered into her rose-scented hair. Here was home. He brought her closer. "I have you."

And he was never letting go. Not for a lifetime.

Epilogue

❦

The miraculous recovery of Lord Benjamin Archer, Fifth Baron Archer of Umberslade would be remarked upon for months, if not years. Indeed many a lady and gentleman could not account for it. The man had remained hidden behind a mask for as long as anyone could remember only to arrive at Lord Leland's exclusive dance party and stroll directly out on the ballroom floor with his lovely wife, Lady Miranda Archer.

A hush of amazement ensued as guests realized the identity of the handsome man waltzing with Lady Archer. Some speculated, rather spitefully, that Lord Archer had never been disfigured, that he'd worn the mask simply to gain attention, a rather sad tactic indeed. But this theory was soon deemed illogical. A man as remarkably handsome and dashing as Lord Archer would not willingly hide such a countenance away for years. No. His recovery was nothing short of miraculous. And one could not help but smile at his good fortune upon watching him glide his wife about the dance floor as if in a dream. It was decided at that moment by many a lady of the ton, that *theirs* would be the first invitation Lord and Lady Archer received the next morning.

As for the couple in question, they realized in an abstract sort of way the stir they created, but it did not truly touch them.

"People are staring," Miranda said, unable to hide her satisfied smile.

His gray eyes did not stray from hers, but merely crinkled at the corners. "Only because I am so handsome." He pulled her a hair's breadth closer. "And they are wondering how you tricked me into to marrying you."

She chuckled, breathless as he spun her with effortless grace. "Undoubtedly. I suspect they are also put out that I have taken the best dancer in the room. I knew you'd be the very devil at dancing." She glared but not very properly, for she was still smiling.

Soft lips brushed her ear as his hand slipped to her lower back, urging her closer. "Yes, but it takes two to waltz, my dear." Her breasts brushed his starched linen, eliciting a soft ripple of shock through the crowded hall. "I should not waltz so well if it wasn't for you in my arms."

She let two fingers of her gloved hand slip past the silken barrier of his wide lapels—propriety be dammed—and he grinned in response. "Then I shall have to stay put," she murmured. "Lest you suffer any embarrassment."

All in all a good plan. And their happiness was a contagion, causing many a couple to dance a hair's breadth too close for propriety's sake. As the night wore on, all wished them well. All save one who stood in a far-off corner watching the couple with a pain-filled heart. *His* dream had not come true, and he wondered if he would ever find contentment. Bone weary, he turned from the room. There was nothing left for him here.

When her repressive marriage ends, Daisy Craigmore is more than ready for adventure. What she finds instead is terror on the streets of London...and an irresistible lone wolf.

Moonglow

Please turn this page for a preview.

Moonglow

Men were already spilling into the alley as Ian charged headlong into the fray. Someone shouted in shock. A woman fainted. A ripple of terror went through the throng of onlookers, heightening the sharp smell of fear. Men both retreated in horror and shoved forward in fascination. Women were quickly ushered away.

Ian shouldered a rotund man aside. The scent of wolf overpowered his senses. Wolf and blood. *Jesus.*

When yet another gentleman stepped in his way, he found his voice. "Move aside! I'm a doctor." Though from the overwhelming amount of blood he smelled, he rather thought his services would not be needed.

The crowd parted, and Ian took in the scene. Bile surged up his throat. Blood was everywhere, coating the walls of the town house, pooling upon the ground, and

running along the cracks between the cobbles. A man—
what was left of him—lay in a tangled heap pushed up
against the wall, his face an unrecognizable hash of claw
marks, his torso eviscerated. Just beyond, a woman had
suffered the same fate, though her face was unmarred.
She'd died first. He'd bet his best walking stick on it.
Already the stench of decay crept over her. The body was
stiff and white in the moon's glow.

Ian crouched low and inhaled. Scents assaulted
him. He let them come and sorted through the miasma.
Beneath the rot, terror, and blood was the rangy scent of
wolf, a city wolf—for it missed the essential freshness of
country air—yet a wolf tinged with something off, bitter-
sweet. Sickness. What sort, he couldn't tell.

"He's past help," said the man beside him. Ian held up a
staying hand and inhaled deeper.

Beyond the filth came a fainter scent—rose, jasmine,
rosemary, and sunshine. Those notes held him for one
tense moment, pulling the muscles in his solar plexus
tight and filling them with odd warmth. It was a fresh,
ephemeral scent that made the beast inside him stir, sit up,
and take note.

A small groan broke the spell. Someone shouted
in alarm. The dead man moved, rolling a bit, and the
crowd jumped back as if one. Ian's pulse kicked before
he noticed the soft drape of blue silk between the man's
twisted legs.

"Bloody hell." He wrenched the body aside. It pitched
over with a thud to reveal the crumpled form of a woman
covered in blood.

"Step back," he said sharply as one wayward man
tromped forward.

"Lud! Is she alive?"

Ian ignored the query. His hands were gentle as he touched the woman's wrist to check her pulse. Slow, steady, and strong. It was from her that the scent of flowers arose. Her fine brow pinched, her features lost under a macabre mask of crimson blood. Ian cursed beneath his breath and drew her near as his hands moved over her form in search of injuries. Despite the blood, she was untouched. The man's blood, not hers. She'd seen it all, however. Of that, he was sure. She'd been the one to scream. Then the man.

He glanced about the alley. This couple had seen the first victim. They shouted, and then they were attacked. Ian brought his attention back to the woman.

She was a handful, lush curves, small waist. He gathered her up in his arms, ignoring the protests of those around. Her head lolled against his shoulder, releasing another faint puff of sweet scent. A curling lock of hair, red with blood, fell over his chest as he hefted her higher and stood.

"She needs medical attention." He moved to go when a gentleman stepped in his way.

"Here now." The gentleman's waxed mustache twitched. "You don't look like any doctor I've ever seen."

The crowd of men stirred, apparently taking in Ian's odd attire for the first time.

Ian tightened his grip on the female, and she gave a little moan of distress. The sound went straight to his core. Women were to be protected and cherished. Always. He stared down the gathering crowd. "Nor a marquis, I gather. However, I am both." He took a step, shouldering aside the man with ease. "I am Northrup. And it would do you well to get out of my way."

Another murmur rippled among the men. But they

eased away; not many wanted to risk tangling with Lord Ian Ranulf, Marquis of Northrup. Those who weren't as convinced, he pushed past. He'd fight them all if he had to. This woman wasn't getting out of his sight. Not until he'd questioned her. And he certainly wasn't letting her tell the whole of London that she'd just survived an attack by a werewolf.

THE DISH

Where authors give you the inside scoop!

♥ ♥ ♥ ♥ ♥ ♥ ♥ ♥ ♥ ♥ ♥ ♥ ♥ ♥ ♥

From the desk of Sherrill Bodine

Dear Reader,

One of my favorite things about writing is taking real people and mixing and matching their body parts and personalities to create characters who are captivating and entirely unique. And of course, I always set my books in my beloved Chicago, sharing with all of you the behind-the-scenes worlds and places I adore most.

But in ALL I WANT IS YOU, I couldn't resist sharing one of my other passions: vintage jewelry.

Thanks to a dear friend I was able to haunt antique stores and flea markets all over the city, rescuing broken, discarded pieces of fine vintage couture costume jewelry and watching her repair, restore, and redesign them. She gave these pieces new life, transforming them into necklaces, bracelets, and brooches of her own unique creation, and it was an amazing thing to see.

I just knew my heroine, Venus Smith, had to do the very same thing, and thus her jewelry line, A Touch of Venus, was born.

And of course it seemed only fitting that Venus's designs end up in Clayworth's department store, the store I created in my previous book, *A Black Tie Affair*, which is a thinly veiled Marshall Fields, Chicago's late great iconic retailer. Of course, the most delicious part is that Clayworth's is run by Venus's archenemy, Connor Clayworth O'Flynn, the man who betrayed her father and ruined his reputation. And yes, you guessed it—sparks fly between them, igniting into a fiery passion.

But this book isn't just the product of my imagination. Readers have been so kind, telling me the most amazing stories that have transported me to fascinating places, and I want to take all of you with me!

When someone shared with me the legend of the "Angel of Taylor Street," I fell in love with the story and couldn't resist using it myself. The Angel of Taylor Street was a person or persons who for decades did good deeds for strangers without ever asking anything in return. I changed the character to the Saint of Taylor Street in ALL I WANT IS YOU, and now it's an important part of Venus and Connor's story.

But that isn't the only one. Did you know there's a private gambling club hidden beneath the parking lot of an old Chicago restaurant, one that's been in business since our gangster days? I didn't either, until someone tipped me off. Of course it is the site of a fabulous adventure for Venus and Connor. It is just a hint of Chicago's inglorious past, but this time it has a positive spin—I promise!

I hope you'll enjoy Venus and Connor's story in ALL I WANT IS YOU. Please come visit my website at www .sherrillbodine.com. I'd love to hear from you!

Xo, Sherrill

Sherrill Bodine

From the desk of Kendra Leigh Castle

Dear Reader,

"Dogs and cats living together…mass hysteria!"

I heard the voice of Peter Venkman in my head a lot as I was writing MIDNIGHT RECKONING, the second book in my Dark Dynasties series. That's because his little quip there is the basis for the story. Well, maybe not the mass hysteria part. But I did want to see what would happen when one of my cat-shifting vampires met a gorgeous woman who wasn't just out of his reach, but out of his species entirely. This is a tale of cat vamp meets werewolf, and relationships don't come with more built-in baggage than theirs.

I love a good star-crossed relationship, as long as it works out all right in the end (I still suffer traumatic flashbacks from *Romeo and Juliet*), but writing one turned out to be more difficult than I'd imagined. I'm perfectly happy to torment my characters from time to time, but the deck was so stacked against these two that even I was sometimes left wondering how they could possibly work things out. You see, Jaden Harrison and Lyra Black are natural enemies. In their world, vampires and werewolves don't mix, period. While the vampires rule the cities, the wolf packs keep to more rural areas, and the enmity between the races is strong despite years of relative peace between them. The wolves think the vampires are arrogant, worthless bloodsuckers; and the vampires think the wolves are wild, unruly, violent beasts. Each race steers clear of the other, so the chances of

Jaden and Lyra ever meeting were incredibly slim. But they did...and it left quite an impression.

If you've read *Dark Awakening*, you'll remember the beautiful she-wolf who stalked off after Jaden insulted her. What she was doing in a vampire safe house was left a mystery, but in MIDNIGHT RECKONING, you'll discover that Lyra has much larger problems than one rude vampire. She's the only child of her pack's Alpha, and the natural choice to fill his shoes when he steps down. There's just one problem: Lyra is female, and werewolf society is patriarchal, with some archaic notions about a woman's place that would horrify most twenty-first-century women. But this is Lyra's family, Lyra's world, and rather than desert them she's determined to make them see her value. She wants to win the right to lead at the pack's Proving...but to do so, she'll need to learn to fight in a way that evens the playing field. Finding someone to teach her seems hopeless as the clock ticks down, until a chance encounter with an unpleasantly familiar face leads to unexpected opportunity...and a very unlikely teacher.

The wolf and the cat together are a volatile mix of confidence and caution, brashness and reserve, unrestrained ferocity and quiet intensity. Their interaction is frowned upon, and a relationship between them is strictly forbidden. But a blue-eyed Cait Sith is hard to resist for even the most stubborn she-wolf, and it isn't long before both Lyra and Jaden start to wonder if there might not be a way around the traditional "fighting like cats and dogs" arrangement. That is, if the forces working against them from within the pack don't end Lyra's chances, and her life, first.

How Lyra and Jaden find their way to each other, and whether Venkman was right about canine/feline love affairs being a harbinger of the apocalypse, is something you'll have to read the book to find out. But if you're a fan of the sparks that fly when opposites attract, you'll want to come along and visit the Pack of the Thorn, where a vampire cat without a cause has finally met his match.

Enjoy!

Kendra Leigh Castle

♥ ♥ ♥ ♥ ♥ ♥ ♥ ♥ ♥ ♥ ♥ ♥ ♥ ♥ ♥ ♥ ♥

From the desk of Rochelle Alers

Dear Reader,

You've just picked up a very special novel, one that has lingered in my heart for ages.

SANCTUARY COVE, the first book in the Cavanaugh Island series, not only comes from my heart but connects me to my ancestral roots.

Set on a Sea Island in the Carolina lowcountry, SANCTUARY COVE envelops you with the comforting spirit of a small town, where the residents cling to old traditions that assure a slower, more comforting way of life. Drive slowly through quaint Main Street, and you'll sense a place where time seems to stand still. Step into Jack's Fish House and be welcomed with warm feelings and comfort food. Sit quietly by the picturesque harbor and listen to the natural ebb and flow of nature.

The Cove draws recently widowed Deborah Robinson into its embrace, offering a fresh start for herself, her teenaged son, and her daughter. Her grandmother's ancestral home reaches out to her, filled with wonderful childhood memories that give Deborah the strength she needs to face her future.

When Dr. Asa Monroe arrives at the Cove, he's at a crossroads. The loss of his wife and young son in a tragic accident has devastated his world, sending him on a nomadic journey to find faith and meaning. And as he spends the winter on the Cove, he discovers a world of peace that has eluded him for more than a year. When he meets Deborah, he realizes not only that they are kindred spirits but that fate might grant him a second chance at love. When friendship gives way to passion, Deborah and Asa find their greatest challenge is hiding their love in a town where there is no such thing as a secret.

The residents of the Cove are loving, wonderful, and quirky, just like the relatives we love even when they embarrass us at family reunions. So come on home and meet Asa, Deborah and her children, and a town full of unforgettable characters who will make you laugh, cry, and long for island living. Sit down with a glass of lemonade, put your feet up, and let life move a little slower. Enjoy the magnificent sunsets, the rattle of palmetto leaves in the breeze, and the mouthwatering aroma of lowcountry home cooking. If you listen carefully, you'll even hear a few folks speak Gullah, a dialect that is a blend of English and African.

And don't forget to look for *Angels Landing*, the second novel in the Cavanaugh Island series, coming in the fall of 2012.

Read, enjoy, and do let me hear from you!

Rochelle Alers

ralersbooks@aol.com
www.rochellealers.com